WINTER FIRE

A Novel

WINTER FIRE

A Novel

RACHEL ANN NUNES

DESERET
BOOK

Salt Lake City, Utah

Library of Congress Cataloging-in-Publication Data

Nunes, Rachel Ann, 1966-
    Winter fire / Rachel Ann Nunes.
       p.   cm.
    ISBN 1-59038-382-6 (pbk.)
  1. Women teachers—Fiction. 2. Divorced fathers—Fiction. 3. Custody of children—Fiction. 4. Children of divorced parents—Fiction. I. Title.
    PS3564.U468W56 2005
    813'.54—dc22
                                    2004021460

Printed in the United States of America   70582

10   9   8   7   6   5   4   3

To my sister Ruth,

for shining hope into a child's life.

You are an example to us all.

Acknowledgments

Thanks to Jana Erickson, Suzanne Brady, Emily Watts, and the other great people at Deseret Book who have made this novel possible. It is a pleasure working with you.

Additional thanks must go to the writers at LDS Storymakers, who are as close as family, for their continuing support and love. How wonderful it is to associate with talented (if sometimes eccentric!) people who share not only my love of the written word but also my values!

Chapter One

Amanda Huntington's quick footsteps echoed eerily in the nearly deserted hallway of Grovecrest Elementary where she taught fourth grade. Though it was barely four o'clock, the school was darker than usual, signaling that clouds had moved in to cover the sun. The artificial lights overhead did little to cut through the resulting gloom. Snow was definitely on the way.

"Did the fire alarm go off?" James Hill emerged from the other fourth-grade classroom and hurried on his shorter legs to catch up to her. "Oh, I know. I bet you have a hot date—eh, greeny?" He called her that because her eyes were green and because she was the newest teacher at the school.

"Not hardly," she retorted. James was always teasing her about finding someone special. He said he couldn't understand why a woman as attractive as Amanda wasn't dating. In the few months she had taught at the school, James, abetted by his wife, had repeatedly tried to set her up with a seemingly endless slew of available bachelors. Amanda wasn't interested.

Her history with men wasn't good. She'd experienced one brief, misguided engagement right after high school, and then last year, worried about growing older, she had nearly married a man she cared for but really hadn't loved—not totally and completely in the way she'd always dreamed. She'd been saved from making that terrible mistake by a chance encounter with an old high school flame, Tanner Wolfe. As they began dating, she discovered that he *was* the man of her dreams—everything she could want. She fell in love, quickly and hard, only to realize too late that he cared for someone else. In the end she had let him go. The experience had been painful, to say the least.

No, for the time being, she was satisfied with her single existence. She alone decided what she wanted to do and when, what she wanted to eat and where, and she was becoming independent. That was good. She hadn't even joined the singles ward in the area yet, preferring a family ward because it gave her the opportunity to get to know her neighbors. It also gave her time to . . . well, heal.

There was a part of her who hoped for—and even planned for—a relationship in the future. Growing up in the Church, she had long envisioned herself as part of a growing family, surrounded by children to love and to raise.

Well, she was surrounded by children every day. That part, at least, had come true.

Twelve long months had passed since she'd said good-bye to Tanner, but, if she were truthful, sometimes she relived the memory as though the events had occurred only yesterday. Oh, how her heart had broken, seeing him walk through her apartment door and out of her life! She wondered if she would always regret letting him go, always regret allowing him to believe she had accepted Gerry's proposal, when the reality was that her love for Tanner had been the determining factor in her refusal. How could she marry Gerry when she had caught a glimpse of true love? Yet how could she make Tanner stay when his heart was elsewhere? When Tanner had married a few months later, she knew she had done the right thing. Part of her wished him the best, but another part had cried into her pillow for months until there were no tears left.

That was then. She was over him—or so she reminded herself for the millionth time.

"So how'd class go today?" James asked.

"What?" Amanda forced herself to return to the present.

"The kids. You know, the ones you teach." James's large nose and receding brown hairline made his bright hazel eyes stand out in his thin face. "How'd it go?"

She smiled wearily. "They were all really restless. And it's only Wednesday. We still have two more days to go before the weekend."

"It's the change in the weather. Once it snows they'll settle down soon enough. You'll see."

Amanda hoped so. She'd taken this post at the end of August when Rilla Thompson had become ill and opted for early retirement. Amanda knew she'd only been offered the job because she'd worked with Rilla at the school last year while doing her student teaching. This was Amanda's first real teaching post, and she worried about succeeding. So far she'd made it to November.

"They're great kids," she said.

James shifted the small stack of papers he carried to his other arm and opened the outside door for her. "Yeah. Lot of energy. Keeps me young." He was barely in his forties, but Amanda laughed as he'd intended, though she didn't find it funny. She'd be twenty-five next month and was just beginning to comprehend how fast the years really did pass.

"Well, it's home to the new baby," James said, taking a step toward his car. "My wife'll be ready for a break. I tell you, we're too old for this again. Eight years between number five and number six. That's just crazy."

"I thought it kept you young," she quipped.

James laughed and unlocked his car door. As Amanda watched him leave, her smile died. At least James had someone home waiting for him.

Maybe it had been a mistake, moving out of her shared apartment in Orem and buying a house in Pleasant Grove. Yet she had wanted to move on with her life—not hang in limbo while she waited to meet someone special. Truth be told, she had come to the point where she didn't even *want* to meet someone special. She wanted to be whole and well. She wanted to depend on herself. Never mind that most of her friends were married. Never mind that her sister, barely two years older, had a perfect husband and three perfect children to live in her perfect house. Yes, three perfect children spaced exactly two years apart—just like their mother had timed her four babies. In another two years, another baby would appear. It was a good thing for Amanda that the oldest of her younger brothers hadn't married yet. At twenty-three and two years off his mission, Mitch was finally beginning to draw some of the heat at family gatherings.

Amanda had her hand ready to open the door to her green Audi when she noticed a change in the sky. The mountains were edged in mist and gloom, but right in the middle there was a break in the clouds where the sun lit up the steep slopes. Her breath caught in her throat, and her spirits lifted. This was why she had moved to the East Bench in Pleasant Grove—so she could view the majestic mountains from her kitchen window every day.

After a moment the clouds closed again, and Amanda slipped inside her car. On the drive home, her thoughts drifted toward dinner. The idea of cooking exhausted her. Once, she had enjoyed cooking and creating something special for a date or her roommates, but living alone had squeezed much of that pleasure from her. She always ate too much and ended up with leftovers that went to waste.

It was more economical to throw a ready-made meal into the microwave oven.

Then she remembered that her sister, Kerrianne, was feeling sick, and with a new two-month-old baby, even her perfect sister might need a little help. The thought of seeing her niece and two nephews brightened Amanda's thoughts. Though she spent much of her day with children, her niece and nephews were the most important children in her life.

It's my stupid biological clock, she thought. Of course, her mother's weekly phone calls and overt questions about her personal life never helped matters.

Amanda made a silent vow to get out more with her friends. Generally, her life was filled with laughter and important things to do. Only in this past month as the first anniversary of her break with Tanner loomed had she become so melancholy.

She whistled to herself as she went inside her small, three-bedroom house. Facing the west and nestled on a hill above newer, much larger homes, the house was her dream. She had the best of a good neighborhood, a low mortgage, and when there wasn't fog, a view to die for. The only thing she regretted was the lack of a garage. Hopefully, the coming winter wouldn't be too severe.

In the kitchen she turned on the gas oven before walking into the attached family room where she put in her new Josh Groban CD. The music bore little resemblance to the new wave rock she had adored in high school, but her tastes had refined as the years passed. A companion she'd had on her mission to Georgia had introduced her to Groban, and now she was hooked. She especially loved the rare songs he sang in French. They were so romantic.

Her smile faltered, but she forced the thoughts aside. So what? She was listening to romantic music alone. That was perfectly okay.

She rummaged through her freezer, finding several small packages of chicken. Hmm, what else did she have? In the refrigerator she found sour cream, milk, and fresh broccoli. In the cupboard she had a large container of rice. Perfect. She would defrost the chicken in the microwave and then rustle up her tasty chicken rice casserole, liberally decorated with broccoli florets and topped with cheese. Her mouth watered.

Kerrianne lived only three streets over, and the meal would still be piping hot when she arrived. Amanda would feed the children and her brother-in-law at the table, take Kerrianne a plate to her room, eat a bite herself while cleaning up, and then play with the children until bedtime. After that she'd come home, call a few friends, and arrange to go out for lunch or dinner over the weekend. She might even go dancing.

Pausing a moment to listen to a particularly beautiful passage of music, Amanda swept up the telephone, pressing the button that held her sister's number in memory. "Hello, Kerrianne? Hi, it's me, Amanda. How're you feeling?"

"Yuck and yuck and more yuck," came Kerrianne's tired voice. "My nose is running like a faucet, and my head feels like it's going to burst."

"Well, I'm bringing dinner, so don't worry about that. I've got it all planned. Remember that chicken broccoli casserole you love so much? Well, if I get started right now, I can bring it over by six."

"Oh, that's so sweet of you, Manda! But Adam's bringing food home. He called a few minutes ago before he left work to tell me he was coming early with dinner."

Amanda's smile faded. "Oh, that's nice of him." Leave it to Adam to play the role of the perfect husband.

"Oh, but I'm sure I'll still be feeling lousy tomorrow. Do you think . . . would you mind bringing your casserole then? The children loved it that time you brought it when the baby was born. If I remember, we ate it for three days. I appreciated it so much!"

"Well, only if it will help." The last thing Amanda wanted was to be an annoyance with her casserole.

"Of course it will! In fact, Adam has a late meeting at the district office tomorrow with some of the other school administrators, and afterwards he has to go to the church for Scouts. If you bring dinner, it will really help out. And if you could stay a bit and help get the kids to bed when Adam's gone, I'd be so grateful. I'll understand if you can't. Believe me, the casserole alone is plenty. They're so picky nowadays, it's hard to find something they love to eat. I wish I could cook as well as you do."

Kerrianne could make table scraps into a gourmet meal, but Amanda was already feeling better at her sister's assurances. The chicken would thaw out better in the refrigerator anyway—that way she wouldn't accidentally cook parts of the meat before the casserole went into the oven. "Okay, I'll bring it tomorrow. And I'll stay for a while. Be glad to."

"You're so good to me."

Amanda felt content as she hung up. Kerrianne always did that for her. No matter how lost or unneeded Amanda was feeling, her big sister turned things around. Humming with the Groban CD, Amanda returned the casserole ingredients to the refrigerator and the cupboard. Hmm, what to eat now that the oven was hot? She didn't want to waste electricity. How about pizza? She had leftovers from Monday when her brother Mitch had picked up take 'n bake. She hadn't eaten the leftover slices yet because she didn't like pizza warmed in the microwave. It just wasn't the same.

"It's fate," she told the pizza, as she threw the pieces onto a round baking pan and slipped them into the oven for an early dinner.

When she returned ten minutes later, worrying about the possibility of having left the pizza in too long, she found smoke snaking out from the cracks around the oven door. "Oh no!" She opened the door and the smoke billowed into the room, momentarily blocking her view. When she could see again, flames engulfed the pizza, growing larger now that she had opened the door and allowed more oxygen inside.

What should I do?

She had never started a fire in her oven before, and several scenarios presented themselves. If she closed the door, would it eventually burn itself out? Or would it burn down the whole house? She couldn't risk that.

Amanda reached in with her oven mitts to remove the pizza, only to watch as they too blackened and started to burn. She released the pizza immediately. At that moment the smoke detector went off, adding its shrill scream to the confusion. Shaking the mitts to put out the flame, she darted to the sink, dumped the singed gloves, filled a cup with water, and threw it on the pizza inside the oven. The water sizzled as it hit the hot metal, sending steam into her face. To her relief, the fire around the pizza seemed to be dying. Amanda threw in another cup of water to make sure.

Finally, she dared to take the pizza out. Underneath the edge, caught between the pan and the pizza and hanging down over the edge, was a smoldering dishrag. She groaned. When she'd thrown the pizza onto the pan, she must not have been paying much attention.

"Of all the stupid things." She shook her head. Kerrianne would never have done something so brainless. This was one secret Amanda meant to keep. If Mitch got a sniff, he'd never stop teasing. Just thinking about that made her giggle almost uncontrollably. She had to admit that now danger had passed, it *was* kind of funny.

Only a little water had escaped outside the oven, and Amanda mopped it up quickly. Then she looked inside, frowning. There was more water than she remembered throwing in. Most of it should have boiled out, right?

Looking at the temperature gauge, she realized that though she hadn't turned off the oven, it was quickly growing cold. She flipped the switch off, gave it fifteen minutes with the door open to cool, and then sopped up the water with paper towels. When everything was returned to order, she turned on the oven. A few minutes were long enough to tell her something was wrong. The stove top was fine, the flames leaping to life when she turned on the gas. But the oven didn't begin to get warm. Had the pilot light gone out?

"Should have used the fire extinguisher," she muttered, belatedly remembering her father had bought one for under the kitchen sink. "Great. Just great."

How much would it cost to repair? Then again, she didn't use the oven that much. Maybe it could wait.

Her eyes fell on the baking dish she had been going to use for her sister's casserole. "Oh, no," she groaned. She *couldn't* go back on her word now, not when she'd practically begged Kerrianne to let her bring dinner.

Maybe if she explained. "It was a huge fire," she'd say. "I have no idea how it started." But that would be a lie.

Maybe she could prepare the casserole and take it to Kerrianne's to cook. But Kerrianne would instinctively know something was wrong, and Amanda wouldn't have time to grade the test she was giving tomorrow if she spent the entire evening at her sister's. What to do?

She'd only bought the house at the end of the summer, and it was her first experience being responsible for appliances. This time there was no owner behind the scenes to ask for help. She ran through the possibilities in her mind. Call her dad. No good. Kerrianne would somehow find out and tell her not to worry about dinner. Call Mitch. Yeah, right. He was worse than she was about being independent. He had barely left home a month ago after two years off his mission. She could call her home teachers, but what could they do besides recommend a repairman?

"I have to get you fixed!" In frustration Amanda kicked the oven door. All she accomplished was to hurt the big toe on her left foot.

What would Kerrianne do?

Amanda grimaced. Kerrianne would have paid attention to what she was putting in the oven, but if there ever was a problem, she'd probably let Adam deal with it—and Amanda didn't have an Adam.

I can do this myself. She reached for the phone book and turned to the repair listings, finding only one for Pleasant Grove. *There, not even a choice. How easy can this be?* Smiling to herself, she dialed the number, glancing at the clock on the microwave. Five minutes after five and the shop was open until six. *See? It's not that hard to be independent.*

"Doug's Appliance and Repair, Blake speaking," came a man's voice, deep and rich. It was a voice that didn't belong at a repair shop but would have seemed more at home on the radio.

"Hi. My oven's broken. Do you make house calls?"

"Yes. We charge thirty-five dollars for a visit, plus parts and installation if we fix anything. What's the problem exactly?"

"Well, I had a fire."

"A fire?"

"Yes, a small one. I accidentally put a dishcloth in with my dinner." She shut her eyes and groaned inwardly. *That* was supposed to be her little secret.

A few heartbeats passed before he replied. "Can you tell me anything else? Exactly what doesn't work?"

Amanda wondered if he thought she was crazy. "I think the pilot light is out or something. It looks good—there's no fire damage—but the oven won't get hot. I think it might not light because of the water."

"The water," he repeated with a low chuckle that sent warm shivers up her spine.

Irritated, Amanda snapped, "So are you coming or not?"

"Sure. Let's see . . . I can make it tomorrow about one. Would that be all right?"

"You can't come tonight?" Amanda hated herself for sounding so desperate.

"You need it tonight?"

"Not exactly. It's just that I work tomorrow, and I need my oven tomorrow night for sure."

"Oh, you need it tomorrow."

Amanda stifled a sigh at his annoying way of repeating half of what she said. "Yes, I'm taking dinner to someone."

"What kind of stove is it?"

"A gas stove."

"I meant what brand. You already said it wouldn't light. Has to be gas."

"Oh. Well, I don't know what brand. Does it really matter?" She walked over to the stove.

"It could. Does the stove top still light?"

"Yes. It's fine."

"Good. A least you won't starve." He gave another of those delicious chuckles.

His attempted joke did not amuse her. "It's an Amana," she said. "I just looked."

"How old?"

"I have no idea. I just bought the house a few months ago. But it doesn't look old."

"Uh-oh," he said. "Can you hold a minute?"

"Yes." She wondered what was so wrong about owning an Amana. Maybe he wouldn't work on that brand.

"You're not supposed to be up there," came his muffled voice.

"Get down now! Watch i—" There was a loud crash of what Amanda imagined came from a box of supplies tumbling to the ground, followed by a brief, high-pitched scream. She shook her head. Was he ever going to come back? What kind of shop did he run anyway?

After a very long time, he returned to the phone. "Hello?"

"I'm still here."

"Sorry about that."

His apology did nothing to soothe her growing irritation. "So, can you come any sooner?" She was calculating the possibility of running home at lunch, or perhaps having her neighbor let him in.

"I leave here at five-thirty. I'll come by then. Would that work?"

Amanda sighed. "Yes. Thanks. I'll see you then." She started to hang up.

"Uh, I'll need your name and address."

Amanda bit her lip. She was a complete idiot! Of course he needed her address. "Amanda Huntington," she said.

"Amanda with a broken Amana," he said, obviously amused.

She laughed politely while making a sour face. What a comedian!

After giving him her address, she hung up the phone before she could embarrass herself further. Not that he would even understand her embarrassment. He was probably a high school dropout, whose only dream in life was to study the latest models of appliances. Amanda bet he wasn't even aware of his incredible voice. Maybe she'd enlighten him. She would, if he was nicer to her when he came.

During the next hour, she changed into an old pair of jeans and a worn T-shirt that said *Number One Teacher*, tidied her kitchen, threw in a load of laundry, and began correcting papers on the floor of her family room. She was lying stomach down on the soft beige carpet, her mind engrossed on the capitals of each state, when the doorbell rang.

She arose, tucking her shoulder-length blonde hair behind her ears. "Yes?" she asked, opening the door.

"I'm Blake Simmons from Doug's Appliance and Repair," said the same voice she had heard earlier on the phone. "I'm here to look at your oven."

He looked like no repairman she had ever seen or imagined. He was taller than she was by several inches and broad-shouldered enough to make her feel small. Long legs were clad in snug Levi's that crinkled at the bottom where they met black work boots, topped by a blue button-down shirt boldly reading Doug's Appliance and Repair. A small oval patch declared *Blake* in red italic letters.

Her eyes wandered to his face. Drop-dead gorgeous he wasn't, but he was more ruggedly handsome than she cared to admit. His cheeks sported a day-old beard growth, and his brown hair was slightly mussed, giving him an adventurous air. He reminded her vaguely of her English professor in college—on whom she'd once had a secret crush. Her heart flopped inside her, something that hadn't happened for a very long time.

"My oven," she found herself saying. Her breath made white clouds in the cold air.

"I am at the right house, aren't I?" Blake's brown eyes held hers, his lips curved in a gentle smile as though perpetually amused.

"Yes." For a long moment, neither spoke. Amanda was intensely aware of him, of the way he steadily met her gaze. She became suddenly conscious of her jeans and worn T-shirt. Why had she chosen that outfit? Not that he was dressed up, but he'd look handsome in anything.

"Okay," he drawled finally. "I guess I'll get my toolbox from the truck."

"Right." She followed him with her eyes, craning her neck to see if he was wearing a wedding ring. She couldn't see one, but a lot of repairmen might not wear a ring for fear of getting their hands caught in a machine. Right? Or maybe he wasn't married. The thought was unsettling.

He had pulled a toolbox from the back of his blue pickup and was heading back over the lawn when her eyes went beyond him to the passenger side of the car. A small face peered out at her, framed with short blond hair.

He had a child.

That meant he was taken.

In that instant of discovery, Amanda realized that she was profoundly disappointed.

Chapter Two

The repairman was back at the porch now, but Amanda gazed at him with a frown. "You can bring your son in, uh, Blake. I don't mind." She wanted to say more, specifically to tell him that he shouldn't have left the child in the truck at all.

He looked startled, as if he'd forgotten all about his son. "Oh, yeah. Thanks." Setting down the large toolbox, he sprinted back to the truck and opened the door with his key. The small boy burst from the cab as though released from a prison. He was wearing a new-looking blue coat, jeans, and small black hiking boots. As Blake shut the door, Amanda caught a glimpse of a rear-facing car seat next to where the boy had been seated.

She showed Blake into the kitchen and offered the boy some crayons and a coloring book. He refused, his bright blue eyes going to the tools Blake was laying out on the counter. Blake pulled the stove out a few inches, leaned behind to unplug it, and then heaved it out farther. Amanda was mortified at the thick layer of dust and crumbs that lay exposed.

"Yuck," she said. "I didn't know that was there."

He grinned. "This isn't half as bad as some I've seen." With a screwdriver, he began to remove the back of the stove. "You said some water was in the oven?"

Amanda bristled. "Well, I had to put out the fire." She had never felt so defensive before.

"Was it a big fire?" asked the boy hopefully.

"Not really," she told him.

"Oh." His face fell with disappointment.

"But it was scary," Amanda hurried to add. "Look at this." She showed him the tips of her oven mitts, still in the sink.

The boy's eyes widened. "Good thing you didn't burn your fingers."

Blake set down his screwdriver and went to work removing the metal back plate. "Don't you have an extinguisher?"

"Yes." Amanda felt herself coloring. "I—it's under—I forgot I had it."

"I see."

Amanda opened her mouth to explain, but nothing came out. What was it about this man? She had always been popular among her peers and had no trouble striking up conversations with strangers, but this man made her feel like a two-year-old playing house in her mother's kitchen. She *never* felt like that. She was always the calm, cool one—even when being dumped by the man she loved.

Blake was watching her, tools in hand, waiting for what she would say. "Never mind." She waved her hand, dismissing him, and turned to the boy. "Hey, I have a cool book about insects, if you want to look at it."

He appeared interested, so she retrieved the hardbound book from her school bag and set it on the square kitchen table. Still wearing his blue coat, the child climbed onto the chair and immediately became absorbed by the larger-than-life images. Amanda returned to her papers, but she sat on the navy plaid couch to correct them instead of on the floor. Once seated, she glanced at the man in her kitchen, but all she could see was the top of his brown head poking up from behind her counter.

Her eyes went to the boy, wondering how long the book could hold the interest of a child so young. He was a beautiful child, but the heart shape of his face, the blond color of his hair, and those blue eyes obviously hadn't been handed down to him by his father. What was his mother like? What type of woman did this handsome repairman love?

Who cares? Amanda forced herself back to work.

After she had been hopelessly trying to correct papers for ten minutes, Blake came out from behind the stove and began removing pieces from inside her oven, his muscles rippling beneath his shirt. She watched him surreptitiously through lowered lashes.

Finally, he emerged with a rectangular part, holding it up for her inspection. "Here's the problem. This actually causes the spark that lights the oven. Looks like metal, but it's very fragile."

"So how did that happen? Was it the water?"

He shrugged. "It's hard to say. These go out all the time. Could have been the water. Or it could have just been time to break."

Amanda guessed it was the water and that he was only being nice. "How much to fix it?"

"About seventy-five, including installation. I don't have this exact one in stock, but I have something down at the shop that will work just as well."

Seventy-five dollars! With the repair visit that was a hundred and ten bucks—all because she hadn't been paying attention to a lousy dishrag. She could forget that new set of books she wanted for her classroom. If only she could go back and cook the pizza again!

She sighed. "Okay, let's do it."

"I'll go down to the store and come right back," he said, straightening.

Biting her lip, Amanda wondered if that meant another thirty-five bucks for a second visit. At least it would be done today. She would pay him and forget it ever happened.

Looking around, Blake said, "If you have any kids, you'll want to keep them away from this while I'm gone."

"I'm not married," she said. "I live here alone." She could have kicked herself when she said it. For all she knew, he was a burglar on his days away from the shop. "My brother's around a lot," she added quickly. She gave a nervous laugh when he nodded and smiled, making her heart feel funny again.

"Come on, Kevin. We need to go back to the shop."

The child glanced up, his blue eyes mournful. "But I'm not done."

"We're coming back. You can look at it then. If that's all right with . . . with Miss—"

"Amanda," she supplied as the child looked to her for confirmation. "Call me Amanda. Of course you can look at it when you come back. Or you can take it with you, if you want," she added impulsively. "To look at in the car, I mean. But I'll need it back."

The child brightened. "Thanks!" He shut the book, held it to his small chest, and propelled himself from the chair. Amanda was glad she'd made the offer.

"Be careful with it," Blake warned.

"I will."

Since the book had already been read by hundreds of children, Amanda didn't suppose there was much harm the boy could do to it. "I'm surprised he's still interested," she said with a laugh. "His attention span is longer than some of my fourth-graders'."

Blake grinned. "He loves books. Sometimes he brings me several dozen at a time to read."

"That's great. How old is he?"

"Four."

"I thought he was about that age. I have a niece who's four." As their eyes met and held, something flowed between them. Amanda discovered she didn't want to look away. Her heart thudded in her ears.

"So you're a teacher?" he asked.

"Yes. I teach the fourth grade at Grovecrest Elementary."

He nodded, and she wondered if he had other children who went there. He didn't look too much older than she was, but he could have married young.

"Are we going yet?" Kevin was already waiting by the door. "I'm bored."

Blake looked toward the child, and the connection between them broke. Amanda was both relieved and sorry.

"We'll see you in a few minutes," Blake said.

Amanda watched them stride across her lawn, the man carrying his toolbox and the little boy clutching her book. Again she tried to imagine a woman in the picture—and failed.

Had she imagined the current between them?

Turning away, she shut the door. It didn't matter. Ring or no, he was obviously married and off limits. Besides, she wasn't ready to become involved with anyone—especially an appliance repairman. Now if he'd been a teacher or an accountant or computer programmer, maybe she would reconsider. If she ever did get involved, it would be with someone more like herself.

❊ ❊ ❊

Blake was glad when they were finally back in the truck and on their way to the shop. His heart had almost stopped when Amanda Huntington had opened the door and stared at him with intense green eyes that were quite unlike any color he had ever seen. He'd been prepared to dislike her, she'd been so vague and annoying on the phone, but seeing her had evoked a different emotion altogether. What's more, she wasn't married. Not that it really mattered. His duty was to Kevin and Mara.

"I like this book," Kevin said from the seat. "Could you buy it for me?"

Blake groaned. "Another book? You'll send me into bankruptcy."

"Bank? That's good. You can get money at the bank."

Blake grinned at the solemn expression in Kevin's eyes, eyes that mirrored his mother's. "How about we try the library first, okay, bud?"

"Okay," Kevin agreed. "But can I keep it for a long, long time?" There was another plea behind this one, a plea Blake doubted Kevin knew how to voice.

"As long as possible."

"Good." Kevin turned back to the book, his brows crunched together. Blake wondered if he had answered well, or if the child's mother would prevent him from keeping the promise.

At the shop he found his sister-in-law getting ready to leave. "Oh, good, you're back," Rhonda said, coming from behind the long desk that spanned one side of the shop. "Doug should be here any minute to pick me up. I thought we were going to have to take the baby home with us."

"No, don't take her!" Kevin glared at Rhonda before rushing over to where the baby stood grinning at them from the portable playpen set up in the used washer section.

"My, my, Mr. Protective," Rhonda said, smiling.

Kevin ignored her. "Hi, I'm back," he cooed to the baby in falsetto. "Yep, your big brother's back." He leaned over to give her a sloppy kiss, causing one of her hands to slip off the edge of the playpen. She swayed but didn't fall. "Did you miss me? Huh? Yes, you did. I know you did. Look, I got a book!" He held it up for her to see.

Blake met his sister-in-law's smile with one of his own. "Thanks for watching her."

"No problem. Mara's an angel. It's Kevin that's a handful. I don't know how you manage to get anything done with him here."

"Practice, I guess." Blake remembered the box of parts Kevin had overturned earlier. "It can be hard."

"And their mother?"

He shrugged. "She'll be back soon."

Rhonda looked at him for a minute, as if contemplating whether or not to believe him. There was a honk outside. "Doug's here. We've got Scouts tonight so I'd better hurry." She grabbed her purse, flew to the playpen to give Mara a kiss, and headed for the door. "I gave her a bottle already and some baby food. She's about ready to sleep. Oh, and check the log. I added another repair to tomorrow's list. We shouldn't book any more till Friday or Saturday because it's just you and Ernest tomorrow. It's Del's day off, and Doug and I have a sales appointment with a hotel manager in the afternoon. I'll be in, though, in the morning. I'm going to start organizing the used parts if it kills me." They both glanced to the far corner behind the used dryers where boxes of old parts looked more like mounds of steel and plastic refuse than anything useful. "I already bought the shelves. Maybe you can help me put them up."

"Sure. No problem." Blake was glad that Doug and Rhonda's last child started first grade this year. The place was much neater since Rhonda had begun working at the shop.

"Oh, and Kevin sweetie, I saved a Twinkie for you. It's on Uncle Doug's desk." She motioned with her chin to the door behind the counter that led into the office.

"A Twinkie?" Kevin said. "Thanks!"

Rhonda blew him a kiss and was gone before Blake remembered

the schoolteacher's oven. Rushing to the door, he saw only the tail-lights of his brother's car disappearing down the street. *Just great,* he thought. *What do I do with Mara now while I fix the oven?*

Mara was holding out one arm, her fingers grabbing the air in his direction, her other hand tightly gripping the edge of the playpen. Blake went to pick her up. She was so tiny that at first he had felt nervous around her. But not anymore. He squeezed her in a tight hug and then scattered kisses on her cheek and neck to get her giggling. She hugged him back, and he breathed in the sweet smell of her hair. He'd washed it himself with baby shampoo just last night. The dress she wore was new, but he'd underestimated the size, and half her diaper was displayed underneath. He'd have to buy another dress and some tights while he was at it.

"Sorry, Mara. Got some work to do." He set the baby back in the playpen on her feet. She grasped the edges with small fists, teetered for a minute, and then fell onto her bottom. Instead of crying, she picked up the soft-bodied doll he'd bought her and put it to her mouth. Should he have washed it first? He'd have to ask Rhonda.

"An igniter, an igniter," he murmured. "Let's see." He started toward the floor-to-ceiling new parts shelves behind the long, counterlike desk, pushing aside a washer drum on the floor that blocked his way. "Keep an eye on Mara, Kevin. I need to get a part for that nice lady." Afterward, he'd decide what to do with Mara while he made the repair.

"Okay." Kevin pulled off a tiny piece of the Twinkie he had retrieved from the office and, standing on his tiptoes, reached into the playpen to give it to Mara.

When Blake was ready to go, he picked up Mara—only to discover that she smelled worse than his garbage can on trash day. Fortunately he was prepared. Mara was a happy baby most of the time and easy to satisfy, but right now she was going through more diapers in a day than *three* babies her age. He figured she'd probably picked up some kind of bug that caused loose bowels. Since she was prone to diaper rash, he had to be vigilant.

Sighing, he grabbed the diaper bag for what seemed like the millionth time that day. Ever helpful, Kevin opened the teacher's book and showed his sister a particularly gruesome bug.

Amanda opened her door to Blake and his son forty-five minutes after they'd left. Outside it was nearly dark now. And colder. "Come on in," she said.

"Thank you." Blake nodded with an amused grin that made Amanda feel like smiling too.

"Can I look at the book?" Kevin asked, shrugging off his coat onto the wood floor.

Blake turned to the child. "Kevin, where is the book? Is it in the car?"

"No. I don't think so." The boy shook his head, staring dejectedly at his boots.

"I don't either. You must have left it at the shop." Blake's voice was weary, but he didn't sound angry. He blew out a sigh, his lower lip jutting out.

Amanda hid a smile.

"I'm sorry," Blake said to her. "I'll go back and get it as soon as I get the part in."

She nodded, feeling awkward. If she hadn't offered to lend Kevin the book, Blake could be on his way home to his wife and warm dinner instead of chasing after paper insects.

Blake went right to work while Amanda found a book about snakes for Kevin. Then she set out a plastic container of magnetic bars and balls for him to build things with in case he grew bored.

"I have to go next door for a moment," she said to Blake. "I'll be right back."

He nodded without speaking. Kevin didn't look up from his book.

Amanda slipped out the front door, jiggling her neighbor's key in her hand. She could feed their birds later, but it was dark and it might snow by the time Blake finished with the oven. Glancing at his truck parked in front of her house, Amanda thought she saw a light inside but decided the illumination came from the passing cars, which were steady this time of night as people returned home from work. Shaking her head, she cut across the lawn to her neighbor's. They were away now on vacation, and she was proud of herself for not relaying that bit of information to the repairman. Not that he was a burglar or anything. You just never knew.

The birds had dirtied their water and tossed out much of their food. "Obviously you're bored," she told the two cockatiels. She refilled the food and washed out their water dishes before replacing them. One bird scolded her, while the other hopped onto her finger. Amanda took it from the cage and softly stroked the blue-gray feathers.

"You must be Bluebell," she said. "Your mate hates me, you know." Bluebell pushed her head into her fingers. Amanda petted her for a while before returning her to the cage. "Sorry, lady. I've got a strange man in my house, and I have to make sure everything's okay. But you keep this up, and I just may get a bird for a pet instead of a dog. Though I can't imagine letting you cuddle up on my bed at night—or that you'll be chasing away burglars."

She put the birds away, all too-aware of the passing minutes. Had Blake finished the job? She hurried outside and across the lawn. Snow had begun to fall, the small white flakes disappearing as they touched the ground. The faint sound of an engine running caused her to pause as she reached her porch. There were no cars passing at the moment, and the sound appeared to be coming from the repair-man's truck. A quick suspicion shot through her. In the five minutes she'd been gone, maybe he'd stolen her valuables and was taking off!

Wait a minute. She didn't have any valuables other than her lap-top computer, and she'd left that at the school. Besides, she knew where he worked.

Yet his truck did seem to be running. Curiously, she walked over to the vehicle, expecting to find the sound carrying from somewhere up the street.

No, it was his truck. And the cab wasn't empty.

Amanda stared in amazement at the baby sitting in the car seat, wrapped in a pink blanket. She might have been pretty when calm, but her face was red and ugly now, her mouth open in a heartrending scream that Amanda could hear through the closed window. This baby was more than upset. Even the top of her head, covered poorly by sparse brown hair, was crimson with her efforts.

Amanda reached for the door. It was locked. Anger surged through her. With no thought but to rescue the poor baby, she ran quickly across the lawn and up to the house, bursting inside with such force that Kevin looked up from the table, startled.

"Hey, you! Blake Whatever-your-last name. Where're your keys?" She had crossed the living room now and was in the kitchen by the table.

"Huh?" Blake was on his knees, head inside the oven.

"I need your keys," she said through gritted teeth. "Your baby's outside screaming her head off. She looks hot. Did you leave the heat on?"

Blake jumped to his feet, dropping something in his hand. It landed on the ceramic tile. "Dang!" he said, stooping to pick it up.

"Didn't you hear what I said?" Anger made her voice sharp. "Babies *die* in too much heat. You shouldn't have left her out there!"

"I heard you!" Blake tossed the piece onto the counter and ran for the door.

Snow was coming down faster now, the flakes beginning to show on the grass. From her porch Amanda watched him open the truck door and reach in for the howling baby. After wrapping her in a blanket, he leaned over, shut off the engine, and came across the lawn.

The baby's screams were only occasional jerking sobs by the time they arrived at the porch, but her face was still red and wet with tears. Amanda stepped back to let them inside.

"It *was* too hot," Blake said.

She could see regret in his face, but she was too angry to care. "You should *never* leave a baby alone in a car. Never! What were you thinking?"

"She was asleep. I didn't want to disturb her." He patted the child's back tenderly, and it wrenched Amanda's heart when the baby gave him a tentative smile through her sobs.

"I didn't realize I'd be this long. I left the heat on because it was so cold."

Amanda didn't accept this excuse. "She was there earlier, I bet," she accused. "When you came before. Does your wife know you leave them in the truck?"

"I don't—" He stopped, his face coloring with his own anger. "Look, I don't answer to you. I did what I thought was best. Turns out I was wrong. I know better now."

"Yeah, lucky for you it wasn't serious," she retorted. "*This* time."

A father should know better, she thought. As a schoolteacher she had learned that she had to imagine every scenario, no matter how far-fetched, to keep the children safe. Their imaginations were miles ahead of her own—or any other adult's, for that matter. Maybe she should call the police on this repairman and alert them to the possible danger. He could be telling the truth, but then again he might be negligent all the time. Who could know for certain?

"Get your coat on, Kevin," Blake said calmly.

Amanda noticed the boy was standing nearby, looking up at them anxiously. "Where are we going?" he asked.

"Back to the shop."

Amanda glanced into the kitchen, where the pieces of her stove lay on the floor and on the counters. "What about my oven?" She had a sinking feeling it was going to remain dismantled. Well, she certainly wouldn't pay his thirty-five dollar fee. Or for the part, either.

"I have to get another part." Blake spoke through clenched teeth, as though trying to maintain his calm. "I broke that last one when you started yelling at me."

"Yelling?" She shook her head. "I was worried about her. That's all." She sighed.

"Well, she's fine now." He held the baby close to him. Her little arms were around his neck, her eyes drooping. Amanda noticed that unlike her brother, she had brown eyes and hair. A definite daddy's girl.

"You're not going to leave her out in the truck again, are you?" Amanda felt compelled to ask. "At the shop, I mean."

He stared at her with those deep brown eyes that made her heart miss a beat. "You think just because I'm a dumb repairman that I can't learn by my mistakes?" His voice bristled with barely concealed anger. "Don't concern yourself, miss. I'll take care of her. Come on, Kevin." He opened the door, and they went out into the snowy night.

For some reason Amanda felt she was the one in the wrong. "Uh, I could watch them while you're gone. I'm mean, since you're coming back." At least she hoped he was coming back.

He turned at the bottom of the stairs. "How do I know you won't call child services or something while I'm gone?"

Amanda felt color seeping into her face. "I'm not going to do that." *Not yet*, she added silently.

There was a hint of a smile on his face, but it did not change the anger she saw in his eyes. "Don't worry, I'll be back. I'm leaving my tools."

He walked away, his back tense and stiff. The perfect snub. Except that he was cradling the baby—and somehow that softened everything.

Not watching them get into the truck, she slammed the door, wondering where she'd gone wrong. She'd done the right thing about the baby. His eyes had seemed sincere when he told her it was the first time he'd left her in the truck alone. But could she be sure? He'd seemed about to leave the older boy in the truck earlier, so why not the baby?

One thing was sure: she'd made him angry. Not a good thing, considering. What if he booby-trapped her stove to explode or something the next time she used it? The headlines would read: "School Teacher Killed in Unfortunate Accident." Or maybe: "Repairman Testifies Accident Caused by Teacher's Stupidity." Yes, that would be more likely. He'd blame the explosion on the water she'd thrown inside the oven.

Ignoring her upset stomach, Amanda sighed and went back to her papers.

Chapter Three

Blake was angry. Furious. No, there weren't even words in the English dictionary to define his feelings. He thought of the woman he'd just left, how those emerald eyes pierced him and made him want to find out everything about her. While he fixed her stove, he'd begun to think that maybe a date with her might be possible—if he explained about Kevin and Mara. And then this had to happen!

Fury flooded him in a renewed wave as he drove through the dark streets to the repair shop. He wasn't angry at the woman—at Amanda. He was angry only at himself.

In front of the repair shop, he took a sleeping Mara from her car seat and stroked her face softly. "I'm sorry," he whispered. "I didn't realize . . . I was stupid. So stupid." He hugged her tightly, and she wriggled in her sleep.

"I thought you said *stupid* was a bad word," Kevin said from the other side of the seat. Blake looked at the boy and noticed he was clutching a book, the second one he'd been reading at Amanda's. Oops.

"It is," Blake said. "But what I did was very bad. I shouldn't have left Mara in the truck alone. I thought it would be okay, but it wasn't."

Kevin shrugged. "Mommy does it all the time."

"She shouldn't."

"I stay and watch Mara."

"She shouldn't leave you, either."

Kevin's forehead wrinkled. "I thought you were going to leave me when we went there before."

"Well, that was only for a minute so I could see what was wrong." But Blake knew both times he'd been wrong. Neither child was old enough to be left alone. Yet what was he to do? He had to work, or they'd really be in trouble.

"I promise I won't be so stu—leave you alone again."

"Okay." Kevin tugged the door open.

After unlocking the door to the shop, Blake carried Mara inside and held her while he got the new part. On the way out, he remembered both Amanda's books.

"Are we going back to the lady's?" Kevin asked in the truck. "'Cause I'm getting kinda hungry."

"I'm going to leave you with a friend. But I'll order you a pizza before I leave."

"Do I know him?"

"Yes, but it's been a few months, and I never left you with him before so you might not remember him. He's really nice, though. And it's just until I fix that oven. I'll be right back."

"Does he have a TV?"

"Yes. I just hope he's home." It didn't escape Blake's notice that Kevin didn't seem concerned to be left with a stranger. As long as there was a television.

He was relieved to see the lights on as he drove up to the small house a few blocks northeast of the shop where he rented a base-ment apartment. Garth lived in the upstairs half of the house and had rented to him for a year now. As bachelors, they had become good friends. Blake bundled a sleeping Mara in her blanket and went out into the falling snow, shivering slightly.

"Man, why aren't you wearing a coat?" Garth said as he opened the door to them after three rings of the doorbell. He was wearing sweats, and his black hair, thinning on top, was wet, as though he'd just stepped from the shower. The sweats didn't do much for the roll that had begun around his waist, but Blake would never tell him so. Garth had a very macho image of himself that Blake suspected had begun in high school when he'd broken his nose defending a girl. That crooked nose and his olive skin—a gift from his Italian grandmother—secured him more dates in a month than Blake had in a year.

"I left it home this morning. Had my hands full, and I didn't want to bother with it. Didn't know it was going to snow." Blake went inside without waiting for an invitation.

"Hey, you got a kid under there!" Garth eyed the blanket with mistrust. "And here I thought you were bringing me a welcome home gift."

"*You're* the one with the fabulous job that takes you to Hawaii—in the winter, no less. And you don't even need the tan, thanks to those Italian genes. What'd you bring *me*?"

"Shells?"

Blake groaned.

"No, really. It's this cool little get-up that looks like a lady in a swimsuit." His brow creased. "Well, I think it's supposed to be a lady. Has seaweed for hair. Hmm. Actually, it looks more like a skinny sea creature they've dried and pasted shells onto. Maybe I should show you. You don't think—"

"No." Blake said.

"Cool. I wanna see it," Kevin said from behind Blake.

Garth's eyes widened further. "Another one? Oh, yes. Wait a

minute, is this Kevin? Wow, you've really grown in the past few months, haven't you?" Garth never forgot a name or a face. "Where you been, buddy?"

"At my grandma's. Mostly. But I like it better here."

"Look, Garth, can you watch them for a minute?" Blake asked. "I'm right in the middle of fixing some lady's oven, and I can't be hauling them with me. Won't be longer than a half hour. Promise."

"He left Mara in the car," Kevin said helpfully. "Her cried. The lady got mad."

"That's enough, Kevin." Blake tousled the boy's hair to eliminate any sting from the words. "Well, Garth, will you watch them?"

His friend lifted his hands. "I don't know anything about kids. You've at least had practice."

"Practice? They've only been here three days."

"*This* time. What's your cousin gone and done now?"

"Shhh." Blake looked pointedly at Kevin. "We'll talk later. Will you do it?"

"Yeah, I'll do it."

"Thanks. I owe you one." He went to the couch and gently laid Mara down. "You'll have to watch her closely," he said, pulling a few pillows from the love seat to put on the floor next to the couch. "She rolled off my couch the first day before I realized she could roll at all. Seems babies do things a lot earlier than I remember with Kevin."

Garth nervously rubbed his hands together. "Get going already. She could wake any minute."

Blake wondered if he had looked that worried when he had first brought Mara home on Monday. "Okay." He hurried to the door. "Oh, Kevin's hungry. I'm going to order a pizza and have them bring it here. I'll pay you when I get back."

"Watch her *and* pay?" Garth sighed. "Next, you'll be wanting free rent."

Blake shut the door behind him. Garth wasn't experienced with children, but he was a good man. They'd be safe. Still, he'd better hurry and get back before Mara woke and decided that her diaper was too clean.

He pulled out his cell phone and brought up the number for pizza delivery.

It was only six minutes to the teacher's house. Blake timed it. He bet he could install the part in ten minutes, including replacing the inner cover, and use only another five to screw on the back that he hadn't needed to take off in the first place. Then six more minutes to get home. Total of twenty-seven minutes. Giving her three minutes to write a check would make it thirty. He decided to waste thirty seconds in the pickup preparing her bill so that maybe she'd have the check waiting for him when he was finished.

He half expected her to have the police waiting to take Kevin and Mara away when he arrived, but there was no sign of visitors. She opened the door, looking better than any woman had a right to look in tattered jeans.

"Oh, you're back." She sounded relieved.

"I took the kids home."

"That's good."

Blake was standing inside her door, staring at her. Her green eyes seemed to root him to the spot. He noticed how her blonde hair, cut to one length in back and feathered gently up the sides, curled at the ends as it rested on her shoulders. Her skin was very white and soft-looking. Earlier, he'd noticed an adorable dimple in her right cheek, but she wasn't smiling now. Her bottom lip was caught beneath her top teeth and from the slightly swollen look of it, this wasn't the first time. He forced himself to look away.

"I'll get right to it," he muttered. "Oh, wait. Here're your books." He shoved them at her.

"Thanks."

He set the repair bill—for only one part and one home visit—

noticeably on the counter and went to work. Now that he wasn't worried about leaving Mara in the truck and hurrying too fast, the job was quickly finished. He glanced at his watch. He'd been away twenty minutes.

"Here." She handed him a check.

"Thank you." He clipped the check to the work order, threw his tools in his box, and started for the door. She trailed after him.

"It's not going to, uh, explode or anything, is it?" she asked, her voice joking but hesitant enough that he could tell she was actually worried.

For a moment he forgot all that had gone before and grinned. "No, I didn't rig it to blow, if that's what you're asking."

"Did you tell your wife what happened?" Her face wasn't soft now, and there was steel behind the question.

She thinks I'm married, Blake realized. But of course! He'd showed up with two children. What else could she think?

"Their mother wasn't home," he said.

Her eyes opened wide. "You didn't leave them alone!"

"No!" He shook his head. "Look, I told you it was a mistake. Kind of like starting a fire in an oven. It won't happen again. But this really isn't your concern."

Amanda nodded and looked away. He saw in her expression that it had been hard for her to ask, but that her concern for the children was paramount. His irritation vanished. He wished he could soothe her worry and tell her the children were safe, that they weren't even his. That he was just learning to care for a baby again. But what was the point? There was a time before Kevin went to his grandmother's that he was with Blake more than with his mother. Who knew what might happen this time? The children were with him for the time being and that meant he was responsible. He should have known better.

I should at least tell her I'm not married. He pushed the thought away even as it came. That was also irrelevant. It wasn't as though they would start dating if she knew. He'd learned that where women of her caliber were concerned, a man's job made a big difference in their dating preferences. He was a degree short of her—for the time being.

The green eyes rested upon him again, and he realized that he had stopped walking halfway to the front door. He wouldn't tell her about the children or his marital status, but he would do something else. "I—" he began. "Look, I am grateful you found Mara. I didn't realize what might happen when I left her there with the heat on. I'm really new at this."

"They are young," she commented, but her expression was reserved.

Yeah, he thought, *but Mara's turning eight months old this week. If I were really her father, I should know not to leave her by now.* He gave a silent, bitter chuckle. Yes, even if he had a degree, he doubted this woman could ever be interested in him now. First impressions were hard to erase.

She opened the door, and he stepped onto the small cement porch. Cold rushed over him, but his body felt too warm from the heat inside the house. "I left the oven on to make sure it would heat up," he said. "Seems to be working, but let me know if it doesn't."

"How long should I leave it on?"

"Doesn't matter. Just make sure it's getting hot."

"Okay. Thanks."

He nodded and strode across her lawn, feeling her eyes trailing him, but when he glanced up at the house after climbing into his truck, he saw the door was shut. Unexplainably disappointed, he looked at his watch. Twenty-six minutes. He would be two minutes later than the half hour he'd promised Garth.

Blake arrived just as the pizza delivery man was leaving, so his timing hadn't been bad at all. At least his dinner wouldn't be cold.

He wondered briefly what the teacher was having for dinner. He bet she knew how to cook. He himself had become a fairly good chef over the past years, at first out of necessity and later on from pure enjoyment, but his class schedule was fairly heavy this semester. He didn't have much time for cooking. With Kevin and Mara around, he'd have to change that—somehow. He wouldn't have taken so many classes if he'd known they were coming to stay.

Garth didn't hide his happiness when Blake entered the house. "She's awake," he announced as though having just won a Nobel Prize. The baby sat on the floor near the couch, with pillows stacked around her.

"She doesn't need pillows when she's on the floor," Blake said. "She sits up just fine."

"Really?" Garth took a pillow from behind her back and whistled when she didn't fall.

Kevin giggled and went to stand beside Blake. "I'm hungry. Can I have some pizza?"

"Sure. Get up to the table." Blake went to the cupboard where Garth kept the plates. "You want some, Garth?"

"Yeah." He was still in the adjoining living room with the baby.

"Better get in here, then. But move those figurines from the coffee table, if they're breakable. Believe me, she can crawl over there and pull herself up far enough to get them. She's already broken everything I didn't move in my apartment."

Garth came to the table, his arms filled with ebony figurines that Blake knew he'd picked up on a business trip to Florida. "Uh, you'd better go check on the baby," he said uncertainly. "There's something on her back."

Blake had an idea what that "something" was. Sure enough, her dress and undershirt were soaked through. "Looks like it's time for a bath and some pajamas," he said. Mara grinned at him, and he found he didn't mind the effort—or the complaining of his famished stomach.

As he bathed and changed Mara in his basement apartment, Blake pondered his life. Had he gone directly to college and not wasted two years working at his brother's shop after his mission, he might have been married by now. Yes, married to Laurie, the only girl he'd ever seriously dated. She'd wanted him to go to college, but he hadn't seen a need. Then. Too late he realized she was right, that he could never make the living he wanted working for Doug. And by the time he enrolled in college, the girls he met in school were too young, too immature—or so he'd felt.

Of course, it hadn't helped his social life that for the past four years he'd been a part-time daddy to Kevin. Paula would leave him for weeks and months at a time—especially after Mara was born. Blake knew his cousin had always wanted a daughter, and when Mara came he'd hoped she would settle down and become a proper mother for both children. Yet after only two months, Paula had begun leaving Mara with her mother in Cedar City, and Kevin remained with Blake in Pleasant Grove.

That arrangement changed six months ago when Paula had come to pick Kevin up one night, so drunk she could barely remember Blake's name. He hadn't let her take the boy from his bed and had threatened to call the authorities. The next day she had come back sober, grabbed Kevin, and whisked him off to her mother's. She hadn't brought him by since. Blake missed Kevin and had been down to Cedar City nearly every weekend to have day-outings with the boy when his mother wasn't around. Mara never went with them on their outings, but Blake had become enchanted with her and had taken to giving her toys. Seeing her face light up was one of the highlights of his visits.

He had still worried about their care, though, because his aunt was old and really too frail to be dealing with the offspring of her youngest child. And Paula . . . well, she was never around much. Then last month when he called his aunt to set up a time to see Kevin, she told him Paula had taken the children away. She didn't know where. Days of worry stretched into weeks until Paula had called three days ago from jail and asked him to pick up the children in Salt Lake City. He had left work immediately to get them.

For his part, Blake had loved having Kevin with him over the years, but the care of a small child had required him to cut back on classes and forgo many opportunities to meet dates. So here he was at twenty-eight, a senior nearly halfway through his last year of college with no wife or even a girlfriend. He was still working at his brother's shop. And now he had two children to care for.

Mara's eyes were drooping again, so he held her close as he fed her another bottle. She was out before it was half-finished. He laid her gently in the crib he had bought years ago for Kevin and, leaving the basement door open, went upstairs to Garth's, reminding himself to call his aunt tomorrow and talk to her about the children. Not that he wanted to turn them over to her, but she'd want him to bring them by for a visit. He was surprised she hadn't already called to arrange a time to see them. Surely Paula had phoned her mother from jail. She would have needed money for bail and had learned long ago that while Blake would bend over backwards for Kevin, he was through giving her cash. His aunt, however, was more easily convinced to part with her retirement funds.

The pizza was cold, but Blake devoured it without heating it up in the microwave. He hated pizza heated in the microwave, and the oven would take too long.

Kevin lay on the couch in front of Garth's huge TV screen, his eyes closed in sleep. Blake checked the clock and saw that it was already eight-thirty. He shook his head, remembering that he still had to study for a test tomorrow night.

Garth came to sit with him at the table. "So, what happened?"

"I left Mara in the car with the heater on while I went to fix a lady's oven," Blake began. "She was so tired, and I was just going to be fifteen minutes. I thought it'd be okay, but she got too hot, I guess, and woke up crying." He shook his head, feeling a renewed surge of anger at his actions. "When the lady told me, I was stunned. Couldn't even move. I kept looking at this part I'd dropped on the floor, thinking I'd broken it and what was I going to do? It was crazy. I've never felt so brainless in my entire life. I shouldn't have left Mara, Garth. I was wrong. I knew it. For a minute, I thought the lady was going to call the police, or something."

"Someone should—and not on you."

Blake sighed. "Paula does need to get her head on straight."

"You're enabling her. She's using you."

Blake gave a bitter chuckle. "Bringing our job home with us, are we?" Garth worked for a motivational speaker, arranging scheduling, which was why he got to travel to exotic places while Blake stayed home to study and change diapers.

"Well, it's true."

"I know, but what . . . well, you don't know Paula like I do." Blake leaned forward, hands held out over the table, palms upward. "We grew up together. She was a sweet kid. My favorite cousin. I don't know what went wrong."

Garth rubbed his forefinger down the slant of his nose, pausing as he always did at the bump the break had left. "I do. It's called substance abuse."

"Yeah." Blake felt bile rise in his throat. He sat back in his chair, folding his arms over his chest. "She called me from the jail and begged me to get the kids from a friend's house. When I got there"—he shook his head—"it made me sick. This was not a place for children—for anyone. Beer cans lying around, a sickly sweet smell—probably pot—and the guy was this skinny, bearded loser who looked like he was whacked-out on cocaine. I was so mad at her for leaving them there. I almost called the police myself."

"You should have."

Blake let his head drop into his hands for a minute. "I know that. I do. But I love her, you know? She's my favorite cousin. We were so close growing up. The two youngest among all the relatives. Doug was in high school when I was born. Same for Paula and her brother and sister." He lifted his head. "I know it sounds crazy, but the Paula I grew up with wouldn't have left her children with a man like that."

"I bet she wouldn't have done drugs, either." Garth's dark eyes were sympathetic. "You're going to have to do something."

"I know." Blake stood. "But not today. I'll have a talk with her when she comes to pick up the kids. With any luck, it won't be until after Christmas. That's almost two months away." He walked over to where Kevin slept on the couch, scooping him up in his arms.

"Hey," Garth said. "Don't you have class tomorrow night?"

"Yeah. A test."

"Well, I'm not really into kids, but if you need someone . . ."

Warm gratitude shot through Blake's heart. "Thanks, Garth. I asked that little girl next door. She said she'd come every Tuesday and Thursday. And Rhonda said she'd take Friday mornings until I find a sitter for days—which I'm going to have to do since Mara's here, too. I can't have her at the shop all day. But basically my school times are covered." He paused and added, his voice thick, "Thank you, though. Means a lot to me—your offer."

Garth grinned. "Yeah, man. Just remember I'm off again this weekend, so I won't be here if you need something. We're headed to California."

"Lucky you. No snow." Blake said goodnight, silently thanking the Lord for Garth's two-car garage. At least there would be no window to scrape before work.

Kevin didn't wake as Blake tucked him into bed, deciding that the four-year-old could sleep in his clothes instead of his new pajamas. He likely wouldn't notice. Paula had never brought pajamas when she dropped him off—or a toothbrush for that matter. Kevin's arrival had always meant a shopping trip. He kissed the little boy, checked on Mara, and then hit the books. Tired to his very bones, he sat at the small round kitchen table so he wouldn't fall asleep.

Less than an hour had passed when a terrified scream pierced his weary brain.

Kevin!

He ran to the children's room. "I'm here, Kevin," he called out. "Don't worry, Uncle Blake's here."

Reaching the twin bed, he cuddled Kevin in his arms. The boy clung to him. "What is it?" Blake asked. Was this a realization of Blake's greatest fear? Had Paula's lifestyle damaged the boy permanently? He mentally kicked himself for not calling the authorities six months earlier. Paula obviously was *not* the sweet girl he'd grown up with. There was no one to protect Kevin and Mara. No one but him.

"The bugs," Kevin moaned. "Bugs all over my bed! They're all over my bed!"

"Bugs?" Blake looked at the bed uncertainly. In the dim light coming from the hall, he couldn't see any bugs.

"Uh-huh. Crawling on me!" Kevin shuddered and buried his face in Blake's stomach.

"Kevin. I don't see any bugs. You had a dream. Look at the bed."

Kevin pulled his face reluctantly from Blake's shirt. "I see them still," he cried. "When I shut my eyes. Lots and lots of bugs! And snakes, too."

Blake rubbed the boy's back. Bugs and snakes? Where had this come from? Then understanding dawned. The books from the schoolteacher's house! One had been about insects, if he'd understood Kevin's babbling in the truck, and the other about snakes. Here

41

he was worried about abuse and Kevin was only dreaming about bugs.

Chuckling to himself, he held Kevin away from him so he could look down into his face. "It was those books at the lady's house, wasn't it?"

Kevin shrugged. "Maybe."

"You want to go to my bed? Or to the couch?"

"Your bed," Kevin snuggled against him, sighing softly as Blake picked him up and took him to the other bedroom.

"There, no bugs here," he said, making a big show of looking beneath the covers. "But just in case, I'm going to leave my magic bug-repellent light on."

"And snakes."

"Yes. My magic bug-and-snake-repellent light. See?" He switched the dimmer on his overhead light low enough for the boy to see but not so bright as to chase away sleep.

"It really is magic," Kevin said, laying his head on the pillow. "But what about Mara? Her might have bugs too."

"*She* might have bugs," corrected Blake. "But I bet she doesn't." He held up a hand to stay Kevin's inevitable protest. "However, just to make sure, I will use another magic bug-and-snake-repellent light for her. Now, where did it go?" He rummaged through his top dresser drawer. "I know I put it here somewhere. Ah-hah!" He held up the nightlight he had used for Kevin the last time he'd come to stay.

"Good." Kevin smiled sleepily.

"If you need me again, call me." Blake said. "I'm right here in the kitchen."

Kevin shut his eyes. Blake watched him for a full minute before going into the children's room and plugging in the nightlight. Mara wouldn't need it, but Kevin would check in the morning. He was protective of his little sister.

Blake sat down before his school books, grinning to himself. Bugs were serious business. How he wished that was the worst thing Kevin would have to face in life!

What would Amanda think of her books now? Blake thought. *Amanda, Amanda.* Her name reverberated in his mind. He didn't really know her well enough to call her by name, but he did all the same. It was a beautiful name, so vibrant, alive, spunky, and so . . . so *her.*

He sighed. It didn't matter what she would think of Kevin's dream because she wouldn't know. If he had told her the truth about the children, maybe he would have been able to tell her. Maybe they would have passed each other in the grocery store and casually chatted about Kevin's dreams. Then he would have asked her out.

Blake started suddenly, realizing that his face was on the cool kitchen table and that he was almost asleep. Almost dreaming . . . of her. Absurd!

He should have told her. Why hadn't he, really? He knew the answer, one difficult to admit even to himself. He hadn't told her because when he looked into her eyes, he'd wanted never to stop. He knew too well that he was ripe for a relationship, hungry for something lasting and permanent. When he fell it would be hard. But now was not the time to lose himself with either success or failure in a relationship. He had to stay focused for Kevin and Mara.

Chapter Four

Being with the fourth-graders at school was Amanda's favorite way to spend time. She loved watching them, loved their innocent way of looking at the world, their unabashed amazement when she taught them something new. She didn't mind their constant questions, their awkwardness, or even their rare bouts of stubbornness. She adored teaching and had wanted to be a teacher for as long as she could remember. She only wished that along with all the secular teaching, she could also teach them of God and the gospel as she did the young women in the church class she taught on Sundays. Most of her fourth-graders were members of the Church, two were even in her ward, but there were a few whose occasional comments showed they didn't have a clear idea who God even was, much less Jesus.

For the past three weeks in science they'd been studying insects. They'd read about them, made illustrations of them, and shared with the class stories they'd written from the perspective of an insect. They had brought insects to class—found around their homes, even at this cold time of year—looked up their names, and discussed their parts and where they fit in the ecology. When the children showed eagerness for more, Amanda had taken to calling pet stores to find new insects. Once she had some odd-looking black crickets shipped to her from the Internet. Her brother Mitch, studying to be a wildlife biologist at Brigham Young University, had also been a great source for unusual insects, most of which he borrowed from his professors.

Amanda knew this was one of her finer science units. Girls who had been afraid of insects before they'd started the unit now eagerly held the bugs. Boys who had smashed them before without thinking now released them unharmed outside—at least in front of Amanda. Today was the last day of study and then on Friday she would conclude the section by giving each child the small insect sticker books she had purchased at her own expense.

As they broke down in groups to study their insects, with several parent volunteers leading the discussions, Amanda found her mind drifting to the man who'd repaired her oven. He had been so irritated with her when she'd asked about his children. She thought he was telling the truth when he promised to take care of them, but had he really? Was it any of her concern? Surely their mother would take care of them.

Or would she?

Before Amanda had started teaching, she'd thought every mother was like her sister, Kerrianne—completely and totally wrapped up in her children and attentive to their every need. By now she'd learned that some weren't. Some mothers didn't seem to mind if their children wore clean clothes or combed their hair. Some mothers never paid attention to their children's homework, either because they didn't think it important or because they had too many other responsibilities. In a few heartbreaking cases, Amanda had found mothers who simply didn't care. What if the repairman's children had a mother like that? After all, they had been with their father at work.

Then another thought came. *Maybe they don't have a mother.*

Hadn't he mentioned a mother? She couldn't remember now. She did remember his face, his name, his eyes like pools of chocolate fudge that made her weak in the knees.

Ridiculous! Chocolate fudge indeed!

She needed to let it go. Or . . .

Or what? Was the Spirit telling her she needed to check up on those children? Were they in danger? Was this an excuse to see their father? *That* could be even more dangerous . . . for her, at least. For all she knew, he was a happily married man who'd made the mistake of leaving his child unattended. Still, there was always the possibility that he was a neglectful father whose children were at risk.

I'll go check on them, she decided. *I'll see for myself that they're okay and then forget it.* She felt immediately at peace with her decision and knew it had been inspired. Saying a silent prayer of thanks, she turned her focus back to her students.

When school was over for the day, Amanda grabbed an extra insect sticker book, looked up the address of the repair shop in the school office phone book, and drove over. Located one block west of the post office, the medium-sized building was sided with huge strips of corrugated metal. A large sign announcing Doug's Appliance and Repair ran half the length of the shop, and an old, white, lidless washing machine by the entrance held a mound of dead plants. There were only two cars in the parking lot, a blue pickup on the far side and a four-door sedan close to the entrance. *Employee and customer?* she wondered.

Now that she had arrived, the assurance she had felt abandoned her, and she thought of a hundred excuses not to go in: the children might not be there, Blake might be angry, he might call the police and accuse her of stalking, the children's mother might think she was trying to steal her man . . . There were others, each more outrageous than the last.

Finally, Amanda grabbed her purse and left her car, glad that the overhead sun had melted all of last night's snow, except in the mountains. The snow had cleared the air, making it smell fresh and new. Biting her lower lip, she entered the shop.

The interior was dark, though she immediately recognized the man behind the long counter bordering the right side of the shop. He was talking to a faintly familiar, rotund lady dressed in a long black sweater, but he looked up as the bells over the door jingled. His mouth froze, apparently in mid-sentence, and then continued on so deftly that Amanda wondered if she had imagined the hesitation. Her eyes wandered over the shop. Sure enough, there was a playpen that held the baby from the night before, and beside it stood little Kevin. Next to him was an older girl she knew well: Natalie Michaels, a child as skinny as her mother was round.

"Sister Huntington!" Natalie shouted, running to her. Kevin trailed behind. Natalie reached Amanda and hugged her. "This is my teacher, Kevin—in the fourth grade. She's my most favorite teacher ever! Her name's Miss Huntington, but I call her Sister Huntington 'cause she's also in my ward. She teaches my sister in Young Women's."

"I know her, too," Kevin said, lifting his chin. "We fixed her oven. I read her books."

"Sister Huntington always has the best books!" Natalie said, her excitement bubbling over. She looked back to Amanda. "Your stove was broken? You didn't tell us."

Amanda smiled. Sometimes the children forgot she had a life outside school, one she didn't share with them. "I guess I forgot." She looked at Natalie. "So do you know each other?"

"We met yesterday. Mom had to pick up a part for Dad, but it was the wrong one so we came back today. Kevin was showing me his baby sister. She is *so* cute. Want to see?"

"Sure." Amanda let the children lead her along a row of

appliances. She stole a glance at Blake, who was still talking to Natalie's mother. Their eyes met and held for the briefest of seconds.

"See?" Natalie was saying. "I love how she can stand up while she's holding on to the edge. And look at her clothes. She's so cute!"

Amanda had to agree that the bright pink outfit really set off the child's brown hair and dark eyes. She also wore pink socks and soft-looking, brown leather shoes. The only thing missing was a bow for her hair.

Kevin was equally well dressed. His dark blue cargo jeans looked so new they were still stiff, and his navy, waffle-woven shirt had obviously not seen many washings. He wore the black boots of the night before, and his longish blond hair had, at least at some point during the day, been combed.

Both children looked well cared for and happy. Amanda felt like an idiot.

"I'm all finished." Natalie's mother approached them. "Oh, hello, Amanda," she said, her dark eyes widening with surprise. "How are you?"

"Very well. And yourself, Shelly?" Amanda didn't know Shelly Michaels well, but she loved her daughters.

Blake had followed Shelly over and was staring at Amanda with a sour expression on his good-looking face. He wore the same blue button-down shirt of the day before—the company uniform—but this time his jeans were black to match his boots. She noticed that today he was clean-shaven.

"You look really great," she added to Shelly. It was true. Shelly Michaels had one of the most classically beautiful faces she had ever seen.

"Thank you, my dear," Shelly said, smiling widely. "You are so sweet. I could always lose a few pounds, but I am feeling well." She paused for a breath and went on. "Amanda, it's good I ran into you here. I've been wanting to talk to you, and there never seems to be time at church." She glanced at Blake. "Amanda's in our ward, you see. Anyway, Amanda, I just wanted to let you know what a wonderful year Natalie's having at school. Last year all she did was complain, but this year . . . Oh, you've really made the difference. Thank you so much! And my Sharon feels the same way about Young Women's. You're really a gifted teacher."

Amanda blushed at the unexpected praise, especially since it was given in front of Blake. "Thank you. I love teaching them both. They're wonderful girls."

Shelly's face beamed. "I appreciate your saying so. Well," she hefted a brown bag containing her purchases, "I'd better get this home if I want to use my dryer tonight. Come on, Natalie."

Amanda watched them leave. She felt Blake's eyes on her but only when Shelly and Natalie left the shop did she meet his eyes. "So you know Shelly Michaels," she said, for lack of anything better to say.

"Actually, my brother knows them. Used to be in his ward. They come in often."

"Always breaking things, huh?" She chuckled, feeling very stupid. "Natalie's that way, too. She's broken three of our insect cages in the past two weeks alone."

He smiled, and the formerly sour expression disappeared. "So, did your oven stop working?"

"Oh, no," she said quickly. His smile was doing funny things to her heart, and she decided she much preferred his sour look. "Not at all."

He raised both eyebrows. "Your washer quit?"

"No. It's fine."

"Dryer? Microwave? Toaster?"

"No. All working. At least they were the last time I checked."

He tilted his head back and stared down at her. "So what isn't working? Are you going to make me name all your appliances?"

Amanda felt her stomach tingle. He was right, this was ridiculous. "I just came to see, uh, if Kevin would like this." She pulled the sticker book from her purse and waved it between them. "He was so interested in my books last night."

Blake studied her, his dark eyes intense and accusing. "You're checking up on me, aren't you?"

"No, of course not. Everyone makes mistakes." Amanda bit her lip. "Besides, I didn't come just for the book."

"Oh?"

She had to think of something fast! If she wanted to be of any use to the children, she couldn't anger him further. "Uh," she began. Could she say she just wanted to know how long it would be until she might have to replace the oven part again? No, for that she would have called. Unless she was in the neighborhood—and what would she be in the neighborhood for? She never really visited this part of town. "I—oh, my stove . . ."

"Yes?" His fists clenched at his side and his stance was rigid, like a tiger ready to pounce. She should have known better than to try to stretch the truth. Not only was it against her religion, but her face always gave her away.

"It beeps," she said.

He looked confused. "Beeps? You mean the timer?"

"Yeah, exactly." She raised the hand that still held the sticker book, motioning in his general direction. "Sometimes during the night, the timer goes off for no reason at all. Scared me to death the first time it happened. Thought it was the fire alarm. It's gone off about five times in the last three months."

"It happened again last night?"

"No, but it will. It always does. There's no telling when. So since we've established a relationship—a working relationship . . ." She groaned mentally at her awkwardness and completely lost her train of thought. "What I mean is, since you repair stoves, I thought you might know what I could do about the timer. Maybe buy a part to fix it, or something." Did her words even make sense, or was she just babbling?

"And you just happened to have that sticker book lying around?"

What was he grilling her for? Was it a crime to offer the child a book? "Yes. I'm a teacher, remember? I was headed this way anyway," she added for good measure, "on my way shopping." There, he couldn't disprove that. Shopping could lead her anywhere. In fact, maybe she would stop by Macey's afterwards so her conscience would feel better. "So you think you might have a part to stop the beeping?"

To her relief, his fists unclenched and his body relaxed. "You'd need a screwdriver to get off the back," he said doubtfully.

"I have a screwdriver—I have a whole set." Never mind that they were the pink ones Mitch had given her for a present a few years back. All the pieces were still pristine in the box, except for the smallest one that she had used to put batteries in an electronic memory game she had bought for her students. That one was lying in her desk at the school. "I know how to use them, too."

He studied her. "I'm sure you do. But it's really hard to say what might be wrong without testing it. Could be a simple loose wire, or the whole thing might need to be rewired." He grinned at her. "That would take more than a screwdriver. So do you want me to come and look at it?"

She sighed. "Not this month. Unless I want to go without food. I bought too many books last month. I was hoping I could just slap a part on—a cheap part—and, voilà, be done with it. Anyway, I can live with it for a while. Never know, it might not even happen again for a few weeks. Here, take this book." She shoved it into his hands.

Kevin had patiently endured this long exchange and now dived for the book in Blake's grasp. Blake held it up. "Hey, bud, don't you remember your nightmare last night?"

Kevin shook his head. "I really, really wanna see the book. Pleeeeease?"

"Nightmare?" Amanda asked.

"He had a nightmare about insects," Blake explained.

"And snakes," Kevin added.

Blake turned on him. "Ah-hah! So you *do* remember!"

"A little." Kevin shrugged his shoulders, his blue eyes pleading. "Can I see the book? Please? I won't be scared. I promise."

"Yeah, not now, anyway." With an exasperated sigh, Blake handed him the book. "Can't ever seem to say no to him," he muttered. "Tell Amand—the lady thank you," he added as the phone on the counter began its shrill ring. "Excuse me a moment." He sprinted across the room and picked up the phone.

"Thank you, lady." Kevin's eyes barely met hers before they fell to the cover of the sticker book.

"You find the stickers inside and match them to the drawings." She pointed to the stickers when he opened the book. "There are facts about each insect underneath the drawings." She frowned. At four he wouldn't know how to read them yet. "Ask your father to read them to you."

"I don't have a father."

Amanda blinked twice, sure she had heard wrong. "What about, uh, Blake?" She looked at the man on the phone.

"He's my uncle, but he'll read it to me."

"Good." Amanda felt confused and more than a little angry at the sudden rush of hope that Kevin's matter-of-fact statement had caused in her heart. Why hadn't Blake told her the children yesterday weren't his? Seemed an easy way to get out of an awkward situation. While she wouldn't excuse his behavior, she would never have worried about the children so much if she had known he was only a temporary caregiver. Her eyes went to the baby. Maybe he wasn't temporary at all. The baby could still be his daughter—she looked like him.

"Well, take care, Kevin." Amanda decided to leave while Blake was on the phone. Since the children were obviously not in danger at the moment, now seemed like a good time to escape.

Kevin didn't look up at her words, his eyes devouring the book and the cool-looking stickers. Amanda hoped they wouldn't cause him nightmares. Funny how worried she'd been about Blake caring for the children when it was her book that had caused the child problems! She couldn't have known that would happen. She usually dealt with fourth-graders, not four-year-olds.

"It won't go off?" Blake was saying as she made her way past the counter. "Are you sure? The water's still leaking all over the floor? Okay, calm down, Sister Fairbanks. I can't understand what you're saying. Can you turn the water off? It's those round handles behind the washer. They look like the ones where you turn on your water outside. Stuck? Can you unplug the washer? Look, I'll be right there. I'll hurry as fast as I can, but I have to lock up the store. One guy has a day off and our other one's out on a call. Doug and Rhonda are in Provo. Just block the water from getting on the carpet with towels or something. I'll get there as quickly as I can." He hung up the phone.

Amanda, hearing the stress in his voice, forgot about leaving. "What's wrong?" she asked.

"An old widow in my ward is having trouble with her washer." Blake was moving toward the children as he spoke. "I tried to get her to end the cycle, turn off the water, you name it, but she just can't get it to stop. She's frantic and crying, so she's not thinking straight. I've got to go over there." He swept Mara from the playpen. "Kevin, we have to leave now."

"I could watch them for you," Amanda offered. "It'll take so long getting the baby into her car seat—here and there. I promise, I'll take good care of them. And the shop, too."

"I can't ask you to do that." He wrapped the baby in a blanket, but she began to cry.

"Mara's hungry," Kevin announced, glancing up from his book. "You didn't give her a bottle yet, 'cause that other lady came in."

"Oh," Blake groaned. "I forgot the bottle." He raked a hand through his hair, shaking his head. He looked at Amanda for a moment, his brown eyes discerning. She felt he was studying her, measuring her worth. "Okay," he said finally. "Thank you. I appreciate it. She only lives three minutes from here. I'll be right back." He put Mara in her arms and started for the door. "The milk is in the diaper bag behind the counter. Kevin knows where. Just add the powder to the water. Oh, and don't let Kevin climb the shelves."

"We'll be fine. Go!"

When the roar of his engine signaled his departure, Amanda went to look for the formula. Mara had calmed down now and was playing with Amanda's hair. "Kevin, I don't see any di—never mind, here it is." She picked up the bag and found several bottles with the water already in them. Amanda read the instructions on the formula can before adding the powder. "Shake well," she said to Mara, who grinned at her and reached for the milk. "Just a second . . . let me shake it a bit and sit down on this chair . . . there."

Mara greedily slurped at the bottle, but she couldn't have been too hungry because not even an inch was gone before she stopped sucking to smile some more.

"You're a cutie," Amanda cooed, enchanted with the baby. "Come on, drink a little more. I see there's some applesauce in the bag. Would you like that instead? Huh?"

Mara grinned again and started sucking.

Amanda stroked her fine dark hair, as soft as silk. "You are so pretty. Aren't you?" *Like your daddy,* she thought. Was he her daddy? "Kevin?" Amanda called. "Could you come here, please?"

"I'm just right here." Kevin came around the counter, stickers in his hands. "These are hard to get out."

"Come here, and I'll help tear them off. You can lick them and paste them in." He handed her the book, and she saw that he'd already ripped two of the stickers in half. "That's okay," she said as she tore them carefully from the sheet. "We'll just paste the two halves right together, and no one will even see that they're ripped." She handed the stickers to Kevin, and he pasted them into the book. "Very nice."

They worked quietly together for a while, and then Amanda said, "Is Mara your sister?"

Kevin nodded. "Uh-huh." He licked the back of another sticker.

"So Blake is her uncle, too."

"Yeah."

"Where's your mom?"

Kevin shrugged, his mouth twisting slightly. "I don't know. Her took us to Larry's on Sunday and then Uncle Blake came to get us on Thursday."

"A week ago? Today's Thursday, you know."

"Then maybe Friday or Wednesday."

A smile tugged the corners of Amanda's mouth. "So how many nights did you spend at Larry's?"

"Just one. I slept on the couch. Mara was hungry. I gave her some of my chips." He paused and then added quickly, "Her didn't choke. I broke them up real small."

"That was smart," Amanda said gravely. She handed him another sticker. Mara was through with her bottle and now looked with interest at the pages of stickers. "No, Mara. You can't touch these. Here, you can have this. We already took the stickers out." Mara happily crushed the paper remnants in her hands. Amanda set down the rest of the stickers and hugged the child, who smelled like baby powder and rose-scented lotion. She was so precious!

"I need another one," Kevin said.

Chuckling, Amanda went to work tearing out the insects, vowing next time to find a sticker book with peel-out stickers.

Chapter Five

Blake felt the worse for wear when he returned to the shop less than twenty minutes later. His hair was on end, one pant leg was completely soaked, and his shirt was dark where it had been spattered with water droplets. To his relief, Amanda and the children were in the shop playing peacefully with Kevin's sticker book. Blake hadn't expected them to be anywhere else, but since he didn't really know Amanda well enough to leave the children with her, he'd worried anyway. If it hadn't been for Shelley Michaels's glowing praise of the woman, he would have taken them with him, emergency or no.

"The water's off," he said. "I had to stay and help her mop it up—that's what took most of the time."

"What was the problem?"

He shrugged his head. "Didn't stay to tear the machine apart. I'll go back tomorrow. Any calls? Customers?"

"Nope. All quiet. I guess Thursday isn't a big day for appliance parts. Then again, you weren't gone long."

"Good."

Silence fell between them. Blake thought of how natural she looked sitting there with Mara in her lap. Her hair was straighter today, which he liked, but her green eyes were the same as he remembered—bright and riveting. She wore silky black pants, topped by a multicolored sweater, definitely more dressy than yesterday's jeans, but she didn't seem worried about dirtying her clothes with the baby.

A loud rumbling sound came from Amanda's lap, cutting through the silence. "Hold her up, quick!" Blake advised. "She sometimes explodes."

Amanda held the baby up. Sure enough, a dark patch was just beginning in the back above the waistband of Mara's outfit.

"Her is stinky," Kevin said, grinning.

Blake sighed. "*She* is stinky, not *her.*"

Kevin lifted his chin stubbornly. "I said Mara's stinky. I didn't say her or she."

"No way, Kevin. You said *her.*" Blake took the baby and said to Amanda, "She has diarrhea. I thought at first it was the diapers—wrong brand or maybe too small, but I've tried eight different kinds in various sizes. It's got to be diarrhea." Balancing Mara on the countertop, he reached for the diaper bag. Mara giggled. "Either that or she has powerful, uh . . . muscles."

"A change in food can cause diarrhea," Amanda said with mirth in her voice.

Blake scowled. "Yeah. I thought as much. I don't know what she was eating before, but according to my sister-in-law, she's on track now."

"Then it'll get better." Amanda ripped out more stickers for Kevin as Blake changed the diaper, a skill he felt he'd perfected over the four days Mara had been with him. He also changed her clothes and put the soiled ones in a plastic bag with the two other sets she had already messed today. This was the last change he'd brought. In fact, it was the last clean thing he had left from the six outfits and five sleepers he had purchased on Monday. When he got home, he'd have to do laundry, and this weekend he would definitely pick up a few more sets of clothes. Too bad it wasn't the season for garage sales. Thank goodness Kevin didn't have this problem or he might have to take out another college loan.

When he was finished, Amanda set the stickers on the counter and stood. "I'd better get going."

"Yeah, you said you were going shopping." This was as close as he would come to saying he didn't believe her. The truth was that if he hadn't been so scared of losing the children, her concern would be touching, amusing even.

Her lips twisted in a wry smile. "I'm sorry if my books caused Kevin nightmares. I hope the stickers don't do the same." She picked up her purse by the chair. "You know, I was thinking that maybe if he knew insects better, held them and learned about them, maybe they wouldn't be so scary. You could read him the sticker book. Or you might . . ." She trailed off, her teeth biting into her lower lip. "I have a lot of bugs at the school. We'll be finishing our science unit tomorrow, but I'll have them until Saturday morning. You could come by and show them to Kevin. He can even hold some."

"You really think that would help?" Blake asked, trying not to stare too long into her eyes.

She shrugged delicately. "I really don't know. I teach fourth-graders, not preschool. But a lot of the girls were afraid of insects, and now they're not. Think about it. You could come by after school tomorrow, if you want. Grovecrest Elementary."

He wanted more than anything to say yes, to have another chance to be near her, but he just nodded. "I know where it is. Thanks."

She turned again to go, then stopped short, her eyes full of curiosity. "Why didn't you tell me they weren't your children?"

He was surprised that she knew. Kevin must have done more than paste on stickers in his absence, the little blabbermouth. Or maybe she'd grilled him. Irritation replaced the attraction Blake felt for her. "Why didn't *you* tell me you really came here to check up on me?"

She threw up her hands, her face turning a light shade of pink, though whether from embarrassment or exasperation, he couldn't tell. "Okay. You're right. I came to make sure they were okay. My conscience wouldn't let me alone until I did. Truthfully, I didn't know what I was going to accomplish. I didn't think they'd be here. I was just following my . . . my conscience."

Her conscience or something else? For whatever reason she had come, Blake was glad—despite his present irritation. "They're here because I haven't found a sitter yet," he told her, cuddling Mara to his chest. "They haven't been with me long, and the sitter I used when Kevin was with me before has moved." He was about to expound on the dangers of leaving children with people you didn't know well when he realized he wasn't a great example in that respect. He'd left Mara *alone* in the car last night and then with Amanda today. Besides, he was preaching to the choir because Amanda was obviously aware of the dangers to children. *Probably a class in college teachers have to take,* he thought. *Signs of Neglected Children 101.*

"So are you their uncle?" Her eyes held him.

Boy, she is gorgeous, he thought, drowning in those eyes. He was having a difficult time maintaining his irritation. *Why isn't she married?* Now that would be the question to ask.

"Well?" she pressed.

"I am their uncle—sort of. They're my cousin's children. But if you want to know the truth, Kevin has spent more of his life with me than with his mother." They continued to stare at one another, and this time there was no denying the electricity between them. Blake felt alive and tingling. What's more, he knew beyond doubt that she felt it, too. Her face flushed deeper, and her eyes were wide with an emotion he couldn't name.

She looked away first, glancing over to where Kevin now stood on a chair by the shelves of parts.

"Get down, Kevin," Blake told him. With a disappointed sigh, Kevin jumped to the carpet.

"I know a sitter for you," Amanda said into the silence.

Her voice was rushed, and Blake wondered if she was anxious to get away from him. What had he been thinking? She was a schoolteacher, and he was an appliance repairman saddled with two children who weren't even his own. He couldn't fool himself that he would measure up to her intellectual standards. Maybe he'd have a chance if he mentioned he was a senior at BYU, where he would soon finish a degree in business management. Maybe if he told her this shop was really his older brother's dream and not his.

Ridiculous, he thought. *She's not here about me.* Even if she had been, there was a pride in him that would only be accepted for who he was—and a big part of that was this shop. He'd spent ten years of his life working for Doug, two during high school, one before his mission, and seven afterward. He'd been happy and content for at least three or four of those years. And the rest . . . well, the money had put him through college.

"Uh, that's okay," Amanda said, her face rigid. "It was just an idea."

"What? No! I'm sorry." Blake struggled to focus on her words instead of the emotions she had evoked. "I wasn't ignoring you, I was spacing off. Sorry. I haven't gotten much sleep lately. Trust me, I'd be glad for a recommendation."

The stiffness left her face. "Mara doesn't sleep well?"

Blake shook his head. "She's fine. It's just that I've been up late getting things done." He didn't want to tell her he'd been studying.

As though sensing his reluctance, she nodded. "And then last night Kevin had the nightmare. I'm sorry for that. As for your sitter problem, my sister has three children, and one's a girl Kevin's age. She's absolutely wonderful with children. I don't know that she'd watch them long term, you'd have to discuss that with her, but certainly she'd do it until you could find someone. She loves kids. I'll give you her number." She grabbed the pen from the counter and wrote down a name and number on a sheet of paper she pulled from the planner in her purse. "Well, good luck," she said. "Bye now, Kevin. Take care of that book! I'm sure your uncle will rip out the rest of the stickers for you." She turned and practically ran from the shop.

Eager to get away, Blake thought with a surge of self-pity.

He looked to make sure Kevin wasn't climbing anything, but the child was seated on a chair looking through his new book. The bells above the outside door rang, and Blake turned quickly, expecting Amanda. What had she forgotten?

A tall, white-haired, barrel-chested man was standing there instead. "Can I help you?" Blake asked, fighting his disappointment.

The man looked at Mara with interest. "Now there's a cutie."

"Thank you," Blake said with a smile, feeling more pride than he should have. After all, he'd had no part in bringing Mara into this world.

The old man chuckled. "Her eyes are so heavy she can't seem to keep them open."

Sure enough, Mara was nearly out. "I'll be right with you," Blake said.

"Go right ahead. Had eight myself. They have to come first." The old man gave him a wink.

Blake went to the playpen and carefully placed Mara inside, covering her with the blanket. She opened her eyes, smiled once, and shut them again. He prayed she would stay asleep.

Business picked up, and for the next hour Blake was kept busy with customers and phone calls, but everything calmed down at five-thirty. Blake had to be at his class by seven, so if Rhonda was late getting back from her sales appointment, he'd close the store early and go home to get ready. He should feed Mara dinner before the baby-sitter came over.

"Can you rip these out for me?" Kevin asked, proffering several bent pages of stickers.

"Sure, bud. While I do, I'm going to call your grandma, so we can go visit her. I keep forgetting to do it."

Kevin scowled. "I don't have to go back there, do I? It's soooo booooring. I like being with you."

With him, Blake, not with his mother. He tousled the boy's too-long hair. "No, you don't have to go back there. At least not now."

"Whew! That's good." Kevin smiled, and Blake felt a tightening in his chest.

From his pocket Blake took out the small checkbook-sized calendar where he kept all his important information. He dialed his aunt's number before beginning to rip out Kevin's stickers. *Darn schoolteacher,* he thought. *She probably planned this torture for me on purpose.* But it wasn't as bad as it looked. He had two ripped out before his ring was answered, and the contentment on Kevin's face was worth the effort.

"Hello?" came a frail voice.

"Aunt Bonny? It's me, Blake."

"Oh, Blakey, I'm so glad you called. I need to talk to you."

"I need to talk to you, too. I'm at work, though, so I may have to put you on hold or hang up, but for right now I have a minute. What's up?"

"I did it. I finally did it." For a moment his aunt's voice lost it's frail quality.

"What did you do?" Blake envisioned all the trouble an old

woman in her seventies could cause, and he couldn't come up with any scenarios that worried him. Even a new marriage sounded more positive than not.

"I called the Division of Child and Family Services."

Blake's heart seemed to drop to his feet. "When?"

"Today. I woke up and knew I couldn't take it anymore." She sniffed hard and took a shuddering breath. "I don't care that Paula's my daughter. I just have to know my grandchildren are okay. I know I can't keep them with my health being so poor, but I'll be darned if I'll let Paula destroy their lives. I talked to Tracey and Hal about it this morning. Hal and his wife can take the kids, if need be. Mind you, they're not exactly happy to, since their kids are in high school already, but they're willing. Of course, if you want to have custody, Blakey, we'd all support you. You and Paula were like twins growing up, and Kevin adores you. The important thing is that they're safe and with family. None of this hiding and taking-off stuff—and dressing those kids like they were orphans. Doing drugs right in my own house."

Blake finally overcame his shock enough to start speaking. "Aunt Bonny, that's why I called. I have the kids."

"You have them?" Aunt Bonny's voice broke, and she began to sob. "Oh, thank heaven! Oh, thank you, Lord!" There were a few mumbled words Blake didn't catch and then, "I've been so worried since you called the last time, wanting to come see Kevin. I prayed real hard about what to do—I've been praying for them every night. Are they okay, Blakey? Tell me they're okay."

"They're fine, Aunt Bonny. Mara has a bit of diarrhea, that's all. I thought you knew they were with me. Didn't Paula call you?"

"She called me all right—on Monday—wanting money. I told her to bring me the kids, and I'd give her some. I also threatened to call Social Services. She hung up on me."

"She was calling from jail," Blake said, "so she couldn't have brought them over. But she did call me—it was on Monday, too—and I went and picked the kids up at her friend's house in Salt Lake. I'm really sorry, Aunt Bonny. I would have called sooner if I'd known you were still worrying about them. I had no idea."

"This morning I called the authorities on her." His aunt's voice was scarcely a whisper. "That's why I wanted to talk to you. They're going to interview you about Paula. They've even contacted the police. Oh, Blakey, have I done the right thing?"

"I've been about to do it myself." Blake could hardly speak through his emotions. "You should have seen where she left them . . . and the guy they were with. It can't continue, Aunt Bonny. It just can't. They're in real danger. I didn't know what I was going to do, but I wasn't going to let her take Kevin from me again. Or Mara, either."

"Then I've done the right thing." Aunt Bonny's voice was calmer now. "She won't have you to blame for it, and if she finds out it was me, then that's how it has to be."

"You did right. It was the strong thing to do," Blake assured her. "We have to think of the children now."

"Will you bring them to see me? I miss them."

"In few days, okay? On Saturday."

"Thank you, Blakey. You're such a good boy. I'll have their things ready for you—clothes and toys and stuff. Paula didn't take much when she left. It's only been a month, so I bet Mara hasn't grown that much."

"She hasn't." Blake didn't want to remind her that with Paula in charge of their food, they'd likely received scant and irregular portions. Paula herself was thin and for the past nine years had thought more of her next high than making dinner. Over the past few days whenever he'd seen other babies, he'd taken to asking their mothers how old they were. By comparison Mara seemed to be a little on the small side for her age. "I could use the outfits," he added. "I bought her some, but a few seem almost too small already. Maybe they shrank in the dryer."

"They grow so fast," Aunt Bonny said wistfully. Blake wondered if she was remembering Paula when she was born.

The bells above the door jingled, and Blake looked up to see his sister-in-law, Rhonda, enter the shop. "Hey, I have to go now, Aunt Bonny, but I'll see you on Saturday."

"Let me know what the social worker says. I'm sure they'll contact you soon. I'll call them right now and let them know you have the children. They can stop the police search for them."

A moment of fear overcame Blake. What if the social worker wouldn't allow him to keep Kevin and Mara? He was single, worked full time, and between Tuesday and Thursday night classes, his Friday morning class, and the Internet class, he also went to school full time. He could cut back next semester, but he was stuck now through mid-December. Not exactly great foster parent material. Yet where else could they go? He knew Paula would fight any attempt to move the children to Hal's or Tracey's. She hadn't spoken to her siblings for years because she knew they were disgusted with her. With good reason, but their attitude had pushed her further away. Only Blake still bothered to try catching a glimpse of the girl they had all once adored.

If the children weren't left with Blake, they'd go to strangers. Strangers who would be paid to house them, strangers who might not love them like Blake did. No, he wouldn't let that happen! He would fight for them. He would *make* it work.

He said a subdued good-bye to his aunt and hung up the phone, turning to face Rhonda. She glanced at the mound of stickers he had ripped out for Kevin during his conversation with his aunt, though he didn't remember having done it. Pushing them over to the boy, he stooped for the diaper bag.

Rhonda came around the counter. "Sorry I'm so late."

"How'd it go?" he asked.

Rhonda smiled, her narrow face almost lost in the voluminous frizz of her brown hair. "How do you think it went? You know Doug."

"I guess that means he got a new contract." His brother was nothing if not a good salesman.

"Yep, sales and service for fifty machines—and that's just to begin with." Rhonda put her purse under the desk. "He's very content."

"Where is he?" With all of Doug's sales appointments and Blake's repair visits and school schedule, he hardly saw much of his brother anymore.

"He dropped me off and then went to the post office. Had some letters to pop in the mail. Any excitement here? You look a little tired."

"Nope, nothing." Depression like a dark cloud settled over Blake. If he lost Kevin and Mara, would the foster family let him visit?

"Nothing?" Rhonda studied him doubtfully. Her hazel eyes swept over the store and, finding nothing amiss, shrugged.

"I have the feeling today is one of the calm days," he said.

"The calm before the storm," she quoted.

He knew neither of them could guess how prophetic those words might become.

"Well, thanks for staying," Rhonda said. "You'd better get going. You have class tonight, don't you? I'll stay a few more minutes and then lock up when Doug gets back. I assume Ernest is still out on a repair?"

"Yeah. He called to say he was heading straight home after his last job."

Rhonda nodded and reached for the repair log.

Blake walked across the room to where Mara lay in the playpen. Sleeping, she looked even more like an angel than usual. Tucking the blankets around her small body, he cuddled her close. A feeling of peace spread through him. The bottom line was that the situation was out of his hands. He would put his trust in the Lord.

Chapter Six

Amanda didn't know why she'd invited Blake and Kevin to see the insects. To her mind, the invitation made her appear to be chasing after Blake, when in reality, she only wanted to help Kevin. Well, maybe not *only* to help Kevin. Yes, Blake was a handsome man, but she wasn't ready for a relationship. She didn't need another failure. Besides, a man with the responsibility of two children—two children not even his own—would not fit smoothly into her life.

She checked her watch and realized that because she had spent so much time at the shop, she was going to be late getting the casserole to Kerrianne's. Her sister would understand, of course, when she told her about Kevin and Mara, but Amanda wasn't sure she wanted to bring them into the conversation. Kerrianne was bound to note her interest in Blake and that attraction was something she couldn't explain. He wasn't even her type. She bet he didn't like to read and had no interest in current events. Probably his idea of a dream vacation was visiting a state fair featuring appliances of the future—if such a thing existed. So why did her heart bang in her chest every time he got within two feet of her?

Wait a minute! What was she thinking? She'd *have* to tell Kerrianne about Blake. She'd given her sister's number to him, and she would have to warn her about his call. *If* he called. Of course, her sister was ill right now, a fact that had totally deserted her mind earlier, like every other sane thought.

Amanda sighed and pulled into her driveway. She had to hurry if she was going to make the fastest casserole in history.

At ten to six, Amanda was on her sister's front doorstep. Her four-year-old niece met her at the door, wearing a white princess dress and a tiara. "Hello, Misty." Amanda smiled at her. "You look so gorgeous!" With her curly blonde hair, blue eyes, and chubby cheeks, Misty always reminded Amanda of a porcelain doll.

"I'm a princess." Misty followed her into the kitchen. "I dressed Benjamin up as a prince, but he keeps taking off his crown."

"Boys!" Amanda commiserated, setting down the casserole and sweeping Misty into her arms.

"It's only 'cause he's so little," Misty said. Amanda hugged her more tightly. Misty was certainly her mother's daughter; there wasn't a mean bone in her body.

"Where is your mom?"

"Upstairs with the boys. She heard the dingdong and told me to open the door."

"And your daddy?"

"He's not home." The sound of the garage opening made Misty giggle. "I think he just got home. Are we going to eat now?"

"Yep. Let's go get Benjamin first."

Misty led the way upstairs to the second floor where the three bedrooms were located. They found Kerrianne sitting in her bed, propped up by several pillows, her long blonde hair hanging loose around her shoulders. She wore gray jeans and a sweater, but no makeup. "Oh, Amanda, I would have come down, but I was nursing Caleb."

"That's okay. You should be resting."

"I'm feeling much better, thank you. It's amazing how much better." Kerrianne lifted Caleb to her shoulder and began patting his back. "My head still hurts, but the pressure in my sinuses is nearly gone. I can even blow my nose now." She pointed to a short wastebasket by the bed which was filled with crumpled tissues.

Amanda laughed. "What a relief!"

Kerrianne grinned, her blue eyes sparkling. Her face looked more like Misty's round one than her own since she had gained so much weight during her last pregnancy, but Amanda knew Kerrianne would eventually get the weight off. Not only had she been blessed with good genes but Kerrianne was addicted to fresh vegetables.

"So how's the baby?" Amanda sat on the edge of the bed.

Kerrianne passed baby Caleb to her. "Perfect. Thank heavens he hasn't gotten my cold—yet."

Amanda cuddled the two-month-old baby, looking so tiny and comfortable in his dark blue sleeper. Caleb's eyes were a milky dark but would likely turn blue before long. The brown hair he'd been born with was already making way for a covering of very fine blond.

A giggle erupted from under the bed. "Is someone hiding here?" Kerrianne asked, winking at Amanda.

"Yes, it's Prince Benjamin," said Misty. She was kneeling by the bed, her head pressed to the carpet. "Come and see." More giggles came from under the bed.

Amanda handed back the baby, smiling as Kerrianne kissed him on the forehead and laid him on her chest. Dropping to her knees next to Misty, Amanda peered under the bed. "I see a boy wearing a purple shirt and a golden robe. Hmm, he has a sword and a shield

69

there on the floor beside him but no crown. Nope, Misty, I don't see a prince. If he were a prince, he'd have a crown."

Benjamin crawled out from under the bed and hurled himself into Amanda's arms. He didn't seem to have understood much of Amanda's speech, but he was happy to see her. Misty plopped a plastic gold crown on the two-year-old's head. He giggled harder as it fell over his eyes.

"Little big, huh?" Amanda asked. "No wonder he doesn't want to wear it. Well, no matter. It's time to eat. Come along, Prince Benjamin, Princess Misty."

"Thanks so much," Kerrianne said from the bed. "I really appreciate you."

Amanda wondered if she would be so appreciative after she told her about Blake and his need for a baby-sitter. She hadn't lied about Kerrianne's love of children, but she seemed to have her hands pretty full at the moment.

Carrying little Benjamin, Amanda left the room. She met her brother-in-law, Adam, just outside the bedroom in the hall. He was a nice-looking man of average height, with a roundish baby face, very short blond hair, and blue eyes. He worked as a school district administrator, and treated Kerrianne like a princess. For this Amanda loved him almost as much as she loved her two brothers.

Benjamin held out his chubby arms to his father, while Misty clung to his legs. He kissed and hugged both children. "I think I'm the luckiest guy in the whole world," he said, winking at Amanda.

"I think so too," she answered. "I've got dinner ready, if you have time before your meeting."

He nodded. "For your casserole, I'll make time. First, I have to see how Kerrianne is doing."

"I'm fine," Kerrianne called from the bedroom.

Adam grinned at Amanda. "She always says that. In fact, the only time in her life she didn't say that was after she'd been in labor for five hours with Benjamin and they couldn't find the anesthesiologist to give her an epidural."

"Sounds like Kerrianne." Amanda took Benjamin from Adam, and he hurried into the bedroom.

"I need a kiss from my beautiful wife!" he exclaimed.

"No, Adam. You'll get sick."

"Then a hug at least."

Amanda caught a brief glimpse of Adam picking up the baby, kissing him gently, and laying him to the side before gathering his wife in his arms for a hug. A longing sprang up inside her, one that had nothing to do with hormones but everything to do with real love.

"Are you okay?" Misty stared at Amanda from the top of the stairs.

"I'm great," Amanda said lightly. "I'm just wondering who is going to eat the most, you or me."

Misty giggled. "Daddy, of course. He's bigger."

Amanda spent the next two hours feeding the family, bathing the children, and finding just the right pajamas. "Okay, go kiss your mom and then it's straight to bed." But it was only after four bedtime stories, three drinks of water, and eight kisses, that Amanda left the bedroom the children shared.

"All tucked in and eyes nearly shut," she reported to Kerrianne with a long sigh. "I don't know how you do it every day. I'm exhausted already." She smiled to show she had enjoyed every minute.

"Oh, come on. You're the one with the hard job. I can't imagine all those fourth-graders. I'd go home in tears every day."

Amanda sat on the bed, not believing it for a minute. "That reminds me. I had a repairman in the other day, and he's apparently become responsible for his cousin's children. I'm not sure if it's temporary or what. Anyway, he mentioned that he needs a sitter quite urgently. He's been taking the children to work." Briefly, she outlined how Blake had left Mara in the truck and how she'd gone to the shop to check on the children and ended up watching them while he went to stop the widow's washing machine from flooding her house. "I thought maybe you'd be interested in earning some extra money—when you get better, of course. They seem like nice children."

"So let me get this straight," Kerrianne said, seeming intrigued with the story. "What exactly did this guy come and fix at your house? And why did you go to his shop?"

Amanda flushed, having purposely left the fiasco of her oven fire out of her story. "Actually, my oven had a problem—gas wouldn't light—but it's all taken care of now. Not a big deal. And I went by the repair shop to find out about a part to stop the timer on my stove from beeping whenever it decides to."

"No, uh-huh." Kerrianne shook her head. "I don't believe it."

Amanda felt embarrassed. Now Kerrianne would guess about her attraction to this guy, and while ordinarily she didn't mind sharing her feelings with her sister, she couldn't face it now—especially when there was no future in these crazy emotions.

"I know why you went to that shop," Kerrianne continued. "To check up on those children—and a good thing, too." She pushed herself farther up onto the pillows, her pale face becoming flushed with emotion. "I'd be glad to watch those kids for him, but I warn you that I'm going to give him a piece of my mind. Ha! Leaving a baby alone in the car—and with the heater on!"

"He knows it was wrong," Amanda said, relieved that her sister hadn't guessed everything. "He doesn't have much experience with babies." Then, remembering his assertion that Kevin had spent much of his life with him, she added, "Or maybe he's out of practice."

"Well, he'd better learn fast," Kerrianne said.

"You don't have to do it, if you don't want to." Amanda reached out to touch the tiny curl of baby Caleb's hand, sleeping soundly on the bed next to his mother. "We could recommend someone else. But I thought . . . well, they're really cute kids, and I didn't want them to stay with just anyone."

Kerrianne smiled, her blue eyes shining with approval. "I'm glad to help. I don't reach out to others as much as I should, and I'm grateful for the opportunity. You did the right thing, Manda. You really did. It's not everyone who would care enough to check up on some stranger's children. You put people first and follow inspiration—that's a quality I've always admired in you."

Amanda was uncomfortable with her praise. She felt funny hearing it called inspiration, though she believed that was what it had been. For whatever reason, even just that minor water emergency, she was supposed to be at the shop today. "You would have done the same thing," she told her sister.

"I hope so. Well, did you give him my number? Good. If he calls, I'll tell him I'll watch them for a few weeks. If it goes well, we'll continue. If not, I'll find him someone really good to take over. The only real worry I have about doing it is that I don't want Misty and Benjamin to feel neglected. They've already been feeling a bit displaced by Caleb, and they have to come first."

"Of course they do. They're your children. But it might actually help, having someone new to play with." Amanda arose and from the nightstand retrieved the plate that had held Kerrianne's dinner.

"It might." Kerrianne's expression became thoughtful.

"Well, I'd better get going. I've got some work to catch up on." Amanda took a step backward.

"Thanks so much for bringing dinner."

"Get better, okay?"

Kerrianne smiled. "I'm planning on getting up tomorrow. I'll be fine."

Amanda said good-bye and started for the door.

"Uh, Manda, wait!" Kerrianne called.

Amanda turned around, pausing by the door. "Yes?"

"You're doing okay, aren't you? I mean, you seem a little different today. Did anything else happen?"

Amanda shook her head and then sighed when she realized Kerrianne wasn't going to accept that answer. "It's been a year since Tanner and I broke up," she said. "A whole year." It seemed like forever.

"Oh." Kerrianne frowned. "That's got to be hard."

Amanda shrugged. "I was right to let go. He's married, and the last time I talked to Savvy, they were very happy."

"How is Savvy?"

Savvy was Tanner's cousin, and they'd become good friends even before Amanda had begun dating Tanner again last summer. "She's in her second year at BYU, but truthfully, I haven't seen much of her. I've felt awkward."

"You shouldn't. Your relationship with her had nothing to do with Tanner."

"I know that." Amanda forced a smile. In fact, she had thought time and time again about setting Savvy up with her youngest brother, Tyler, as soon as he got home from his mission in January. There was no one she'd rather have as a sister-in-law. She'd even set Savvy up once with Mitch, but there hadn't been any attraction or interest from either. Her brother Mitch was into animals big time, while Savvy, studying to be an astronomer, was interested only in the sky.

"It's not like Savvy's going to talk about Tanner all the time."

"No, but she is a reminder that he's gone on with his life, while I'm still in the same place."

"No, you're not!" Kerrianne shook her head. "How can you say that? You're a full-fledged teacher now with your own class, you bought a house—that's moving on. So what if you haven't found the right guy yet? You will, and when you do, you'll understand why it took so long to find him."

Amanda felt her melancholy evaporate. Talking to her sister was like opening the curtain to the sun. Besides, if the truth were told, she wasn't pining after Tanner anymore. She might not be ready for another relationship, but emotionally she *had* moved on.

She hurried back to the bed, set down the plate, and gave her sister a hug. "I love you, Kerrianne," she whispered.

"I love you, too."

Chapter Seven

On Friday afternoon, Blake felt a tremor of worry as he hung up the phone and sank down on a chair behind the counter at work. He had a four-thirty appointment with the social worker at his apartment to discuss care of the children. To his relief, there had been no mention of removing Kevin and Mara from his home, but since the children were now wards of the state, an inspection had to be made of the premises before he could be given official custody. There would also be a questionnaire and an interview. That was what worried him.

"Bad news?" Rhonda looked at him from the new parts shelves where she was letting Kevin help her store the items that had arrived in the mail that morning.

He shook his head. "I'm not sure. It's the social worker assigned to Paula's case. She's coming over this afternoon."

"I'm sure it'll be fine."

Blake sighed. "It's just that . . ." He broke off, noticing Kevin watching him closely. "Kevin, could you go check on your sister in the playpen for me? I bet she's waking up and wants a bottle."

"I'll go see." Kevin rushed around the counter. Blake smiled at his eagerness. Kevin loved his sister, no doubt of that.

Blake met Rhonda's eyes. "It just that sometimes I wonder if they wouldn't be better off with someone else, you know? They need a full-time mother or father who's not always at school or work."

Rhonda shook her head so hard her frizzy mop fell over her thin face. "Oh, no. Don't go there. You're the only father Kevin knows. Mara, too, for that matter. You do everything a father would do for them. You're the one who loves them. It might be different if Paula had the guts to give them up for adoption, but you and I both know Paula will never allow that. It's all about her, when it should be about the kids. That's what you've got to remember. It's about Kevin and Mara, not you—and they need you." Rhonda's voice became softer. "It's not like you have to do it alone. Doug and I are here. They're our relatives, too, and we may not be able to give them a home, but we want to be here when you need us."

"I know. You've been great. Especially you—taking care of them for me this morning while I went to school, letting me bring them to the shop, watching them while I go out on repairs. I really appreciate it."

Rhonda sighed. "I only wish I could do more, I really do. Even with the five I've got, I might be willing to take them in if Doug was, but he's finished with that time in his life. Now that Scotty's finally in first grade, he's looking forward to being free to go where he wants when he wants . . . and having me with him." She shook her head, eyes full of memories. "It was quite a setback for his plans when Scotty came seven years after we'd decided to quit having children. Don't get me wrong, he loves little Scotty like crazy, but he's feeling his age, especially since Catharine got married and had a baby so young. Being a grandfather is a wonderful thing, but it made him think twice about aging and all the things he wanted to do in his life."

"I know, I know. I understand. I just wish I'd finished school earlier, or that I—" Blake stopped. True, he hadn't pursued a wife because he'd been busy with school and Kevin, but even if he had, he couldn't really support a family working here. At least not with any degree of comfort, and he didn't want to pinch pennies for the rest of his life. Of course, that would all change once he finished school and found a good job as a business manager, but for now there was no sense in voicing regrets to Rhonda who had never been anything to him but kind.

Rhonda shrugged and turned back to her work. "While you were on the phone, Doug came out of the office. He wants to see you. Don't worry, I'll keep an eye on the kids and the desk."

Blake smiled his thanks and went into the office. Fridays were normally his favorite days at work because he was only there a half day, most of which he spent out on repair calls instead of stuck in the shop, which he had begun to find less and less enjoyable as the months wore on. *Only six more months,* he told himself. *One and a half semesters. In a few months, I can begin sending out resumés.*

Doug looked up from his computer and smiled. Blake smiled back, remembering a time when Doug had not been in such a good mood after battling with the "newfangled contraption." Over the past two years, the computer had proven its worth.

"You wanted to see me?" Blake asked.

"Yeah, it's about the kids."

Blake sat down heavily in the chair by the desk. "Today's the last day they'll be here. I've got the names of several sitters. I called a few, but there's one more I'm going to call today as soon as I get off. She comes very highly recommended." He hadn't really been impressed with the other women over the phone, and he wondered what Amanda's sister would be like.

"That's not it." Doug leaned back in his chair and put his hands behind his head, looking much like their father—from what little

Blake could remember of their father—who had died when Blake was thirteen. Doug's dark hair was peppered at the temples with gray, and the spare tire around his waist had begun to spread. He had never been a handsome man, but he'd always had presence. He was good at repairs and a fantastic salesman. During his early life, he had sold everything from chocolate bars to cars. After a successful mission to Peru, he'd opened his shop and begun doing what he did best. Hard work had paid off well enough to hire two full-time workers and one part-timer. He had a nice house, two nice cars, and owned his shop free and clear. Blake was a little in awe of his brother—he'd gone after his dream and won.

"I'd like to pay for the sitter," Doug said. "Until you're out of school."

Blake couldn't hide his surprise. Doug was a good brother, but he wasn't overly generous. "You don't have to do that."

"I want to."

Blake wondered if his conscience was working overtime, or if Rhonda had been twisting his arm. "What I meant was that it might not be necessary. I just talked to the social worker—oh, that reminds me, she wants to meet at four-thirty, so I'm going to have to leave early today."

Doug nodded assent. "Del's here and Ernest is due back from his last repair job soon. We'll be fine. In fact, you can take off now. It's almost three, and no doubt you'll want to clean up before she comes."

Blake chuckled. "You got that right. I just started thinking the same thing. I didn't have time to do any dishes last night or this morning because of school."

"That's understandable. Now what were you saying about the social worker?"

"Well, she said since Kevin and Mara were going to be wards of the state that eventually I'd receive some money for their care. I was thinking that money might pay for their sitter. It'll take a few weeks to get the checks coming, though."

Doug rubbed his jaw doubtfully. "From what I've heard, it's not a huge amount. You'll need it for food and clothes and unexpected expenses. You shouldn't have to worry about paying the sitter, too."

Blake considered his brother's offer. He was reluctant, not only because he wanted to be independent but because he didn't want to owe more than he already did to Doug. His brother had paid for his mission, had given him a temporary place to live when their mother had died after his mission, and he had given Blake a job. While that job hadn't exactly been the future Blake had believed it could be when he was twenty-one, it had paid his rent, bought clothes for him and Kevin, and provided his college tuition.

"Take it, Blake," Doug urged. "Kevin and Mara are no more your responsibility than they are mine, except by your close relationship with Paula."

Blake didn't exactly agree. He was also responsible because he had fallen completely and hopelessly in love with the children. In a way he couldn't explain, they were part of him.

Doug leaned forward abruptly, the wrinkles around his eyes becoming more noticeable. "Look, Blake, I know this shop didn't turn out to be what you wanted in life—and maybe you're right about leaving. I was raised in a world where the salary I give you was a good one. I know things have changed, lifestyles, expectations . . ."

"Prices . . ." Blake prompted.

A smile crossed Doug's lips. "Yeah, prices. At first I was really disappointed that you decided to go into another career, but for what it's worth, I've come to terms with your decision. You've given me a lot of good years here, and I never offered you partnership. I never . . ." He shook his head and fell quiet. Blake realized that this was as close to an apology as he would ever receive.

"Okay," he said. "I'll accept your help. And I am very grateful. I still have next semester's tuition to look forward to."

Doug laughed and relaxed again in his chair. "Look forward to . . . Yeah, that's one way of saying it. I think I'll use that on Rhonda when I tell her the dentist left a message on our voice mail a minute ago—something about scheduling her for a root canal."

Blake winced in sympathy. "Wait till I leave, okay?"

Doug stood up and put a hand on his shoulder. "I'm proud of you, you know? I really am."

Blake nodded. "Thanks." They might not always agree, but they were brothers and they loved each other.

In the shop, Del was helping a customer at the counter, and Rhonda was talking with another one in front of their top-of-the-line washing machine. Kevin was at the playpen handing Mara a toy, which she promptly tossed back onto the floor, giggling in delight when he bent to pick it up again.

"Her is playing with me," Kevin said as Blake approached. The boy was grinning ear to ear.

"That's great, bud. You are one awesome brother." Then the adult in him kicked in. "But remember to say 'She is playing with me' instead of her."

Kevin shook his head, his chin lifting stubbornly. "Uh-huh. It's her."

"Really, Kevin. I wouldn't lie to you. It's she."

"Anyway, I said Mara. I didn't say her or she."

Blake gave up, opting instead to praise the child with what he was doing right. "Okay, do it again. Show me."

Kevin gave Mara the ball. She threw it out, giggling like mad when Kevin put his hands on his hips and pretended to scold her. Then he picked the ball up and the game began again. Blake watched for a while before stopping them so he could change Mara's seemingly eternally dirty diaper and give her a bottle to drink on the way

81

home. Instead of wrapping the blankets around her, he put on the new little pink coat Rhonda had brought in this morning.

In the truck, Kevin was looking at his insect sticker book again. "Haven't you had enough of that book?" Blake asked. Last night Kevin had once again awakened him with dreams of insects crawling over his bed. No snakes, at least, but Blake had spent an hour curled up next to him in his twin bed so he wouldn't be scared. Then Mara had awakened long enough to mess her diaper. In all, it had been an active night. No wonder Doug wasn't up for starting over.

"I like bugs," Kevin said. "Are we going to that lady's school to see some? Her said we could."

Blake didn't think Kevin had been paying attention when Amanda made her offer. Apparently, he was mistaken. Again. Getting this parenting thing down wasn't as easy as it looked. He couldn't believe how much things had changed in the six months Kevin had lived with his grandmother and mother.

He glanced at the clock on his dash and made a rapid decision. "She should be getting out of school about now. Maybe we could zip on over, take a peek at those bugs, and then get home."

"Yay!" Kevin's blue eyes lit up, and his smile filled his whole face.

"We can't stay long," Blake warned. "Only ten minutes. Fifteen, tops. We have to get home quick because we have someone coming over."

"Who?" Kevin asked, his voice carefully neutral. "Is it my mommy?"

"No." Blake waited several heartbeats before asking, "Do you miss your mommy?"

Kevin cocked his head, considering the question. Then he shrugged. "I don't think so. I want to stay with you."

"You can stay with me and still miss your mommy."

"Oh." Kevin smiled. "I do like it when Mommy sings to Mara. But her doesn't sing to me anymore."

"That's because you're such a big boy now."

"*You* sing to me."

Blake hardly thought that "Itsy Bitsy Spider" and "Popcorn Popping" really counted. "Shhh, just don't tell anyone," he said in a loud whisper. "I think I'm probably too old, too."

Kevin giggled. Mara, finishing her bottle, threw it on the floor of the truck and grinned with them.

The halls of Grovecrest Elementary were thick with children. "Looks like we got here about on time," Blake said.

"Where do we go?" Kevin clung to his hand, awed by the swarm around him.

"Hmm. We'll have to ask." Blake stopped the first adult he saw and requested directions to Amanda's classroom.

When they walked into the room, she was standing by a student who sat in a desk. She leaned down, her blonde hair spilling forward, as she pointed at something in a book. The child nodded and smiled before marking the place and slamming the book shut. "See you tomorrow," Amanda called. At that moment she saw Blake and froze for a fraction of a second before her smile widened, dimpling her right cheek. She came over to meet them.

"So," she said. "You decided to come in and see the bugs."

"Where are they!" Kevin asked, his eyes searching the room.

"Along the windows there."

Kevin gave a whoop of excitement and hurried over to the several dozen cages.

"Hello, Mara." Amanda held out a finger to the baby, who grabbed it eagerly. "I see you have on a cute little coat today." She chuckled. "She's adorable."

"My sister-in-law got the coat," he admitted. "I forgot about the weather when I was shopping. I was focused on clothes and blankets, I guess."

"Well, you've had a lot on your mind."

"You can say that again." Blake didn't want to take his eyes from her. She looked so beautiful in the emerald skirt and jacket that exactly matched her eyes. Yet there was something more than just her looks. He felt another connection, a familiarity. Mentally, he shook his head, bemoaning the fact that the only woman beside Rhonda with whom he seemed to have any meaningful contact was also a woman who thought he was completely incapable of taking care of children. Or had he convinced her yet? Thinking of the approaching visit with the social worker, he hoped so.

By the window, Kevin was making loud noises of appreciation. Amanda walked toward him. "We can't stay long," Blake told her. "I have an appointment."

"Okay." Amanda opened the first cage. "These are ants," she said, catching one on her finger. "It won't bite you." She gave Blake a meaningful glance that told him there were ants that most definitely did bite, but she wasn't about to explain that to Kevin. "Hold out your hand. It may tickle a bit."

Next, they stood in front of several jars and cages holding crickets, grasshoppers, a spider, and even a praying mantis. Some insects, like the mosquitoes and the flies, they just looked at in their jars, but most they were able to hold. Blake had never seen such a variety. "My brother's studying biology at the Y," Amanda told him. "Half of these are his or belong to his professors."

"Is he going to take them back then?" Kevin asked.

"Yep. Tomorrow morning, bright and early."

Time flew as it always seemed to when he was with Amanda. When Blake checked his watch, he was startled to see that it was five minutes to four. "Oh, no."

"What is it?"

He stared at her in horror. "My appointment with the social worker—it's at four-thirty, and my apartment's a wreck!"

"Your appointment is with the social worker?"

"Yes." Laying Mara down on a table, he began to change her diaper as he explained about the impending visit. "I only hope she overlooks the mess," he finished, pushing Mara's arm into her coat. "Come on, Kevin. We've got to run."

Amanda grabbed her purse and coat, shut off the light, and followed him out. "I can help," she said. "It might be good to have someone to take the children into another room in case you need to talk to her alone."

A part of Blake wanted to demand why she would do this for him, but he was almost afraid of the answer. For the children, of course. Yet his heart didn't want to hear that. Besides, he wanted her company—and not only because he didn't want to face the social worker alone.

"Thanks, I'd appreciate your help," he accepted. "I don't want to lose—" He broke off, catching Kevin's intent stare. "What I mean is, I need things to go smoothly."

Amanda nodded, her eyes sympathetic. "I'll follow you over."

At home, Blake parked in the garage, and before he had Mara out of the car seat, Amanda was standing by his truck. A door in the garage led to both the upstairs and the downstairs apartments. "I didn't have any time to wash the dishes," he explained on the way inside. "And I don't have a dishwasher in this place."

"You, an appliance repairman, don't have a dishwasher?" A smile tugged at the corners of her mouth.

"Hey, I had one in the last place. I haven't really needed one here." He grimaced. "But now I guess I'd better put in an order."

"I guess so." Amanda took off her coat and with difficulty packed it into the already full closet next to his and Kevin's. "Look, I'll do the dishes while you get started on the rest since I don't know where anything goes."

Blake glanced around, seeing the small apartment as she must see it—a pigsty. Toys and empty popcorn bags were strewn over the carpet. Various packages of new diapers littered the love seat. The entertainment center he was usually proud to tell people he had made now had numerous videos and books out of place, lying haphazardly where he'd left them. Even from where they stood, he could see dust on the TV. The connecting kitchen was every bit as disastrous. The linoleum was littered with bits of cereal, and several used diapers, rolled up into tiny bundles, sat outside the cupboard under the sink, waiting for him to throw them away. The stacks of dishes in the sink and on the counter were bigger than he remembered.

The bedrooms weren't likely any better. He seemed to remember plastic hangers from Kevin's and Mara's new clothes in a corner and more of Kevin's old toys that he'd unpacked for Mara. The beds definitely weren't made. He'd been too tired last night even to put away his own clothes. And the kitchen . . . well, it was too late now to hide the apartment from her.

Amanda didn't seem too shocked to realize he lived in a pigsty. He wanted to tell her it was only because his life was so hectic, but she was already filling one of the stainless steel sinks with water. "Kevin," she called. "If you pick up your toys really fast, I'll let you help with the dishes."

Blake blinked as Kevin filled his arms in record time. "I thought you didn't have any children," Blake said to Amanda.

She turned around and grinned. "I'm a schoolteacher, remember? And I have a niece and two nephews."

"Just put the toys in a stack by the entertainment center," Blake told Kevin.

They worked steadily for the next half hour. Blake gathered up the unused diapers from the couch and stuffed them in the top shelf of the coat closet. His backpack of textbooks barely fit under the coats. Since Kevin was making progress on the toys, Blake headed for his bedroom. He didn't figure the social worker would look in his dresser drawers, so he shoved everything on the floor inside them, including several empty baby bottles and a stack of books. Then he made a quick job on the bed. Not bad. In the children's room, he threw all the toys in the crib before deciding that might be seen as hazardous and instead stacked them in the corner where they just covered the plastic hangers from the new clothes. He had to get a proper toy box soon. The last one he had taken down to Cedar City to Kevin's grandmother.

Next, he gathered up the children's dirty clothes and stuffed them into the washer, making a mental note to go back and divide the lights from the darks before turning it on. He should probably remove the spoons and the scraps of paper he had seen among the clothes as well. Grabbing the vacuum from the hall closet, he made a quick tour around the apartment.

In the kitchen, Amanda had finished the dishes and was sweeping the floor. Kevin stood on a chair and was drying the cups, stacking them in the cupboard when finished. "Good job, bud," Blake said. "I didn't know you were such a great help. Now I know who can help me do the dishes every day."

"Me." Kevin grinned ear-to-ear. The cup in his hand slipped, but Amanda let go of her broom and caught it before it hit the ground. "Whew!" Kevin breathed a sigh of relief. "Her caught it!"

"*She* caught it," Amanda corrected him.

Kevin looked at her adoringly. "*She* caught it," he repeated.

"Hey, why don't you believe me when I tell you it's *she*." Blake put his hands on his hips.

"Amanda's a teacher, ya know," Kevin said seriously. "I have to listen to teachers."

Blake fought the urge to smile. "Oh, you do, huh?"

"Yep. Teachers are smart."

Amanda shot Blake a triumphant glance before handing Kevin back the cup. While she resumed sweeping, Blake found a rag and began removing layers of dust from the entertainment center and the television. As he cleaned, he mused that he couldn't even remember having turned it on this week except to put on a video for Kevin.

"I think we did it," he said a few minutes later, looking around the apartment with satisfaction. "Oh, wait!"

"What?" Amanda stared at him. "You just went totally white."

"The bathroom! I forgot the bathroom!"

"I can do it."

"No!" He knew he'd left not only his clothes but the children's lying about, not to mention his deodorant and shaving supplies. "I'll get it. But could you change Mara?" He looked to where Mara sat on the floor in the living room, playing with her shoes.

"You just changed her at the school."

He sighed. "I know, but believe me, she needs a diaper change. She *always* needs one. She's been going through at least ten dirty diapers a day. I'm beginning to think she has some sort of a virus. In fact, I'm taking her to the doctor on Monday. To tell you the truth, if I have to change another diaper right now, I think I'll—" Blake looked at Kevin's interested face and decided not to say "sell her to the gypsies."

"You'll what?" Amanda's green eyes danced.

He grinned. "We'll . . . I'll . . . I'll have to buy some more hand lotion. My hands are getting a little chapped from washing them so much." He held them up for her inspection.

"Yeah, right." Amanda went over to Mara. "Let's get you changed, shall we?"

Blake gathered everything in the bathroom, shoved it into the dryer, and went back to wipe off the sink. The doorbell rang as he was considering the dirty ring in the bathtub. He opted for closing the curtain. At least the toilet itself didn't look too bad. On his way out, he picked up bits of toilet paper Kevin had used as a tent for his Lego dinosaurs and stuffed them in his pocket. Belatedly, he looked down at himself. No time to change from his work clothes.

Oh, well, he thought. *She'll ask what I do anyway.*

Amanda and Kevin had opened the kitchen door that was the only other entrance to the apartment besides the garage door that led into the living room. One part of Blake noticed that Kevin's hair was way too long. He should have asked Amanda if she knew how to cut it. But when would they have had time?

His muscles tensed as the social worker stepped into the kitchen.

Chapter Eight

I'm Erika Solos from the Division of Child and Family Services. DCFS for short," the woman said to Amanda. She was a tall, graceful-looking woman, with a thick waist, a rather large nose, and beautiful almond-shaped eyes. Cut in the latest style, her short black hair framed her face becomingly. The stylish cut made Amanda wish she had done something with her straight hair.

"Hello. I'm Amanda Huntington," she said, stepping back. "I'm a—a friend of Blake's. This is Mara, and Kevin is this big boy right here." She was rewarded by a wide grin from Kevin. "Please come in. Blake's just in the other room."

"Actually, I'm right here," Blake said, coming from behind her.

Amanda could tell he was nervous, and for some reason this weakness endeared him to her. One more plus to add to the expanding list of items in his favor, at the top of which was how good he was with children. Not even the disarray of his apartment had dimmed her growing opinion of him. Hadn't her own house been much worse after an evening alone with her niece and nephews?

Well, minus the hordes of diapers, of course. Blake hadn't been kidding when he said he'd tried everything to stop Mara's leaks.

"Nice to meet you," Blake said to the social worker, offering his hand. "Won't you come into the living room and have a seat?"

"Thank you." When Erika moved across the kitchen, the appearance of grace vanished. Her elbows stuck out at right angles from her body, and her feet stumbled briefly where the carpet met the linoleum.

"I can take the kids into the other room," Amanda offered as Blake led the social worker to the love seat and then brought a chair from the kitchen for himself.

"I'd like to talk to them a minute first, if you don't mind." Erika slapped her briefcase on her lap and opened it. Once again, she was the picture of grace. "Plus, I have some forms for you to fill out, Mr. Simmons."

"Please, call me Blake."

As Amanda passed Blake to sit on the love seat with the social worker, Mara kicked her legs and held out her arms to him. Smiling, he reached for her, checking her diaper before placing her on his lap. Kevin stood next to Blake's chair, watching the social worker with wary interest.

"Have you heard from Paula?" Blake asked, accepting several papers from Erika.

Erika nodded. "I talked with her this morning for quite some time." She shook her head and frowned so Amanda assumed it had not been a good conversation.

"Is my mommy still in jail?" asked Kevin. "Because I want to stay here. I don't like my grandma's house so much. It's boring."

Erika smiled. "Actually, your mother is not in jail right now, but that's what I'm here for—to make it so you can stay here with your . . ." She looked at Blake for help.

"Uncle," he supplied. "Paula and I are cousins, but we were as close as siblings when we were young. Uh, if you'll excuse me a minute, I'll get a pen so I can start on these papers." He went into the kitchen and opened a drawer. Then he shut the drawer and went to the front closet. Amanda knew that wasn't a good idea.

"Wait, I have a p—" she started to say.

Too late. The diapers stuffed in the closet came tumbling down from the top shelf where she'd shoved them after they'd fallen on her when she'd changed Mara's diaper earlier. With an embarrassed exclamation, he began stuffing them back up with one hand, the other still holding Mara.

"I have a pen," Amanda said again. She darted a look at the social worker and was relieved to see she was watching Blake's attempts with amusement.

"Attack of the diapers!" Blake exclaimed when more diapers showered over him. He set Mara down on the floor and began putting them back again.

Amanda giggled. At least he'd kept his sense of humor. Reaching for her purse next to the love seat, she found a pen and also a small book about babies that she had read to her niece and nephew the night before. "Look, Kevin," she said, proffering the book. To Erika she added, "He likes books." To her surprise, Kevin took the book, climbed into her lap, and began looking at the pictures. Amanda put her arms around him loosely and then freed one hand to stroke his hair. He really did need a haircut, but he was adorable.

"For starters," Erika began when Blake was back in his chair, with Mara playing on the carpet in front of him, "Paula knows the children are here and you are her choice—if anyone is to have temporary care of them. The necessity of anyone keeping them is something, however, that she is disputing. But we'll discuss that in a minute. First, I'd like to talk to Kevin about his life with his mother and with you."

"Okay, but . . ." Blake glanced at Kevin pointedly.

Erika smiled. "I understand. Don't worry, I've done this before."

"Of course." Blake began filling out the papers.

"Kevin, you were staying at your grandmother's before you came here, weren't you?" Erika asked.

Kevin looked up from his book. "No. We were at Shaunda's and Barb's. And sometimes at Loony's. I didn't like it there at all."

"Did you have your own room at these places?"

He nodded. "We slept on the couch. Mara slept in her car seat. We brought it in the house."

"What did you eat?"

He shrugged.

"Were you hungry or full?"

Everyone waited for his answers, but Kevin was suddenly shy. He turned around and whispered to Amanda, "I was hungry sometimes. My stomach hurt. Mara cried a lot, but I let her suck on my fingers. It was yucky. I told Mommy I wanted to go back to Grandma's. Then her got me some crackers with peanut butter. I love those a lot." The whisper carried across the room. The social worker's lips tightened, and Blake, his pen no longer moving over the papers, looked ready to explode.

"Let's talk about your grandma," Erika said gently. "Did you like staying with her?"

"Yes, but it was boring." Kevin was no longer whispering.

"Why is that?"

"There's nothing to do. Grandma doesn't like me to go outside 'cause her doesn't have a fence."

"Oh, and you go outside here?"

Kevin shook his head. "It's too cold now, but I will when it's warm. We have a fence."

Amanda noticed Blake staring at the window in the kitchen. There wasn't much to see but a metal-lined window well. He looked about to speak but then clamped his lips shut. Amanda wondered what was out there that worried him.

"Did you see your mom a lot when you were at your grandma's?"

Kevin shrugged. "Yeah. Sometimes. Her sleeps a lot."

"Did she wake up when you went to bed?"

"No. Her wasn't home."

Wasn't home? Wasn't home when? One night, two? More? Amanda didn't like the picture she was beginning to form of Kevin and Mara's mother. What mother could bear to be away enough at night that a four-year-old child would consider it a way of life? From the tight expression on Blake's face, she knew he was thinking along the same lines.

"So do I get to stay here?" Kevin asked hopefully.

"Do you like it here?"

"Yes."

"Why?"

Kevin thought for a moment. "I like Uncle Blake's truck, and I like my bed and my new coat. It's really warm. Mara doesn't cry much here. Uncle Blake cooks good food, and he bought *two* jars of peanut butter. One has nuts in it."

Erika smiled. "Is that all? What else do you like?"

"He sings me songs." Kevin clapped his hand over his mouth so his next words were garbled. "Oops. I wasn't supposed to tell."

Erika glanced at Blake, whose face had turned crimson. "What weren't you supposed to tell?" she asked.

Kevin looked at Blake, who nodded. "You can tell her. It's okay."

"He sings 'Isty Spider' and the popcorn song at night when we go to bed. He does the best actions. He's so silly." Kevin grinned, eyes shining.

Amanda met Blake's gaze. "You sing?" she asked, a smile tugging at her lips.

"Only for Kevin." The color was fading from his face, but his jaw was clenched, his discomfort plain to everyone in the room except Kevin and Mara.

Amanda tried to stop smiling but failed miserably. To cover up, she tickled Kevin until he giggled. "Stop!" he shouted. "Stop! I need to go potty."

"You're just trying to escape," Amanda accused. She let him wriggle from her grasp.

Still giggling, he fled the room. Seconds later they heard the bathroom door slam shut.

Then Mara's diaper exploded.

Amanda laughed helplessly at the expression on Blake's face. "Oh, no," she said. "Looks like you'll need another diaper."

"I left the diaper bag in the truck," he said, holding Mara up so the leak spreading up her undershirt wouldn't get on the carpet if she decided to roll over. He glanced at the closet with a look of despair.

"She has diarrhea," Amanda explained to Erika. When Blake scowled at her, she quickly added, "She had it before she came, and he's taking her to the doctor on Monday just to make sure it's nothing serious."

Erika shook her head and leaned back on the love seat, her smile wide and friendly. "Relax. Children get diarrhea. Mara here certainly doesn't look like she's a neglected child—at least not here. She's happy, well dressed—both children are—and they obviously love their uncle. Mara's a little on the thin side, but I'm sure she'll fatten up. From what I've seen so far, there's nothing to preclude Blake from being their foster parent."

Blake's expression lightened, and Amanda could see that he was fighting tears. A lump developed in her own throat.

"But I do need to see their room and bathroom, and I'd also like to know a little background."

"Background?"

"When you started to take care of Kevin and so forth. I talked quite some time to your aunt, but I'd like to hear your version."

So would Amanda. She glanced at Blake, who still held Mara aloft.

Blake nodded. "Okay. Let me change her first, if you don't mind."

"I'll do it," Amanda volunteered. "And when Kevin's done, I can keep him in the other room."

"It probably won't be necessary." Blake handed Mara to her. "He seems to have the opposite problem from Mara. He spends an eternity in the bathroom. I'll go check on him in a minute."

Amanda opened the closet and a half dozen diapers rained down on her. Mara giggled, and Amanda shot Blake a smile. She decided to leave them on the floor. "Easier to use this way," she mumbled. Carefully, she pulled off Mara's clothes and cleaned her back before laying her on the carpet next to the tub of wipes.

"So how often have you had the children?" Erika asked Blake, hiding her own smile behind a carefully French-manicured hand.

Blake took a deep breath, letting it out slowly. "Well, the first time Kevin came to stay with me he was about six months old, just a little younger than Mara is now. At first Paula would leave him for an evening, and then it was a day or two. By the time he was a year old, he'd be staying at least a week at a time. The longest she ever left him during that time was about three weeks. She'd start missing him terribly and come to see him." He paused for a moment and then rushed on. "Whatever else Paula's doing, she loves Kevin and Mara very deeply."

Erika nodded. "Her love for her children is not in question. I know she cares for them. So what happened after he was a year old?"

"Same thing. One week, two weeks away, then a week here, maybe three. When he was with her, I'd call and check up on him or go see him. Even bought her a phone line." He snorted and shook his head. "Learned the hard way that I had to block the long distance."

"What was the longest time Kevin ever stayed with you?"

Blake rubbed his jaw in thought. "Six months—might have been seven. It was when she was pregnant with Mara."

"And after Mara was born she came and got him?"

"Yeah, when Mara was a few months old. But she was on something, or maybe drunk, so I didn't let her take him. I threatened to report her. I was serious. The next day she came back sober and took him to her mother's, where she'd been keeping Mara. She accused me of trying to take her son away and basically forbade me to see him again."

Amanda could see how much his cousin's actions had hurt Blake. She wanted to go over and hug him, but how could she? It wasn't like they had a real relationship. She finished changing Mara's diaper and scooted closer to the chair where he sat. Mara needed another outfit, but she didn't want to miss this.

"They were at your aunt's how long?"

"Five months. And I'm sure you already know that I did go down to see Kevin despite what Paula said. She was never there, though I know her mother told her about my visits. Then last month Paula disappeared with the children. My aunt and I have been very concerned."

"With good reason." Erika folded her hands atop the closed briefcase in her lap. "From what I've been told by the police, Paula and the children have mostly been staying in a rundown house on the outskirts of Salt Lake City, with no heat and nothing edible in the refrigerator. There were no bathing facilities. Drugs and alcohol were found in the house. Paula resisted arrest and became quite vicious with the police officer. The resisting arrest charges have been dropped, and she hasn't been charged with possession because there were others in the house, including the owner, who is being charged, but the police believe she was definitely a part of it. Unfortunately, they don't have proof."

Blake shook his head, looking sorrowful. "I don't know how she got this way. Sometimes I can't even believe it's happening at all. This isn't the girl I grew up with. I promise you, she would be horrified at herself now. I just wish she'd change her life. If not for herself, then at least for the kids."

"Unfortunately, she doesn't see that she's doing anything wrong," Erika said. "I spent over an hour this morning explaining it to her, but she really doesn't get it. Our goal is to help her—eventually—but right now we need to focus on what's best for the children."

Blake twirled Amanda's pen between his fingers. "She'll want them back."

"Yes," Erika agreed. "She thinks that everyone—you included—are trying to take her children from her. Of course, I told her that wasn't the case."

"I'll bet she wouldn't listen." Blake cast Amanda a despairing look. "It's always the same thing. That's why she's managed to alienate every single member of her family . . . and mine."

"Except you," Amanda felt compelled to say. *Loyal,* she thought. She could add *loyal* to his list of good qualities.

"Her intentions are good," Blake continued with a grateful look in Amanda's direction, "but she's . . . ." He took another deep breath before plunging on. "Whether they've charged her or not, she's using drugs."

"We know that." Erika leaned forward, her almond-shaped eyes grave. "I've seen it time and time again. Before she can get Kevin and Mara back, she'll have to take drug tests and also arrange a suitable place for them to live. Meanwhile, because she took them from her mother's and didn't leave any information on their whereabouts, and because she has no job or property, we feel she may be a flight risk. What that means is that she is not allowed to see the children without supervision. Either you must be with the children when she's with them or we'll assign a mediator to have supervised visits."

Blake stood and began pacing. Amanda had known him long enough to see that he was battling with himself over something he wanted to say. After thirty seconds of silence, he spoke. "That might not turn out to be as easy as it sounds. Sometimes Paula's rather . . . well, it could get ugly."

Erika wasn't surprised. "Believe me, I know."

"It's the drugs." Blake's voice was pained.

"It's the drugs," Erika repeated. "Wherever drugs are concerned, things can quickly get out of hand. If necessary, we can issue a restraining order so she can't come around here at all. I made it very clear to her this morning when I talked to her that if she made this difficult for you we'd be forced to put them in a foster home somewhere she doesn't know about."

"What do you mean by difficult?" Amanda asked.

Erika sighed. "Oh, I've seen it all. They'll show up at odd hours—often drunk or on something—beg to take the children by themselves, call all the time to try to make secret meetings with the children or just to hang up. Basically, they make any normal life for the foster parents impossible. That's why we sometimes have to issue restraining orders."

Blake shook his head. "I don't think that'll be necessary—at least not yet. I'd like to try to work it out with her." His voice didn't hold much hope, and again Amanda felt the urge to comfort him. What a messy situation! Quite different from the scenario she had envisioned when she'd discovered Mara screaming in the overheated truck.

The sound of a toilet flushing made them all look toward the hallway. "I'd better make sure he washes his hands." Blake went down the hall and into the bathroom.

Erika looked at Amanda. "So, have you known Blake long?"

"Not really. But from what I've seen, he's really good with the children, if that's what you were asking."

"Actually, I was wondering if maybe you two were romantically involved."

"Us?" Amanda felt her heart skipping a beat, as her mind raced through possible reasons for the question. "Are you worried about us being . . . improper in front of the children?" Amanda wasn't satisfied with the word *improper,* but she wasn't willing to be more specific.

"Oh, not at all," Erika said. "You look like two responsible people. But since having a bachelor be a foster parent isn't very usual, I just thought if there was a chance of you two becoming engaged or getting married, that it might make his position stronger in case there was a competing family request for custody. That may even be reason enough for a judge to continue to award Mr. Simmons custody if his cousin goes to court before she's really ready to get the children back."

"She could do that? Before she's ready, I mean."

"Well, we're going to do everything we can to see that she is completely fit before awarding her custody, but it might not be enough. She could clean up just long enough to convince a judge that they would be better off with her than with a single man."

"So she'd get them back and nothing would have changed?"

"A judge might believe she deserves another chance. Especially here in Utah. They are very reluctant to take children from a mother. Children really do need a mother figure, you know."

Amanda made a rapid decision. "I am very interested in Blake. I . . . if things work out . . ." She trailed off, shrugging and blushing miserably.

Erika laughed. "I thought I felt the chemistry between you two. I knew I was right."

She most certainly *wasn't* right, but Amanda couldn't let her know that. What was she talking about? Chemistry? Bah!

Blake returned then with a new outfit for Mara, saving Amanda from further embarrassment. While he took Erika on a tour of the apartment, Amanda sat on the couch and read the insect sticker book to Kevin and Mara.

"Did you have another nightmare last night?" she asked after the second page.

"I guess."

"You did?" She gave him a sympathetic grin. "Hmm. Oh, wait a minute." She leaned over and grabbed her purse. "I just remembered. At school today we made these really cool bug bracelets from bug-shaped beads, and I have one for you." Actually, she had two that she'd made for Kerrianne's children, but this was more important. She found the bracelets in the zipper pouch and pulled one out.

"Cool!" Kevin fingered the odd-shaped beads that had been painted to resemble tiny ants, beetles, grasshoppers, and ladybugs. "It's mine? Really?"

Amanda nodded but didn't let him take it from her hands. "There is one thing, though," she said in a mysterious voice.

"What?" Kevin's eyes were huge.

"It's magic."

"Magic?" There was no skepticism in his eyes as there would have been in an older child's.

"Yep, it's a magic bug bracelet. If you wear it, no bugs can come anywhere near you. If you get near them, they'll run away as fast as they can." She was pretty proud of this last addition. If he were to try it out on any hapless bugs, he'd find it very true.

"What if you *want* to hold a bug?" he asked.

"Well, you'll have to take it off first because they can't stand it. They'll run away. They can't even come in your dreams, I'm pretty sure."

He pulled at it again, and she let him have it. "Do you want me to put it on?" she asked. He nodded.

When she was finished, he showed it to Mara. "Look, it's my magic bug bracelet." Mara grinned and tried to pull it into her mouth.

"Stop that!" Kevin said. His voice was firm, but Amanda noticed he pulled his arm gently away so as not to startle her.

"Well, that looks good," Erika was saying as they came from one of the bedrooms. "I'll just take those papers with me and get them processed. Meanwhile, if you do take the children to the doctor, the dentist, or something like that, it'll all be covered by the state since we're responsible for them now."

"Thank you," Blake said.

Amanda stood and walked to the door with them. "Nice to meet you."

Erika smiled. "You too. Good luck with your future." She winked.

Amanda could feel Blake's eyes on her and knew he was wondering what they had talked about when he was in the bathroom with Kevin. Her face burned. Why did she have to be so transparent?

"I'll stay in touch." With that, Erika Solos was gone, and Amanda was left alone with Blake and the children.

"That went well," she ventured.

"What was she talking about at the end there?"

"Oh nothing really." Amanda sat down at the kitchen table and folded her hands together. "I've been thinking, though, about Mara's diarrhea. My sister always gives her kids some clear liquid she buys in big bottles at the store. I think you should get some."

Blake wasn't buying any of her evasion. He sat down next to her. "What did she mean by good luck with your future?"

"Of course, you probably already have some," Amanda continued.

"No, but I'll go get some just as soon as you tell me what she meant."

Stubbornness, Amanda thought. *There's one for the list against him. Right after his profession.* When she got home, she was going to write up the list of his good and bad qualities to prove to herself that any relationship with him was not only a bad idea but entirely out of the question. Never mind that she had noticed all the interesting books on the shelves of his entertainment system. Books that proved he wasn't as intellectually deprived as she had first suspected or as she felt his job indicated.

Then again, what did it really matter, anyway, what job he had? If he was happy at it and could make a living, the more power to him. Her grandfather had been a farmer. A simple man, to be sure, but she had never known a wiser one. Or one who was more content with his life. Besides, Blake's smile was incredible, and his eyes were like pools of . . . No, forget any mention of chocolate.

"Well?" he prompted, holding her with his stare.

She sighed. "Okay. She said that if there were to be a problem, like one of your relatives trying to get custody from you—"

"That won't happen. Everyone's happy to let me do the work."

"Well, then. It doesn't matter. Let's go look at Kevin's new magic bug bracelet."

"What else did she say?"

Amanda darted a glance at Kevin, but he was on the floor by the kitchen door with Mara, searching for an ant to serve as an experiment for his bracelet. "She said it was possible your cousin might be able to get custody back before she was ready if she could convince a judge that a bachelor couldn't care for the children as well as she could."

"And?"

"Well, she also said that if you were to, you know, have intentions of getting . . . uh, involved . . . married even, that might help your case. I was a little concerned so I guess I sort of let Erika think that we were, um, well, interested in perhaps becoming involved." Too late Amanda realized he could actually be dating someone else and that she could have greatly complicated matters. She wished she could sink into the ground and disappear.

A smile spread over his face. "I see. I see. Well, you did the right thing. Thank you."

She looked at him suspiciously. His words definitely did not match the gleam in his eyes. "Uh, you're welcome."

"I really do appreciate it," he went on. "I'm glad you care so much about what happens to Kevin and Mara. Of course, this brings up an entirely different dilemma."

Here it comes, she thought. "Oh?"

"You see, I'm not used to lying, and letting someone believe something that's not true is lying."

"Oh, I see. So letting a person think a couple of children are yours when they're really not would be a lie." *Ha, two could play at this game.* Amanda was suddenly enjoying herself.

"They are mine—my responsibility."

"Okay," she conceded. She was sure if she held out on that line of questioning, he'd ask her if she'd gone shopping yesterday after her visit to his shop, and she'd have to say no.

He grinned. "So as things now stand, I see no other choice than for us to go out."

"On a date?" Amanda found herself returning his smile.

"Yes. I'll make an honest woman of you." He leaned back in his chair, obviously proud of himself.

"When would this date be?" Amanda asked.

"As soon as possible. Tomorrow night?"

"I don't know. I was thinking of going dancing with a friend."

"A friend?"

"A *girl*friend." Amanda hadn't actually called a friend yet, but before Blake had shown up she had planned to call Savvy right after work.

He lifted his shoulders and shook his head. "I guess you'll have to tell her you've changed your mind. You know how important being honest is."

"Maybe."

"Oh?" He raised an eyebrow.

"I'll go out with you tomorrow *if* you'll do something for me."

"Fix the timer on your stove?"

"Nope. I'm not telling you what until you agree." Amanda smirked at him, daring him to accept.

"Okay, deal."

"I'll go out with you tomorrow only if you'll sing 'Itsy Bitsy Spider' to me." She grinned triumphantly.

Blake blinked. He shook his head, whether in rejection of her demand or disbelief, she couldn't tell. "You've got to be kidding."

"Nope."

"Nope?"

She shook her head.

"Well, I don't know if I can do that." His voice was low and sent shivers up her spine. He was no longer smiling.

She was about to kick herself for being so coy when he leaned toward her. Because she was also leaning forward, he was close now— too close for the good of her pounding heart. Only a mere three inches separated their faces. Amanda saw him glance at her lips and instinctively she glanced at his. Long seconds ticked by. Amanda usually waited a good long time before allowing any of her dates to kiss her, if she ever allowed it, but somehow this moment with Blake was different from any she had experienced before. *Yeah, right,* she thought. *That's because he's not even a date.* The space between them closed . . .

"Dang!" Kevin shouted in their ears.

Blake and Amanda jerked upright and stared at Kevin who was

now standing by the table. "What?" Blake asked, his chest expanding as he took an exasperated breath.

Amanda fought her acute disappointment.

"I can't find any ants." Kevin held up his arm to Blake's face. "I was trying to make them run away with my bracelet, but I can't find any here."

"See?" Amanda said brightly. "It's working already!"

Kevin stared at the bracelet for a moment. "Wow," he said. "I wish I'd had this bracelet when I was with my mom. There was lots of ants there."

His comments brought Amanda back to reality. "I'd better get home." She went to collect her purse.

Blake looked disappointed, which made Amanda feel slightly better. "Wait," he said, going with her to the door. "What about our date?"

"Mara's stinky," Kevin announced. "Her smells real bad."

Amanda grinned, although part of her was close to tears. She wasn't ready for a relationship. She didn't even want one. She should tell him that. Instead she said, "Call me." With a little wave to Kevin, who was sitting beside Mara on the linoleum floor, she fled.

In her car, she laid her forehead on the cold steering wheel. *That was close,* she thought. *Too close.* Still, she had to admit, if only to herself, that every word she'd said to the social worker had been absolutely true.

Chapter Nine

Blake had just returned from the store where he'd bought some of the clear liquid Amanda had recommended. Mara seemed to like the taste and began guzzling her bottle while he decided what to make for dinner. Normally, he didn't mind cooking, but now he felt exhausted. Besides, it was Friday night. He was young and single—he should be out on a date having fun, not slaving over a hot stove.

A date with Amanda?

No way am I going to sing "Itsy Bitsy Spider" for her. He grinned at the absurdness of the request. *Especially not before our first date!*

"So what should we eat?" he asked Kevin.

"Pizza?" suggested the boy hopefully.

"I was thinking of something a little more nutritious—and less expensive."

"Donuts?"

"Yeah, right." He rolled his eyes, making Kevin giggle.

"How about chicken and potatoes? We'll put it in the oven and in an hour or so it's ready to eat with that bag of salad we bought."

"But I'm hungry now."

"Tacos then?"

Kevin nodded. "I want soft shell."

"Okay, but you have to have lettuce and tomatoes on it. Or at least a salad on the side."

"Salad." Kevin looked at Mara who was lying on the carpet by the love seat. "What about Mara?"

"Oh, I got vegetable and chicken something-or-other for her." Blake held up the baby food bottles. He wasn't sure if he should feed her anything other than the clear liquid, but he certainly wasn't going to starve the child. If she wanted food, she was going to get it.

Kevin frowned. "Her doesn't like vegetables. Her spits them out."

"*She* spits them out. And that's because she's never had my spinach soup."

"Can we make that tomorrow?"

"Sure." Blake took out a pound of lean hamburger and began frying it in a pan. He wasn't actually positive that tacos were more healthy than pizza, but at least they included fresh vegetables. He tried to get Kevin to eat as many as possible.

The phone rang, and he picked it up from the kitchen counter. "Hello?"

"Blake? Thank heaven I found you! It's taken me hours to get your number!"

"Paula?" Blake glanced at Kevin, who was watching him with wide eyes.

"Yes, it's me," came the irritated response. "I've been trying and trying to reach you. I had to call Mom to get your number."

"My number hasn't changed." He always made sure of that, just in case Paula needed to contact him. "I guess you lost it during the last six months."

"What's that supposed to mean? It's not as if you didn't get to see Kevin. I know you were visiting."

"Your mother's too old to take care of him. He should have been with me."

"He's *my* son!"

"How much were you even there?"

"None of your business!" Then Paula repeated the phrase, this time punctuating it with a few swear words that grated on Blake's ears.

Fighting irritation, he said calmly, "What do you want?"

"What do I want?" Paula's voice rose two octaves. "I want my kids, that's what." Again she swore colorfully.

"Paula, if you continue to talk like that, I'm hanging up. I will. Now, I've got Kevin here waiting to talk with you, so let's get to the point."

"Okay," Paula sounded like she was talking through gritted teeth. "What I'm saying is, I'm coming to pick up the kids."

"You can't do that. The social worker said they have to stay here. But you can come see them any time you want."

"Any time I want," she screeched. "They're *my* kids, Blake. Mine. Not yours, not the—"

"No swearing," he warned. "I'll hang up." He winked at Kevin to show him there wasn't a problem. Kevin tried to wink back, but both his eyes shut with the effort.

"They aren't the state's children."

"No, but they have custody now. They told me that if I don't follow their rules, they'll find another foster family. Then you wouldn't be able to call or see them whenever you want."

"That's crazy! They're mine! Come on, Blake, it's me, Paula. Let's forget all these idiots. You know I'm a good mother. I'll come get the kids and disappear. They won't blame you."

Blake kept his voice calm. "No, Paula. I can't do that. I promised."

"Your promise to them is more important than me being with my kids?" Bitterness oozed from every word.

"No, my promise to Kevin and Mara is more important. They deserve a good home."

"I give them that! They're my whole life!"

"I know you love them. But let's be honest, Paula, they had no heat where you were living, and no food in the refrigerator."

"I hadn't gone shopping yet!"

Blake turned his back to Kevin, who was still trying to wink, holding down one eye while he opened the other. "You left them with a stranger overnight," he snarled softly into the phone. "When I picked them up, they were starving."

"I was going to get them, but the stupid police hauled me in for nothing." Paula burst into another torrent of swear words.

Blake hung up the phone. "Your mother's a little upset," he told Kevin. "Don't worry, she'll call back. Can you get out the tomatoes for me?"

He fried all the hamburger, grated the cheese, and diced the tomatoes before Paula called back. "I want my kids," she said without preamble.

"You can see them anytime. You can come by tonight if you want."

"I can't. I have something else to do."

Blake wondered why he felt surprised. Yes, Paula said she wanted to come and get the children, but he couldn't even count the times when she had promised to come and hadn't. It had gotten so bad that sometimes he wouldn't even tell Kevin when she planned on coming.

"What about tomorrow?" he asked. She could go with them to see her mother.

"No, I'll come on Sunday."

"What time?"

"Around ten. I can stay until about five. I have something to do later."

"We have church at one-thirty," Blake told her.

"At one-thirty?"

"I know, it's an odd schedule, but there's some new development in our stake boundaries and four wards are using our building until the new chapel's done."

"Do you even have to go?"

"Yes."

"Why?"

"Because I do." He wasn't going to justify anything to her.

"You could go alone, and I could stay with the kids."

"I can't do that."

"I won't take off with them. You know that."

Blake didn't know any such thing. "I can't. And they should be at church anyway. They need a schedule."

"You think I don't know that? Besides, visiting their mother is more important than church. *I'm* more important."

Blake had to fight to control his anger. "Paula, that's the problem. Don't you see? That's putting your needs first, not theirs."

"You're trying to steal my kids!" she yelled in his ear. "You can't find a girl and get your own so you have to steal mine!"

Almost, it was as if he could see his cousin as the innocent girl she had been, pointing a finger at him accusingly. His heart ached for that girl. "I don't want to steal your children, Paula," he said calmly. "I'm just trying to help. I'm here for you, like I've always been. Would you prefer that I tell the social worker I don't want to be involved?"

"No, no." Paula began to backpedal as fast as she could. "Not at all. I'm grateful to you, really I am, Blake. I just wish you weren't such a stickler for the rules."

"That's who I am. I'm doing my best. But, Paula, it's up to you now. You show up at their counseling sessions, take their drug tests, get a job, arrange a nice place to live, and you'll get custody back. It's as simple as that." Or it should be simple. For someone using drugs, he knew, nothing was simple. Paula hadn't been able to hold down a job for years. After a couple of weeks, she was always fired.

"I'll have a place next week. And I'll be doing the rest, too."

"Okay, then. See you Sunday at ten?"

"I might be a little late. Never know if my car's going to start."

"We'll be here till one-twenty and then after four."

"Okay. Let me talk to Kevin."

"All right." Blake handed the phone to Kevin.

The child put the phone to his ear. "Yeah," he said. "No. Yeah. I love you, too. Okay. Mommy, can I stay here for a while? Uncle Blake's making spinach soup tomorrow." He smiled. "I like it. Yeah." His smile vanished. "On Sunday? Am I going with you? Oh." He nodded. "Okay. Bye, Mommy."

Blake had set out their plates with the warmed flour tortillas on the table. "So what did she say?"

"She said she's coming on Sunday." The round blue eyes began to water, and his voice was choked as he added, "I don't want to leave yet."

"You won't, Kevin. I promise you, the next time you go with your mommy, you're going to have a nice warm house, and a nice baby-sitter, and your mommy will go to work. She won't drink anymore." Knowing Paula, Blake felt a moment of despair. How could she ever accomplish such things? *If she loves these kids enough, she can do it,* he thought. *I have to remind her on Sunday that she's not alone. The Lord can help her find her way back.*

"Will I see you when I go live with her?"

Blake reached over and gathered him into his arms. "Oh, yes. Wherever you are, I'll be close by. No matter what. We're like two of the three musketeers."

Kevin seemed satisfied with that. "Mara's the other musket-ear. Can we watch that show again?"

"Sure. Why not?"

"Tomorrow?"

"We're going to your grandma's tomorrow, but if we get up early and go, we should get home in time. We can stay up late since church isn't till after lunch."

"Yay!"

After dinner, they played several games of Memory. Blake made sure to lose every other hand. He had to try less hard to lose now since Kevin was really improving. *In another year, I might actually have to work at winning,* Blake thought.

When they tired of the game, they changed for bed and brushed their teeth. "Come on, I'll tuck you in," Blake said.

"Will you sing?"

"Sure." Blake sat with Mara on the edge of Kevin's bed and sang Kevin's favorite songs. Doing so reminded him of Amanda and how she'd asked him to sing her "Itsy Bisty Spider." Crazy. No way he'd do that. Was it just an excuse for her to refuse him?

Then again, it had been her idea to let the social worker think they were dating. He smiled as he remembered. What was so wrong with that? He *wanted* to date her—he'd asked her out. And she'd said to call.

So he'd call.

But he wasn't singing that stupid song to her. He wouldn't tell her about his schooling, either. She'd have to accept him as he was.

After changing another diaper, he settled Mara in her crib and then gave Kevin a final hug and kiss before turning out the lights.

He didn't go to the phone right away. He went first to the dryer and removed the array of bathroom items he'd put inside, making a mound by the machine. The collection in the washer made the pile grow. He put in a load of Mara's clothes so she'd have something clean to wear the next day. All her undershirts were stained, and he sprayed them several times before adding non-chlorine bleach. Funny the tricks he'd picked up over the years raising Kevin.

He thought of Paula and the smile on his face died. So many clothes he'd bought for Kevin when he'd been with him, but each time the child had returned with only the clothes on his back. Sometimes Blake wondered if Paula had hocked the better items to pay for her habits.

Shaking his head, he closed the washer and started the cycle. It was time to call—or not. The thought of Amanda made him strangely happy, as though she were here in the room, her bright green eyes smiling up at him.

He had to call her. He knew he wouldn't be able to sleep until he did.

Chapter Ten

Amanda knew it was childish, but she made the list on a page in her journal.

Blake Simmons

Pros	Cons
can fix appliances	boring job (probably low-paying)
persistent, doesn't give up	stubborn
good with children	acts like a child
can change diapers	shoves things in closets
can make bottles	forgets to wash dishes
loves books (has a lot of them)	messy house
is kind to old widows	was rather rude to me when I found Mara
uses a car seat	left Mara in the truck ALONE! (no sense?)
loyal	enables his cousin's bad behavior
Kevin and Mara	Kevin and Mara
responsible	very occupied

works hard	*probably isn't around enough*
is dang good-looking	*makes me worry about my hair*
eyes like pools of chocolate	*eyes like pools of chocolate*
	(makes it hard to think!)

She shook her head. This was getting her absolutely nowhere. Each of the pros had an opposite con. Maybe it was true that many people cited the exact same reasons for divorcing as they did for marrying, only worded differently.

He had, at least, asked her out. Yes, she had messed that up by requiring him to sing the song, but she had told him to call. If he did, what would she say? Getting involved with him didn't seem like a very good idea. Did she want the responsibility of two children who didn't belong to either of them? A relationship was hard enough—throwing two children in the mix could make it impossible. Never mind that they were adorable. Never mind that she could feel her biological clock ticking louder every year. Never mind that she'd take Kevin and Mara in a minute if the situation were reversed.

She sighed and propelled herself off her plaid couch to the phone lying on the kitchen table. The number came to her without difficulty, though she hadn't dialed it for months.

"Hello?"

"Hi, Savvy. It's me, Amanda." She returned to the couch and sat down.

"Amanda! I just about thought you'd dropped off the face of the earth. Where've you been?"

"I bought a house in Pleasant Grove. I decided it was time to put down some roots and quit waiting for Mr. Right to appear and sweep me off my feet."

Savvy gave a little groan. "Don't I know it!"

"Hey, you're what—barely nineteen? You're too young to think like that."

"I know, I know. It's not like I want to get married—I'm really into my studies right now. But it would be nice to *want* to marry the guy who's asking."

"Someone asked you to marry him?"

Savvy giggled. "Actually three guys did—from my ward. It's like it's a contest or something to see who can get married first. They don't seem to even care that I'm carrying an extra ten or fifteen pounds."

Amanda snorted. "That's because it's in all the right places!" Savvy had always been a little weight conscious, but her rounder curves went perfectly with her sunny disposition.

"You always did know how to cheer me up."

"Well, I called to see if you want to go dancing. Tomorrow, maybe." There. If Savvy said yes, she wouldn't be able to go out with Blake even if he did call.

"Tomorrow? Oh, I'd really love too, but I can't. They're having a family dinner at my uncle's, and I'm invited. Apparently, there's going to be a special announcement. You'd think they could wait until the end of the month when we're all together for Thanksgiving, but no, it has to be now. I think it's Tanner and Heather's announcement, since he's the one who made me promise to go. My guess is that Heather's pregnant. They've been married almost a year now."

Tanner with a baby? Only last year had Amanda envisioned what their child might look like, hers and Tanner's. Just as she'd dreamed of their wedding and becoming a part of his family. Now he and Heather were having a baby. She waited for the familiar sadness to envelope her, but she felt only happiness for her old boyfriend. "That's really great," she said. "I know Tanner's been waiting a long time for this. I bet he's in seventh heaven."

"You can say that again. That's why it's not really a secret. Those two are going around acting like crazy idiots, slinging names at each other out of the blue. Would you believe Tanner actually suggested

Zebediah? Heather couldn't stop laughing." Savvy paused, abruptly more serious. "You're okay with this, aren't you, Amanda? I mean, with the way things worked out?"

Amanda didn't know how she *couldn't* be okay with it. After all, the choice hadn't really been hers. She had seen plainly that Tanner was in love with Heather, and she couldn't bear to be second-best. "Yeah, it's fine," she said. "I'm really happy for them. Tanner's a wonderful guy, and Heather's perfect for him."

"I'm glad you think so, because I was beginning to worry that we wouldn't be friends anymore because of him. You haven't really responded to any of my invitations since you stopped dating Tanner, and then you moved, and I didn't know how to reach you."

"I've been really swamped this past year," Amanda said. "And I'll be honest, it did take me some time to get on with my life, you know. I mean, Tanner wasn't the right guy for me, but it's still hard to be alone. I'm almost twenty-five and all my friends are married and having children."

"And that's another strange thing. Tanner thinks you *are* married. I knew you wouldn't get married without telling me, but he was so sure."

Amanda smiled. She hadn't told Tanner she was getting married, just that dating him had made her understand her feelings for Gerry. And it had. She'd learned she couldn't marry someone she didn't love at least as much as she loved Tanner. "Well, I was dating someone, but that didn't work out," she said to Savvy. "I discovered I didn't really love him. It wasn't fair to him. I hear he's engaged, though. Might even be married by now."

"See?" Savvy said. "Then you *do* know what I mean. It'd be nice to find the right guy so you could stop having to worry about ending up with the wrong one! Hmm, I'm not sure that's right, exactly. I'm sure all those people who're getting divorces didn't all know they were marrying the wrong person."

Amanda started laughing. That was what was so great about being with Savvy. She was always amusing. "You think too much," she told her. "So when are we going dancing? That is, if you can take time off from getting all those proposals."

"Oh, I can squeeze you in. How about next Saturday?"

"Deal. But I'll only pencil you in my planner—in case one of your home teachers decides he has to propose before the other one does. Just remember the answer is no. I'm saving you for Tyler, and he doesn't get off his mission until January."

Savvy giggled. "Oh, I've missed you, Amanda."

"I've missed you, too." Despite the nearly six-year gap in their ages, they were very much alike.

"Well, I'd better get back to my books."

"What, studying on a Friday night?"

"I know, it's sad." Savvy didn't sound upset. "I just love school. Science is so interesting! And my astronomy classes—well, I'd rather go to those than do just about anything else."

"Your poor home teachers!"

"Yep. I guess until I find a guy that's more fascinating than black holes or fission, I'll stay wild and single. Well, at least single. My books are too heavy to take on any wild adventures. I only wish my roommates could understand that."

Laughter bubbled up again in Amanda's throat. She felt so much better now. "Well, don't feel too bad. My excitement for the week was starting a fire in my oven and calling a repairman."

"Really?"

"Yeah, really. And he just happens to be the most handsome guy on the face of the planet."

"No!"

"Yes." Amanda pulled her feet up on the couch as she warmed to her story. "Here I am in my old jeans and T-shirt, practically drooling over this guy. When we look at each other, there's a connection, you know? Electricity. Then I spy his kid in his truck."

"Oh, no!"

"Yes. And guess what? He asked me out. Not right then, but today."

"What? He's got a nerve asking you out when he's married!"

"Well, he's not. Wait till you hear the rest." Amanda recounted the week's adventures, including Kevin's nightmares and Mara's constantly exploding diapers. She dwelt only briefly on the reasons Blake had the children and told her nothing about his cousin. Time enough for that later. When she finished her tale, Savvy was giggling madly.

"You actually asked him to sing?" Savvy managed through her giggles. "I've got to remember that one."

"I didn't mean to, but he was just so cute when Kevin told us about the song. He turned bright red."

"So what are you doing on the phone with me? Huh?" Savvy asked. "I bet he's trying to call you right now."

"I don't know. Maybe I'm afraid."

"Of what? He sounds like a nice guy."

Amanda's laughter was gone now. "Yeah. I just don't think I can go through losing someone special again."

Savvy was silent for a long minute. "I'm sorry, Amanda. I know it wasn't fun losing Tanner. Heck, he's my cousin—by marriage at least—and I would have married him in a minute if there'd been an ounce of attraction between us. But what if for now you didn't look at Blake as something permanent? Just go out, have fun. With his responsibilities, he probably needs some fun. There's no reason you can't be friends."

"You're right." Amanda nodded, though Savvy wasn't there to see. "I guess I've been thinking about this the wrong way. There really is no reason we can't be friends. He could use some help with the children."

"Exactly. Once you know him better, you can decide what you want."

"Thanks, Savvy. It's good to have someone to talk to. If I'd told Kerrianne or my mother, they'd already be planning my wedding."

"What about Mitch? I bet he's taking some of the heat off you."

"Oh, yeah. You should hear them. 'Mitch, darling, what about that Olsen girl? She just got home from her mission. Why don't you ask her out?' Or 'Mitch, will you be having anyone special come for Christmas?' It's a living nightmare. Mitch is fit to be tied. Hey, maybe we should take him dancing with us."

"Okay," Savvy agreed. "Just don't tell your mother we're all going together or it'll be *my* wedding in the works. We've been down that road before—Mitch and I will never be more than friends. Still, he's fun to go dancing with. Only tell him to leave his lizard home this time. It definitely didn't help."

"I will. I promise."

A few minutes later, Amanda hung up the phone smiling to herself. Yes, she had neglected her relationship with Savvy way too long. Most of her older friends might be occupied with their new families, but Savvy was mature for her age. At least she had goals in mind that didn't always involve settling down and raising half a dozen children. Not that Amanda was against the idea—she herself wanted more than anything to have a family—but it was hard to talk about it all the time when it didn't look like a marriage was even in her future.

Amanda changed into her pajamas and began considering popping corn and putting in the five-hour video version of *Pride and Prejudice*. It was her favorite of all time—a rich, haughty man falling in love with a poor, down-to-earth young woman. Perfect.

The phone rang and she froze. No one called her anymore after nine unless something was wrong.

Or it could be *him*.

Amanda's heart pounded. "Well, answer it," she told herself. She dived for the portable phone where she had left it on the couch after her conversation with Savvy. "Hello?" she asked, trying to sound casual.

"Hi. It's Blake."

He hadn't needed to tell her. She recognized his deep voice the minute she heard his first word. Thank heaven she couldn't see those eyes.

"Hi, Blake. What's up?"

"I'm glad you're home."

She remembered it was Friday night. Maybe she shouldn't have answered the phone so that he might think she was out. *Ridiculous*, she thought, *I'm finished playing games*. Besides, she had to admit, she was glad *he* was home, too, instead of out with someone else.

"I just got the kids to bed," he said.

She smiled to herself. *A little hard to go out when you have two children*. "That's good. Any nightmares?"

"Not so far. Kevin really likes the bracelet. Thank you."

"Just something I had in my purse, left over from school. I was glad to give it to him. He's a cute kid." She waited to see what he would come up with next. Surely he hadn't called her to tell her he'd put them to bed.

"I tried the magic bit with a light, and it worked a little. Maybe the light and the bracelet, along with holding the bugs today, will do the trick."

"I hope so."

"Me, too. Oh, and I bought some of that clear stuff," he said. "Mara seemed to like it okay. The bottle said it might take a day or so."

"Then you should know soon enough if it works."

"I'll be grateful if it does—I've changed more diapers this week than I can count." He paused before adding, "That reminds me. What was the idea with the diapers in the closet? Did you rig them to fall on me?"

She laughed. "No. I wouldn't do that. Well, I might have, but not when the social worker was there! When you asked me to change Mara before she came, I couldn't find your diaper bag, and then I remembered you stuffing the diapers in the closet. I tried to get one down, and suddenly it was raining diapers. I was lucky to get them all back in. I don't think I've ever seen so many diapers in my life!"

"I've been desperate," he admitted with a chuckle. "I thought if I found the right diaper, I wouldn't have to do so much laundry."

"It was worth a try."

They both fell silent. Amanda hated the awkwardness that reared between them. It was almost enough to make her wonder if she really wanted to start dating again.

"Uh," he said.

Could he be having a hard time himself? She considered the idea. He was very good-looking, but having Kevin to care for and a job that often demanded late hours might have put a damper on his dating prowess.

"Yes?" she asked. "Was there a reason you called?" If she were a more modern girl, she'd just ask him out!

When he spoke, his voice was tense. "It's about what we discussed earlier."

"Diapers?" she asked with feigned innocence.

"No, not diapers! About going out."

"Oh, you mean making it so I wasn't lying. Okay, when?"

"Just like that. You aren't going to make me sing?"

She laughed. "No. I'll let you off the hook this time."

"That's a relief." The tenseness in his tone was gone.

"So, is it tomorrow?" she asked. "Are we going dancing?"

"Uh, I can't tomorrow after all."

Amanda felt a sudden lump in her throat. Had she misunderstood him? Maybe he hadn't really been asking her out at all. Maybe he'd been talking about confessing to the social worker. No, he'd mentioned the song. She tried to replay the conversation in her mind but couldn't recall a single word.

"Oh, some other time then." She kept her voice light.

"I'd like to go out tomorrow," he said, "but I forgot that I promised Kevin's grandmother I'd take the kids to see her. We're leaving early, but it's almost a four-hour drive to Cedar City, and I'm not sure we'll be back even by six or seven. I was going to order a pizza when we got back. Plus, I promised Kevin we'd watch *The Three Musketeers*."

"*The Three Musketeers*?"

"Yeah, he loves the old ones. I recorded them from the TV. Since he'll probably sleep all the way home from Cedar City, he'll be up past ten or more."

"Sounds like a long day." Amanda was feeling better. At least she hadn't misunderstood his intentions, and he did want to ask her out.

Blake sighed. "Yeah. To tell you the truth, even if I hadn't promised Kevin we'd watch the show, I'd probably be too exhausted to go anywhere." He groaned. "Man, I'm getting old!"

"I know what you're talking about. Sometimes after a day with my fourth-graders, the only thing I want to do is curl up and sleep. That's why I usually go out on Saturdays and not Fridays."

Another awkward pause grew between them. "Well, I guess you could call your girlfriend," he said. "You know, go dancing."

"Actually, we're going next week instead. She had a family dinner crop up. I think I'll stay home and watch *Pride and Prejudice*. The nineties version."

"That's five hours!"

She was surprised he knew. "And every second is great. I've seen it six times."

"Well, if you thought you could tear yourself away, you could come over and hang out with us. The guy I rent from has this huge TV screen in his living room. He's out of town, but he lets me use it whenever I want." His voice was casual, too casual. Amanda knew the invitation hadn't been easy for him to extend.

Friendship, she reminded herself. *If he were Savvy, I'd accept in a minute.*

"Hey, that might be fun," she said. "I haven't seen any bad sword fighting for a while."

He chuckled. "You've seen good sword fighting then?"

"Guess not, but one can always hope. Oh, and I'll bring the popcorn. Just give me a call when you get home."

"Okay. I'll order pizza."

Another awkward pause. Boy, she hated this! "Well, I guess I'll see you tomorrow," she said. "Good night."

"Good night."

She hung up the phone. Why was her heart racing? Of all the foolish things for it to do. He needed a friend. She needed somewhere to go. That was all.

Chapter Eleven

Amanda tucked a small box of microwave popcorn bags into her purse before she went out to the car. Blake had just called and offered to pick her up, but she had reminded him that the children would likely be asleep before the movie was over and driving her home wouldn't be convenient.

She felt as nervous as the day she'd had her very first date. Where had all her confidence gone? In high school, she'd never worried this much. She'd even tried on three different outfits before deciding on a newer pair of jeans and a fitted blouse with ruffled ends on the long sleeves. The color was the sky at noon, a vibrant blue. She knew it didn't match her eyes the way green did, but the soothing color normally had a calming effect.

Not today. Her stomach was in knots.

Blake answered the door with a pajama-clad Mara in his arms. She smiled and launched herself at Amanda. "Hey, she likes you!"

Amanda hugged Mara, making kissing motions on her neck to make her giggle. "She's so adorable." Her smiled faltered.

"What is it?" Blake asked.

Amanda looked up at him. "I just thought . . . I mean . . . her mother . . ." She looked around but didn't see Kevin. Lowering her voice, she said, "I just don't know how her mother can bear to be away from her."

"I know." Blake shook his head. "I think the same thing every day. I know it kills me when I can't see Kevin, and I already feel the same way about Mara."

"Diapers and all?" Amanda tried to lighten the mood.

He chuckled. "Yeah, diapers and all."

She took off her coat and handed it to him, along with the popcorn from her purse. While Blake was popping the corn, Kevin came from the bathroom. "Amanda!" he said, running to her. "It worked! It worked! The ants didn't come in my bed last night."

"That's wonderful!" She hugged him.

"I *knew* it would work," he said.

"So did you have fun at your grandmother's?"

He nodded. "We got my toy box. And Grandma had some clothes for me and Mara because we didn't grow too big. See those pink pajamas Mara's got on? Uncle Blake put them on just now. Mara really likes them. Her was sucking on them."

"*She* was sucking on them?" Amanda gently tried to correct his grammar.

"Yep. When Mara sucks on them, that means her likes them."

"I think you're right. Babies love to suck on things they like." Amanda sat down on the couch and drew him over to stand in front of her so she could look into his face. "But remember to say 'she was sucking on them,' not *her.* You almost always use *she* at the first of a sentence."

"*She,*" he repeated. "Or *Mara?*"

She grinned. "Exactly. You are one very smart boy."

"My mommy's coming tomorrow," he announced then. "Well,

her *said* her was coming. But I'm not going back with her. Or Mara, either."

Amanda looked toward Blake, who was coming from the kitchen holding a large metal bowl full of popcorn and a cardboard pizza box topped with a small stack of plates. He nodded in confirmation. "Well, that'll be fun," she said, though Blake didn't look very happy.

Kevin spun away from Amanda. "I'm putting in the video. Okay?"

"Okay," Blake said. "Do you remember the right way?"

"Uh-huh." In fact, Kevin proved adept at working the video player.

"I'm going to meet your sister tomorrow," Blake said, sitting on the love seat beside Amanda. Leaning over, he put the pizza box on the floor with the lid wide open, keeping the popcorn on his lap out of Mara's reach. "We're going over after church. I wanted to meet her and help the kids feel comfortable with her before they actually go to stay on Monday."

"They will love her," Amanda said with confidence. "She's excellent with kids. You should see all the crafts she does with hers. But, tell me, how did she sound? She was sick this past week—I don't know if I mentioned that."

"She told me, but she sounded good. I know she's well enough to go to church because she mentioned it on the phone when I asked what time we should come."

"Then she's better. She'd tell you if she wasn't. She's very up front about things."

He grinned. "Like her sister?"

Amanda hated the way his expression made her want to smile back and how his eyes made her want to never look away. Worse, her stomach was doing flips. *We're going to be friends,* she reminded herself. *I am here to help with the children.*

Kevin was back, and he snuggled between them on the love seat, telling Mara that the film was going to begin in just a minute. He showed her the remote control in his hand, but Mara was busy chewing on the straps of Amanda's purse.

"I thought we were going to watch it on your friend's television," Amanda said to Blake.

He made a face. "We were, but then I got to thinking about the food and the kids. My friend's a bachelor, so maybe it's best if we stay down here."

"Wise decision."

"I thought so."

There was a brief silence as Kevin dug his hand into the popcorn bowl on Blake's lap. "Wait!" Amanda said. "Stop eating that right now! It's not finished."

Kevin and Blake looked at her, mouths slightly ajar. "Why?" asked Kevin.

Amanda reached into her purse and drew out a brown bag of M&Ms. "It's missing these, of course."

"Mmmmm!" Kevin bounced on the love seat.

Amanda ripped open the bag and poured the candies over the white popcorn kernels. "They'll sink to the bottom, but if you get at least one with every handful, it'll change the way you look at popcorn forever."

Blake shook his head. "I think you're just trying to cover up the fact that your popcorn is 94 percent fat-free."

"Ah, you noticed. It's healthier, you know."

"And M&Ms are healthy?"

Amanda shrugged. "For chocolate, I'll take my chances."

"Yeah!" exclaimed Kevin, diving a hand into the bowl. Mara tried to follow his lead and fell on top of Kevin. Both giggled.

"Can she eat popcorn?" Amanda asked.

Blake's brow creased. "Probably not. She doesn't have any teeth yet. But I already fed her a bottle and some spinach soup."

"We ate spinach soup for lunch at Grandma's," Kevin added, his mouth full of popcorn. "It's sooooo good. Uncle Blake maked it for us. It has beans in it. We brought some home to eat tomorrow."

"Sounds yummy." Amanda made a face at Blake behind Kevin's back. The soup most definitely *didn't* sound yummy. *Can make children eat spinach soup,* she mentally added to her list of pros. Opposite this, she would write: *likes spinach soup.*

"I'll make it for you sometime," Blake said, ignoring her look. "It's good."

"If you say so." She wished she didn't feel such a delight that he planned to see her again.

"Can we watch the movie now?" Kevin waved the remote in his hand.

"I forgot the drinks." Blake handed Kevin the popcorn bowl and went into the kitchen, returning in a few minutes with root beer in cans for everyone, except Mara, who had water in a spill-proof Sippy cup. Blake put a plate with pizza on the floor and set Kevin's root beer on a book nearby. "There you go, bud. You can turn on the video now." Kevin plopped onto the floor and pointed the remote at the TV. Mara scooted into his place on the love seat to be nearer the bowl of popcorn. Blake set the bowl on the floor behind Kevin so everyone could reach it except Mara.

The movie came on, but Amanda couldn't follow the plot, if there was one amidst all the sword fighting or the talk about sword fighting. She and Blake began breaking off tiny pieces of pizza crust for Mara and occasionally giving her half an M&M. She didn't choke once, and Amanda suspected the baby was accustomed to eating more foods than Blake knew.

There was a surreal aura about the evening. She, Amanda Huntington, twice failed at love, on a love seat with a good-looking man, a baby between them and another child sitting on the floor nearby, eating pizza with root beer and popcorn with M&Ms.

I'm here for the children. Amanda had to remind herself that at least five times because every time she glanced over at Blake, he was looking at her with eyes larger and darker than any brown M&M.

Blake couldn't get over how perfect the evening seemed. He could almost think they were a family. It seemed that in a few minutes they'd put the children to bed and snuggle on the couch together to watch the rest of the film, stealing kisses during the slow parts. Amanda was everything he had ever hoped to find in a wife. She had a wry sense of humor, was creative and kind, and attractive to boot. Every time she looked at him, his insides felt funny and his knees went weak. But could she like him? She seemed to. She liked Kevin and Mara, that was easy to tell. From the first, she'd been concerned about them. Since he couldn't imagine his life without some connection to Kevin—and now Mara—that was a plus in her favor. Or was it?

An uneasy feeling came to rest in the pit of his stomach. She had come to the shop to check up on the children. What if her interest now was more of the same? What if she felt obligated to continue playing the good Samaritan? Wasn't that a lesson they had both learned in church? The pizza in his mouth tasted funny, and he hurried to swallow it.

When the first show had ended, Mara's eyes were drooping and her head had fallen onto his thigh. "I'd better put her in bed."

"Wait, you haven't changed her all evening," Amanda said.

He grinned. "That's right, I haven't. I changed her right before you came, but she's due." He rolled the half-asleep baby over, sliding out from under her. Carefully unsnapping her pajamas, he checked the diaper. "Nothing! Maybe it's over." He couldn't believe how happy he was not to clean up more mess.

"Yay!" shouted Kevin.

"Shhh, we don't want to wake her." Blake picked Mara up and rocked her in his arms for a few minutes until she was sound asleep. "Kevin," he said, "why don't you go brush your teeth while I put Mara in her crib?"

"Okay."

"You need help, Kevin?" Amanda asked.

"No, I can do it."

Mara nearly awoke when Blake put her down, so he stayed and patted her tummy for a while. When he returned to the living room, Kevin was in his place on the love seat, his head propped up on the armrest. Blake dropped to the floor instead. He didn't mind, though he couldn't see Amanda as well from here.

Kevin's excitement didn't wane, and Blake began thinking the boy might still be awake when Amanda left. Maybe that was a good thing. But as the ending credits rolled across the screen, he saw that Kevin had at last given up the fight with his heavy eyelids.

"Why don't you take him to bed?" Amanda said. "I'll clean up a bit."

"You don't have to."

"I know." She looked at Kevin. "The way his neck is kinked, I'd be sore for a week if it were me."

He laughed. "Don't I know it." He lifted the child in his arms.

When Blake returned, Amanda had picked up everything in the living room, including Kevin's misplaced kernels of popcorn. She had also stacked the dishes in the sink.

"You don't have to do those," he said.

"Oh, I'm not. I make a habit of never doing dishes after midnight. I never know what I'll drop."

"It's after midnight?" Blake checked the clock on the wall by the sofa.

"Not yet, but it will be before we could finish." She yawned, covering her mouth in a gesture he found extraordinarily attractive. "I better get going."

Scooping up her purse from the floor by the couch, she started for the kitchen door.

Blake retrieved her coat from the closet. "Thanks for coming."

She stared at him, and he felt he was drowning in the green sea of her eyes. He found he didn't care. Let him drown, as long as she was with him. He took a step toward her, his eyes searching her face, hoping for clues to her feelings.

"You're welcome." Her voice came softly. He could find no refusal in her face, though her eyes again had the strange expression they'd held at the shop.

"I enjoyed myself," he said.

The distance between them closed, and the emotion intensified in those green eyes. *What is she feeling?* he wondered. He wished he knew—or that he could ask.

"Me too. I really liked being with the children. They're great kids."

Her words hit him like a slap in the face. She liked being with the children. The children, not him.

"Blake," she went on, "if you ever need any help—you know, someone to watch them—I'd be glad to help."

"You would?" Even to his own ears, his voice was thick.

"Yes. What are friends for?"

The nail in the coffin! he thought. *The kiss of death! Friends.* She wasn't interested in him. He was someone worthy only of friendship.

"I'm sure it'll be fine," he said. "Thanks for the offer."

"I mean it." She looked up at him, puzzlement etched on her face. "Is something wrong?"

"Wrong? No. Why?"

"You just . . . your voice . . ." She shook her head. "Well, I had a good time. Thank you."

Despite his hurt feelings, Blake felt himself soften. To be fair, she'd never given him the idea she was interested in him. "Good night," he said. "Stay in touch."

Immediately, he wished he hadn't added that last sentence. It was too much like what people said when they knew they weren't going to see one another again soon. But it was too late to recall the words. She was gone, and Blake was left alone with his doubts and self-recriminations. He should have at least kissed her. If he'd kissed her, then he'd know for sure if there was any future for them.

Chapter Twelve

Blake was furious at his cousin—again. He was so angry he thought it might be a good thing Paula hadn't shown up, even late, because he would have strangled her if she had. Then where would Kevin and Mara be? In a foster home with strangers.

"I don't think Mommy's coming." Kevin looked adorable in his dress pants and white shirt and tie. Blake had wanted to buy a suit, but he hadn't been able to justify the expense—yet. He wouldn't be in school forever. Mara looked equally adorable in the burgundy velvet dress that had been in the box of clothes Aunt Bonny had given them yesterday, complete with white tights, black shoes, and a bow for her hair that Blake was sure would not stay on long.

Not only had he wanted to dress the children up for church but he'd wanted to show Paula he could take care of her children, that they would be safe with him until she was able to be with them herself.

Except she hadn't bothered to show up. He'd waited, like he always did, and now sacrament meeting was almost over. He'd missed the most important meeting, missed taking the sacrament, which would have helped him endure the hardships of the coming week, the extra burden he had taken on, however willingly.

"Come on," he said. "Let's go to church. Primary won't be over yet."

"Goody!" Kevin ran to the door. He loved Primary and hadn't been able to attend the past month since he'd left his grandmother's house. Mara crawled across the linoleum after her brother. Blake picked her up and put on the coat Rhonda had given her.

At church he took Kevin to Primary and introduced him around. But when he tried to take Mara to Sunday School with him, she quickly became restless, so he headed to the nursery to see if they'd let her play with some toys. Blake thought how fortunate it was that the bishop had released him from his calling as Sunday School teacher when he'd gone back to school full-time this year. He'd loved the calling and had been reluctant to leave it, but the bishop promised to offer him another position in the spring when his classes were over. Given his new situation in life, Blake could see that the bishop had been inspired. One more thing to do right now might have driven him insane.

His ward was a family ward, and though he'd had every intention after Paula had taken Kevin to begin attending a ward for singles, he'd been so busy with work and school that he'd put off going. He'd even stopped going to the singles' dances to drive to Cedar City to be with Kevin. Besides, Blake loved being surrounded by families, despite the pangs of jealousy he sometimes suffered. That would all change once he was graduated. He'd find a woman who liked children and marry her.

Thoughts of Amanda filled his head. He loved the way she tossed her head when she was annoyed, the way her dimpled smile filled his heart, the way her green eyes . . .

Stop it! he told himself.

This was working up to being a very lousy day.

The children in the nursery, especially Mara, brightened Blake's black mood. There was something about playing cars and dollies and singing fun Primary songs that made it impossible to stay angry.

When church was over, Blake left the building, feeling for the first time since his parents had died that he was part of a family. The children had attracted much attention, and people had been quick to offer support. A few even remembered Kevin from before, because he had been staying with Blake when he moved into the ward. Blake whistled on his way to the truck. Mara giggled and put her hand over his lips, patting them to vary the sound.

Back at the apartment, Blake pulled the spinach soup from the refrigerator and began reheating it for an early dinner. His aunt had insisted he take home the rest of the large batch he'd made at her house the day before, and now Blake was grateful for it. Mara could even eat the soup if he blended it up a bit first.

"Okay, you have to change your clothes," he said to Kevin. "You only have that one nice shirt for church, and spinach might not be so easy to get out."

"Does Amanda like spinach?" Kevin asked, his mind obviously elsewhere.

"I don't think so."

"I think her would like it if we gave her some. It has beans."

"You think *she* would like it."

"I said Amanda would like it," Kevin insisted.

Blake snorted a laugh. "Whatever."

Kevin grinned up at him. "I like Amanda."

"She's nice." Blake turned from him and reached into the cupboard for cups and bowls.

"It's like her purse is magic."

"What?" Blake set the bowls on the table.

"Her purse. Her has a lot of things in it. Like my sticker book and my bracelet." He shook his wrist and watched the bugs move.

"And M&Ms?"

"Yep." Kevin grinned up at him. "But I like my bracelet the best."

"Well, right now you'd better go change, or I'll eat all the soup."

Kevin glanced at him in disgust. "You can't eat all that soup. It's too much."

"Maybe I'm starving."

"Can we bring some to Amanda?"

"I don't think so. We can make it another time for her."

Kevin's brow furrowed. "What if we don't? What if we never see her again?"

"Well . . ."

"Please, Uncle Blake?" Kevin's blue eyes stared up at him. "Please? I want to give her something."

"Yeah, but spinach soup?"

Kevin's face fell. He turned to leave the kitchen, but Blake stopped him, unable to bear his disappointment. What did he care if Amanda liked his soup or thought he was an idiot for bringing it over? What mattered was Kevin's desire to share.

"We'll take some over later on our way to see your new baby-sitter."

Kevin's entire demeanor changed. He began jumping up and down. Mara, sitting on the carpet in the living room, giggled.

"Go take off your shirt," Blake ordered, "before I change my mind. And lay your clothes out nicely on the bed when you're finished."

Laughing, Kevin fled the room. Blake turned his eyes on Mara. "Okay, dear, it's your turn." She was on her hands trying to crawl, but the skirt of her dress made her efforts in vain. At his words, she pushed herself into a seated position and held out her arms. Blake's heart filled with tenderness. *Only a week, and she has me eating out of her hand,* he thought.

He was picking her up when the doorbell rang. Blake froze, wondering who it might be. A dread settled in his heart.

Sure enough, he opened the door to find Paula standing there, one hand on her slender hip and the other reaching out to bang on the door. "Oh, you're home," she said.

She hadn't changed in the half year since she'd taken Kevin from him. Her tiny figure was still tiny, her heart-shaped face was still unlined and childlike, her once-dark hair was still bleached in the way that he disliked, and her blue eyes, so much like Kevin's, were still as large and sleepy. The sleepy aspect, he knew, came from whatever she was on, but other than this, she had none of the telltale marks of a drug and alcohol user. Most of her friends appeared old, but she remained eternally young. He wondered when her lifestyle would finally catch up to her.

"You're late," he said, opening the door wider to let her in. The stale smell of cigarette smoke wafted inside.

"I was here earlier, but you were gone."

He looked at her, wondering if she was telling the truth. Sometimes it was hard for him to tell. "We were at church."

She focused on Mara in his arms. "Hello, sweetie," she cooed. "Mama came to see you. You look so pretty. Come here, come on. Mommy's missed you terribly!" Mara held out her arms, smiling ear-to-ear so Blake relinquished her to Paula. "Where's Kevin?" Paula asked, her eyes searching the room behind him.

"Changing his clothes. I told you we had church."

"You could have waited a few minutes for me." Paula hugged Mara tightly to her chest and then relaxed her hold as the child started to struggle.

Blake made his voice hard. "We waited an hour."

"Oh." Paula glanced up at him, her sleepy eyes empty of expression. "Well, I must have missed you." She laughed. "It's this darn weather," she said, choosing her words carefully for Blake's sake. "It's so cold I can't seem to get anywhere on time."

Blake had actually thought the weather was rather nice, seeing as it was already November. "That reminds me," he said, walking with Paula to the love seat. "Your mother and I were talking about what to do for Thanksgiving. She wanted to know your plans."

She made a face. "I don't know. I don't want to make the trip down there right now. I'm sort of busy. Besides, I really don't want to spend any time with my mother. All she does is preach at me." She made a show of playing with Mara, who giggled with delight. There was an obvious affection between them, and in that moment, Blake could well imagine her as she might have been had she chosen another path. A strange longing in her behalf swelled in his chest. Couldn't she see what she was missing? If only she could catch a glimpse of how things could be!

"I can come over on Tuesday night," Paula said.

Blake shook his head. "I can't."

"Why not?" Paula frowned, and even then her face was unlined. "You said I could see them whenever I wanted." Tears gathered in her eyes.

"Because I have school, that's why."

"Can't you miss a class?"

He shook his head. "Not this one. I'm nearing the end, Paula, and it's a three-hour class. Missing one is like missing a whole week."

"Well . . ." She patted down Mara's dress before brightening suddenly. "I can stay with them while you go."

"You know I can't do that. If they found out, they'd take the children away."

Her lips drew into a pout. "They won't find out. Honestly, Blake, you act like it's their *right* to take away my kids."

Blake didn't reply.

Her face flushed with anger. "I can't believe you think that I'm not a fit—"

"Hi, Kevin," Blake interrupted her. "Looks who's here. Your mom."

Paula turned and held out one arm, the other still securely around Mara. "Oh, baby! I've missed you! Come here on the couch and give Mommy a hug."

Kevin hugged his mother tightly.

"I missed you so much," she said.

"I missed you, too," Kevin answered.

Paula shot Blake a triumphant glance. "I bought you some peanut butter crackers, but I left them home. I'm sorry. I'll do better next time, I promise."

Blake wondered how many times Kevin had heard that excuse. For himself, he knew he'd heard it enough times to last his entire life.

"Okay. But I'm not going there, am I, Mommy? I want to stay with Uncle Blake for a while."

Blake didn't stay to see how Paula took that statement. He went into the kitchen and began ladling soup into bowls.

"You're going to stay here a few more days," he heard Paula tell Kevin. "Maybe a few weeks. But I'll have you come back really soon. You and me and Mara will all be together again. You'll have a nice room just like you do here. Does that sound fun?"

"Yes," Kevin agreed. "You wanna see my bug bracelet? It's magic."

"Time to eat, Kevin," Blake called. "Want some soup, Paula?"

She followed Kevin to the table. "No, thanks," she said, making a face. "Looks like you cut up seaweed or something."

"Nope, spinach. Well, if you don't want some, you can at least feed it to Mara. I blended some up for her." He wasn't surprised that Paula refused his offer of soup. She never ate enough. He'd worried about that during her pregnancies, but each child had been miraculously healthy. Paula had at least stopped smoking while she was pregnant.

"Do you have a bib?" Paula asked.

"Yes, but on second thought, let's change her clothes. I don't want that dress stained."

Paula laughed. "You sound like a mother." Kevin's snort of amusement sent spinach soup from his spoon onto the table.

Blake ignored them. "Prayer first, bud. Will you say it? Then I'll go get a change of outfit for Mara."

During the prayer he began to worry that Paula would take off with the children while he was in the bedroom. How cynical and suspicious he'd become! Still, better safe than sorry.

"Paula, why don't you go get her changed?" he said when Kevin was finished. "I want to eat my soup while it's still warm. Her clothes are in Kevin's room in the top drawer of the dresser. There's also some in the dryer."

Paula was only too happy to play mommy. When she was gone, Kevin wrinkled his nose. "Her smells funny."

"That's because she smokes," Blake answered, betting that Kevin had grown accustomed to a smokeless environment over the past week. "And you're right, it does smell funny."

Kevin nodded sagely and dug into his soup.

A short time later, Paula came from the hallway carrying Mara. "Blake, I just remembered something. Some friends and I are having a birthday party on Saturday for a friend of ours. They're bringing their families, and I want the kids there. I'd like to spend more time with them. Is that okay?"

"What time?" he asked.

"At one."

"Where? I'll need the address."

"I could just pick them up."

He stared at her in frustration. Didn't she get it? Was her brain so fried that she didn't understand that the state had custody of her children? "I'll drive," he said shortly.

"I'm not exactly sure of the address right this minute, but I'll call and give it to you later."

"Okay." Blake took the ladle and helped himself to more spinach soup.

Paula stayed exactly one hour and then, promising to see them on Saturday, whisked out of the kitchen and vanished into the darkening night.

Blake glanced at the clock and saw that he had twenty minutes to get to Amanda's sister's house. Her name was Kerrianne Huntington Price, and he wondered if she was anything like Amanda in person. He had been so impressed with her on the phone that he'd hired her on the spot.

"We have to get ready to meet your new baby-sitter," he said.

Kevin looked up from the floor where he was playing with a puzzle. "Can I carry the soup?"

"Soup?"

"Yeah, for Amanda."

Blake sighed and went to find a container.

Chapter Thirteen

Amanda's day had not been going well. During her church meetings, she kept thinking about Blake and what a wonderful time they'd had the previous evening. Wonderful, that is, until it was time for her to leave and there had been all that awkwardness at the door. Had something she said upset him? She thought so, though she couldn't pinpoint exactly what. She didn't even remember what she had said because she'd been too busy trying to stop the pounding in her heart. Not even Tanner had evoked such emotion! She didn't know how much more of it she could take.

Not that it mattered. He wasn't likely to call her again.

She sighed and went to her CD player, punching a button. She ordinarily didn't listen to any music on Sundays unless it was related to the gospel in some way, but every now and then she made exceptions for Josh Groban. Sometimes listening to his exceptional voice was all she needed to forget something that was bothering her.

Like how much she wanted to see Blake and the children.

Josh Groban's voice filled the living room. She listened to the first song, not in the least disturbed that she couldn't understand a word.

Her favorite song was next. "Gira Con Me Questa Notte"—which she learned meant "Wanders with Me Tonight"—and she turned up the sound to a near ear-shattering level. The sound reverberated off the walls and seemed to enter inside her very being, carrying her away. Good thing she didn't live in an apartment building, or she'd bring in complaints from the neighbors for sure, despite the sweeping beauty of the music.

She sat on the plaid couch, closing her eyes and letting her body sway to the soaring strains. The song ended and the next began. Beginning to feel a trifle hot with all the emotion and swaying she was putting into the music, she decided to open the door and stand on the cement porch for a while and stare out over the valley below. It was dark enough that the wonderful array of lights would complete the beautiful music.

Pulling open the door, she stepped out into the night—right into the arms of Blake Simmons. Her eyes opened wide as she tried to backpedal, tripping over the step into the house and losing her slippers in the process. She would have fallen hard on her backside had it not been for Blake's quick hands on her arms. He pulled her upright, holding tightly to her. A tingling sensation raced into her skin, through her veins, and lodged somewhere in her heart. He let her go almost immediately—way too soon, in her opinion.

"I—uh—I—" she stammered. Her rapid breath made clouds of white in front of her face.

He said something, but the music blasting from the house was too loud to make out his words. She shut the door behind her.

"You surprised me," she gathered her wits enough to say. He looked far too handsome in his suit and tie. Distinguished. Except that his brown hair was mussed as usual.

"I knocked, but there was no answer." His grin was uncertain.

Amanda felt heat seep into her face. "I didn't hear. I was listening to some music."

His glance toward the door was amused. "Yeah, I noticed."

Silence fell between them. Amanda thought she would be content to stand here and stare at him all night, never mind the cold that penetrated her short-sleeved Sunday dress. She didn't even try to put back on her house slippers, though her feet clearly felt the cold cement.

"We brought you some soup," Blake said at last, motioning beside him. For the first time, Amanda noticed Kevin standing there holding a clear plastic container. The substance inside looked very dark.

"It's spinach soup with beans." Kevin held the container up to her.

"Oh, thank you." Amanda accepted the offering.

"Kevin insisted on bringing it over," Blake said, leaving her no doubt as to his opinion on the matter. She wished she could fling it back in his face.

Kevin grinned. "It's real good."

"I appreciate it, Kevin. I really do." At least she had no doubts as to where she stood with the four-year-old. "You are a very sweet boy." Kevin stuck his hands in the pockets of his coat and beamed.

"Well, we'd better go." Blake thumbed at his truck which sat in her driveway, the doors open. "We left Mara strapped in her seat. We're going to meet your sister." He was already down the steps and walking toward the truck by the time he finished speaking. Kevin ran after him.

Amanda didn't have time to respond before they were in the truck and backing down the drive. A wild urge to follow them in her own car to Kerrianne's arose in her mind, leaving just as quickly. No—she couldn't.

She watched the truck disappear down the street before turning slowly and going inside her house. Heat from the container of soup warmed her hand, though the rest of her was freezing, especially her feet. The music went on, rising in ever more beautiful crescendos. She barely noticed, except to realize that the music wouldn't allow her to think. Still holding the warm container, she went to the CD player and plunged the room into abrupt silence.

Looking at the dark soup, she noticed, as Kevin had promised, that there were beans on the bottom, swirling around as she tilted the container.

Yuck, she thought. *There's no way I'm eating this slop, and what's more, if Blake thinks he's impressing me with his cooking skills, he is sadly mistaken.*

Or was that his intention? Maybe he was trying to scare her off.

What was it with her? She wanted only to be friends, yet she was peeved at him for not pursuing her. Or was she peeved because he had shown interest?

Nothing made sense.

Feeling suddenly very sad and alone, Amanda set the soup container on her table and went to find her tennis shoes and her long dress coat. Maybe a brisk walk in the moonlight would clear her head so she could think straight.

She walked for at least twenty minutes, and though her emotions toward Blake were still undecided, she felt much calmer. For one thing, she'd decided the soup was nothing more than Kevin's idea, one Blake had likely agreed to reluctantly—not because he was angry at her but because he hadn't wanted her to read anything into the offering.

Well, she wouldn't. She would pour the soup down the drain and forget it.

As she stood at the kitchen sink getting ready to do just that, she decided she had better at least taste it in case Kevin asked—provided she ever saw him again. She took a spoon, dipped it in, stirred it, and sipped.

"Mmm." Her eyes opened wide. It was good! Shaking her head

in disbelief, she took another taste, dumped the soup into a bowl, and put it in the microwave. Warmed up, it proved even tastier.

She was tipping the bowl to get every last bit on her spoon when the phone rang. Swallowing, she ran for the phone lying on the table beside her couch.

"Hello?"

"Hi, Manda."

"Kerrianne—hi." Amanda was immediately curious, wondering how the meeting between Kerrianne and Blake had gone. *Calm down*, she told herself. She couldn't ask outright, unless she wanted to raise her sister's suspicions. She'd have to let it come out naturally in the conversation. "How's it going?"

"How's it going? How's it going? Is that all you have to say?" Kerrianne's voice came too loudly through the phone. "You didn't tell me he was so handsome!"

Amanda bit her lip. "Who?" she forced herself to ask.

"Who? Blake Simmons, that's who. The guy is gorgeous. So handsome! Why didn't you tell me?"

"I guess I didn't notice."

"I can't see how you didn't. I did. And he's nice, too. Definitely devoted to those children. He's even interesting to talk to. You should have heard the conversation about education that he and Adam got into. He sounds very smart. I can't believe you haven't noticed that, either."

"Well, no." Though now that she thought about it, Blake did seem to speak intelligently about everything that came up. Then again, had they talked about anything but children? She admitted to herself that she was too busy worrying about where their relationship was headed to pay much mind to their conversation.

"Well, I did. In fact, the moment after he left, I thought, 'Too bad he's only a repairman, or he'd be perfect for Manda.'"

Amanda felt an uneasy chill run up her spine. "What do you mean by that?"

"Just that you rather like your male friends to . . . well, be educated."

"Is that wrong? It's nice to have them understand something of the world. But that doesn't mean I look down on people who haven't gone to college. There are a lot of smart people who've never gone to college." Again, Amanda thought of her grandfather and his farm.

"What I mean is that you don't see his job to be important."

Amanda was offended. "His job is important! Without appliances, how would people live?" Even as she spoke, she knew her defense was lame. She pulled her feet onto the couch and scowled at the carpet.

"Yeah, but it's not teaching or working in an office."

"Are you saying I judge men by their jobs?" Amanda demanded.

"Well, not exactly. Maybe you just aren't attracted to men without jobs that require formal education."

"That's not true."

"Come on. I know you and Tanner really hit it off, but the fact that he was an executive in his father's company didn't hurt matters at all. And that's at least one of the reasons Gerry could never measure up. Oh, I know you said you didn't love him, but *why* didn't you love him? He was attentive, strong in the Church, good-looking, and obviously gone on you. But he was a construction worker who didn't give a darn if he knew what was going on in, say, an education bill, or if he knew the proper way to address a letter."

Amanda was shocked. Was she so shallow? Had she determined that she was too good for someone who might not have had the opportunity of receiving an education? "Well," she said after a long pause, "I'm sure Blake is man enough to stand up for himself whether or not he has a job that requires an education."

"He certainly can," Kerrianne agreed.

Amanda didn't reply.

"Now don't be mad, Manda. I was just pointing out that you are attracted to powerful men."

"You make me sound like a snob."

"No, not a snob." Regret filled her sister's voice. "I just meant . . . well, a man chooses a certain job because of who he is. And to some degree, he becomes who he is because of his job. You seem to be attracted to the type of guy who has a, well, a white-collar job—as opposed to manual work. Does that make sense? Either type can be a good man, depending on a woman's taste. I thought it was too bad that Blake, this really good-looking, nice, father-type, wasn't the kind of man you'd go for. That's all."

Stated that way, it didn't sound so horrible. Amanda could live with the fact that she was attracted to men with jobs that required degrees, not because of the job itself, but because the type of man she yearned for just happened to desire that type of job.

So where did that leave her and Blake?

Exactly nowhere.

I don't look down on what he does for a living, she told herself. *I'm just not attracted to him.*

Yeah, right. And I think he's ugly, too.

Boy, was she a liar. She needed to repent—and soon. Still, the truth remained that he wasn't her type, which meant she wasn't his type, either.

"Manda? I didn't mean anything bad by it," Kerrianne said. "Forgive me? Please?"

"Of course. It's forgotten."

"If it were me, however," Kerrianne continued. "He's one man I wouldn't mind taking a look at—if I wasn't already married."

"Kerrianne!" Amanda didn't know what bothered her most, her sister's confession or the surge of jealousy that shot through her heart.

"Oh, don't worry, I'm definitely not looking."

"That's a relief," Amanda said dryly.

"I do wonder sometimes . . ." She trailed off.

Amanda wasn't sure where Kerrianne was going with this. "Wonder what?"

"I mean, I only had a year of college, and I didn't like it much. And Adam, well, he's talking about going back for his doctorate. It's kind of intimidating. I worry—I worry that he'll outgrow me."

"Nonsense! You're an intelligent woman."

"Yeah, but I haven't been to college, and I don't even like to read. Adam loves his books."

"He loves *you*. And you do read, whether you enjoy it or not. You always know what's going on in the world."

"I try to keep up with him, that's all."

Amanda had never heard her sister sound so unsure of herself. Odd that Amanda would be the one to comfort her "perfect" sister. "Adam loves you," she repeated. "That's plain to see. No, he adores you."

Kerrianne gave a little laugh. "He does, really. Don't mind me. I'm sure it's just the hormones talking. I'll be more stable once a few more months go by. Having a baby can make you crazy, you know?"

Amanda didn't know—at least not from personal experience— but she agreed anyway.

"I really do have a good life," Kerrianne continued. "I guess that's why I wish you could find someone like Adam."

"I'm sure I will some day." Amanda spoke the words without conviction.

"Well, anyway, those kids were adorable. Misty took right to Kevin, and you should have seen her bringing dolls and blankets for Mara. She so wanted Caleb to be a sister. Now she has a little girl to play with—at least during the day."

"If it becomes too much for you—"

"Don't worry, I'll make sure. I have someone in mind to watch them if I can't do it."

"Thanks. I really appreciate it." Amanda lay back on the couch, relaxing now that she was sure Kerrianne wasn't going to talk about the possibility of a relationship between her and Blake. "Their mother doesn't seem very responsible. It makes me happy they'll have you."

"Well, they have Blake, too, don't forget. From what I see, he's really good with them."

Amanda sighed internally, glad she had not confessed her attraction to her sister. Kerrianne would be hard to control if she thought she had a matchmaking opportunity.

"I have to go," Kerrianne said. "Adam's got the table set for dinner."

Amanda bade her sister good-bye and hung up the phone.

Going into the kitchen, she found herself tipping the container that had held the spinach soup into her mouth to get every last drop.

Much later, hours after she had turned out the light in her bedroom, a shrill sound pierced Amanda's awareness. She sat up, holding a hand over her pounding heart. *The smoke alarm?* Reaching for the phone, she considered calling the fire department.

She sniffed the air, but there was no acrid smell of smoke.

Oh, it's that stupid stove again.

Wearily, she climbed from bed and padded barefoot into the kitchen. She pressed the *clock* button, changing the timing mode back to the display of the hours. The clock read 1:38 AM. Stifling an urge to find her old baseball bat and beat the appliance to smithereens, she stomped back to bed.

Chapter Fourteen

Blake never remembered being so tired. When he wasn't at work that week, he was at school or with Kevin and Mara. In his "free" time late at night, he did homework or read the lessons his Internet teacher had posted. He didn't know how much longer he could keep up this schedule, but surely he could make it at least until the semester was out. Then he would think about stretching out his last semester, taking only one or two classes. It might take another year that way, but he couldn't see any other option.

There was no regret in his heart as Blake mentally made this sacrifice. As tired as he was, as overwhelmed as he felt, the time he spent with Kevin and Mara put everything into perspective. He adored every minute with them. He wouldn't send them away for all the sleep and study time in the world.

Being a "single parent" wasn't easy, though he had learned the routine well enough since Kevin's birth. Two children, he soon discovered, didn't mean double the work but triple or quadruple. Sometimes all he could do to maintain sanity was to shake his head and laugh.

Then young Julianna from next door called on Thursday at the last minute to tell him she couldn't baby-sit after all that night, and he couldn't find one laugh left inside.

After he made a few phone calls, his desperation grew. Rhonda and Doug weren't home, Garth from upstairs was on a date, and all the neighbors he thought he could trust with the children didn't answer their phones. Even Kerrianne's number was answered by her voice mail. He hung up without leaving a message.

What am I going to do? He couldn't miss school that night—not when he was as far behind as he was.

Maybe he could take the children with him. Kevin might be okay in the hall with some crayons, and Blake could hold Mara by the door so he could still hear and yet not disturb the others. He'd seen young women do it before at BYU, and when the babies invariably cried, he'd always felt a rush of irritation at their lack of preparation. In his view, they should have found baby-sitters or finished their education at another time. After all, he was paying for his education and deserved a distraction-free environment. Now he felt guilty for those past thoughts. Had the woman been as desperate as he felt tonight?

"Get your shoes," he told Kevin. "I think you'll have to go with me."

"Okay." Kevin looked up from the book he was thumbing through.

Mara was lying on the floor, chewing on her fist. Her nose was running, and she'd been irritable. Kerrianne told him she might be teething and that the crankiness could last for weeks. Blake prayed she'd be good. At least the diarrhea hadn't returned.

She began to cry and rub at her eyes as he put on her coat.

"Her's tired," Kevin said helpfully.

"Not as tired as I am."

Kevin shrugged. "Then let's stay home."

"I *have* to go. And I can't leave you home alone." Even if he didn't stay the whole time, he might be able to evoke some sympathy from his teacher and the offer of detailed notes from one of the other students.

"Amanda will come over." Kevin was looking at his bracelet. "Her likes us."

"*She* likes you," Blake said through gritted teeth, his patience completely sapped.

Kevin smiled up at him, his blue eyes wide and innocent. "I know. So can we call her?"

"Call her? Call her? Why not?" Blake threw up his hands. He'd tried so hard that week *not* to think about Miss Amanda Huntington, the green-eyed enchantress who wanted only to be friends. "Why shouldn't I call her? After all she seems to care for you guys just as much as I do."

You just want to see her again, said a voice inside his head.

"I do not!" he growled aloud.

Kevin and Mara stared at him uncertainly.

"Never mind," he said more softly. "I'll go call her right now."

She picked up on the second ring. "Hello?"

"Hi, Amanda. It's me, Blake."

"Hi, Blake. How are you?"

Was it his imagination, or did she actually sound happy to hear from him? "I'm fine. Well, actually, I'm rather in a bind tonight. I have to leave, and my baby-sitter cancelled at the last minute. I can't find anyone to help out. I called my sister-in-law, Kerrianne, my neighbors, even the president of our ward's Relief Society."

"And then you called me."

This time the tone of her voice was definitely annoyed. But was she irritated because she was last on his list of people to call or because he'd asked her to watch the children at all? He decided to do as many good men before him had done—pretend he didn't hear the irritation.

"I'm so sorry to disturb your evening," he said in a rush. "I know you've got millions of things to do, but I didn't know who else to call. There aren't many people I'd trust with the children. I'll understand if you can't watch them. I can just take them with me, but . . ." He was still reluctant to tell her about his class. "Well, it's really hard. They'd be miserable. I'm already going to be late. I'm supposed to be there at seven but—"

"I can watch them."

"You can? Thanks so much." Relief swept through him.

"It's nothing. I told you on Saturday I'd be glad to help out."

"Well, I hope I'm not ruining anything—like a date or something." He could have kicked himself for saying the words.

"No, I wasn't going out."

He felt even more relief. "Okay, I'll bring them over."

"How long are you going to be gone?"

"Till ten-thirty. About four hours."

"Then I'll come to your place. Kevin and Mara will need to go to bed before you get home."

"Oh, I couldn't ask you—"

"Aren't you late already? I'll be right there. I'm walking out the door now."

"Thanks. I owe you one."

"Right." She hung up the phone.

Blake had just enough time to stuff the mess in the living room under the cushions on the couch, load his backpack into the car, and change Mara for bed before Amanda arrived at the back door, carrying both her purse and an off-white book bag. She looked wonderful in a soft brown dress that accentuated her narrow waist. Her blonde hair was caught back in a clip today, making her high cheekbones more prominent.

"Can I come in?" She smiled at him, her right cheek dimpling.

Realizing he was staring, he stepped back from the door and let her into the kitchen. "They're all fed and ready for bed," he said. "But Kevin needs to brush his teeth."

"What about Mara's diaper?"

"All clean. The diarrhea hasn't returned. She's tired, though."

Mara crawled over to the door, mumbling and whining. Amanda picked her up. "It's okay, sweetie."

"Even though she's not hungry, she may want a bottle before she sleeps. I always hold her while I feed it to her, and she usually drops off in a few minutes." Blake didn't look at Amanda as he spoke, feeling the heat rise to his face. Why should he be embarrassed that he held Mara each night until she slept? In his mind, babies deserved to be rocked to sleep.

"So I guess you feed her formula," Amanda said.

"Yeah, it's there on the counter."

"I know how to make it," Kevin informed her.

Amanda grinned at Kevin. "Then you shall certainly help me. We're going to have a super time tonight," she promised. "I brought you a great bedtime story! It's about pirates."

"Yay!" Kevin jumped up and down, his eyes radiant.

Amanda smiled at him before turning her emerald gaze on Blake. "Shouldn't you be going?"

Problem was, Blake didn't *want* to go anymore. He wanted to stay here with Amanda and the children. "Yeah," he made himself say. "Kevin knows my cell phone number if you need it. He can even dial if your hands are full with Mara." Having no excuse to stay, Blake took his keys and left the apartment.

Well, at least he's not dressed up, Amanda thought as she watched Blake leave, his dark hair slightly standing on end in the front as though he'd been rubbing above his forehead. At first she had been excited when he'd called—inordinately so, to her mind—but when he'd asked her to baby-sit, her disappointment had been hard to hide. Not that she didn't want to help him, but because she'd wanted him to want *her*. Instead, he wanted her to watch the children so he could go out.

Out where? On a date? She could only assume so since he had completely avoided telling her where. Even though he was only dressed in jeans, topped by a navy and maroon sweater, he looked too good to be going to the grocery store. On the other hand, he wasn't dressed up enough for a church meeting—unless it was being held at a member's house.

"Where's the book?" Kevin asked. "What else do you have in your purse?"

Shrugging aside her lingering disappointment, Amanda settled on the love seat with Kevin and Mara. "Well, I was going to save it until after the pirate story, but now that you mention it, there might be something interesting in my purse."

She pulled out three postcard-sized puzzles of insects in their natural environments. Kevin eagerly dumped out the first one on his lap. "Cool, cool," he said, fingering the pieces.

"We can't forget our snack." She handed him a small white package. "No study of insects would be complete without *tasting* them!"

Kevin's eyes widened, but he started giggling when he saw that the insects in the package were made of fruit.

"I most particularly like the flies and beetles," she informed him gravely. "They are the best."

Kevin eagerly tasted each one as Amanda helped him put together the puzzle. While they worked, she wondered if he would enjoy the astronomy section she was doing with her class now—with Savvy's help—as much as he seemed to enjoy the insects. With only a small effort she could simplify the information for Kevin.

"My mommy like puzzles," Kevin said, glancing up at her and then back down to his lap.

Amanda felt her smile fade. What was she thinking? She didn't know how long Kevin and Mara would be with Blake, much less if she would see them again. The thought made her somehow deeply sad.

"She likes puzzles, huh?" she said.

"Yeah. Her helped me to do some once. It was fun."

Amanda had to ask, "Do you miss your mom?"

He shrugged. "I wish Mommy could live with us. But I'm gonna stay here with Uncle Blake." He put in a piece and then added, "I'm going to see her Saturday. We're eating lunch."

"That sounds nice."

He smiled and nodded.

Amanda felt something poking her from under the couch cushion, making her perch slightly awkward. She stood up and pulled off the cushion, revealing two picture books, a math textbook, several scraps of paper with scribbled equations, a broken pencil, an eraser, dried orange peels, and several wrappers from granola bars. A few toys poked out from under the other cushion.

"Uncle Blake didn't have time to put stuff away before you came," Kevin explained.

"I see." Amanda smoothed out the mess a bit, put the couch cushion back on top, and sat down. She would let Blake keep his secrets.

They completed all three puzzles twice and then read the book about pirates. Mara was fussing by then, and Amanda let Kevin help her make a bottle. She began reading another book to the children, but before she was halfway through, Mara was asleep, most of her milk still in the bottle.

"I'll put her in bed if you can put the bottle in the fridge," she told Kevin.

"But can we read the rest after?"

"Of course. I brought a bunch more books, too."

"Put on the nightlight," Kevin called after her. "Mara gets scared sometimes. It's magic like my bracelet. It won't let bugs come."

"Okay." Amanda hid her smile in Mara's hair. The baby didn't stir as she put her in the crib and tiptoed from the room, stopping to flip the switch on the nightlight by Kevin's bed.

She was barely out the door when the phone rang. *Probably Blake checking up on us,* she thought.

Kevin got to the phone first. "Hello? Oh, hi, Mommy." He listened for what seemed like a long time to Amanda and then, "No. He's not here. Uh-uh. I'm not alone. Amanda's here. No, big like you. Julianna was coming but then her couldn't. Okay." Kevin handed the phone to Amanda.

"Hello?" Amanda said.

"Hello, I'm Kevin and Mara's mother, Paula."

"Hi, Paula. I'm, um, Blake's friend."

"I'll bet." Paula's giggle was all out of proportion to the comment, and Amanda wondered if she had been drinking. "Well, I need to leave a message for Blake."

"All right. Just a minute, let me get a pen." Amanda rummaged through her purse for her planner, her fingers feeling suddenly very slow and unwilling to cooperate. "Got it. Go ahead."

Paula rattled off an address, transposing the numbers once and having to repeat it after verifying the correct address with someone else. "I can't believe he wouldn't leave the kids with me tonight," Paula added in a conspiratorial voice. "In fact, I can't believe this whole mess, especially the state keeping me from my kids. I don't know how much Blake told you but—" Paula launched into a story so different from what the social worker and Blake had told Amanda that she knew it could only be a lie.

"Thank heavens you have Blake to watch the kids till you get things worked out," Amanda said brightly, not knowing what else to say and not wanting to offend the woman. Doing so would only make her mad at Blake.

"You sound like such a reasonable person," Paula gushed, pausing to take a noisy drink. "I sure hope you and Blake . . . I mean my cousin is such a good-looking guy. It's about time he found a nice woman."

"Oh, we're just friends."

"Really? That's too bad. He really does need a girlfriend." Paula's last words were slurred, and Amanda could barely understand them.

"Well, nice talking to you," Amanda said.

"You, too. Put Kevin on again, would you? I want to tell him something."

"Okay." Amanda covered the receiver and looked over at Kevin who was lying on the carpet in the living room trying to fit the puzzle pieces into the small cardboard holder. "Hey, Kev," Amanda said softly, "Blake lets you talk to your mom, doesn't he?"

Kevin nodded. "When she calls."

"Well, she wants to talk to you again."

He jumped up and ran to take the phone. "Hi? Yeah. Okay. Yes, I love you." A sudden frown creased his forehead. "But I want to . . . I know . . . well, you could stay here with . . ." Kevin fell silent, his lips quivering with threatening tears. "Okay. Bye, Mom." He hung up the phone and went to put it on the kitchen table, his shoulders heavy.

"Kevin," Amanda said, "what's wrong?"

His little face crumpled. "Mommy said her was going to get me out of here fast. Take me far away where no one can find me. And . . . and . . . her said some bad words about my uncle." With that he burst into tears.

Amanda ran forward and hugged him, her eyes smarting. "It's okay, Kevin. Really. If your mom does take you away, soon, I'm sure things will be different with her. She'll spend more time with you, and you'll get to come and see your uncle all the time. They both love you, you know."

Kevin nodded through his tears, allowing Amanda to soothe and comfort him. They cuddled up on the couch and read through all her books several times until he fell asleep in her arms. Amanda stroked his soft cheek. "I'm so sorry," she whispered. "I'm so, so sorry." Never before, not in all her training as a teacher, had it been so clear that some children didn't have a proper chance to be children at all.

She carried Kevin to bed and tucked the covers around him.

Back in the living room, she began grading papers from school. The high-pitched ringing of a phone drew her attention—not the phone on the table but the cell phone in her purse. "Hello," she said, when she finally found it under all the junk she'd stuffed inside.

"Hey, it's Savvy."

"Oh, hi."

"So are we still on for Saturday? I tried to call you at home. Glad you left your new cell number on the answering machine."

"Yes, I've finally come into the new age."

"So where are you? I mean, can you talk?"

"Yeah, I can talk. I'm—I'm at a friend's."

"Oh?" Savvy's voice trailed upward more than necessary for a simple question. "Any *friend* I know?"

"I'm baby-sitting, okay?" Amanda let her disgust show. It still stung that Blake hadn't called her all week except to watch the children. "Not that I mind, really," she added quickly. "Next to my niece and nephews, I don't think there's cuter kids in the whole world."

"So tell me all about it," Savvy said eagerly. "Is this the first time you've seen him since we talked?"

"No." Amanda told her about watching the video Saturday night and about the soup he'd brought on Sunday.

"Sounds like things are going well. Not too intense, but steady."

Amanda wasn't sure if that was good or not. "I don't know," she said. "He seemed rather peeved with me on Saturday. Not the whole night, just at the end."

"Well, tell me exactly what happened."

"I'm not sure. I told him that if he ever needed someone to watch the children, I'd be willing to help out. He thanked me, and I said something like 'What are friends for?' I thought everything was fine, but he got weird after that. Distant, rather."

"Friends? You actually said *friends?*" Savvy's tone showed her disbelief.

"Yeah. So? What's wrong with that? Being friends is a good thing. Besides, you and I discussed this. We decided that friends was where I needed to go at this point."

"Well, obviously it's not where *he* wanted to go."

"Savvy!"

"Why else did he act that way?"

Amanda thought about it, and a warmth spread through her. Was he really interested in her? Had she unintentionally sent the wrong signal?

Wait a minute, she thought, *I do want to be friends.*

Yes, but maybe, just maybe, not *only* friends.

"Guys hear the word *friendship,* and they back off immediately," Savvy said. "Believe me, all I have to do is mention the word *friend,* and that's it."

"Even right in the middle of a proposal?"

Savvy giggled. "Especially in the middle of a proposal. I swear, all the males here at BYU are really searching for Miss Right. Too bad my name is Miss Hergarter!"

They laughed together, and then Savvy spoke again, "Look, I think you should invite the guy to the dance with us. I mean, if your brother's coming—you did ask him, didn't you?"

"Yes. He's coming."

"So we'll be one guy short. You never know what kind of odd-balls we might need to get away from at the dance."

"I thought the whole point was going to meet someone."

"No, Amanda, the whole point is to *dance*."

Amanda crossed one leg over the other and let her body sink farther into the love seat. "I can't ask him."

"Why not? The guy needs a break. If Mitch is going along as a friend, why couldn't he? He's probably going crazy now with no time alone with other adults."

"Yeah, well, how do I know he's not out with some woman right now?"

"Maybe he is. You could always ask him to bring her along. Size up the competition, so to speak."

"Savvy!"

"I'm kidding. Seriously, what do you have to lose? It's not like it's a real date or anything, just some friends going out dancing."

"Well . . ."

Sensing that Amanda was weakening, Savvy went in for the kill. "So you'll do it? You never know how much fun it'll be until you try. If it doesn't work out, what's the problem?"

She's right. Amanda would never know how much fun she could have with Blake if she didn't try. Besides, there was that slight matter of the electricity between them. What if they went their separate ways and she never found out where their relationship might have led? But Savvy was wrong about there being no problems if it didn't work out. Amanda had lost the man she thought she loved once before.

"Okay," she said. "I'll ask him—as a friend."

"Don't you *dare* use the word *friend!* I mean, you can say 'some friends are going dancing and do you want to come,' but don't ask him to come 'as a friend.'"

"I get it, I get it." Amanda rolled her eyes, but excitement pounded in her chest. She was going to ask Blake out! That's what it all boiled down to. *So what's the big deal,* she thought. *I'm a woman of the twenty-first century.*

"I'll pick you up Saturday at seven," Savvy said. "No use in getting there before eight. Or do you want to eat first?"

"I don't know. I mean, who'd pay? It's going to be awkward enough at the dance. I know. I'll ask Mitch to bring a pizza, and we'll eat at my place before we go to Salt Lake."

"Okay, I'll come at six-thirty. Nothing like getting to know each other a little bit before we go." Savvy's voice held laughter in it now. "You never know, I may take one look at your repairman and fall madly in love."

Amanda doubted that—Savvy was far too interested in astronomy. Would that subject even interest Blake? She was uncomfortable with the rise of jealousy in her chest. "Whatever," she said aloud. "See you Saturday."

"Bye." Giggling, Savvy severed their connection.

Amanda set her cell phone on the love seat beside her. Instead of returning to her papers, she removed her hair clip, curled up on the couch, and began practicing how to ask Blake about Saturday. All the scenarios she tried sounded desperate to her. She closed her eyes to think better, realizing how utterly tired she felt. The broken timer on her stove had gone off at three that morning, and she hadn't been able to get back to sleep.

I'll just rest my eyes for a moment.

A short time later, she stirred only slightly when in her dreams she heard the click of a door opening.

Blake hurried home as soon as class let out. His blood rushed faster through his veins as he turned up the street to his apartment.

By the time he parked the truck and went inside, he couldn't say if he was excited or dreading to see Amanda. His feet practically ran to the door, though, and he did nothing to stop them.

Inside his apartment, he found Amanda asleep on the couch, cheek on the armrest, legs drawn up, arms on top of each other and pulled in close to her body. Her hair was out of its clip, cascading over her face. Her feet were bare. He stepped quietly to her, hardly daring to breathe, reluctant to wake this sleeping beauty. She stirred, mumbling something. Blake thought he heard his name but attributed it to wishful thinking. He reached out to touch her cheek, to smooth the hair from the white skin, but stopped before his hand made contact.

Stepping back, he went to the closet and stored his backpack, glad to see that he'd used enough diapers from his stash so none of them fell. Turning back to the couch, he took a deep breath. "Amanda. Amanda!"

She opened her eyes and blinked several times. "Oh." Pushing herself to a sitting position, she covered a yawn with her hand. "I must have fallen asleep."

Blake felt his own mouth copying her yawn. "Yeah, they have that effect on me, too."

"I'll bet. So, are you all finished?"

She's curious about where I've been! Blake didn't know why that was important to him, but it was. "Yes," he said with a grin.

She shook her head, smiling back at him. "Well, I guess I'd better get home." She began gathering papers and books, shoving them into her bag.

Blake felt a panic surge through him. He didn't want her to go just yet. "How'd it go?" he asked.

"Okay. They were angels . . . except when . . ." She finished with her books and met his eyes. "Well, Kevin's mother called. Left an address for you. It's on the table."

"Thanks." He knew by her frown that there was more to the story.

"Look, I know it's none of my business, but do you let her talk to Kevin without listening in? He said you did, so I let him."

"Yeah, he talks to her—when she bothers to call. She's only called once since they got here this time. I guess twice, if she called tonight. Why, was it a problem? Was she rude?" Blake made a mental note to have hard words with his cousin if she had treated Amanda poorly.

"No, not to me, but . . ." Her brow puckered. "Well, according to Kevin, she said something about getting him out of here and taking him far away. Also, she apparently said some bad words about you."

"Swore, more like, I'll bet." Blake's anger was growing.

"Kevin cried after she hung up." Amanda made a sympathetic face. "I had to read a lot of books to calm him down."

Blake strode across the living room and into the kitchen, his teeth clenched. He had an urge to grab the paper with the address on the table and rip it to shreds. *How dare Paula do this!* he thought. But Paula always dared everything. Paula answered to no one except herself.

Until now, he thought. At least the state had become involved.

"She seems to be confused," Amanda said, coming to stand next to him. "Her account of what happened the night the police arrested her doesn't match anything I've heard before."

Blake immediately became aware of her closeness, of the light perfumed scent that surrounded her. He longed to gather her into his arms and bury his face in her hair for comfort. Reining in his emotions, he turned to her. "What'd she say?"

"She said that a friend of hers had a little party, but it was crashed by some people they barely knew. She claims those people brought the drugs and that she tried to get them to leave, but they wouldn't. In the end she supposedly called the police—or cops, to use her words. She said one of the policemen who came, uh, acted inappropriately with her and when she called him on it, he arrested her, too.”

Blake shook his head, frowning at the address on the table. “It’s a lie. She always lies, even when she doesn’t have to.” He heaved a sigh. “She lies so much that I doubt she even knows what the truth is.”

“I’m sorry.” She laid her hand on his arm, and a shiver curled up his spine.

He met her gaze, drowned in those green eyes. “Thank you. I appreciate that. I also appreciate your being honest with me. As for Kevin, I’ll get another phone, let her know I’m listening in.”

“She won’t like that.”

He shrugged. “This isn’t about her. It’s about Kevin.”

“You’re doing the right thing.”

“Am I?” he said, almost to himself. “I hope so. Sometimes I worry that it’s all in vain, that she’ll go into the custody hearing the state has set in January and walk out with the children. Then it will start all over again.”

“Are you so sure she won’t reform?”

“I don’t know. I *want* her to get her life together, but I think she has a long way to go.”

“Maybe all this will be the catalyst to bringing her back.”

Blake sighed. “Or maybe it’s only the beginning, and Kevin will be a teenager before she ever realizes it’s her fault he keeps going to jail.”

“Oh, don’t say that!” Amanda’s voice was passionate. “He has you. Remember?”

Blake shook himself and tried to smile. “I’m sorry. It’s been a long day. I usually try not to focus on the negative. It’s just . . .” He stared intently at Amanda, willing her to understand. “It’s just that I love Kevin so much—and Mara, too, now. I wish . . . I wish they could both have a normal life.”

Amanda's hand tightened on his arm as she nodded with understanding. Then she removed it, and his skin felt cold there, the heat from her touch gone.

"I think you need a break," she said, her tone brightening. She took her book bag from her shoulder and set it on the table.

"Got one tonight." He thought of the ten pages of notes he'd written in class and added, "Well, sort of."

"Some friends of mine," Amanda continued, as though he hadn't spoken, "are going dancing on Saturday. Why don't you come along?"

Stunned, he blinked and sat down in a chair. *Where did this come from?* he wondered. Then, *Yes! she's asking me out!* He stifled a grin. "Will you be there?"

"What?" She toyed with the straps on her book bag.

"You said some friends were going. Are you going, too?"

She nodded. "Yes, I thought that was implied. Tonight when I was talking to my friend about Saturday, she thought . . . I thought you might . . . it would be fun to . . . it's a change . . ."

Blake loved how her face flushed as she searched for words, how her eyes seemed to turn a darker green. "I'd love to," he said, ending her torment. "Should I drive?"

"No. My friend, Savvy, will. We're meeting at my house at six-thirty for pizza first. If you want to come then, that would be good. Or we can pick you up around seven on our way to Salt Lake." The last words were added hurriedly.

"Pizza? I'm there," he said. "That's one of the four main food groups, isn't it?"

She laughed. "For me, it is. Oh, yeah, and Savvy has some younger sisters if you need a sitter for Kevin and Mara."

Blake hadn't even considered what he'd do with them. "My sister-in-law might be willing. She likes taking them every now and then. I'll ask her. Oh, that reminds me." He reached out and picked up the address from the table, noting that it was written on the same type of narrow paper she'd given him with her sister's number. "I have to go to this lunch with my cousin earlier in the day, but I should be back way before then." Even if the lunch with Paula got off to a late start, it couldn't possibly last past three.

"Okay, then." Amanda hefted her book bag, slinging it over her shoulder where her purse already dangled. "See you Saturday."

Blake watched her walk to the door. "I think you're missing something," he said, looking at her bare feet.

She followed his gaze and again flushed a bright red. "Yeah, my shoes. I think I left them by the couch." Going into the adjoining room, she collected them quickly.

This time he retrieved her coat and walked her to the door. The tension between them was palpable. Almost. Blake thought if he reached out and touched her, a fire would burst into existence and burn down the whole house.

"Good night," she said.

He had to clear his throat to reply. "Good night. And I owe you one. I won't forget."

The minute the door closed he uttered, "Yes!" and did a victory dance that included jumping and waving his hands about wildly. All the fatigue and the depression brought on by Paula's phone call to Kevin vanished. He had a date with the beautiful and accomplished Amanda Huntington! What's more she had asked *him!* She might have started this relationship because of the children, but now he had a chance to show her what he had to offer.

Fly and soar, he thought, *or crash and burn. The moment of truth is fast approaching.*

Doubts and questions followed quickly on the heels of his elation, but for tonight he shoved them to the back of his mind. Another interesting idea was forming in his head. He suddenly had a plan to pay Amanda back for watching the children, and Kerrianne might just be able to help him pull it off.

Chapter Fifteen

Amanda lay in bed that night, inundated by thoughts of Blake and his reaction to her dancing invitation. Yes, there was a rather strange look in his eyes when she'd asked, but he'd agreed to go. He'd also flashed her the engaging grin that made her want to laugh.

She had done okay, all things considered, especially since she hadn't had much practice asking guys out. Of course, maybe she shouldn't have gone to sleep on his couch, but that wasn't entirely her fault. *That dratted timer!*

What had he thought when he'd found her asleep? *I hope I didn't snore,* she worried. *Or have my mouth open.* Yuck. Probably—that was just her luck.

And where had he been, anyway?

None of my business.

She sighed and shut her eyes tight, willing sleep to come.

The next day Amanda felt sluggish from lack of sleep. To make matters worse, a freezing rain had poured intermittently throughout the day, keeping the children in for recess. By the end of school, she felt so drained that she could barely muster a feeling of relief when the last of her fourth-graders left the class room. Though it was a Friday and in the old days she had usually been the first one with a date, she found that today she was actually looking forward to an evening alone. All she wanted was to go home and crash without excuses to anyone.

Visions of a hot bubble bath lured her through the soggy streets to her house. After her bath she would heat up the spaghetti from last night and curl up with a blanket and eat in the family room while she watched *Pride and Prejudice*. She might even fall asleep.

Hey, she thought to herself, *I might even fall asleep here in the car if I'm not careful.* The heater was hot now, and she was a little too comfortable.

Then she saw the blue truck parked outside her house, and all her sleepiness faded.

Blake!

Oddly, the truck was empty.

The rain had turned to snow, and she was glad that tomorrow she didn't have to teach. Scraping snow and ice off her car in the mornings was not something she enjoyed. She really needed to think about building on a garage—or a carport at the very least.

What is Blake's truck doing here?

Amanda entered the side door of her house with her key. She spied Blake immediately across the room in the kitchen. He wore jeans and a blue work shirt, his face unshaven.

"Hey, you're in my house," she said, more curious than annoyed. "Alone."

He grinned. "Yeah, like you were in my house alone."

"I was baby-sitting."

"I was fixing your stove." He held up his tool box. "Didn't take much to fix your alarm. It was only a loose wire—fortunately. Not like the stove I had to completely rewire yesterday."

She couldn't believe it. "You fixed my stove? You mean, no more being jolted from a sound sleep? No waking up thinking it's the smoke alarm and that I'm going to burn in my bed?"

He arched a brow. "That bad, huh? Nope, no more. At least it appears to be all right. Let me know if you have any more problems." He started for the door.

"Where're you going?"

"Back to work."

"But how did you get in?"

"Kerrianne opened the door. She was here a minute ago, but one of the kids had dance or something so she had to leave. I told her I'd lock up."

"Oh." Amanda didn't know what to say. "Uh, thanks. What do I owe you?"

He lifted one shoulder in a half shrug. "Nothing. It was no problem. I had a break between two of my appointments, I called Kerrianne, and we stopped by, that's all." He frowned briefly. "Only you weren't supposed to come home yet. It was supposed to be a surprise. I left a card."

Amanda strode to the counter and picked it up. "Surprise!" she read aloud. "The timer on your stove should be all right now. Thanks for watching the kids on such short notice last night. From Blake." She looked up from his masculine script. "You didn't need to do this."

He smiled at her. "Yes, I did. I wanted to."

"Thank you."

He didn't reply for a minute. The tension between them was back, and Amanda imagined sparks leaping the gap between them.

"Well, I'd better go," he said. "I only do half days on Fridays, but I started late today, so I still have a couple hours left to work."

Amanda walked him to the front door and watched him speed away, all thoughts of a quiet evening gone from her head.

❀ ❀ ❀

After his last service visit, Blake returned to the repair shop. Only Doug and Rhonda were there, and Doug was talking with a customer near the dryers. Rhonda smiled at him as he entered, her frizzy hair looking more wild than usual. "All through?"

"Yeah." He yawned as he went around the counter and sat down in the chair next to her. Glancing at his watch, he realized he still had a few minutes before he could leave work and head over to Kerrianne's for the kids.

"I missed watching them this morning while you were at school," Rhonda said, correctly interpreting his gesture. "After a week of having them underfoot, it seems weird them not being here at the shop, though I know Doug's glad to have everything back to normal. How're they liking their new baby-sitter?"

Blake leaned back in his chair, stretching out his legs and placing his hands in back of his head. "They adore her. In fact, there's probably only one person they like more."

"You?"

He looked at her, surprised. "Oh, yeah, I guess, but I was actually thinking of someone else."

Rhonda's eyes narrowed. "Okay, spill the beans, Blakey boy. You're looking way too happy for someone I know for sure spent half of last night studying and the other half comforting Kevin from a kidnapper nightmare. Who is she? And when did you have time to meet anyone? I know that every second you weren't working or studying this week you were changing diapers and hanging out with two certain children. Come on, tell me everything."

Blake couldn't help grinning. "Well, there is this one woman I sort of like."

"Ah-hah! More. Tell me more."

"What's to tell?" Blake shrugged.

174

"Duh. Like who is she, where you met. Did you ask her out? How many times have you seen her? And did you kiss her? Details. I need details." Rhonda's eyes gleamed.

Blake shook his head at his sister-in-law's exuberance, though his own emotions were flying high. "Her name is Amanda Huntington. I met her last week when I fixed her oven, and then she came into the shop the next day—last Thursday. The kids and I stopped by her school on Friday—she's a teacher, by the way—and she was with us when the social worker came over. Then we sort of had a date on Saturday, and Kevin insisted on taking her soup on Sunday. Last night she watched the kids while I went to school."

"And?" Rhonda's thin face was eager.

"No, I didn't kiss her."

"Oh." Rhonda gave a disappointed sigh.

"But she did ask me out for tomorrow night." Blake looked at Rhonda, both of them grinning like a couple of children. "That reminds me. Can you watch the kids while I go?"

"Yeah, I can do that. Be glad to." She paused, studying his face. "You really like her, don't you?"

Blake nodded. "She's beautiful, intelligent, creative—everything I ever wanted. Except . . ." His smile faded. He pulled in his legs and put his arms on his lap.

"She sounds perfect. So what's wrong?"

"I'm not sure she's interested in me."

"Why on earth not?" Rhonda was outraged. "Is it because of the kids?"

He shook his head. "Actually, I think she may like me *because* of the kids."

"That doesn't make sense."

He shrugged. "She may just want to be friends. I mean, there seem to be sparks between us, but sometimes she gets this really strange look in her eyes . . . I don't know what it is. I think I'm not good enough for her."

"What do you mean not good enough? You're smart, you've almost finished school, you earn a good living. You're handsome, funny—everything *she* could want!"

Blake managed a smile at her impassioned defense. "I think she might feel she's above me. In station, I mean. She's got a degree. I don't."

"Are you sure you're being fair?" Rhonda said. "She's not Laurie."

The name shot through Blake's body, seeming to touch every part of him with a sense of remorse, of remembered pain.

Laurie. No one had mentioned her name for years.

He'd met Laurie a year after his mission, during the time he had still believed he could make a lifetime career at the repair shop. Laurie hadn't agreed. In the end she had left their six-month relationship, taunting him for his lack of ambition. No way would she spend the rest of her life trying to stretch each penny. His dreams of their future had been shattered that day, and for a long time he thought he would never recover. Yet, in a way, she had caused him to look inside himself and see what *he* really wanted instead of what Doug had always planned for him. When the pain of losing her had dimmed enough, Blake decided that maybe she was right. Doug had been his hero far too long; maybe it was time he made his own choices. He decided to go to college and find his own dreams. Laurie never knew—would never know.

Later, when Kevin had come to stay with him, Blake no longer thought of Laurie every day. That was when he realized that she couldn't be the love of his life or he would still miss her. He began to hope for someone better. Still, the memories seared into his heart weren't happy.

"I know she's not Laurie," he said, taking a deep breath. "But she comes from a family that really values education. Her father has several degrees and is an executive at some big PR firm, her mother recently graduated with a family science degree, Amanda herself has a degree in education, and her brother is going to be a wildlife biologist. The only one who doesn't have a degree—besides her younger brother who's on a mission—is her older sister who married young. That's Kerrianne, the woman who's watching Kevin and Mara. She may not have a degree, but her husband is talking about going back for his doctorate."

"So?" Rhonda lifted her shoulders. "You fit right in. You're almost finished with your degree."

Blake stared at his hands—rough and scarred from years of repairs. "I didn't tell her about school."

"What?" Rhonda's voice rose to a screech. Across the room Doug and the customer looked over at them, and she immediately lowered her voice. "What do you mean you haven't told her about school?"

"I wanted her to like me for who I am." Even as he said the words, Blake knew they sounded feeble. But he also knew he needed a real relationship, not one based on his education level. If Laurie had truly loved him, she would have seen past everything else. She would have seen that he would eventually find his way. Moreover, his happiness would have been more important to her than money.

"Isn't going to school a part of who you are?" Rhonda asked fiercely. "And your desire for a better financial future? Though repairmen *can* earn a very good living, thank you very much." She gave a disgusted shake of her head.

Blake opened his mouth to explain, but Rhonda was too worked up to listen.

"Not telling her your plans for the future is like her not telling you she's a teacher and letting you think she works as an exotic dancer or something. You certainly wouldn't be interested in her then."

"It's not the same thing. Repair work is a respectable career."

Rhonda rolled her eyes. "Yes, but your plans for the future are also a part of who you are. Didn't I just say that? Aren't you listening? She deserves to know what she's in for."

Blake knew Rhonda had no idea how it felt to be rejected in the way he'd been rejected. Still, some of what she said made sense. "I'll tell her," he promised, "but only after I'm sure she really likes me, that she's not just sticking around because she likes children."

Rhonda sighed. "I guess you'll do what you have to do." She mumbled something under her breath.

"What?" he asked.

"I said, 'If you'd kissed her, you'd know whether or not she likes you.' A kiss doesn't lie."

"Rhonda," he moaned.

"It's the truth." With that Rhonda stood up and went into the office.

Blake stared after her.

Chapter Sixteen

On Saturday afternoon, Blake sat in the truck outside the address Paula had given Amanda. He'd already been to the door three times, but Paula had not yet shown up. Her friends inside assured him there was going to be a party and that it would start any minute. They invited him to wait with them. Taking several breaths of the thick secondhand smoke in the air—some of which he suspected didn't come from tobacco—he declined. Since then he'd been driving around the neighborhood, checking back periodically. It was cold outside, but at least it wasn't raining or snowing.

"I'll be right back," he told the kids. He sprinted to the door of the run-down house, only to learn that Paula had still not arrived.

"What do you say to a hamburger and fries?" he asked Kevin when he was back in the truck. Mara was getting fussy, and Blake knew he needed to do something to distract her.

"With a shake?" Kevin asked, not showing any surprise or concern at his mother's continued absence.

"Sure."

Blake drove to the nearest McDonald's and took them inside, inwardly fuming at Paula's negligence. Over the years he'd missed work, school, and even church waiting for her. Today was the last day. He was finished with waiting. Now that he was officially Kevin and Mara's foster parent, he was in this for the long haul. He was determined to make life as normal as possible for the children. He had to! And normal did not include waiting for a woman who always put herself first.

He ordered their food, still fuming inwardly about his cousin. She drove while drunk, left her children with drug addicts, couldn't hold down a job, and didn't stick around to be a mother. She said things to her son on the phone that caused him to have nightmares about kidnappers.

It stops now, he told himself. *After today, if she wants to see the children, it will be on my terms, not on hers.*

When they'd finished eating, they drove back to the address one last time to leave Paula a message. To Blake's disappointment, his cousin had arrived. She helped him take the children inside the house, blithe excuses tumbling from her lips. Her jittery movements made him nervous.

"Oh, Mommy's so glad to see you," she gushed to Kevin. "I see Uncle Blake cut your hair. Did you have to make it so short, Blake? Well, no matter, you're a cute boy, no matter how short your hair is. You take after me." She giggled at that. "Come on over here, every-body. Look at my darlings. Aren't they just the most beautiful kids you ever saw? Somebody get that sack I brought. Get out the peanut butter crackers for my son. He loves them, you know."

On and on she talked. Her friends gathered around as Blake stood near the wall, watching. Smoke curled from cigarettes up to the ceiling, alcohol flowed freely, the music was too loud. Lunch consisted of chips and cookies. A man sat on the couch showing Kevin how he could touch his nose with his tongue. There was a lot of bare skin, as though some of the party-goers thought it was sum-mer. A woman was telling about a fight she got into at the grocery store where she worked. An older man talked about losing his wel-fare check on a game of cards. Every other word on the air made Blake wince. A girl who looked about fourteen was making eyes at both him and the old man who'd lost his welfare check.

Blake's heart felt like lead. Couldn't Paula see that this environ-ment wasn't healthy for the children? He imagined Kevin and Mara growing up smoking and doing drugs. He imagined them learning about life from people who would never teach them how to work but rather would instill in them the self-important philosophy that soci-ety owed them a living.

He couldn't let that happen. He would have to *make* Paula see.

"Okay," he said over the noise. "It's time to go."

Paula's sleepy eyes opened wide. "What? But you just got here."

"No, *you* just got here. We've been here since one." Blake picked up Mara from the floor where Paula had placed her moments after entering the house.

"I—uh—but—" Paula stuttered. "Uh—you haven't eaten!"

"We ate at McDonald's after we waited two hours for you." Blake looked at Kevin. "Get your coat." Holding his nearly empty package of peanut butter crackers, the child obeyed without protest or expression.

"Blake, come on," Paula cajoled, casting an amused glance at her friends. "Don't be mad. Be a sport."

He shook his head. "I'm finished being your sport."

Paula's heart-shaped face turned crimson. She opened her mouth to speak, but seeing the interested stares of her friends, she opted to save face. Smashing her cigarette in a dish, she jumped to her feet. "I'll walk you out."

Once alone, she started in on him again. "I can't believe you,

Blake! The state takes away my children, and you can't even let me spend any time with them!"

"*You* were the one who was late," Blake said calmly.

"My car broke down!" she screeched. "That wasn't my fault. And I slept in a bit."

There was a time when he would have felt sympathy, but he was beyond that now. "Ever hear of a phone? You know my cell number. I would have picked you up at any time."

The guilty look passing briefly over her face told him she did know his number but she had been occupied elsewhere. At least she had some honesty left.

"Believe it or not, I have a life," he added. "I have somewhere I need to go tonight. That's another reason we can't stay."

"You just want my kids!"

"Paula," he warned, dipping his head toward Kevin.

Her lips tightened, but she fell silent. As he put the children into the truck, she kissed them, told them she loved them, and promised to see them soon. The moment he shut the door, she whirled on him.

"Admit it. You're trying to steal them. Why, Blake? Why? Those kids are my life! My whole life!"

Blake drew her away so Kevin wouldn't be able to hear any of their conversation. "Your life, your life," he gritted, his back to the truck. "That's all I hear from you. Your life. This isn't about you, Paula. It's about those children. And I'll be hanged if I'm going to watch you destroy *their* lives." He flung an arm toward the house. "Is that what you want for them? Do you want them living off hand-outs, swearing like sailors, killing their bodies with drugs and alcohol, living in sin? What about a real family life? What about an education? A job?"

"I'm a good mother!" The red in her face deepened.

He shook his head and said the words that were long overdue.

"No, Paula, you're not." He raised his shoulders and hands in an exaggerated shrug. "That's where you're wrong. The Paula I know and love, the Paula I grew up with, wouldn't let her children down like this. The Paula you once were would sooner die than say things on the phone to her son that make him have nightmares about being kidnapped."

"I didn't—" She broke off and then started again, her voice low and deadly. "I want my kids, so help me, Blake. I'll get you if you don't help me. I'll burn your house down. I swear, I will. I'll *hurt* you." She glared at him, eyes furious, her small fists clenched at her side.

Blake shook his head. "No, you won't. Not as long as I have the kids. Because as much as I think you've been a terrible mother, as much as I've learned that I can't believe a word you say, I know you love Kevin and Mara. I *know* that. You'd never purposely hurt them. So what you have to do now is open your eyes and see that you *are* hurting them. You need to get your head together and be there for them. As for the rest—well, I'm not afraid of you. That's all I'm going to say." With that he turned his back on her and strode away, the image of her furious face etched into his brain.

"Is Mommy okay?" Kevin asked as he climbed into the truck.

"Mommy's fine," Blake said. "She's just a little disappointed that we can't stay. Next time, we're going to have her come to our house."

"Good," Kevin said. "Because those people were weird."

Blake had to agree. "More than you know, bud. More than you know."

Amanda was a bundle of nerves when Savvy arrived at her house, looking great in her simple jeans and a fitted jacket that went well with her ample curves. She was a full head shorter than

Amanda, with long white-blonde hair that fell to her waist. Her lively, sky blue eyes shone from a smooth white face, marred only by a small, almost undetectable scattering of red blemishes on her forehead near her hairline.

"It's so good to see you again!" Amanda hugged her friend tightly.

Savvy grinned. "I've really missed you."

"I'm glad you're early," Amanda said. "How do I look?" She framed her face and hair with her hands.

Savvy arched a brow. "How do you look? Wonderful! I like the way you've layered your hair up the sides, and those bangs become you. I've been thinking about doing that myself." She touched her forehead. "Bangs would hide all signs of the chocolate I've been eating. Could you lend me a little cover-up or base? I forgot to use it at home."

Amanda went to the bathroom where she handed Savvy a stick of cover-up. She watched her friend put some on her finger and rub it into her forehead, almost completely hiding the tiny red dots. It didn't make much difference to her overall appearance, Amanda thought, because Savvy was beautiful, regardless. She wasn't slender, she wasn't tall, she didn't wear a lot of makeup, her hair was straight, but she was beautiful in a wholesome, classical sort of way. Amanda had long wished she could grow out her bangs, but she didn't seem to have the forehead for such a style.

"What about my clothes?" Amanda asked. "Think I should change into jeans like you?" She smoothed her silky black pants.

"No, those pants are good. I wish I had the flat stomach for them. But that sweater . . ." Savvy frowned. "Don't you still have that really cute green blouse? I swear that thing makes your eyes really stand out."

"Yes." Amanda snapped her fingers and ran to her bedroom. She had the blouse tucked in the back of her closet. It was made of silk and fitted, though not so tight as to be immodest or uncomfortable. When she looked in the mirror, she knew she looked good.

"You like him this much?" Savvy asked, smiling from the doorway.

Amanda's will to deny everything immediately faltered. "I once compared his eyes to chocolate," she confessed.

"Chocolate?" Savvy gasped in feigned horror. "What about our agreement that you not get too involved?"

Amanda shook her head. "I don't know."

"Well, for chocolate, I'd take my chances." Savvy grinned at her. "Forget the fear factor."

Amanda's thoughts exactly—*if* she didn't have a heart attack first.

Mitch arrived next, balancing two steaming pizzas. He was the tallest in their family and a little on the lean side. His brown hair was quite different from the missionary haircut he'd once sported but still short enough to be barely acceptable to their mother. His bangs, parted near the middle reached clear to the bottom of his ears, falling forward at times as he dipped his head during the conversation. Today he wore baggy dress pants that helped hide his thinness and a blue sweater that made his eyes appear a deeper blue than normal. In all, Amanda thought her brother was a nice-looking man.

Amanda hugged him as he kissed her on the cheek. Mitch was her favorite brother, being less than two years her junior. Since her birthday was in early December and his in late August, growing up they'd only been one year apart in school.

"You look extraordinarily beautiful tonight," Mitch said, giving her a bow that reminded Amanda of decades gone by when people had commonly said such things to their siblings. "Your eyes look so green." His gaze shifted to Savvy. "Hi, Savvy. You look lovely, too. I'll have to be fending off the men tonight, I see. Don't worry, though, I think I'm up to the task."

"I'm sure you are," Savvy said dryly.

185

Amanda glanced at the clock. It was just after six-thirty, and Blake was nowhere in sight. "You two get started eating while it's hot," she said. "We don't want to run too late."

Mitch went to pull out a stack of plates from the cupboard. Then he folded himself onto the plaid couch in her family room and began eating. Savvy joined him, but Amanda sat on the floor without a plate. She was too nervous to eat. What was taking Blake so long? Had something happened?

At last the doorbell rang, and Amanda went to answer it. "Sorry, I'm late." Blake grinned apologetically. "I had a little car trouble on the way home from Salt Lake today."

"Is everything okay?" She noticed the four-door sedan parked in front of her house. She was sure it didn't belong to Savvy or Mitch.

"I had to borrow my brother's car, but it'll be fine. I'm good at fixing things."

Amanda invited him in, noting that like her brother he wore dress pants and a sweater, though he filled his clothes out considerably better than Mitch. He had chosen brown shades instead of blue, which made his skin look almost olive and his dark eyes more like chocolate. Her knees felt oddly weak.

He was giving her the same perusal. "You look fabulous," he said.

"So do you." They stood there in the doorway for a full ten seconds, the cold air blasting in, until laughter from the family room called their attention. "Oh, let's go meet the others," Amanda suggested weakly. She shut the door, and he followed her into the next room. It felt odd to Amanda not to have Kevin and Mara tagging along.

"This is Blake, everybody," Amanda announced. "Blake, this is Savvy, a good friend of mine. And this is my brother Mitch." Savvy nodded from her seat on the sofa, but Mitch bounced up and shook

Blake's hand. Savvy winked at Amanda while they were occupied, signaling her approval. Delight spread through Amanda.

"Have some pizza?" Mitch asked Blake, heading toward the table. "It's a little cold, but I can just slip it in the microwave for you and Aman—"

"No!" Amanda and Blake said at the same time.

"I'll heat it in the oven," she added. "I hate microwaved pizza."

"It changes the texture of the crust," Blake agreed.

Mitch shook his head, grinning. "I never thought I'd ever meet anyone else with an aversion to microwaved pizza." He put two slices on a plate and took them to the microwave for emphasis. "You two were made in heaven for each other."

There was a brief, awkward silence, and then Savvy added, "at least pizza heaven. You two should start a restaurant." Everyone laughed.

Amanda heated one of the pizzas in the oven, and it was only five minutes after seven when they piled into Savvy's little red Subaru. "Oh, wait, I need to get something." Mitch hurried to his car, grabbed a plastic sack, and climbed back in the car. Amanda, in the backseat with Blake, wondered what might be inside the bag, but Blake's closeness drove the thought from her mind. He smiled at her and she smiled back.

"How are Kevin and Mara?" Amanda asked, as Savvy drove toward the freeway.

A shadow passed over his face. "They're fine. They saw their mother today, but she was two hours late. We had to wait, mostly in the truck. It was irritating, to say the least."

"That's not fun." Amanda shook her head with sympathy.

"On the bright side, she threatened to burn down my apartment."

Amanda opened her eyes wide. "She did what?"

"Oh, she didn't mean it. She'd never hurt the kids. As long as they're there, I'm quite safe."

Amanda wondered again why Paula hadn't been charged with drug possession. Maybe if she had gone to jail, the children could have a better life with Blake. As it was, things would continue to be difficult. "Doesn't sound like she cares about wasting your time."

"That's it exactly. I think I'm going to have to ask for supervised visits." He made a face. "That's where the social worker comes to get the kids, takes them somewhere and stays with them while Paula visits. The way it's going—the way it's always been—I can't have a life. She expects me to drop whatever I'm doing whenever she feels the urge to see the kids."

"You'd think she'd understand that she's making things tougher for herself," Amanda mused.

"She doesn't. She sees only what she wants to see." Blake's jaw tightened, and he looked out the window at the passing lights.

Amanda felt his worry. Reaching out, she placed her hand over his, trying to offer comfort. He turned toward her, smiling again. Then his hand turned and grasped hers. Amanda's heart seemed to skip a beat. He held her hand in the darkness all the way to the dance club.

The music at the club was loud for Amanda's current taste, and some of the dancers were more scary-looking than she remembered from her college days. She danced every song with Blake or Mitch. She was surprised that with Blake there was no awkwardness or lag in the conversation. They laughed together often. When she wasn't dancing with Blake, he was either dancing with Savvy or watching from the sidelines. Once, she saw a very pretty girl ask him to dance, and he spoke with her for a minute, shaking his head and pointing in Amanda's direction. A warm feeling of gladness spread through her when the girl, not in the least offended, laughed and went to dance with someone else.

At every slow dance, Mitch disappeared, leaving Blake with Amanda. Wonderment filled the air between them. When she saw Mitch coming their way again near eleven, she waved him off with the hand behind Blake's back. Mitch gave her the okay signal and faded into the crowd. Amanda couldn't see Savvy and guessed she was dancing with one of her many new admirers.

Amanda and Blake danced into a corner that was darker than the rest of the floor. Everything was painted with magic—the whirling lights, the colors of the dancers' clothes, the shining floors. Blake's eyes bore into hers, and Amanda felt she knew him in a way she had never known anyone else—as though she could see into his soul. The whole world stood still.

"Amanda," he said, his voice slightly hoarse.

"Yes?"

He didn't reply, but his face bent toward hers. Joy surged through her, but it was followed by the same old fear. She stared at him, suddenly wishing she could run fast and far—to go anywhere so she wouldn't have to look into his eyes and feel this aching hope. She wished she could lock her heart in a box and hide it away where no one could find it and break it.

His movement toward her stopped. "What are you thinking?" he whispered, seeming surprised at his own question. He was so close that Amanda plainly heard him, could feel his warm breath on her cheek. "I've seen that look in your eyes before. Tell me—what does it mean?"

She couldn't look away and she couldn't lie, any more than he could have held back the question. This was the moment of truth, the moment they had both known would come since they first felt the electricity between them. "I—I'm afraid," she answered, her voice softer than his. So soft she knew he would have to read her lips to understand the words.

"Of what?"

"Of losing it again."

Emotion filled his face. She felt tears rise in her eyes, saw them in his. He shook his head very slowly. "We won't."

He hadn't promised the world. He hadn't sworn undying love, but his simple assurance gave her courage.

His head lowered, and their lips met in their first kiss. The noise and music around them faded. They were alone. The kiss briefly deepened before Amanda pulled away, her heart thumping furiously. She was glad he wasn't holding her tightly enough to feel that pounding, though at the same time she wished she could feel the beat of his heart. If his expression—dazed, tender, loving—was any indication, his heart was pumping just as fast as hers.

And that's when Amanda knew.

She *knew*.

There was no looking back. This was *it*.

She put her hand in his, feeling as though she were soaring above the clouds. His strong fingers tightened over hers, their eyes still locked. His head lowered once more.

"What!" came an outraged voice, breaking through Amanda's euphoria. "I didn't know it was against a public ordinance! For crying out loud, it's just a gerbil!"

"It's a mouse!" a girl nearly screamed. "Or a rat! It tried to nibble my hair!"

Amanda and Blake turned to see two burly men escorting Mitch to the exit, a girl with long blonde hair glaring after them. An interested crowd was forming by the girl.

"You go with him," Blake said, laughter dancing in his eyes. "I'll find Savvy."

Reluctantly, Amanda pulled her hand from his warm grasp and hurried after her brother. Shortly, they found themselves out in the cold, Mitch murmuring words of comfort to a little brown creature that did look rather like a fat, furry mouse.

Amanda shook her head. "Did you have to bring Hiccup?" she said after briefly eyeing the creature.

"What, you'd rather that I'd brought Dizzy? Now that would have been a disaster."

"I didn't want you to bring either of your gerbils." She held up a hand before he could protest. "Nope, not the lizard either. Or the frogs."

Mitch shivered. Already the skin on his face was turning red, and small welts were appearing as his acute sensitivity to cold kicked in. "Here, hold her." He gave her the gerbil before donning the coat the bouncers had thrown at him on the way out.

Amanda looked anxiously toward the door. If Savvy didn't appear soon, she and Mitch would have to find some place to get out of the cold. Though Mitch was dressed warmly enough that his breathing shouldn't become a problem, he was going to have serious hives. Mitch zipped up his coat, scratched his neck, and then reached for Hiccup.

"I'll hold her," Amanda said. "Put your hands in your pockets to keep them warm."

"I will, but she'll go in, too. Remember, she's a desert creature. She's probably as allergic to cold as I am."

Amanda snorted. "The desert sometimes gets pretty cold at night from what I hear. Isn't that when gerbils are mostly awake?" But she gave up the creature, figuring it would warm his hands. Besides, what if she dropped it? They might never find it out here, and her brother would be heartbroken.

Mitch put the gerbil in his coat pocket. With his other hand, he scratched at his neck again. "At least it's not raining or snowing." He wasn't exactly right. There were a few white flurries, and the playful breeze was very cold.

"There they are." With relief Amanda waved to Savvy and Blake as they emerged from the dance club.

"I can't believe you!" Savvy gave Mitch a disgusted look. "I thought you learned your lesson last time with the lizard."

"I did," Mitch insisted. "That why I brought Hiccup."

"It's not a zoo," Savvy said.

"Yeah, but you never know who I might meet. The girl I'm going to marry will love my animals as much as I do."

Savvy rolled her eyes. "We'd better get you in the car before you scratch your skin off."

Blake looked at Amanda, a question in his eyes. As they followed Savvy and Mitch to the car, she explained. "My brother has something called cold urticaria. Basically, it's an allergy to cold, or rather, sudden changes to cold temperatures."

"I never heard of such a thing."

She shrugged. "Neither had we. He was diagnosed one time when we went waterskiing when he was about fifteen. He had a very severe reaction and almost died for lack of air. Hasn't been able to go in cold water since without a dry suit. That's like a wet suit, only it doesn't allow water inside."

Blake shook his head. "Too weird."

Amanda laughed. "That's my brother, summed up in two words. Weird. But he's wonderful, too. Keeps us all young. He's twenty-three but acts about seven."

"I like him," Blake said. Their hands touched as they walked, and he grabbed her cold hand with his warmer one.

At the car, Savvy was insisting that Mitch put Hiccup in her cage—which just happened to be in the plastic sack he had smuggled into the car earlier. Amanda and Blake slid into the backseat, still holding hands.

As they sat there, Amanda began to wonder if she had only imagined what had occurred between them. The heavy feeling in the hollow of her stomach warned her that she had only just stepped on the ride. Now if she could just hold on.

Chapter Seventeen

Amanda wasn't surprised when she received a phone call from Blake after work on Tuesday. He'd called on Sunday just to talk, on Monday he'd invited her over for family night, and he had called her again on Monday night after she returned home. Under the very curious stares of Kevin and Mara, there had been no more kisses, but Amanda was willing to take their relationship slowly. She couldn't remember ever having felt this way about a man before. She didn't care what he did for a living, what he wore, or if he had custody of *ten* children that weren't his.

"Hi, Blake," she said, enjoying the way his voice seemed to reach into her very being.

"I have a favor to ask." His voice was hesitant now. "I was going to call my sister-in-law, but Kevin begged me to call you instead."

"What is it?"

"I have to go somewhere, and I can't take the kids. I usually have the neighbor girl baby-sit, but I . . . well, I started getting worried this morning, what with Paula's outburst on Saturday, that maybe I shouldn't leave them with a child. I really didn't think she'd come here without asking, but I suddenly find I'm not so sure. Maybe this is the Spirit warning me. Ordinarily, I'd shrug it off as my own imagination, but Kevin and Mara . . . well, it's too important to *not* listen to. Paula knows I won't be here tonight."

"She knows?"

"Yeah. I, uh, always have to go somewhere on Tuesday nights. Thursdays, too."

Ah-hah! Amanda thought. "And where is that?" she asked.

"Uh . . ." He trailed off, obviously not wanting to share more information.

A spurt of anger shot through Amanda. She didn't expect him to check with her for every little thing, but he *was* asking her to watch the children. She had a right to know where he was going. She had a right to know if he was seeing someone else. He had kissed her, after all. He had said, "We won't"—whatever that meant.

"Don't tell me," she said, feigning cheerfulness. "You're going to AA meetings? Or maybe Weight Watchers. Yes, that must be how you keep so trim."

"Actually, I've got school."

Relief flooded through her. "School? You have school? Why didn't you tell me? I thought you had a da—uh, never mind."

"You thought I had a date?" He chuckled. "That's rich. Who'd want a date with a guy who works too much and is caring for his cousin's children."

"Me, I guess," Amanda said.

His chuckle grew into full-blown laughter. "That's one thing I love about you, Amanda. You don't take the easy way out."

"What do you mean?" She didn't know if she should be offended or pleased. He had, after all, mentioned "love."

"I was thinking of that night you discovered Mara in my truck. You were so angry at me. You weren't going to back down, no matter what. I was almost afraid you were going to call the police right then and there."

"The thought did cross my mind."

"I bet. Then you came to the store to see how they were."

"Well . . ."

"You were right to do so," he said, suddenly serious. "You never know these days." He fell quiet, and Amanda knew he was thinking about his cousin.

"I'll be glad to watch the kids," she told him softly.

"Thanks. I didn't want the girl next door to have a problem with Paula, you know?"

"Yeah. Well, don't worry. Even if she does show up, I won't let her take them."

"Exactly." The smile was back in his voice. "Still, maybe I should bring them over there."

"And keep me from seeing what else you have stuffed under the couch cushions?"

"Hey, I was in a hurry. I cleaned it up later."

She laughed at his embarrassment. "Well, your place is better because they'll need to go to bed before you come home. See you in a few minutes."

Only after they hung up did she begin to wonder about his school classes and what he was studying. Washing machine repair? *It doesn't matter,* she told herself—and found that wasn't exactly true. It did matter and he should have told her. She needed him to feel he could share his dreams with her, regardless of what they were.

Amanda's tire was low, so she had to use the electric pump her father had given her several Christmases ago. She arrived barely in time at Blake's apartment. She noticed his brother's car was still parked out front and that his truck in the open garage had the hood up. She went around the house to the back entrance.

Blake put Mara in her arms right after opening the door. His eyes lingered on her as he slung his backpack over his shoulder.

"What do you have in your purse?" Kevin asked eagerly.

"Yeah, what?" Blake winked at her, but she noticed he made no move toward the door. For family night she had stuck finger puppets in her purse for the children. Both had loved them, but Blake had enjoyed them every bit as much.

"Aren't you going to be late?" Amanda asked, smiling at him. If she had to wait until later to hear about his classes and his plans for the future, he'd have to wait to see the delicious candy turkeys she was going to make with Kevin in honor of Thanksgiving next week. "Better hurry. You don't want those young whippersnappers down there making jokes about how slow older men are."

Blake groaned. "Don't remind me. I *am* the oldest in the class." He glanced at her purse again and then at her face. Without warning, he planted a quick, solid kiss on her mouth. "See you later."

Amanda watched him leave, holding Mara tighter in her arms.

The evening went well. Making the candy turkeys took longer than Amanda expected, but that was because as much candy found its way into their stomachs as into their creations. Finally, they had turkeys for each of them, including Blake.

Mara had fallen asleep in the high chair. After gently washing bits of marshmallow from her hands and face, Amanda picked her up. "I'm going to take her to bed," she whispered. "Then we'll read some books. I brought a few, but you can go and get any others you want." Kevin had quite a nice collection of books on the bottom shelf of the entertainment center.

When she returned to the room, Kevin was standing in the middle of the kitchen, staring at the door. His eyes were wide, his face scared. "What is it?" she asked.

He pointed to the door. "Someone's trying to get in." Sure

enough, the knob wiggled, and a loud thump sounded on the other side of the door.

Amanda reached out to Kevin. "It's okay." She took his hand, pulling him toward the table, reaching for the phone.

The doorbell rang, sounding loud in the quiet. "Let me in," came a woman's muffled voice. "I want to see my kids!"

"That's my mom." Kevin took a step toward the door and then stopped and looked at Amanda with a question on his face.

The voice outside the door had gone silent, and Amanda pondered what she should do. Maybe she should let Kevin's mother in to see him for a minute. But what if she hadn't come alone? What if she tried to take the children? Amanda didn't know much about drug use, but she knew enough about Paula to know she wasn't stable.

And she had threatened Blake. Or at least to burn down his apartment.

Paula began to pound on the door. "I know you're in there! I know it!" A few foul words punctuated her exclamations. "Open up and give me my kids! Come on. I know Blake's gone. I know it! Just give me the kids and I'll leave. You can say I forced you to do it." When Amanda didn't answer, a stream of muffled curses came through the door.

"I think my mommy's drunk," Kevin said, showing no emotion at the fact.

Amanda fought the sadness that came with his statement. She doubted whether her niece, Misty, even knew the word *drunk*, much less the meaning.

More banging and cursing. The door shook with the force behind it. Amanda cringed.

Kevin put his hand in hers. "Let's go get Mara and hide under the bed or in the closet," he said. "Let's pretend we're not home. Mommy will go away and come back later."

Amanda could hardly see through her tears at his practicality. "I don't know about hiding," she said, "but it's a good idea to go to your room." She took the phone with her, debating whether to call the police. She decided to call her brother instead, not wanting to cause Kevin more stress. There was also a lingering worry in her mind that Paula might somehow be able to convince the police that the children were supposed to be with her and that she might disappear with them before the true circumstances were untangled. Mitch could get here in only a few minutes if he was home.

Thankfully, he answered on the second ring. She explained the situation quickly, making him promise to be careful when he came over. "I don't think she's dangerous, but I don't know if she's alone."

"Stay tight. I'll be right there."

"Okay, hurry."

"You don't have to call anyone," Kevin said from the closet where he was clearing space for them to hide. "Mommy always goes away. Grandma and I used to hide when her comed home drunk. Tomorrow her will come back—and maybe bring me peanut butter crackers."

"What about when you lived with your mom?" Amanda asked.

He shrugged. "Sometimes I hided under the bed. But Mara doesn't like it. Are you going to pick her up now?" He glanced at the crib anxiously, and Amanda saw the fear he had hidden behind his pragmatic suggestions.

"No, I think we'll let her sleep. Don't worry, though, my brother's going to come and talk to your mom. Everything's going to be fine. We don't need to hide. We're safe. Come, sit on my lap here on the bed. I'll read you a book."

They could still hear the banging at the door. Amanda figured the man upstairs who rented the apartment to Blake must not be home or he would have called the police by now. *Thank heaven Blake didn't leave the kids with that young baby-sitter,* she thought, sending up a silent prayer.

With a last glance toward the closet, Kevin snuggled into her lap and opened the pages of a book. Amanda began to read aloud. Mara didn't stir at the sound of her voice, the light, or the banging.

After a while the pounding ceased, and Amanda went into the kitchen, wondering if she dared open the door. A knock came and then a voice. "It's me, Mitch."

"Wait on the couch, Kevin," Amanda said. "Gather all the books you want me to read."

"Can I see your brother?"

"Yes. I'll bring him in." Amanda opened the door, eyes going past her brother. No one else was there.

"She's gone," Mitch said.

"Did you see her?"

He nodded and kept his voice low as he explained. "I told her I was investigating a disturbance. She said someone had kidnapped her kids. I asked her if she wanted me to take her down to the station to file a report. She swore at me and left."

Amanda glanced at Kevin, who stared at them with interest from across the room. "Thanks for coming. I was worried there for a moment."

Mitch chuckled without real mirth. "She was wasted, that much was obvious. I'm glad you didn't open the door."

"Well, come on in. Kevin wants to meet you." Amanda noticed her brother's face was already turning red from the cold. Several pea-sized welts stood out on his cheeks.

Mitch immediately made friends with Kevin. Amanda smiled as Mitch, without using a book, told Kevin the most outrageous true stories involving animals that he had learned while studying wildlife biology.

"And the bear really, really just walked away?" Kevin asked, his eyes huge in his small face.

"Yep. When that woman started yelling at him, he knew he had to leave or get screamed to death."

Kevin giggled. "Funny bear."

"Yep, animals are fascinating creatures."

"You know a lot about animals. Is that your job?"

A frown crossed Mitch's narrow face. "I thought it was, but to tell you the truth, Kevin, I've discovered that many wildlife biologists don't end up working with animals at all. They do research on computers, spend their time in a lab, or teach at schools." His eyes met Amanda's. "In fact, I've been thinking about changing my major to zoology. They face many of the same work challenges, but at least that way I could work for a zoo or someplace. Slightly more of a chance to work with animals."

"You should do that," Kevin agreed, sounding grown up. "I want to work at the zoo, too."

Amanda was about to add her approval to Kevin's when Mitch's coat began swaying violently on the back of the chair in the adjoining kitchen where she had hung it earlier. "Looks like Dizzy woke up," Mitch said. "I forgot she was there."

"Mitch!" Amanda jumped up and ran into the kitchen. "I swear, you're going to kill these animals one of these days. You just can't go around with them in your pocket like that."

Mitch beat her to the coat. "I know, I know. That's why I've put Dizzy in her plastic ball and not just in my pocket. It's a small one, but enough to protect her and to let her breathe. It's just like the one I had Hiccup in at the dance the other night." Mitch grinned at her. "You didn't know I took a ball to the dance, did you? Of course I did. I wouldn't risk hurting any of my pets." He let Dizzy out of the plastic ball and showed her to Kevin. "My gerbils love going places with me, but I have to be careful. They squish very easily, and if something were to happen to them . . ." He shook his head gravely, finding it unnecessary to finish the sentence.

Amanda sat on the couch and watched Mitch and Kevin play with the gerbil on the kitchen floor. They were still at it when Blake arrived home. His eyebrows rose at Mitch's presence, but he crossed the room and shook hands. "Brought Hiccup along, I see."

"Actually, this one is Dizzy," Mitch said, holding the animal up so that Blake could see the white stripe on her head that differenti- ated her from her sister. "She's a little more rambunctious. Uh, sorry about those little pellets on your floor here. I guess she couldn't wait until we got home. They sweep up quite easily, though."

Blake stared at the gerbil refuse. "It's okay," he said faintly, look- ing back and forth between Mitch and the floor.

Amanda took his hand, enjoying his touch, and led him to the children's room on the pretense of checking on Mara. Out of Kevin's hearing, she explained what had happened, Kevin's reaction, and Mitch's part in the whole mess.

Even in the dim illumination cast by the nightlight, Amanda saw Blake's color deepen with anger. "I can't believe this," he said, drop- ping her hand and walking over to the crib where Mara lay sleeping. "What am I saying? Of course I believe this. I felt something was going to happen. I know what Paula's like. I just hoped—" He shook his head, glancing over at her. "This leaves me no recourse. I have to file a restraining order. I can't have her popping in like this, mak- ing threats. She'll have to do her visiting at an assigned hour with the social worker. If I'm going to take care of Kevin and Mara the way they need to be taken care of, I have to be out of the middle."

Blake's hands on the side of the crib turned white with the force of his grip. Amanda put her hand over one of his. "I'm sorry," she ventured.

"It's just . . ." he began. "I know it might be hard to understand, but I *love* Paula. We were such good friends growing up, closer than brother and sister. But then her dad died, she fell in with the wrong crowd, and—" He shook his head. "In a way I feel responsible. If I had been a better friend, if I had made her see what she was doing wrong."

"You can't make other people's choices for them," Amanda said.

He looked at her, his dark eyes filled with sadness. "I know that, I guess. But sometimes it doesn't make it any easier. Kevin and Mara deserve so much more."

Amanda hugged him, offering the only comfort she could. "It'll be all right."

For a long moment they stood there, lost in their own thoughts.

"Well," Amanda said finally, trying to lighten the mood, "I think we'd better go keep an eye on Mitch. There's no telling what else he might have in that coat of his."

Smiling in appreciation, Blake let her lead him from the room.

Chapter Eighteen

The man who delivered the letter late Thursday morning was cute—even if he did have really short hair and wore a suit. Paula liked the way his wide chin seemed so strong and sure. She liked the way his blue eyes lit up curiously as she identified herself, as though he thought she couldn't possibly be who she said she was. Blushing, she ran a self-conscious hand through her hair, knotted by last night's party and this morning's sleep, glad that she was wearing the black jeans and crop top she'd been wearing last night instead of her pajamas.

"Here," he said, thrusting the envelope into her hand.

"What is it?" Her long fingernails poked under the flap. She was surprised to see it wasn't sealed.

"A restraining order," the man said.

"You're a cop?" She felt betrayed. He'd admired her; she knew it. And now this.

He didn't answer but walked away.

As she read the document, her anger grew. *How dare Blake try to keep me from my children,* she fumed. *How dare he! The liar! He said I could see them whenever I wanted. He's nothing but a filthy, stinking liar who's trying to steal my kids. MY kids, not his. They're MY LIFE, not his. The ugly, lying . . .* Inwardly, she raged on, using every curse word she knew and making up a few more. When words weren't enough, she went into the kitchen and smashed dishes until Kim came from her bedroom and made her stop.

"I hate him!" she screamed. "They're *my* kids!"

"What happened?" Kim's blonde hair, cropped close to her head, didn't need combing, so she always looked calm and orderly. Unlike Paula, whose long hair reflected her every mood.

"My cousin filed a restraining order!" Paula snorted in disgust. "I can't go near him or his apartment now. I can't even call. And of course that means I can't see my kids except with a social worker staring at us."

Kim shrugged, her face looking hard and worn in the stark light coming in from the window. "I told you not to go there the other night. We all did. You were too gone to listen."

"I just wanted to see them for a minute. I'm dying without them!" Why didn't her friend understand? She had her own son, whom she protected quite fiercely—to the point that she wasn't much fun anymore.

Kim's patience was wearing thin. "So, get someone to beat him up."

Paula shook her head. "It's gone too far. They'd know it was me." She didn't add that despite it all, she still loved Blake. And if she wanted to be completely honest—which she wouldn't be in front of her friend—she knew he loved her.

"Then do what you have to do to get them back. That's what *I* would do. Jump over whatever hoops, do whatever they say. Get them back. Then your cousin won't have a say."

"They want me to do a drug test," Paula said dully. "I've been trying to stay away from it, you know, since they took the kids. But it's hard. I've been drinking a lot to get by."

"What kind of drug test is it?"

Paula shrugged. "Urine, I think. That's what they gave me at the police station."

"Then it's no sweat. Most of that stuff only shows up for a week in your urine. And there's those drug detox products Loony's always bragging about. He claims they work."

"So if I tested in a week, I'd be clean?"

Kim tiptoed through the broken dishes and shut the cupboards Paula had left open. "As long as it's not a hair test. I hear they do that sometimes, too. Especially in a custody case. Loony might know something to help that. I heard someone say once that the hair test can tell if you've stopped so maybe that'd be enough. I know for sure that alcohol only shows up for a couple of days."

Paula began to feel a kind of hope burgeoning in her chest. She could stay clean for that long, couldn't she? If it meant she could have her kids. "Yeah, I think I can do it."

"Well, fine." Kim's eyes narrowed. "But I don't want you drunk again in front of my kid, remember? That was the deal when I let you stay here. That and rent."

"Loony set me up with a job at his uncle's car shop. I'll have rent soon."

Kim turned her back on Paula. "Don't break any more of my dishes—and clean up that mess."

Paula watched her leave, depression taking the place of her dwindling anger. "I need my kids," she whined to the empty room. Tears streamed down her face.

Kim was right. There was only one way to get her children back—and to make Blake pay. She *didn't* have a problem with substance abuse, not even a little one. She just liked to enjoy herself occasionally with her friends. But she would sacrifice that comfort for the time being—if that's what it took to get Kevin and Mara back. She'd take their drug and alcohol tests. She'd get it all out of her system if it killed her.

A small smile played on her lips. Blake would even be proud to hear of her progress—at least until he realized that once she was in charge, she was *never* going to let him near her children again. They were *hers*, and she was going to take care of them.

Chapter Nineteen

On Saturday Blake was out in the garage fixing his truck. The timing belt had broken on his way home from Paula's lunch party last week, and he hadn't found time before now to replace it. Blake had bought the needed parts the day before, and between him and Garth, they had all the necessary tools in the garage.

While Garth worked on his car because he didn't trust "those people" at the shop to get it right, Blake's reasons for doing his own repairs were multiple. First, he enjoyed using his hands. His mind could wander as it pleased or focus on specifics—in fact, he'd memorized a lot of his schoolwork while tinkering on the truck. He also worked on his truck because of necessity. There were so many other things he'd rather spend money on, especially since Kevin and Mara had come to stay with him.

This morning, Mara was in her crib sleeping and Kevin was in the garage "helping." Blake knew he had a solid two hours to work on the truck because Mara would sleep at least that long. Of course, he'd go and check in a while to make sure. The thought made him smile. He was beginning to feel he could do this parenting thing.

"Uncle Blake, can I play with Tara?" Kevin was standing at the entrance to the garage, looking over at the neighbor's house.

"Where will you be?"

"I want to take her in back to see the swing you and Garth put up yesterday."

"Let's see, I fixed the broken fence. And I got rid of all those boards with the nails in them. Sure, go ahead." Both items had been demanded by Erika Solos from DCFS when she had stopped by last week to deliver some papers. Blake had finally found time to comply.

He chuckled as Kevin ran next door, remembering how Garth had acted like an excited little boy last night when he'd brought home the swing and presented it to Blake and Kevin. "Hey, if we're going to have kids here," he'd said, "we need a swing set."

Blake was very grateful for his friend's gift. He'd called Amanda and invited her to the big swing-raising event. They used Garth's flood lights to see in the dark, and their fingers were chunks of ice when they'd finished. Afterwards, Amanda's hot chocolate, made from powder in small bags she had pulled from her magic purse, had felt like fire in their hands. A good fire. One that matched the new-found feeling in Blake's heart.

Garth had seemed taken with Amanda, and she obviously liked him, but Amanda hadn't let Garth's charms draw her away. She had left no doubt as to her preference. She liked Blake. Better yet, she liked him for who he was. Maybe she was even falling in love. He knew he was totally gone. He'd never felt this way for a woman before, hadn't known such feelings were possible. Now he finally understood the Lord's commandment for a couple to be married and to be one. With Amanda he felt he could achieve that spiritual union.

The only difficult moment between them since the dance had been her irritation at him for not telling her about his pending graduation from BYU, but after Paula's drunken visit, it hadn't been so important to either of them.

Things were going so well that Blake could easily imagine their future together. The two of them in a house, complete with a garden and a seventy-two-hour kit. Going to church on Sundays, making dentist appointments, shopping for groceries. Vacations on the beach, curling up before a fireplace, walks in the rain.

Somehow Kevin and Mara were always a part of these dreams, but he didn't examine that too closely. He hadn't heard from Paula in the four days since he filed the restraining order, though the social worker was scheduled to take the children to see her on Monday. He didn't know how he felt about that. He had been so furious with his cousin on Tuesday for scaring Amanda and Kevin, but now that his initial anger had subsided, he wished he could talk to Paula, make her understand. Still, he knew he'd made the only wise decision available. Someone had to be responsible. Talking to Paula would only give her an excuse to curse at him.

"So how's it going?" Garth stood in the doorway to the house. He was still wearing his pajamas, and his hair was plastered to his scalp, making the thinning on top more apparent.

Blake set down his wrench. "Okay, so far. How'd your date go last night?" After they'd finished putting up the swing, Garth had gone to the movies, picking up a date on the way. He'd invited Blake and Amanda along, but Blake didn't want to take the kids out so late, and Amanda needed to turn in early since she had a "date" at the temple this morning with her family. She didn't invite him to come along, and he didn't ask, though he would have loved to go. He wanted to let their relationship progress at a natural pace. Not everyone was ready to get married after only two and a half weeks.

Garth shook his head. "Not good. I don't think we'll be seeing each other again. It's just not working." He shrugged.

"That's too bad."

Garth grinned. "Well, not really because just now I got a call from a woman I met last weekend. I think she might be The One."

"If I had a dollar for every time you've said that in the past year, I'd be able to pay a mechanic to fix this thing." Blake kicked a wheel.

"I mean it this time."

"Yeah, sure. If I had money for *that* phrase, I could have bought the swing set you gave us myself. Now where's that timing light you had? I'm going to need it soon."

Garth pointed in the general direction, and rubbing his protruding stomach, he went back inside in search of breakfast.

No sooner had the door shut than the new cordless phone Blake had left on the single cement stair started ringing. *Amanda?* he thought, though he knew she was still at the temple. He wiped his hands on a rag and went to answer.

"Hello?"

"Hi, Blake? It's Erika Solos, from DCFS."

"Oh, hi. What's up?" He hadn't expected to hear from her on a weekend.

"I wanted to let you know," she began, her voice grave, "that Paula has agreed to drug testing and has been given a new court date—sooner than we expected."

"That's good, right?"

"Well, that depends. If she can manage to convince a judge that all this is a mistake, that she was just down on her luck for a while, and she can prove by taking a drug test that she's not abusing, or at least that the levels in the test are low enough that she can say she hasn't been using since the children were taken away, she may be able to get custody back. Especially since in the court's eyes this is a first offense."

Blake swallowed hard. He hadn't thought about that, only about her agreeing to be tested for substance abuse. "What about counseling? I thought you said she had to attend counseling first."

"I said she'd have to at least begin counseling before she got the kids back. Yesterday she voluntarily came in for her first session. She's also apparently changed her housing status. She's staying with a woman who has a steady job *and* a five-year-old child. What's more, Paula claims she's starting a new job next week. Now with these changes, I'm worried that the judge will see no reason not to award her custody."

Her hardened tone made a bitter taste rise to his mouth. "Isn't that what we want? I mean, the kids *should* be with her if she's ready to take care of them, shouldn't they?"

The social worker sighed. "Yes, that's the goal, but I find it hard to believe that your cousin would suddenly decide to do exactly what we've asked. She's fought us at every turn. She's used crude language—when she actually made it to our offices—and she's threatened about a dozen lawsuits. I just can't believe anything has changed so quickly. I've worked with people like her a long time, and I've learned to listen to my instincts. So trust me on this when I say that I don't know what changed, but Paula is more worried about getting back at you than being with her children."

That Blake could believe. There was nothing worse than Paula's fury, and he knew from seeing her relationship with her siblings that Paula could hold a grudge forever. He'd always avoided being in her line of fire—mostly because there was a genuine love between them—but now, at least in her eyes, he had done the inexcusable.

"It was the restraining order," he said, sighing.

"Most likely," Erika agreed.

"Even if she got the kids back, you'd be checking up on her, right?"

"Oh, yes. Make no mistake about that. The only problem is that sometimes, if they're determined enough, they'll move. Maybe to another state, even."

"But wouldn't she still have to report to a social worker?"

"It depends on what the judge says and on how well she's behaved. That's even assuming she cares what the judge orders her to do. Once she has the children, she might just disappear."

Fear shot through Blake's entire being. He would have to pay a price for getting the restraining order. He knew that. Paula would see to it. But he hadn't considered that when it was all over, she might not allow him to see the children as much as he had in the past. "She loves those children," he said, feeling somehow strangled by the words. "If she can straighten up . . ." The sentence was too hard to finish.

"I know she loves them." Erika's voice was softer now, more human. "But she's not ready. A few months or a year and maybe she would be. Addictions don't clear up in a matter of a few days or even weeks. It usually takes that long for them to admit to an addiction. What worries me is if they're determined, people can fake that they're cured for short periods of time. In the end, if they haven't really gone through the proper steps, it comes back with a vengeance. I don't want Kevin and Mara in her path when that happens. She's not ready. I *feel* it."

Blake shared the same feeling. This miraculous recovery was another of Paula's lies. "What can we do?"

"Well, we have a strong case, too. Strong enough, I think, to at least convince the judge to allow status quo for a few more months. That's all we'll need to see if Paula really is serious about her changes."

"I don't know. She can be very convincing. She'd sooner lie than tell the truth."

Erika snorted. "I've learned that for myself. And she does have a very sweet, convincing face. Certainly she doesn't look like a woman with substance addiction—which is terribly unusual. Normally, I can tell just by looking at them that they're addicts."

Maybe Paula isn't that bad off, then. A tiny hope sprang to life inside him.

"If you and Amanda go in there," Erika continued, "and present a solid front—uh, you are still dating, aren't you?"

Blake allowed himself a small smile. "Yes. She doesn't know it yet, but I'd marry her tomorrow, if she'd have me."

Erika chuckled. "That was fast."

For Blake it didn't seem fast enough. He felt as though his life hadn't really begun or even mattered until the day Amanda walked into it, but he wasn't going to tell that to Erika Solos.

"Well," she began again, "if you and Amanda are there, along with your brother and his wife, and as many of their kids as possible, and if Paula's mother and siblings are also there backing you, the judge will realize there is something to our claim—no matter how sweet and convincing Paula is."

"When is the new hearing then? Do you know?"

"Mid-December. That gives us about three and a half weeks."

Blake felt himself relax slightly. For a moment he'd been worried that Paula had been able to get a hearing for next week. Three and a half weeks got him past Thanksgiving at least.

"Thank you, Erika," he said.

"Oh, one more thing. Paula wants you to call her. She knows she can't call you because of the restraining order, but she wants to talk to you. You don't have to, but I promised I'd tell you."

"I'll think about it. I would like to try to judge for myself if she's serious."

"No offense here, but would you be able to tell?"

"I don't know. I *think* I can usually tell when she's lying. Maybe because we were so close."

"Well, be careful. If she's fooling even herself, you may be fooled as well."

"Okay, thanks." Feeling rather deflated, Blake hung up the phone and went back to work on his truck.

After a while, depressing thoughts of Paula were pushed away as his mind roamed over a jumble of subjects and came to rest on Amanda. He began whistling. He'd told her he would call today and talk about plans for tonight. Would it be too late to get a sitter? He enjoyed the time they spent together with the children, but he had romance on his mind tonight. Maybe a nice dinner—provided he had the budget for it—or perhaps a movie. He'd even be willing to see the latest chick flick, if she wanted. He didn't think he'd be paying much attention to the movie anyway, not with her soft hand in his.

Before long, the engine was running, and Blake aimed the timing light inside the hood, trying to see if he'd have to adjust the belt further. So far it looked good. He shut off the engine and stepped from the cab of the truck, blinking in surprise when he saw Amanda sauntering up the drive.

She looked beautiful. The sun, which had come up with no cloud covering that morning, reflected off her golden hair. Her brown leather coat opened in front to reveal a gauzy off-white floral-patterned dress that swirled down around her ankles. Her feet were clad in thick-heeled pumps.

"Hi," she called. "Thought I'd stop by on my way home to see how you were doing."

"Almost done." Blake became aware of his own disheveled appearance. His hands and arms were streaked with grease up to his elbows, his old jeans and heavy sweatshirt were equally marked, and his hair was likely to be oily since he hadn't showered that morning.

"Great. Want to go out for lunch? My treat. We'll take the kids." She looked around. "Where are they anyway?"

214

"Kevin's playing out back and Mara's sleeping."

Amanda came closer to him, wrinkling her nose. "Of course, if we go to lunch, you'll have to clean up first." Still, she came closer, pausing only when they were separated by less than an inch.

Blake wished he could take her in his arms, lower his lips to hers, tell her about his daydreams of their future. But now certainly wasn't the time. Instead, he lifted his hands, pretending to lunge for her. Laughing, she stepped out of his reach.

While he was storing his tools, she went to the back of the garage where a door led to the yard. "I don't see Kev," she said.

A sinking sensation filled Blake's stomach. Glancing at his watch, he saw that it'd been at least an hour since he'd heard Kevin and his friend out back. Not to mention the fact that he'd never gone in to check on the sleeping Mara.

He crossed the garage and called out into the yard. "Kevin! Amanda's here. Come quick! We're going out to eat!"

"That'll get him." Amanda smiled, but her brow creased when there was no immediate answer. "Could he be next door?"

Blake shook his head. "He knows not to go over there without asking. He was playing with the neighbor girl, though. I saw them at least an hour ago, sitting on that step by the phone. I thought they went out back."

"There's no phone there now." Amanda was looking at the step.

Blake was beginning to panic. Had Paula come and snatched Kevin while he wasn't looking?

"I bet they went inside," Amanda said. "Either here or at the neighbor's. The sun may be out, but it's kind of cold—even if they had coats. I know my kids at school can't stand more than fifteen minutes in the cold."

Now that she mentioned it, Blake's fingers were rather frozen. The rest of him, too, even though he had on a second sweatshirt under his thick blue one. He nodded sharply and walked to the door, wiping his hands on a rag. "If he's not there, we'll call the neighbors."

They went through the outer door and down to his apartment. The minute they opened the door, high-pitched screaming met his ears. "Mara!" Blake ran through the living room to the kids' bedroom, Amanda on his heels. There they found Kevin and his friend Tara standing by the twin bed. On the floor near the bed lay Mara, her face wet and red from crying. A chair from the kitchen stood by the crib.

Blake swooped her up in his arms. "It's okay, honey. Uncle Blake's here. It's okay, sweetheart." Mara's tears didn't stop.

"Her falled off the bed," Kevin explained.

Blake glared at him. "And what was she doing *on* the bed? You got her out of her crib, that's what! You should know better than that, Kevin. You could have killed her!"

Kevin's blue eyes filled with tears. The phone dropped from Tara's hand to the floor as she edged toward the door and escape. Blake let her go. Kevin was responsible here, not her. He opened his mouth to say a few more choice words to Kevin, but Amanda had sat down on the bed and put her arms around the child, holding him close. Her green eyes challenged Blake.

"Don't blame him," she said. "*You're* the one who was watching her—watching them both. If Mara was in here all alone, that was your fault. How many times did you check on her?"

"She was sleeping," Blake protested. "Kevin was outside. I never thought . . ." He stopped. Amanda was right. *He* was the adult in the situation. He shouldn't have left Mara unattended so long. He should have kept a better eye on Kevin and Tara. It was all his fault. He'd thought he'd been doing so well at parenting, but his neglect, however unintended, had put them both at risk—again. He opened his mouth to tell her he was sorry, that he hadn't wanted it to turn out this way, but she spoke first.

"Is Mara okay?"

Whatever words Blake wanted to say died in his throat. He examined Mara, whose sobs were fewer now, comforted by his touch, but he couldn't find any marks on her. "She looks all right. Just shaken." Blake was shaken, too, and his stomach felt queasy.

"Mara wanted out," Kevin said in a very small voice, looking up at Blake with his mother's eyes. "Her was happy on the bed. Then her falled." He started sobbing. "I didn't want to hurt her!"

"Shhh," Amanda said. "Blake knows you were just trying to help. But next time you should go tell him if Mara's awake."

Guilt washed over Blake anew. He knelt down before Kevin. "I'm sorry, bud. Amanda's right. You shouldn't have gotten her out, but it's my fault. I wasn't keeping a close enough eye on either of you."

Kevin broke from Amanda and buried his head in Blake's chest next to Mara. The baby stopped crying and reached for his hair. For a long moment, Blake held Kevin and Mara tightly. "It's okay," he whispered. "It's okay." But he didn't know if he believed it himself.

"If we're going out to lunch," Amanda said when at last Kevin pulled away and began playing with Mara, "I think we'd better let Uncle Blake change."

Kevin's eyes widened. "Are we going to the place with those big slides?"

Amanda gave a slight grimace, which she quickly replaced with a smile. "Well, that's not exactly what I had in mind, but I suppose— yes. I'll make an executive decision and take you there."

"Yay!" Kevin laughed. Seeing his delight, Mara laughed, too. "Her likes it," he said.

"*She* likes it," Blake and Amanda said together.

"I said Mara." Kevin gave them a withering look and left the room.

Blake was still clutching the baby. There was a streak of grease on her pajama sleeve that he didn't know if he'd be able to get out later, but she was okay—despite his mistake.

"It gets easier," Amanda said, placing a hand on his sleeve. "In another month or two, you'll know exactly what Kevin's capable of and predict what he might do. And you'll get in the habit of either checking on Mara every few minutes or having her where you can hear her."

"I don't know how women do it," he said, relieved that she didn't seem angry with him anymore.

"Well, probably because it happens slowly. You've had Kevin on and off, but you never had both of them before. I know when I got this teaching job—it's my first solo deal, you know—those kids surprised me at every turn. I'd never dreamed they could come up with so many unusual circumstances." She grinned. "Of course, sometimes they were good surprises, but some were potentially dangerous."

"Dangerous?" Blake asked. In his arms, Mara struggled to get down, obviously having decided she no longer needed comforting. He put her onto the floor, where she promptly picked up the phone and began sucking on the end.

"Like not understanding that they should stay away from broken glass, not watching to see if fingers are in the door before they shut it, or daring each other to swallow odd objects." She shook her head, a smile on her lips. "Every week they still come up with something new, but I've learned to avoid most everything that's potentially dangerous—and still have fun."

Blake took the phone from Mara, replacing it with her favorite stuffed dog. He climbed wearily to his feet. "Maybe they would be better off with Paula."

A swift intake of breath told him she hadn't expected this vein of thought. "You might have a lot to learn—we all do—but that doesn't mean they'd be better off with her."

"He could have dropped Mara on her head."

"But he didn't, did he? And now you know what he's capable of. He won't surprise you like that again. You'll find yourself transferring this experience to other situations."

He snorted. "Like giving her whole grapes?" He had caught Kevin doing that this week and had warned him about her choking.

"Something like that. The point is, they're getting regular meals and good care—and you love them."

"Paula loves them," Blake felt compelled to say. Could it be that the children might really be better off with his cousin? After all, his lack of attention today could have been fatal.

"Enough to go sober?" Amanda stood up from the bed. She shrugged. "I guess that remains to be seen."

"She might get them back sooner than I thought." He explained what Erika had said to him on the phone. "With school and work, I'm worried she'll make a good case for neglect on my part." He took her hand, feeling the softness of her skin compared to his work-roughened one. "Will you go with me to the hearing, Amanda?"

"Of course," she said, her eyes glittering with unshed tears. "I'd be glad to."

He went to hug her, and then, remembering his greasy clothes, he stopped and pulled off his outer sweatshirt. He hugged her for a wonderful moment, breathing in the flowery scent of her hair. When he drew away, her green eyes held his. He bent down for a kiss. All the insecurity about his parenting skills seemed to evaporate.

Too soon she broke away, though he knew it was for the best. Despite his very strong attraction to her, their relationship was too important to mess up. Something this good was meant to last for eternity—and that meant having patience.

"So, are we going to lunch?" she asked.

"You'll wait for me to clean up?"

"Sure. You go ahead. I'll watch the kids."

A short time later, Blake was ready to go. He walked into the living room and discovered Amanda had dressed Mara in a burgundy outfit that emphasized her dark hair. Until he saw her, Blake had forgotten that he'd left the baby in her pajamas.

Amanda was on the phone. "It's your aunt," she said, holding up the cordless receiver. "Something about Thanksgiving. I was trying to take a message, but she really wants to talk to you."

"Blakey?" Aunt Bonny's voice came from the phone, sounding tinny and very frail.

He took the phone and put it to his ear. "Hi, Aunt Bonny. What's up?"

"Well, I've decided I just don't feel up to having Thanksgiving here this year, and Tracey was sort of wanting to stay home, so we thought we'd do it at her place. They're buying me a plane ticket for Monday. Hal and his family are going there, too. They're driving up later in the week. You're invited, of course."

"Thanks, but I don't think I can make it to Idaho right now. You go and have fun. It'll be good for you to get away."

"You always were such a sweet, polite boy, Blakey. Of course, I knew you could always go to Doug's, or I never would have dreamed to make plans with Tracey."

"Don't give it a second thought. Go and have fun. When you get back, we'll come visit."

"I'll look forward to it." Then her voice altered, becoming the cautious voice of a woman who had too often been disappointed. "I heard from Paula yesterday. She sounds a bit better. Maybe."

"Yeah. I'm hopeful," he said. "We'll see."

"You dating that girl who answered the phone?" Aunt Bonny asked, her voice back to its normally blunt, if frail, state.

"Yes, I am."

"Is it serious?"

Blake glanced at Amanda, who was putting on Mara's pink coat. Feeling his gaze, she looked over and smiled. "I think so," he said.

"Good. I like her. She sounds nice."

"She is. I'll see if I can bring her the next time we come to visit."

"I'd like that. Good-bye, then. Tell the kids Grandma loves them. And pray, Blakey. Pray that Paula will see the light."

Blake hung up the phone, forcing a smile.

"What's wrong?" Amanda asked, not fooled.

He shrugged. "I just feel sorry for her. She's been through a lot."

"What was all that about Thanksgiving?"

"Aren't we going to Grandma's?" Kevin piped up from the table where he was scribbling in a coloring book that looked suspiciously new—and about the same size as Amanda's purse.

"Oh, she's going to Idaho instead. But that's okay. We'll have our own feast." He grinned at Amanda, an idea coming to his mind. "We should stop and buy a turkey today," he added. "Give it time to thaw out so I don't burn the outside again like I did last year."

Amanda's forehead wrinkled. "Wait a minute, she told me something about you going to your brother's."

"Yeah, but what she didn't know is that my brother and his wife already have plans with her side of the family—which they made only after I told them I was going to my aunt's."

"Oh. I see."

No, she didn't, not yet, but he would help her. He walked to the table and stared over Kevin's shoulder at the snake he was coloring. "It's really all right. I have some ancient secret family recipes somewhere, and we'll have a great dinner—provided I can find them. Though I think someone left out the sugar in the pumpkin pie recipe. And I never did like the stuffing—whoever heard of stuffing that contains gelatin?" He winked at her. "I'd invite you over, but I know you'll be with your family."

Her eyes narrowed. "Ancient family recipes—are you trying to wangle an invitation to my family's dinner?"

He laughed. "Actually, yes. How else am I ever going to make you introduce your family to me?"

"Hey, you know Kerrianne, you've met Mitch, and Tyler's on his mission. There's only my parents left."

He met her eyes, suddenly serious. "Exactly."

She smiled. "Okay, consider yourselves invited."

"Don't you have to ask someone?"

"No. Believe me, my mother will be only too happy to have visitors. But I warn you, before the evening is over, she'll have you choosing a date for our wedding."

Blake grinned. That would suit him just fine. "You're too sensitive," he said. "I'm sure your mother is just as level-headed as her daughter."

Amanda started laughing and shaking her head. "That," she said, "is exactly what I'm afraid of. You don't know what you're getting into."

Chapter Twenty

Paula Simmons felt as though her head was going to burst. A week. It had been an entire week since she had tried to visit her children at Blake's apartment. Tomorrow she would have her first drug test.

"I need to know if it'll work," she said to Loony, holding the bottle in her hand. "I did some research and found that some drugs show up even after two weeks or more."

He shrugged. "You can never be 100 percent certain, but it should do—especially since you've been clean all week." His gray eyes in the acne-scarred face met hers. "But are you going to be able to hold off?"

Of course she could hold off. It wasn't like she had a problem. "I'm fine," she said shortly. Her head pounded in her skull, echoing the lying words.

Actually, she had done well since receiving the restraining order, staying home over the weekend, drinking only the barest amount of liquor to get through the rough spots. At first it had almost been easy, but by Monday simple abstinence had transformed into this terrible yearning, this pounding headache. Her hands shook, and she felt like screaming and crying all at once.

Yesterday, when she'd gone for her supervised visit with her children, the acute cravings had momentarily fled. Mara, dressed in an adorable pink playsuit, had been absolutely loving in the intense, temporary way of babies the world over. Paula had delighted in Mara's hugs and smiles—until her interest was stolen by the toy Paula had brought for her. Even then she had enjoyed watching her daughter play.

Kevin had spoiled it by being more aloof. He politely accepted the peanut butter crackers she gave him, but his eyes had watched her every move, as though he *knew* she was faking and that at any moment she would explode.

What he couldn't know was how very close she had been to doing just that. Or could he sense it after all? Her head hurt so terribly, and the pressure was so blinding that she was amazed she could hold it in at all, that a scream didn't escape her throat each time she opened her mouth. For a brief moment, she'd wanted to slap Kevin. Slap him as hard as she could to alleviate her suffering. The thought frightened her. She'd never hit him before. Yelled, yes. But never hit.

Staring into his blue eyes, she wondered for the first time in her life if it wouldn't have been better for him if she had given him up for adoption as her mother and bishop had urged. She hadn't been ready to be a mother when he came—wasn't ready now, if she was truthful. But she believed then—still did—that girls who gave up their babies were taking the easy way out. So she ignored her mother, her siblings, her bishop, and even Blake. She'd kept Kevin. From the moment they'd put him in her arms, she loved him—madly, desperately at times, but she'd loved him. His return love made up for the gaping loneliness that constantly preyed on her soul.

But what if she had made the wrong choice for both herself and Kevin?

Remembering her son's expression as he stared up at her, a single tear slipped out of her left eye.

"Hey, there's no need to worry," Loony said, running a hand through his very short brown hair, bleached white on top. "I'll get you through this. I have other products. Stronger ones."

Paula gripped the bottle until her hand hurt. "I don't need anything more."

She *could* make it until the test tomorrow. She would do it for her children. For Kevin. Once she passed the test, once she had proven to herself that she didn't have a drug problem, she would take a little something to buoy her spirits and get her through her first day at her new job. Not that she *needed* it, but what was the point of not taking anything when she really didn't have a problem with addiction? Never mind what the social worker thought. Loony's concoctions would help get her through future tests.

In three more weeks, her children would be back with her, the awful days of forced separation behind them for good. They would have been with Blake for forty days by then, as she'd counted out on the calendar, but that would mean little in the long life they would have together. Kevin and Mara loved her, and she was going to have a great life. Blake, of course, would be sorry for his part in separating her from her children. Very sorry. Paula's headache abated slightly at these cheery thoughts.

"Okay, it's your call." Loony shrugged, tucked his lanky figure into his tan, knee-length coat, and left the house.

Paula went into her room and collapsed on her bed, pulling the covers over her head.

Only one more day.

Chapter Twenty-One

Blake couldn't believe he was going to be late to Thanksgiving dinner with Amanda's family. He'd been so pleased with himself for eliciting an invitation to their celebration, but now he wasn't so sure. Mara had woken up cranky and cried on and off all morning. She was probably teething, as Amanda had suggested last night when she watched the children at her place during his study group. Half an hour ago, he had given Mara some pain medication for babies that Amanda had bought, and she had calmed down at least marginally. Unfortunately, she had a blow-out diaper and she'd soiled her outfit—after she'd already managed to spill her bowl of breakfast mush on her first set of clothing.

And Kevin. Blake had to shut his eyes so he wouldn't explode at the colorful drawings Kevin had created with markers on the kitchen wall while he was occupied with Mara.

How easy it would be to get ready without the children around! He'd simply shower, dress, grab a piece of toast, and drive to Amanda's parents' house in Alpine where they had agreed to meet. So simple. So utterly simple. But not now. There was breakfast and diapers and dirty clothes—and a wall to wash. Why hadn't he ever appreciated his freedom before?

"Are you mad?" Kevin asked, looking up from the wet rag Blake placed in his little hand. Tears stood out in his blue eyes.

Blake shook his head. "Not really. I am disappointed, though. You know better than to draw on the walls."

"I was making it pretty." Kevin's lower lip jutted out, quivering slightly with an onslaught of tears.

Blake's irritation vanished. He pulled Kevin into his arms and hugged him tightly. "It's okay, bud. I'll help."

"Mommy says I'm going to live with her in a few weeks," Kevin whispered in his ear. "Do I have to?"

Blake swallowed hard. If Paula got her way, he'd have all the freedom he wanted. He could jump into the truck and take off with no diaper bag or car seat. Kevin's books wouldn't be strewn across the seat. There would be no more walls waiting to be scrubbed down. "Don't you want to live with your mom?"

Kevin was silent a long time. "If Mara goes, yes. But I think we should stay here."

"Then I'll try my best to keep you here." Blake rubbed Kevin's hair. "But even if you go live with her, I'll see you all the time."

Kevin gave him a small, sad smile. "I love my mommy," he said, "but, you know"—his voice became even softer—"I sometimes wish that Amanda was my mom."

Blake didn't know what to say to that. With all his four-year-old wisdom, Kevin seemed to know not only what he wanted but what was best for him.

"Come on, let's leave this wall and go see Amanda. We can clean it later."

Kevin threw down his wet rag. "Okay," he said, brightening. "I hope they like you. 'Cause if they don't, they won't let you marry Amanda."

Blake chuckled. "Amanda's a big girl. She makes her own choices."

Yet even as he said it, Blake worried that they wouldn't like him. What had Amanda told her parents? What would they think about Kevin and Mara? *They can't help but fall in love with the children,* he reasoned, *but they might not be so understanding if they think Amanda will have to deal with them for very long.* And despite all the headache this morning, Blake wanted more than anything for them to stay with him forever.

They had put on their coats and were just about to leave the apartment when his phone rang. He debated whether or not to pick up but decided it might be Amanda calling to see what was keeping him.

"Hello?"

"Hi, Blakey. It's me, Aunt Bonny."

"Happy Thanksgiving," he said, touched that she would remember him. "How's it going?"

"Wonderful. There's some snow here, but everyone is so . . . Oh, Blakey, Paula came. She actually came!"

Blake felt his heartbeat falter. "She did? I can't believe it."

"Me, either. She showed up without telling us she was coming. Got a ride from a friend who was coming to Blackfoot. They have to leave in the morning."

"How does she look?"

"Well, that's just it, Blakey, she looks great. She's talking to Tracey and Hal as though they haven't been at odds for the past ten years. You should see it. She's practically got them eating from her hand."

"Does she . . . is she . . ." Blake stumbled over the words.

"She's drinking some," Aunt Bonny said, "but she says she's passed a drug test. She's acting quite normal."

Blake knew this was good news for their family, but for some reason hearing it only brought a heaviness to his heart. "So do you believe it?" he asked "You think she's really changed?"

There was a silence over the phone during which Blake's heaviness grew. "I know it sounds disloyal," Aunt Bonny said in a near whisper, "but I think . . . well, I've seen this before. I can't help but think it's an act. At one point she was telling us how they plan on testing her every week for a while, and there was this . . . I don't know . . . tone in her voice. More than anger. Maybe disgust, or something. It made me feel like she has something to hide. And she's angry, Blake. Very angry—at you. She's halfway convinced Tracey and Hal that you've dreamed all this up to take her kids away. I told them I was the one who called DCFS, but she keeps saying you put me up to it."

Blake knew how convincing Paula could be. "That doesn't matter," he said, though it did. "What's important is if she's really turned the corner."

"I don't know. I really don't. There's something in her eyes that's not quite right. But I can't tell you how good it's been to see my kids together." Her voice became teary as she uttered these last words, and she sniffed several times before continuing. "I just want to believe so badly that it's real."

"We all do," he said.

"Well, she wants to talk to you," his aunt said. "She's just come into the living room where I am and sees that I'm on the phone. She's walking this way. Do you want to talk to her? She said earlier that she can't unless you agree."

Blake's eyes fell on Kevin and Mara who were crawling in circles around a farm set he had bought them, pretending to be animals. Both still wore their bulky coats. "Okay, I'll talk to her," he agreed, feeling he owed it to Kevin and Mara to see for himself how their mother was progressing.

"Hello, Blake?" Paula's voice came on the phone.

"Hi, Paula. How are you?" At the sound of his mother's name, Kevin froze in his play. Sitting down, he turned his face toward Blake.

"I'm doing really good," Paula said, her voice sugar-sweet, "but I'd hoped you'd call me before now. I told Miss Solos I wanted you to call."

"I've been busy," he said.

"Well, you should be very proud of me. I finally took your advice and made up with my sister and brother. In fact, they've promised to come for the custody hearing to speak in my behalf."

"I see." Blake did see. Whoever was advising Paula must have told her how important her family's support was to her case. "Your mom said you went to the drug testing?"

"Yes." The sweetness evaporated. "That was not fun, Blake." The way she said it held him responsible. "But I passed—and I'll pass next week, too. See if I don't."

"I want you to pass," he said.

She chuckled. "I'll bet. Well, I will pass, whatever you want." Her voice lowered and hardened, sounding more like the woman he knew. "What's more, I won't even have to change my lifestyle to pass."

"What do you mean?"

"Nothing, Blake, absolutely nothing. But I'm going to get my kids back. I'll stop at nothing."

"That's what we all want, Paula," he said, fighting the sick feeling in his stomach. "When you're ready. Meanwhile, they're doing fine. I guess that's what you wanted to talk to me about, isn't it?"

"What? Oh, of course." Her tone softened. "How are my babies? Tell them I miss them so much."

"You can tell Kevin yourself." Blake hesitated before adding, "I'm staying on the line, just so you know." He turned his back on Kevin and went into the living room for the cordless phone he had purchased for just such an occasion.

"I never imagined you could be such a jerk," Paula snapped.

"I just want to sleep," he countered, his voice low. "Kevin doesn't need any more nightmares about being kidnapped."

Before she could respond, he said loudly, "Kevin, your mom wants to talk to you."

Kevin came right over. "Hi, Mommy," he said into the receiver. "Where are you?"

"I'm with Grandma in Idaho. I wish you could be here with me."

"We're going to eat with Amanda."

"Amanda? Was that the lady I talked to on the phone that once?"

"Uh-huh."

"So, is she your uncle's girlfriend?"

"What does that matter?" Blake inserted.

"They kissed once," Kevin said helpfully.

Paula laughed. "I'm glad your uncle finally has a girlfriend. Maybe now he can get married and have some children of his own. You would like some cousins, wouldn't you, Kevin?"

Kevin scrunched up his brow, thinking. "No," he said at last. "I have Mara. And Misty and Benjamin—and Caleb, even though he's so tiny."

"They're friends," Blake explained, not wanting to bring up the fact that DCFS felt it was better for the children to go to a baby-sitter than to be with their own mother.

Paula laughed. "I love you, Kevin," she said. "You and Mara. You know that, don't you?" Blake heard the ring of truth in those words as he hadn't in any of the others she'd said so far.

"I love you too, Mommy." Kevin answered.

"I'd give anything to be with you," Paula added. "But I'll see you really soon."

"Okay."

"Bye, sweety. Give Mara a kiss for me."

"I will."

"Wait," Blake said, taking Kevin's phone. He was more confused than ever. Was Paula's recovery for real? She was obviously angry with him, but she seemed sincere in her desire to make things good for her children. How could Blake know the right way to progress? *I need more time,* he thought. Only time would tell the truth. He would pray for that.

"What?" She sounded annoyed.

"I just wanted—Paula, wouldn't it be better to wait on the custody hearing just a bit? I heard you started a new job. I know how hectic that can be. Finding a sitter while you're gone—that's a huge expense. They really are fine here. I—"

"I need my children," she said shortly. "I will *not* wait. The more I sit back and let it happen, the more justified *those people* will feel in taking them from me."

"I'm only trying to help—to do what's best for them . . . and for you."

"Well, you're not helping, Blake. You're just being a stupid jerk." Paula hung up, leaving Blake shaking his head in frustration.

In the living room, Kevin bent over Mara. "Here's a kiss from Mommy," he said, planting one on her forehead. Mara grinned. Kevin looked up at Blake. "Now can we go to Amanda's? My tummy's hungry."

"Sure. Let's hurry." There was nothing Blake could do at the moment about whether or not Paula would regain custody, but he could try his best to make a good impression on Amanda's family— if he hadn't ruined things by being so late. Picking up Mara, he hurried out to the truck with Kevin.

All the way to Alpine, he worried about what would come next.

Chapter Twenty-Two

A manda was in her parents' living room waiting for Blake and the children. She had debated what to tell her family about her Thanksgiving guests, but in the end, she had left a message on her mother's answering machine, telling her only that she was bringing a few friends. She knew her mother wouldn't mind the extra company. Over the years Amanda had brought a wide variety of friends and all had been welcome. Still, that morning as she carefully dressed in her shimmering black pants and holiday sweater, she wondered what her parents would think when Blake arrived with two children in tow.

Probably that her head needed to be examined.

And they might be right.

She knew they wouldn't be impressed with his current career—that was sure. They'd wonder if she was out on another rescue mission that had resulted in many strange friendships in the past. But it wasn't like that. At least not anymore.

Amanda sighed. True, she was spending a lot of time baby-sitting lately. With work and school, Blake kept busy. She hadn't had a moment alone with him since their date almost two weeks before, though she spent a lot of time with him and the children. Romance had certainly taken a backseat. Not that she didn't love spending time with Kevin and Mara—she did—but she worried secretly that he might see her now as only a friend. Where once that had been her plan, now she wanted him to notice *her* and not her motherly abilities.

Yesterday, she'd had the kids at her house while Blake went to study group. In her journal list of his attributes she had added *will have a better job soon* under the pros and *studies too much* under the cons. And then she sighed. Her evening with Kevin and Mara was good, though, and she'd been almost reluctant to let them go home with Blake. "Make sure he wears his warm pajamas to bed," she'd told him. "And here's some teething medication we went to buy. I think Mara's teething."

"You sound like a mother," Blake had teased, the twinkle in his eyes sending a delicious shiver up her spine.

The truth was at that moment she'd *felt* like a mother. "Well, everyone needs a mother," she'd teased back. "Even you."

There was a noise, and they'd turned to see Kevin watching them from the open door, all bundled up in his hat and gloves, an odd expression in his eyes.

Amanda had knelt down next to him, concerned that her comment might have upset him. "Oh, honey. I only meant that everyone needs some nagging. Especially Blake, since his mommy's in heaven. But I know that no one can take the place of your mother. I just like being with you guys."

Kevin nodded solemnly. Then he surprised her by wrapping his arms tightly around her neck. Amanda found it impossible to speak past the sudden lump in her throat. She'd carried him out to Blake's truck, clipped on his seat belt and waved good-bye, not even missing—at least until later—the good night kiss she hadn't received from Blake.

"Are they here yet?" Kerrianne came in from the kitchen where she had been helping their mother with last-minute preparations for the meal. Amanda was to have been here earlier to help as well, but she'd overslept after a restless night and had been late. Thankfully so, she realized now, since there hadn't been time for questions regarding the identity of her guests.

Amanda spied the blue pickup. "He just drove up now."

"He?" Kerrianne turned an interested face to the window, squinting in the weak sunlight coming through the panes. "But that's . . . hey, it is. It's Blake and the kids!"

Amanda's heart jumped. "Uh, yeah."

Kerrianne put an arm over her shoulder. "You are such a sweetheart. I didn't even think that they might not have some place to go—and I'm their baby-sitter!" She ran to the door, calling to Kevin and Blake before they reached the steps. "Come in, come in! I'm so glad you could come."

Kevin hugged her briefly before running past her to Amanda. "Did you bring your purse?" he asked brightly.

Amanda grinned. "Of course. But let's wait a bit, okay?"

"Okay."

"Here, I'll help you off with your coat," Amanda said to Kevin, not meeting Blake's eyes. "Just put it here on the couch with the others."

Blake greeted Kerrianne, who immediately took Mara from his arms, and then turned to Amanda. "I'm sorry I'm late," he said.

Amanda lifted one shoulder. "It's fine. We're just putting the food on the table now."

An awkward silence fell between them. They'd become accustomed to exchanging a hug each time they met, but Amanda, acutely aware of her sister's interested stare, didn't move toward him.

"Come on," Kerrianne urged, tossing Mara's coat onto the couch. Blake added his own to the growing pile.

Amanda and Blake followed Kerrianne into the large kitchen. In the attached dining room, her family was beginning to gather around the banquet-sized table. Her mother was setting down a gelatin salad, Mitch lounged against the wall talking to Adam, who held a guitar in his hands, and Kerrianne's older two children were already seated. Only her father and the new baby were nowhere in sight.

Misty bounced on her chair for joy when she spied Kevin. "Oh, good! Come over here. We have room." She raised her voice. "Grandma, I want him to sit by me!"

Her mother, Amanda noticed, wasn't listening. Her eyes were fixed on Blake and the children. "Amanda," she said, her smile showing too many teeth to be natural, "aren't you going to introduce us?"

Amanda didn't like the gleam in her mother's blue eyes, the one that so clearly radiated disapproval over Amanda's choice in men. Divorce simply wasn't in Jessica Huntington's vocabulary, and Kevin and Mara's presence could only mean a divorce.

"Mom, this is my—uh, friend, Blake Simmons. Kerrianne is carrying Mara." At the sound of her name, Mara giggled and held out her arms to Amanda. Grinning, Amanda took Mara from her sister. "And that big boy over there with Misty is Kevin." Amanda didn't explain further, taking some obstinate kind of pleasure in keeping their familial relationship a secret. "Blake, this is my mother, Jessica Huntington."

"Nice to meet you," Blake said, crossing the room and holding out his hand. "Now I see where Amanda gets her looks."

"Oh." Her mother shook his hand, a slight flush covering her cheeks. Amanda studied her mother, trying to see her from Blake's perception. She had short blonde hair teased in the latest style, and her makeup was artfully applied. Though she had gained weight in the past few years, a careful choice of clothes, like the flowing yellow dress she wore today, minimized her size. She was, Amanda thought, a striking woman at fifty.

"Except for the eyes," Blake added. "They're blue instead of green."

"My dad has green," Kerrianne volunteered. "Manda and Tyler take after him. Of course, you won't be seeing Tyler yet. He doesn't come home from Bolivia until January."

"Hey, Blake." Mitch came around the table and shook his hand. "Good to see you again."

Adam was right behind Mitch, offering his hand. "You look different without your uniform," he commented.

Blake did look nice, Amanda noticed belatedly. He wore black dress slacks and a white dress shirt covered by a black and brown sweater with diamond designs, giving him the casual air of a successful businessman.

"Grandma," Misty said, her voice annoyed. "Didn't you hear me? I said I wanted Kevin to sit by me. We *always* eat together."

Jessica looked from her children to her son-in-law and then to her grandchildren, becoming aware that everyone in the room seemed to know Blake and the children except for her.

"So, Blake, you decided to brave the lion's den and eat with us," Mitch said, seating himself at the table.

"Lion's den?" Blake asked. "You got it all wrong. *My* kitchen is the lion's den. At least the mess resembles it most days."

"Kids have a way of making life interesting." Adam strummed a chord on his guitar before placing it carefully up against the wall. Kerrianne put her hand in his and led him to a chair.

"This is certainly a beautiful house," Blake commented, his eyes pausing on the thick crown molding surrounding the top of the wall where it met the high ceiling.

Mitch snorted. "It's a palace compared to my apartment."

Kerrianne laughed. "Or even compared to my house."

"How long have you known Blake?" Jessica asked Amanda, picking up a fork and setting it closer to a plate.

"Yes," Mitch said, leaning back in his chair lazily. "Tell us, Manda. How long have you known Blake?" His eyes glinted with amusement. Amanda knew all too well how happy he was that she had diverted their mother's attention from his single status.

"Three weeks." Amanda said, glaring at her brother. "Are we about ready to eat? I'm starving."

Jessica tore her gaze from Blake. "As soon as your father gets here," she said. "He's in his office on the computer."

Adam chuckled. "Another rare stamp is up for auction on eBay," he explained. "He's waiting to see if he wins the bid."

"My father collects stamps," Amanda explained unnecessarily. "He's always holding us up."

"That's a relief." Blake moved closer to her. "I was worried that you'd be waiting on me. We had a . . . a difficult morning."

"It's her teething, isn't it?" Amanda asked, glancing at the baby in her arms. "Kevin doesn't seem to have a cold."

He nodded. "Yeah, it's the teething—and something else you don't mention when you're about to eat. Plus, did you know Kevin's a budding artist? My kitchen wall may need a new coat of paint."

"Oh, no," Amanda commiserated. "Well, at least the teething pains should be okay once the teeth break through." She pulled up Mara's lip and examined the upper gums in front where they looked redder than normal and slightly swollen. Blake leaned in to look with her, and Amanda could smell his now-familiar cologne. In fact, all her senses were suddenly working overtime. As she released Mara's mouth, Blake took her hand, and for a brief, intense moment there was no one else in the room but the two of them. Amanda wet her lips nervously.

"Well, I . . ." Jessica eyed their linked hands with a helpless dismay Amanda thought was amusing—given the fact that her mother hadn't stopped matchmaking for her since she'd left high school. "I—I should get your father." She scanned everyone around the table. "Mitchell, you'd better have whatever it is poking its nose out of your pocket in some kind of cage before I get back. And wash your hands!" With a last despairing glance at Amanda, she fled the room.

"That went well," Mitch said. "Kids, want to pet Hiccup?" he added, taking a gerbil from his shirt pocket. Cooing with excitement, the children scrambled to his side.

Adam went for his guitar. "I think they'll be a minute. Let's sing some songs." When everyone murmured assent, Adam began playing a Christmas melody. Mara kicked to get down, and Amanda let her crawl on the carpeted floor to the other children, seated now around Adam's chair.

"That guitar is his pride and joy," Amanda whispered to Blake. "When he was younger, he was going to be a musician. Now he plays for fun. He makes up all sorts of love songs for Kerrianne—and she loves it."

Blake raised an eyebrow at the way Kerrianne draped herself over the back of Adam's chair as he played. "Maybe I should start playing an instrument if it gets that kind of result."

"Maybe you should," Amanda said, letting a sound of exasperation escape her throat. "You could work it in sometime after midnight when you're finished with school. Or maybe squeeze it in every morning before you wake the kids to take them to Kerrianne's."

Too late Amanda realized her frustration was showing. Before she could apologize, his hand tightened on hers, and he led her into the kitchen around the wall that partially separated the two adjoining rooms.

"I know life is crazy right now," he said in a low, intense voice, "but it won't always be like this. I—I don't know what else to say. Only, Amanda, I've never felt this way about a woman before. At night I lie awake worrying that we'll miss our chance because of the chi—"

"Shhh." She put her fingertips over his lips to stop the flow. "It's okay. I'm sorry. I didn't mean—I know it's a lot to deal with right now. It's frustrating sometimes, but I honestly don't mind."

"I talked to Paula this morning." Briefly, he described the call, his aunt's reservations, and his own gut feeling of unease. "If Paula gets back the children, it would leave us more time, but . . ." He left the sentence unfinished, a pained look in his eyes.

"She won't get them back. At least not until she's ready. As for the children, I love their being with you. That's not a . . . a problem for me in our relationship." Amanda fell silent. How could she confess to a man she'd only known for three weeks that she wanted not only to be with him but that she wanted to be a mother to Kevin and Mara—children who weren't even his? The idea that she could feel this way was insane. Her mother had every right to think she'd lost her mind.

Blake came closer. She lifted her face to his, fully expecting a brief peck on the cheek, but his lips found hers, gently at first and then with more pressure. Amanda found she didn't want their kiss to end, never mind that her family was on the other side of the wall.

A gasp and a low clearing of the throat pulled them apart. "Mom, Dad," Amanda said, trying to catch her breath. She didn't look either of her parents in the eyes, focusing instead on Kerrianne's new baby lying asleep in her father's arms. "We didn't hear you."

"Obviously," her father said dryly. Then he grinned his customary irrepressible grin that vaguely reminded Amanda of Blake's smile. Big, balding, and blind without his thick glasses, her father hadn't aged as well as her mother, but what he lacked in looks, he made up for in humor and friendliness. This was part of what made him so successful at the PR firm where he was a top executive.

"This is my father, Cameron Huntington," Amanda said, knowing her face must be bright red.

Cameron nodded. "That I am. And you there, mauling my daughter, must be Blake. My wife told me you were here." His voice was deeper than expected when one first looked at him. It was a voice that inspired trust and reason. One that could sing, too—and not just the many lullabies Amanda had enjoyed as a child. Cameron was particularly good at hymns and had sung in the church choir for many years.

"Blake Simmons," Blake confirmed, offering his hand. "Nice to meet you, Cameron."

"You, too." Cameron shifted baby Caleb to his other arm and shook Blake's hand. "At least I think I'm glad," he added, giving them a wink. With a hand on Blake's shoulder, he led him into the dining room. Following them, Amanda sensed her mother's eyes on her and began to feel guilty. She should have called to warn her, to explain the situation. For all Jessica's eccentricities, she was a wonderful mother and didn't deserve the worry.

"It's about time, Dad," Mitch said, looking up from the furry animal in his hands. "We could have used some help here setting up the table."

"Hey," Cameron hefted the baby, "I was doing my share watching little Caleb here." Kerrianne reached for her baby, but Cameron waved her off. "Still my turn," he said, sitting at the head of the table. "You can have him after the prayer when it's time to dig in." Amanda laughed with her family, knowing her father's love for a good meal.

"Mitchell, I said out!" Jessica stared at the gerbil.

"Aw, Mom. He's so cute." Mitch's words were echoed by Kevin and Misty. Even two-year-old Benjamin said, "Coot, coot."

"You've been telling me that for twenty-three years," Jessica said, "and my answer has always been the same. Not at the table. Now, children, to the bathroom to wash your hands. No, not you,

Benjamin, I'll clean yours at the kitchen sink. Hurry now, kids. Scrub hard. And Adam, since Grandpa here has his hands full, would you get the turkey from the warmer? It's carved and ready to go."

Amanda smiled as she watched her mother take charge. She'd always been the backbone of the family, getting all of them where they needed to go at the right time. Amanda picked up Mara. "Mom, do you still have that old high chair you used for Benjamin?"

Jessica's face was impassive. "It's in the storage room. Mitchell will go get it since he's going to find a cage and wash his hands."

Sighing loudly, Mitch left the room, mumbling something about "germ-frightened humans" to his furry friend. Amanda sat down at the table, still holding Mara. Blake settled in the seat beside her.

"So, did you get the stamp?" Adam asked, coming in from the kitchen with a huge platter of sliced turkey.

Cameron's round face lost its grin. "Nah. A guy beat me out at the last minute. I was just about to put in a bid, but I couldn't get it in quick enough." His chin dipped toward the baby. "Had my hands kind of full."

"Well, I'm sure you'll get the next one." Adam took Benjamin from his grandmother. "I can wash his hands."

"Ah, but this might have been once in a lifetime chance," Cameron said wistfully.

"So's holding that baby," Blake put in with a grin. "I can see that just from the three and a half weeks I've had Mara. They grow and change so fast."

Here it comes, Amanda thought.

"Only three weeks?" her mother asked. "Where was she before that?"

"I—you didn't know?" Blake looked at Amanda, who gave him a sheepish grin.

"She wasn't home when I called," she explained.

Kerrianne burst out laughing. "Now I understand why Mom's

acting so weird! Mom, this is Blake, the guy I'm baby-sitting for. Kevin and Mara are his cousin's children."

Cameron boomed a laugh. "Oh, that's funny! And we thought—" He broke off as Jessica placed a hand on his shoulder. "Well, never mind what we thought."

"So you're the repairman?" Jessica asked, relief in her voice.

Kerrianne slapped her leg. "You thought they were romantically involved, didn't you?"

There was a sudden silence in the room. Then Cameron said, "Well, you usually are romantically involved when you start kissing in your parents' house."

Kerrianne's eyes widened, and her mouth gaped open. "You were kissing? Kissing?"

"Well," Amanda began.

"I never would have thought," Kerrianne looked at Blake. "No offense, but she usually goes for the corporate type, you know what I mean? I guess she finally succumbed to your good looks."

"I guess," Blake said, looking uncomfortable. Amanda felt her heart sink. Over the past week, they had talked a lot about his frustrations at the repair shop, and she knew his job was a sore point with him.

"Well, he won't always be a repairman," she put in hastily. A glance at Blake revealed that she had said the wrong thing.

"It's an honest job," he said.

"I didn't mean—"

"What she meant," Adam said, coming from the kitchen with Benjamin, "is that after next month, Blake'll have only one semester left before finishing his degree in business management."

"That's what I meant," Amanda said with relief. "Though it wouldn't matter to me if he stayed in repairs." Even as she said it, she saw the question in Blake's eyes. Would she really have been attracted to him if he hadn't other ambitions? She couldn't say.

Maybe she wouldn't have because then he wouldn't be the Blake she had come to know.

"He's graduating soon?" Kerrianne looked from one to the other, amazed. "Amanda, why didn't you tell me? Or you, Blake?"

"It never came up," Blake said, as Amanda shrugged.

"And Adam—you knew." Kerrianne frowned at her husband, her hands on her hips.

"You didn't?" Adam asked.

Mitch came into the dining room with the high chair, followed by Kevin and Misty. "What did I miss?" he asked. "You're all staring at each other like something big happened."

"Nothing," Jessica said. "Did you get rid of that animal?"

"Yes, but you hurt her feelings, I'll have you know."

"Something did happen," Kerrianne put in. "Blake is graduating in the spring in business management."

Mitch arched a brow. "Cool. I'm impressed. Congratulations!"

"That's not all," Kerrianne said with the tone of one who has an important secret. "Amanda and Blake were *kissing*."

Mitch shrugged. "About time." When Kerrianne wasn't looking, he winked at Amanda and gave her the thumbs-up signal.

Cameron laughed. "Let's get this show on the road before I starve to death. Everybody, take your seats."

Mitch set the high chair between Blake's chair and the foot of the table where their mother would sit. Amanda passed Mara to Blake, who settled her in the chair. "Bk! Bk!" the baby said.

"She's started saying my name," Blake explained.

Amanda smiled, and she saw her mother's face soften as she sat down next to Mara.

"Okay, this is how it works," Cameron said. "You say one thing you're grateful for before I say the blessing on the food. No long-windedness, please. The turkey is getting cold. I'll start, and then we'll go around the table to my right."

"Benjamin, come sit by Mommy," Kerrianne said to her son who was perched on the edge of Misty's chair. "No, you can't stay there. There's a chair here between Mommy and Daddy. I'll need to cut your meat." Benjamin capitulated with good grace.

"I'm thankful for all of you, of course," Cameron began, "and for the gospel. But today I'm also thankful for—"

"I thought we were supposed to be brief," Mitch muttered.

A brief scowl crossed Cameron's face, but he continued without response. "Today I am most thankful that the growth I went to the doctor for turned out to be benign so that I can be here to watch you all for many days to come."

The jovial mood at once took a somber tone. Amanda could tell that neither of her siblings or her brother-in-law had heard this before, either.

"Misty, you're next," Cameron said. "What are you grateful for, child?"

"I'm grateful to come to see you and Grandma today. Okay, you go now, Kevin."

Kevin, suddenly shy, looked to Amanda seated next to him. "Last night Kevin colored a picture of what he's thankful for," she said, holding up a drawing retrieved from her purse where he had put it the night before. The crayon scrawl showed a tall figure with two smaller ones. "He's grateful to be with Blake." She handed the picture to Blake, touched at the obvious wish in the boy's heart.

"Your turn, Amanda," her father said.

What should she say? The truth was that she was grateful for Blake, too—and the children. Her life had gone from rather ordinary to very exciting. But she couldn't say that here. Her feelings for Blake were too deep and personal . . . and too new to share. "I'm probably most grateful for how well my job's working out," she said instead. "Many teachers have a more difficult time their first year."

All eyes turned to Blake. "I'm very grateful to a fire in a stove," he drawled, fixing his eyes on Amanda's. She felt heat seep into her face.

"Well, what's that supposed to mean?" Mitch grumbled good-naturedly. "Is it just me, or does a guy get a little education and start speaking in tongues?"

Continuing to look into each other's eyes, Blake and Amanda ignored him.

At the foot of the table, Jessica cleared her throat. "My turn. I'm grateful Tyler's almost home from his mission. I miss having all my children together."

Next to her, Mitch straightened. "Well, I'm grateful I've changed my major to zoology and that most of my old credits will still count." He smiled at Blake. "I was going to graduate in April like you, but now I'll have to wait until the end of summer term—if I cram in a few extra classes." A murmur of approval ran through the group.

Now it was Adam's turn. For a moment he said nothing and then, "I am grateful today for my testimony of the Church and for the sacrifice of my Savior. Lately, I've felt as though I'm finally getting to know Him and really comprehend the love He has for me and my family." His eyes met Kerrianne's over the head of their small son seated between them. Amanda felt a stab of envy at their relationship, which to her was the epitome of what a family should be.

"It's your turn, Benjamin," Cameron said.

"Amen," the two-year-old pronounced, eyes glued to the platter of meat. Everyone laughed.

"Well, I'm grateful for our new baby," Kerrianne said next. "Caleb has reminded me how close heaven really is."

"Very good," Cameron said, nodding his head in agreement. "Now that we've waited enough time so our once-hot turkey is only marginally warm—the way we apparently like it—I will now say the blessing." Around the table, heads bowed.

The dinner itself was excellent, and the conversation relaxed.

Still, Amanda felt the occasional odd glance from her mother, though she could not determine the reason for the look. She had expected her mother's worry to vanish upon learning the children weren't Blake's. Jessica did seem to like Blake, and in a few minutes of questioning found out more about him than Amanda had learned in the first two weeks she'd known him. Yet Jessica didn't begin linking their names together or make innuendos about a possible future together. This confused Amanda—and she wasn't the only one. Mitch and Kerrianne exchanged several questioning glances when their mother wasn't looking.

After the meal began to wind down, their mother asked, "So, Mitchell, are you dating any nice girls yet?"

"Oh, no," Mitch said with a groan. "Back to that are we? I promise you, Mother, if I ever start dating *nice* girls, I will bring them home to meet you."

"Well, what does that mean?" Jessica asked, tucking her chin close to her neck and raising her shoulders slightly. "You'd better not be dating any other kind of girl."

Amanda shook her head. "He's teasing, Mom. He can't get a date that likes animals, that's all. Don't we have dessert? I hope everyone saved room."

Jessica stood. "There's plenty of dessert. Five kinds of pie, in fact. Amanda, if you'll give me a hand in the kitchen?"

Great, Amanda thought. *That means she wants to say something privately about Blake.* Aloud, she said. "Sure."

Once in the kitchen, Jessica began setting pies on two serving trays. "He seems nice," she said quietly.

Amanda relaxed. "I think so," she agreed. "And Kevin and Mara are adorable."

Jessica's lips tightened, as though trying to prevent words from escaping. They came anyway. "That's what I'm worried about," she said. "Are you dating him because you like him or because you like the sense of family he represents with the children?"

Amanda set a pie on the tray nearest her. "What are you saying, exactly?"

"Nothing. It's just that all your life, you've tried to rescue people the way Mitchell rescues stray animals. I would hate to see you make a decision driven by your desire to help him with the children—or to mother them."

Amanda shook her head. "I can't believe this, Mom," she said, keeping her voice low so those at the table wouldn't overhear. "You always say I should forget Tanner and find someone else, and when I finally do, you think I'm in it for the children?"

"Isn't that true? From what I've heard Kerrianne say about the way you two met, it *was* about the children."

Amanda thought for a moment about the facts she had shared with her sister. Yes, she had made it seem as though she was only interested in Kevin and Mara. In fact, that was what she'd tried to tell herself at the beginning. Yet there was much she'd left out of her story—the electricity between them, the pounding of her heart at his closeness, the way his grin made her feel so incredibly happy. Yes, she admired him because of his willingness to care for Kevin and Mara, but that was only a small part of it.

Wasn't it?

Could it be the electricity had occurred because she knew he was safely out of her reach? No, it couldn't! She wasn't imagining the way she felt when their eyes met. How could she explain this to her mother?

"Mom," she said. "I don't know where my relationship with Blake is going, but I do know I've never felt this strongly about any man I've ever met."

"Not even Tanner Wolfe?"

"Not even Tanner Wolfe."

Jessica smiled, though her eyes remained cautious. "Well, then," she said. "Maybe I'll have to ask him what he's doing next spring. He'll be out of school then, and spring weddings are very popular, you know."

Amanda grinned and shook her head. This was more like her mother. "Maybe you should just let *me* take care of that. Mitch, however, really could use some matchmaking."

Yet as they returned to the dining room together, Amanda worried that maybe there was a grain of truth in her mother's worry. Not from her side, of course, but from Blake's. Was it possible he liked Amanda only because of what she felt for Kevin and Mara?

Chapter Twenty-Three

Amanda knew it was probably a stupid thing to do—wasting a Saturday morning to drive up to Salt Lake and search for a woman she had never met. But Blake was so worried about the children that she felt someone *had* to do something. Anything. So she'd looked in her planner and found an indentation of the address Paula had given her to pass on to Blake. With very little effort, she was able to re-create the address and drive to Salt Lake.

More than two weeks had passed since Thanksgiving. Weeks that Amanda had thoroughly enjoyed. Each day after teaching, she'd found herself at Kerrianne's playing with the children for a few hours, usually leaving just before Blake arrived. She'd wanted to start taking them home, but by silent agreement, she and Blake had left the arrangement alone. There was no sense in changing their schedule if they were to be returned to their mother at the coming hearing. Though the social worker was confident of the outcome, Blake remained worried, and his fear made Amanda worry, too. She had done a lot of research on the Internet and had learned that for all the ways authorities had invented to test for drug usage, there was always some degenerate or money-hungry person coming up with a way to try to beat the system.

She and Blake were in limbo, really, existing only day to day. There was no talk of their future, though Amanda was falling further each day for Blake—despite not being able to spend much time with him because of his schedule. She had to be content with snatched moments, phone calls, and weekends under Kevin's watchful eyes. They had even celebrated her birthday at a kid-themed pizza restaurant, where Blake and the kids had given her a beautiful silver bracelet.

Her relationship with the children, however, had blossomed. She learned that Kevin loved macaroni and cheese and anything containing peanut butter, but he wouldn't touch lasagna and always left half his tuna fish sandwich on the plate. That he liked watching *George Shrinks* but hated *Teletubbies*. She knew Mara had finally stopped eating paper bits on the floor but couldn't resist anything resembling a button. That she'd gobble cooked spinach, potatoes, or applesauce, but turned her face away at carrots and squash—or anything else suspiciously orange. Amanda read to them, played games with them, and sang to them.

Logically, she knew she shouldn't do any of those things, that she shouldn't develop a relationship with them. If they went to live with their mother, their absence would cause her a lot of endless pain. But she couldn't bear *not* to fill their blatant needs. They loved her, she knew. And she loved them.

"Ah, here we are," she said aloud, pushing aside her disquieting thoughts. She came to a stop at the address, wrinkling her brow at the unkempt lawn and run-down house. From Blake's description, this was where he had taken the children to see their mother for the so-called "lunch."

Amanda took a deep breath and walked to the house, noting the scraggly grass beneath a light layer of snow. An old mitten and a milk carton were wedged in the dried weeds lying against the side of the cement porch. Her knock wasn't answered, so she rang the bell. Once. Twice. At last the door opened to reveal a thin, shaggy-haired man about her own age, rubbing sleep from his eyes. "I'm sorry," she said, "but I'm looking for Paula Simmons. I really need to talk to her."

The man shrugged. "She ain't here. She don't live here."

"Oh, do you know where she lives?"

His close-set brown eyes narrowed. "You a friend?"

"No. I—it's about her kids."

"Oh." His lips briefly turned upward in a smile. "Cute kids."

"Yes, they are."

"You a social worker?"

Amanda shook her head hurriedly. "Oh, no. I'm just a friend of her cousin's. The one who's watching her children."

"Oh, that jerk."

"Not really. He's just trying to help. He wants to do whatever he can to get Paula . . . uh, to see that they're all happy." Amanda stopped talking, seeing this man didn't really care enough to listen. He was staring out blankly into the street behind her. "Anyway, do you know where I can reach her?" She was beginning to have second thoughts about coming here. Maybe she should have talked to Blake first. At least he could have found Paula's address for her.

The man nodded. "Works at an auto repair shop. Doubt they're open since it's Saturday. So she's probably home still sleeping." His pointed glance left her no doubt that he'd much rather be pursuing the same course.

"You don't have her home address?"

He sighed. "Okay, okay. I got her address inside somewhere. Come in a minute. You look like a nice lady, so I'll give it to you. But don't bug her, okay? And don't tell her I gave you her address."

"Sure. Great. Thanks." Amanda waited in his small front room as he disappeared somewhere. She took in the tattered couch, the stains on the rug. The obvious remnants of several meals.

"I haven't cleaned up yet today," the man said, reappearing at her elbow in much less time than she'd expected. "Here's the address."

She smiled. "Thanks. I really appreciate it."

"No problem."

Breathing a sigh of relief when she was finally back in her car, Amanda pulled out of the driveway. The interior of the car was cold again, and she flipped on the heat.

What am I doing? she asked herself. She didn't even know what she would say to Paula.

The address was only five minutes away, but the houses were nicer here and newer, if still small. Amanda double-checked the address and shut off her engine. The clock on the dashboard told her it was after ten. Still plenty of time to be at Blake's by noon. They were going out for a little shopping, then dinner, followed by a trip to the Christmas tree lot. Amanda already had her fake tree up, but Blake wanted a fresh one.

A slender blonde woman in sweat bottoms and a T-shirt opened the door. Her hair was too short and her face worn, but she was smiling. A young, dark-haired boy in a sweat suit was behind her, wrestling on the carpet with a puppy.

"Is Paula Simmons here?" Amanda asked.

"Yeah. She's sleeping." She gave Amanda a once-over and apparently deciding she was harmless, she continued. "Come on in. I'll go wake her up."

"Mom, aren't we going?" the boy asked, brown eyes looking at them in disappointment.

"Sure. You can go on outside and warm up your muscles. I need to get my sweatshirt on anyway. It's cold out—even for running." The boy grinned and then headed for the door without meeting

Amanda's eyes, ducking around her and darting outside, the puppy hot on his heels.

Amanda shut the door behind them. This place, she noticed, had an entirely different feel from the last house. Though sparsely furnished, it was clean and smelled good. *And it has a puppy,* she thought. *Kevin would love that.* Of course, the idea of Mara crawling around on the same floor as a puppy who was still likely potty training didn't bring a pretty picture to her mind. Even so, Mara would adore tugging its ears.

The woman returned in less than a minute, pulling on a sweatshirt over her head. "She's coming. Go ahead and have a seat." With that, she was gone.

Amanda waited on the green couch for a full five minutes before a tiny figure wearing a short-sleeved pajama top and shorts appeared from the hallway. The unlined, heart-shaped face was covered by a long mass of flyaway blonde hair, whose dark roots clearly showed the blonde came from a bottle and not nature—most likely an in-home job at that. Kevin's innocent blue eyes stared out at Amanda, freezing her for a moment in time that felt like an eternity.

"Do I know you?" the woman asked, her voice full of attitude. This was the woman who had been late for almost every visiting session with her children and the social worker and who hadn't even bothered to show up the last time. Amanda remembered how Kevin had taken in her absence stoically, not once revealing his true feelings. She and Blake had taken him out for ice cream when Erika returned with him and Mara that day. Double scoop.

"Well?" the woman asked. "Do I know you or don't I?"

Amanda stood. "No. Well, we talked once on the phone. At least I think it was you. You have Kevin's eyes. Or he has yours, rather."

Paula relaxed visibly. "You must be the girlfriend." She plopped down on one end of the couch, bringing her feet up under her.

"Well, Blake and I *are* dating." Amanda sat down on the other end of the couch. She shook her head. "I can't get over how much Kevin looks like you. His hair's a bit different color, but his face . . . I bet your younger pictures look just like him."

Paula grinned. "Yeah. We could be twins. My hair used to be white blonde like his, but it kept going darker and darker. I bleach it now. I'm about due for another shot."

"I've thought about highlighting mine, but I never get around to it."

"That's because you're still so blonde." Paula reached toward the end table by the couch, pulling half a pack of cigarettes from the drawer. She pulled one out with her long fingernails. "Having kids makes it go dark."

"I've heard that. My sister has three children—but she was always darker, even growing up." Amanda expected her to light up, but Paula seemed perfectly content for the moment, holding the cigarette between her fingers. Amanda was grateful.

Silence fell as Paula toyed with the cigarette, her eyes unfocused, the lids smeared with old mascara. "Well," she said finally, "why are you here?"

Amanda took a deep breath. "To tell you the truth, I don't really know. I just . . . well, I've spent so much time with your children lately . . ."

"Getting in the way, huh?" Paula snorted. "I knew he'd get tired of them."

Amanda sat a little straighter. "No, it's not that at all. Blake adores those kids. He does everything with them. You should see him with them."

"Well, I can't, can I? Not with that restraining order." Her pretty mouth was a thin, tight line.

"He didn't know what else to do after you came over that night." Amanda stared into the blue eyes. "You really scared Kevin. He—he wanted us to hide under the bed. He told me that's what he always did when you . . . when you did that."

"You were there?" Paula's fingers stilled in her lap.

"Yes. And I—well, I'm an adult and it scared me, too."

Paula recovered quickly. "There was nothing to be scared of!" she said, tossing her head. "Nothing! I'd never hurt my children. I *love* them." Her expression darkened as she added bitterly, "I bet he's told you different."

"On the contrary! Ever since I met Blake, he's always told me— and the kids, too—how much you love them. Always! And he talks a lot about you two growing up. In fact, he says that the Paula he knows would be—" Oops, maybe she'd better leave that part out.

"Would be what?" The blue eyes lost their unfocused stare. "What's he saying about me?"

Only the truth would do. "That the girl he knew would be very upset to see her children in such a situation."

"With a mother who drinks and does drugs, I suppose." Paula's voice showed her scorn.

"Yes." Amanda lifted her chin, unwilling to back down.

Paula untucked her feet and stood abruptly. "You can tell Blake it didn't work. I'm not backing down on this. I'm not waiting. I don't have a substance abuse problem, and I'll do whatever it takes— *whatever*—to get my children back where they belong."

Amanda arose more slowly. "He doesn't know I'm here. I came because he's so worried all the time. He's torn between wanting to believe that you're ready to take back the children and the fear that you aren't."

"He has no right to worry about that. It's not his concern."

"He has every right!" Amanda retorted, her anger sparked. "Every right! You gave him that right when you began leaving Kevin with him so much. You were the one who decided to drink and do drugs. All Blake wants to do is to make sure Kevin and Mara are safe."

"They'll be safe with me! Now get out!" Paula tossed her unlit cigarette to the floor, stomped to the door, and threw it open.

"Please," Amanda said, following her to the door. Crisp December air blew in from outside, dousing her irritation. "Don't. I didn't mean to upset you. I just came because, well, if the situation were reversed, I'd want you to come to me."

"Oh?" Curiosity flared in Paula's eyes. At that moment she looked so young, too young to be the mother of two children, though Amanda knew Paula was a year older than she was.

"I never thought I could care about someone else's children," Amanda hurried on. "You know? I mean, I love my niece and nephews, but I care every bit as much for Kevin and Mara." Amanda prayed for Paula to understand. "I'm so grateful I've had the chance to know them. They are the most precious children, and I can well imagine how heart-broken you've been without them. If I were in your shoes, I'd fight every bit as much as you are fighting to get them back. Because when they weren't with me, I'd wonder if they were okay. If someone was loving them and taking care of them. I actually do that now, you know, when they're with Blake and I'm not there. I worry they might need something that . . . well, that only I can give. It's crazy, I know, when Blake's doing so well with them—and they're even not my children. But that's why I'm here." Amanda wiped impatiently at the tears cascading down her cheeks, thankful that Paula was listening. "I want you to know your children are receiving good care. That Blake loves them like his own—maybe even more so because of his feelings toward you. And the rest of us who know Kevin and Mara also love them—we'll do any-thing we can for them. I wanted you to know that. Especially in case . . . well, in case you did need more time to get things ready and let the children stay with Blake longer. That's all."

Paula studied her for a moment without speaking, the anger

seeping from her face. At last, she gave a little sigh. "You really love my cousin, don't you?"

Amanda lifted one shoulder. "I think so. I don't know. Regardless, it's all true—what I said about him taking care of Kevin and Mara."

"I know Blake takes good care of them. Just like he always took care of me, growing up." She gave a half smile. "He was two years older, you know, and I think I was half in love with him. Imagine that, my own cousin! He was so . . . so good. So fun. So responsible. I looked up to him. He's always been there for me. Except now."

"He's still there for you." Amanda's voice was hoarse with emotion.

Paula shook her head, her smile dying. "I need my kids."

"I understand." If the thought of losing Kevin and Mara was so terrible to her, Paula must be in pure torture.

"Maybe," Paula said softly, holding Amanda with her eyes. "Or maybe you don't. I gave up a lot for those kids. It hasn't been easy."

"I believe that," Amanda said.

Paula seemed gratified at her response. "Mara's name came from the Bible, you know. I was reading it when I was pregnant, trying to stop myself from smoking. I'll always remember that day. There was a lake or something called the waters of Marah with an H on the end. Marah meant bitter. That was how I was feeling then. Anyway, the people couldn't drink, and they'd been without water for something like three days. Then with God's help, Moses made the waters sweet—I think he threw a tree or something into the water—and I knew right then that was what would happen to me. Mara would come and the hardships I was having and all the bitterness I felt at my life would go away."

"And did it?"

Paula's gaze dropped to the carpet. "For a while," she whispered. "For a while after she was born healthy, it did."

"I'm glad." Amanda stepped past Paula and out onto the cement porch, realizing there was nothing left to say. "I guess you'll be there to visit them on Monday." It would be the last supervised visit before the hearing.

"Of course." Her chin went up defensively. "I only didn't go last time because my car broke down."

"Well, thank you for your time." Amanda turned and went down the few porch stairs.

"I'm still going to fight him on Wednesday," Paula called.

Amanda nodded. "I know." She walked to her car. The door to the house slammed as she slid into the relative warmth of her car. She reached to close the door.

"Wait!" shouted a distant voice.

Amanda stood again on the driveway and looked around, wondering who had called out. A neighbor woman to her husband or children perhaps? Sound traveled well on such cold mornings, especially in areas like this where the only trees were new saplings. Then down the street she saw Paula's roommate and her little boy running toward her. Amanda waited.

The puppy reached her first, shaking all over in delight and licking her shoes. When he jumped up on her, Amanda was glad for her jeans. "Down, boy," ordered the child.

"Go on up the street a bit," the woman told him. "Stay where I can see you." When the boy and dog whirled away, she turned to Amanda, tension on her pale, worn face. "Thanks for waiting."

"You wanted to talk to me?" Amanda rested her hand on the top edge of the open car door.

She nodded. "I wasn't going to, but . . ." She shook her head. "You're here about Paula's children, aren't you?"

"Yes. I'm dating her cousin, and I guess you might say I've fallen in love with the children. I wanted to tell her how well they're being cared for."

"I'm glad." The woman looked furtively up at the house, as though making sure they weren't being observed. "The thing is . . . I was trying to help her get them back. That's why I let her stay here. But . . ." Again the wary glance at the house. "But Paula's not ready to get them back. She's not. I know she's thinking that everything's going to fall into place, but she doesn't even have a sitter or money to pay for one. My boy's in school already, and that's when I work. I have a couple weeks off now, and she's asked me if I'd watch her kids until she arranges something. Problem is, I don't think she *will* arrange anything. Or at least anything I'll feel good about. And I have to return to work. I love my boy too much to let anything separate us again. It took me four years to get clean. Four years! And I don't believe Paula can change so quickly. Many nights she doesn't even come home. In the past couple of days, I've been talking to her friends—ones who've known her longer than I have—and it's always the same story. They got stuck with the kids while Paula partied. As much as I need her rent money, I can't sign up for that. My life is just barely straight now. I can't be responsible for Paula's children."

"Did you tell her that?"

"Yes. I told her. She just shrugs me off. She might be planning to quit her job and live off the state. I don't know. But she's not at all what I expected when I let her stay. I thought she wanted to turn her whole life around—she said she did. That's not what I see happening now. She thinks she's getting custody of her kids and then going back to her old ways. That's ridiculous! I think it's going to get a lot worse before she realizes she has to change."

"Would you be willing to say that in court?"

"Are you kidding?" The woman shook her head. "I'm not *that* crazy. I've seen her when she's mad. I can't risk it now. Not with my son in the picture. If you tell anyone about this and it gets back to her, I'll deny it." She looked up at the house, and Amanda did, too. The windows stared back at them like watching eyes. "But I'm not testifying *for* her, either," the woman added. "I made sure I had something else important planned that day with my own lawyer."

Amanda smiled "Well, thank you. It does help to know we're try-ing to do the right thing. What's your name, anyway?"

"Kim Harper."

"I'm Amanda Huntington." She extended a hand. "Nice to meet you, Kim."

"You, too. Good luck."

"Thanks." Amanda had the feeling she was going to need it.

Darkness had already fallen as Blake lifted the Christmas tree into the back of his pickup. Amanda was still debating whether or not to tell him of her visit with Paula, as well as Kim's startling revelation. She didn't see what good it would do, since they couldn't make Kim give a statement, and Blake already felt that fighting for Kevin and Mara was the right thing to do. Telling him, Amanda reasoned, would only worry him more. At least the visit and Kim's words had settled any concern she'd had over keeping Paula from her children.

"There," Blake announced, dusting his hands on his jeans.

"Oh, yeah!" Kevin bounced up and down with excitement. "We got the biggest one!"

"Well, it might look that way from way down there," Blake joked, "but it is the best, that's for sure."

"Mara likes it, don't you, Mara?" Kevin said.

In Amanda's arms, Mara giggled through the hand she had wedged in her mouth. She was much happier this past week since she'd cut her two front top teeth.

"All aboard," Blake said, ushering them into the truck. Inside on the floor were plastic bags stuffed with toys Blake and Amanda had taken turns buying and putting in the truck while the other had waited in another part of the store with the children. Kevin eyed them with unconcealed excitement.

They drove to Blake's apartment and spent a happy hour decorating the tree with a box of ornaments Blake brought in from the garage. Mara fell asleep on the carpet by the time they were finished, and Kevin's eyes were heavy. While Amanda put Mara in bed, Blake helped Kevin brush his teeth and change into his pajamas. Before long the child was fast asleep on the couch, face toward the glittering tree.

Amanda helped Blake wrap the presents. "If they leave, maybe I'll send the presents with them," he said. The sadness in his eyes broke Amanda's heart.

"You don't know the judge will decide in her favor."

"It wouldn't be bad at all if I knew she was clean," he said, "or if I knew she'd continue to let me be in their lives. I would feel a lot easier if she had any intention of raising them in the Church—or any church, for that matter! Anything but the world she seems to be in now."

"We'll fight. We'll buy more time."

His hands paused above a shiny gold bow. "You're going to be there?"

"Of course." She smiled. "I promised I'd be there. I've told you that five times already. I'll meet you there at ten to ten, sharp. I'll just get my substitute started at the school and drive down."

"I really appreciate it. From what my aunt tells me, my other cousins are going to be there supporting Paula."

"But not your aunt?"

"No. She's hopeful, of course, but she says she doesn't feel good about Paula's sudden change. She knows Paula too well. So I'll have my aunt, Doug and Rhonda, and some of their children. And you." His smile sent warmth to her heart.

Suddenly, she was in his arms, and they were holding each other tightly. "It's going to be all right," she murmured.

"I know. Everything has been right since the day I met you. I love you, Amanda. You know that, don't you?"

Tears started in her eyes for the second time that day. How right it was to be with him, and how bright their future seemed. "I love you, too," she said.

From the couch, Kevin sighed in his sleep.

Amanda shivered, trying to push aside the odd feeling of fear as she saw for a moment not Kevin's little boy face but his mother's.

On Sunday Blake and the children went to Amanda's for dinner as they had begun to do more and more often since Thanksgiving. Kevin had taken to saying she was the "bestest cooker in the whole world." Amanda enjoyed every moment with them but couldn't help feeling their time was limited, as though somehow she was only borrowing someone else's life—a life that consisted of a mother, father, and two wonderful, if sometimes cranky and rambunctious, children.

Sunday, Monday, and then Tuesday went by in a blur. Tuesday night Amanda watched the children at her house while Blake was at school. When he picked them up, Mara cried because she was tired and didn't want to leave Amanda. Blake had to play peek-a-boo with her before she laughed and held out her arms to him. Then she wanted nothing to do with anyone else, burying her tired little face in his shoulder.

"I'll see you tomorrow," Blake told Amanda.

The words were loaded. Tomorrow they would know if the children would stay or leave. Tomorrow they would know if it was okay to complain, at least a little, at the difficulty of taking care of someone else's children, or if they would be longing for the children and saddened by memories of the days they *had* complained.

"I'll be there," she assured Blake. She kissed Mara's cheek and bent down to hug Kevin, who was having a hard time keeping his eyes open, despite the nap he'd taken at Kerrianne's that afternoon.

"Bye, Kev," she said. "Don't forget your alphabet letters. You know, to stick on the fridge."

Kevin ran to get them—or stumbled, rather. "They came out of the purse," he informed Blake.

"How did I know?" Blake opened the door and took Kevin's hand. "Good night, Amanda." There was more in his eyes, but now was not the time.

Tomorrow.

Tomorrow they would better know where they were heading, what to plan for.

"Good night." She watched his truck drive into the night.

She slept poorly, tossing and turning with dreams that featured Paula carrying Mara on her hip, a cigarette in her hands, the smoke curling into the baby's face. Next to her, Kevin wrestled on the floor with a puppy that grew so fast it would soon smother him.

Finally, Amanda left her bed and made herself hot chocolate and toast for breakfast, watching through her window as the sun rose slowly and majestically over the valley. The call came at seven-thirty.

"Manda," said a strangled cry.

"Kerrianne? What is it? You sound like you've been crying."

"It's Adam. The police just called. They hit him." Fresh tears slurred her words. "He was on his way to work, just going up to the district building, and some guys in a truck hit him. Oh, Manda, they say it's bad. I've got to go down there. I have to be with him!"

"Where're they taking him?"

"To Provo. Utah Valley. They can't deal with it at the American Fork hospital." She took a shuddering breath. "I'm so afraid."

"I'll be right there. I'll drive you. Call mom to meet us there."

Grabbing her purse, Amanda flew out the door, thankful that because of the biting chill it hadn't snowed and her windshield didn't need scraping.

Chapter Twenty-Four

Blake looked around for what seemed like the hundredth time. Where was Amanda? Any minute now the hearing would begin. He felt for his cell phone and then remembered—again—that he'd had to turn it off when they entered.

"Where is she?" Erika whispered.

He shook his head, eyes wandering again over the courtroom. Next to him was Erika Solos, the social worker. Doug, Rhonda, their oldest daughter, Catharine, and Aunt Bonny sat behind him. Behind where Paula would be seated were her siblings, Hal and Tracey, with their spouses. Kevin and Mara were in another room being watched by one of Doug's children.

"Maybe she won't show up," he whispered hopefully, eyes watching the door. "She doesn't usually."

But today she did.

Blake hardly recognized her. She wore a modest two-piece suit dress that, while slightly large, as though borrowed from somewhere, made her look responsible and confident. Her face wore only the lightest touches of make-up, instead of the heavier colors he was accustomed to seeing on her, and her fingernails were cut short. The biggest surprise was her hair, now a light brown, combed neatly and caught in some kind of a clasp in the back that exposed the heart-shaped face to advantage. Shock reverberated through him. He hadn't seen her hair this color since junior high. The overall image was very appealing. This was not a woman who used drugs. This was not a woman who needed help with her children.

Paula caught his gaze and smirked at him, as though clearly reading his thoughts. He knew at that moment she was faking every-thing.

"We have to get more time," he whispered to Erika, fighting the sinking feeling in his chest. He knew without a doubt that if Paula left here with the children, they'd only be back here in the near future—if she didn't disappear with the children altogether.

Oh, Amanda! he thought, wishing he could feel her comforting hand in his.

The attorney assigned by the court to be the child advocate entered the room, and the court came to order. Aunt Bonny gave Blake an encouraging smile.

The judge was a short, broad-shouldered man with black hair that was only beginning to show a little gray. His large brown eyes looked even larger behind the wide metal-rimmed glasses. "I've read the arguments for both sides," he said without preamble, "but I'd like to hear brief statements. Miss Simmons, you may begin."

Paula stood, politely thanking the judge. Without taking another breath, she launched into a sob story of a woman caught in the wrong place at the wrong time. "My children shouldn't have been taken away from me, Your Honor," she concluded. "I'm very grate-ful to my dear cousin for all his help, but I am able to take care of my own children. And he wants that, too. He knows how much I love them."

The judge turned to Blake. "Is this true?"

Blake stood. "She does love them," he said, "but I'm not convinced . . . I think she needs more time, that's all." He shook his head. "If you could have seen where she left them when she went to jail . . . I'm afraid it might happen again."

"She's passed three drug tests," the judge said, shuffling a few papers. "I do show here, though, that you missed one testing appointment two weeks ago, Miss Simmons."

"My car broke down," Paula said.

Blake shook his head. How many times had he heard *that* excuse over the years?

Erika stood, catching her suit awkwardly on the edge of her briefcase lying on the table. "Your Honor, if I may?"

"Go ahead."

"Miss Simmons also missed the past two weeks of supervised visits with her children. She has been repeatedly late to the other visits and to counseling sessions."

The judge looked at Paula. "Well?"

"My car," she said, hanging her head.

"Your car." The judge shuffled a few papers. "Is this car trouble going to be ongoing?"

"Oh, no, Your Honor," Paula said, eyes large and earnest. "The car shop I work for has fixed it up for me now. It'll be fine. My children will have a ride to wherever they need to go."

Erika raised a finger. "Yes?" the judge asked.

"We are not disputing that the children should be with their mother sometime in the future. What we ask for is a delay to be sure she *is* capable of taking care of them. You'll see in the documents that she has left the older child with Mr. Simmons often in the past for very long periods of time—once for five months. She has also left the children with her mother for extended periods and repeatedly with other friends. Mr. Simmons is the most stable relationship Kevin has. I strongly recommend that the children remain with him until we show for sure that Miss Simmons will act in the best interests of her children. There is the matter of the restraining order to consider."

Paula was shaking her head. "Please?" she raised her hand.

"Go ahead," the judge said. Blake sat down.

"I'm sorry about that. I really am. I was just so desperate to see my kids. It's been so long now that I've been separated from them. Over a month—forty days, to be exact. I recognize that I've not always been the best . . . I mean, I've not always made the right choices, but I've really, really examined myself. I will do what is right for them. I promise."

Behind Paula, Tracey raised her hand. When the judge nodded, she arose. "I'm Paula's sister, and I can testify in her behalf. We haven't talked for ten years, but all that's changed. Before I would have been with the others on this issue, but I know things are different. I *know* it."

Blake jumped to his feet. "With all due respect, Your Honor," he said, "I don't see how Tracey can know so much when she lives in Idaho and has only been talking to Paula since Thanksgiving."

"That's true!" Aunt Bonny said from her chair. "Don't let my daughter's sweet face fool you. I know what Paula's like, and while I want to believe in her, I'm not convinced this change is permanent." She twisted toward Paula. "You only came to see the kids a dozen or so times when I had them for all those months. Blakey came more than you did! And when you did come, you only came because you needed money from me. Admit it."

"I've changed, Mother. Can't you see that?" Paula asked, casting a glance at the judge that pleaded for sympathy.

Aunt Bonny shook her head. "I thought so at first, but now I see only a selfish woman who thinks about herself rather than her children."

"That's not true!" Paula buried her face in her hands, apparently too overcome with emotion to speak further.

"Order!" the judge commanded with an ugly frown. "Please talk only when I ask you to do so."

Blake raised his hand.

"Go ahead, Mr. Simmons."

"I'd like to ask for a hair drug test before she takes the children and then again next month. That's all. Please, Your Honor, I can't—" Blake's throat choked and he couldn't speak further.

Paula lifted her tear-streaked face, looking young and innocent. "Your Honor?"

"You may speak."

"My baby's growing up without me! She turned nine months last week. She'll be walking soon. Taking her first steps." Paula's blue eyes pleaded with him, with the whole room. "I appreciate all my cousin has done—I do! But he works and goes to school full time. My baby needs more care, a woman's care. She needs *me*. Please. I'm ready to be their mother."

Blake was himself nearly convinced at her performance and had to give the judge credit when he only nodded and began questioning everyone in the room. Doug and Rhonda testified to the excellent care Blake gave to the children, claiming that he spent every free moment with them. Aunt Bonny told how he visited each week when they'd been living with her, spending more time with Kevin than Paula ever had. "He was the only one in the family who was willing to be a father to them," she added, giving her son, Hal, a pointed look.

Erika mentioned that Blake had a girlfriend who loved the children as well. A girlfriend, she hinted, who might soon become much more than that.

"And where is she?" the judge asked.

Blake shook his head. "She couldn't be here," he said, as a little part of him died. How could Amanda do this to him? He felt betrayed. "But, please, Your Honor. I love my cousin—every bit as much as I love her Kevin and Mara. I'd never go against her if I thought for a moment it would be okay. I just don't know that." Blake looked at Paula. "Please, Paula. Only a month more. Let's wait until then and see how you feel."

Paula shook her head.

Next, the judge questioned Hal, who testified to Paula's miraculous change. Tracey repeated her earlier statements. Blake wanted to protest that they, who had not been willing to develop a relationship with Kevin and Mara, had no right to have any say in their future.

Finally, the child advocate who represented the children stood at the judge's request. He said that Kevin appeared to love his mother and seemed happy to see her during their visits. He pointed out that Paula had a good place to live and was holding down a promising job at the auto repair shop. Blake had talked with the attorney only once and wished now that he'd had the opportunity to invite him over to see how well *he* did with the children. *Please don't let it be too late,* he prayed.

The judge destroyed that idea when he began to speak. "There is no question in my mind that Mr. Simmons has provided a healthy and stable environment for the children. You are to be commended. However, Mr. Simmons's care is not at issue here. What is at issue is whether or not Miss Simmons has the ability to care for the children, as is her right as their mother. I think she does. She has passed drug tests, gone in for counseling, has found work and a good home for the children. She has also shown herself to be an eloquent young woman."

Paula beamed at the approval, while the ache in Blake's heart and stomach grew.

"However," the judge continued, "sometimes everything is not as it appears on the surface. It concerns me that Miss Simmons missed some of her scheduled visitations, and even more so that her own mother does not think her fit, a feeling until quite recently shared by the rest of the family. So, while today I am returning custody of Kevin and Mara to Miss Simmons, I expect her to continue weekly counseling and urine drug tests for the period of two months, after which I will review this case and determine if any further action is necessary. Meanwhile, I sincerely hope, Miss Simmons, that you prove to both your mother and cousin that you really are ready to take on your responsibilities. I also hope you will continue to allow them access to the children since they have been primary caregivers."

"Oh, I will, Your Honor. Thank you so much!" Paula wiped a tear from her pale cheek.

"Bailiff, when she's ready, you can take Miss Simmons to her children." The gavel echoed the pronouncement with a hearty bang.

Blake was stunned. He'd done his best, but Paula had won. He felt Erika touch his arm sympathetically, but his attention turned to Paula. She was smiling at him. *Maybe this is right*, he thought. *Maybe this time will be different.* He walked slowly over to where Hal and Tracey and their spouses were congratulating Paula.

"Thanks so much for being here," Paula was saying to them.

They nodded and murmured politely when Blake approached, before backing away to give him a private moment with Paula. He tried to smile but failed. "I'll get you their clothes," he said. "I can come over right now, if you want."

She glanced at the others and then back to him. "No," she said in a low voice. "I don't think so."

"What? But, Paula, you told the judge—"

"I told him what I had to," she retorted.

"Then at least let me come next week. I have their Christmas gifts." Tears sprang from his eyes, but he didn't care.

"You stole my babies away, Blake," Paula sneered, her mouth twisting into ugliness. "I won't forgive you for that. You should have been on *my* side."

"I was on *their* side!" he said through clenched teeth, not wanting to make a scene but having to defend himself.

"Blake, you will never see me or the kids again." She turned her back on him.

"Paula," he pleaded.

She whirled on him. "You can say good-bye, and then maybe you'd better go find your girlfriend. Something very serious must have happened to keep her away. I know how she feels about Kevin and Mara."

"You . . . what? I didn't know you knew Amanda."

Paula grinned at his discomfort. "Didn't she tell you? She came to see me on Saturday. Tried to get me to delay the hearing."

"I didn't know that." Despite his disappointment, Blake began to feel marginally better, knowing Amanda had tried to do something for him.

"Too bad it didn't work." Paula turned away, heading for the bailiff.

"I'm sorry, Blakey." Aunt Bonny took his hand in hers.

"I'm sure she didn't mean it—not letting you see the kids," Doug added.

"You heard that?"

"Yeah," Rhonda said. "Too bad the judge didn't."

"Even Paula wouldn't be that selfish," Aunt Bonny said. "It would be too inconvenient."

Still, Blake doubted she'd let him keep Kevin and Mara for any extended stays. "I'd better go after her." He took a step toward the door. "I need to tell Kevin."

Paula was already with the children, making a noisy reunion scene while Tracey and Hal looked on. Mara was enchanted with the attention and began giggling. Kevin smiled when talked to, but his eyes, when they met Blake's, seemed very old and somber.

"Hey, we'll stay right in touch," Blake said, kneeling down in front of him.

"I know," Kevin murmured.

Blake was touched at his trust.

"Come on, honey," Paula said to Kevin. "We're going out to lunch."

"Can Uncle Blake come?" Kevin asked.

"Bk, Bk," Mara cooed.

Blake blinked hard.

"No, he has to get back to work," Paula's eyes dared him to make her a liar. "Besides, Uncle Hal invited us. He's paying."

"Oh."

Blake hugged Kevin hard, slipping his cell phone into the pocket of Kevin's coat. "Call me if you need to," he said. "You remember how to turn it on? And the number?" The battery was newly charged, and while it wouldn't last forever, it was something until he could be sure Paula was going to let him visit.

"I remember," Kevin said with a nod of his head.

Blake stood and kissed Mara, who held out her arms to him. Paula pulled her back. "No, Mara. We're going to eat now. Say bye-bye."

"Bk!" Mara said, wiggling her fingers for him to take her.

"I'm sure the social worker will be able to tell you the address where you can send their things," Paula told Blake.

He watched them leave, Mara in Paula's arms and Kevin sandwiched between her and Tracey. Kevin looked back at Blake and lifted a small hand in farewell. They walked out the glass doors and were gone.

Blake shut his eyes for a moment as the pain rolled through him. Wasn't it absurd to feel this way? After all, life would go on, and he would see the children as much as possible. Visiting wouldn't be the same thing, but he would make it be enough. If Paula really was back on the right track—he so wanted to believe that she was!—then everything would be fine.

Help me, Father, he prayed. Warmth spread through him, giving him the strength he needed to leave the courthouse.

He didn't go back to work—he couldn't. Instead, he bought some boxes and began packing the children's things. Tears flowed freely as he folded Mara's little outfits. When he looked at Kevin's clothes, he found himself remembering when Kevin's clothes had been as small as Mara's. Paula had brought him back before; she probably would again. Why was it so hard this time to let them go?

He thought it might have something to do with Amanda and how together they had made up sort of a family, but he didn't want to examine that idea right now. He was too angry with her for not supporting him at the hearing. She didn't even get to say good-bye to the children.

Yet remembering what Paula had said about Amanda's visit, he called her house, the school, and even Kerrianne's. Nothing. Not even her cell was picking up. Where could she be? But his thoughts couldn't focus on this for long. The house was so quiet, so empty. Suddenly, he did remember feeling this way the last few times Paula had taken Kevin. When he had begun suspecting that she was slipping further and further into substance abuse, it had been increasingly difficult to let him go.

Keep them safe, Father, he prayed. *Please.*

Over the Christmas presents, he paused. No need to pack those. Surely Paula would let him visit the children for Christmas. When four big boxes and a mound of toys piled on the living room floor under the silent Christmas tree seemed to mock his efforts, he called the number Erika had given him. He would ask Paula if he could drop by. She might have changed her mind about his coming already. There was no answer, so he left a message.

He stared into space. Time passed. Thinking again about

Amanda, he willed himself to move, but his muscles refused. He sat on the carpet by the boxes—staring, or sometimes touching the plastic toy piano Rhonda had bought for Mara. Maybe he shouldn't send all the toys and clothes. Maybe they would be back soon. But he didn't want that, did he? He wanted Paula to love them and care for them as a mother should. As much as he had—did.

The phone rang. His muscles rebelled as he sprang for the phone on the kitchen counter. "Hello?"

"Hi, Uncle Blake."

"Kevin! Is everything all right?"

"Yes."

"Did you eat? Was it good?"

"Uh-huh. I got full. But Mara didn't like it. Her cried. We had to buy her formula."

"Is she okay now?"

"Her is sleeping."

"That's good. Where's your mom?"

"In the kitchen."

"Is she . . . okay?"

"Yes. Uncle Hal and Aunt Tracey are talking to her."

Blake knew that meant at least Paula was sober, not celebrating her victory in her usual manner.

"That's good. You call me anytime, you hear? When I'm not here, I'll have the calls forwarded to work. And I'll send you the charger for the phone when I bring your stuff. I'll put it inside that box where you keep your sticker collection. Okay? Until then keep the phone off unless you need to call me." He was grateful now that Kevin had been so curious about his phone and that he had taken the time to explain, to let him practice dialing.

"I want to come home," Kevin said.

"I know. I'm sorry. But give it a shot, okay? Your mom loves you."

Kevin sighed. "I know but—"

A protest and the sound of a brief scuffle came through the phone. "Blake, is that you?" Paula sounded furious.

"Yeah. It's me."

Paula swore so loudly Blake had to hold his ear away from the phone. "I should have known," she finished. "You need to leave us alone."

"I just wanted to talk to you about their clothes."

"Send them in the mail. If you come near us without my permission, I swear *I'll* get a restraining order."

"Paula, please."

"Get out of my life, Blake!"

Blake heard Kevin wail before the phone went dead.

"It's okay," Blake told himself aloud. "She's just mad. When she calms down, she'll know that they need to see me. That is, if she's really clean."

That, of course, was the root of the problem. He knew she wasn't clean.

Blake fell to his knees on the linoleum and began to pray again. He prayed for Kevin, for Mara, and for Paula. He prayed for comfort.

Chapter Twenty-Five

Amanda was living in a nightmare. She wanted to scream and cry at the unfairness of it all, but she had to be strong for Kerrianne, who couldn't stop crying and who clung to her like a small child.

More than half the bones in Adam's body had been broken, the heavy truck squishing his car into so much scrap metal. He was lucky to be alive. They had rushed him into surgery and were still working on him when Amanda and Kerrianne arrived at the hospital. Hours passed slowly—agonizingly so.

Their mother took the children home, except the baby who would need to nurse soon. Mitch and their father arrived. Kerrianne continued to weep.

"He's awake," a nurse finally reported. "You can see him for a few minutes." Her serious demeanor told Amanda there was little hope, but Kerrianne gave a sigh of thanks. She jumped to her feet, placed little Caleb in Amanda's arms, and followed the nurse. Their father and Mitch went along to give Adam a blessing, to urge him back to health—if that was the Lord's will. They returned shortly, both looking discouraged.

Amanda watched the clock on the wall. Since they didn't allow cell phones in the hospital, she used the pay phone to try to call Blake. No answer. *What happened at the hearing?* she wondered.

Kerrianne was gone exactly twenty-nine minutes. When she returned, her face was devoid of color and wet with tears. She said nothing but sobbed into their father's shoulder.

Amanda repeatedly blinked back her own tears, but one freed itself and slid down her left cheek. She held Caleb tightly. Next to her, Mitch reached out and touched Caleb's chubby hand. The baby moved gently in his sleep. Amanda bit her bottom lip hard, until she tasted blood.

Kerrianne's sobs filled the whole room. And still they waited.

Later, Kerrianne went to see Adam a second time, but he didn't wake again. At just after five o'clock, he died. Kerrianne's tears suddenly dried, as though the doctor's pronouncement had been a bucket of sand thrown on a small trickle of water. *Or maybe,* Amanda thought painfully, *she has cried out all her tears and can't cry any more until her body makes new ones.*

"I want to see him," Kerrianne said, lifting her chin, daring the doctor to deny her. Of course, he let her—let all of them. Amanda watched as Kerrianne kissed her husband one last time. She didn't cry. Amanda wondered where she found the strength.

Their father drove Kerrianne home from the hospital. Amanda knew Mitch would go there, too, and their mother with the children. Still stunned and unbelieving, Amanda went home to grab a change of clothes and to call her principal about letting the substitute stay one more day.

Alone, she let out the flood of bitter tears she had been holding in for what seemed an eternity. Adam—gone. Her sister's perfect life—gone. It seemed so unfair.

She thought of Adam singing songs at Thanksgiving, strumming his guitar, the children at his feet.

Never again.

Yet hope was alive. Alive in the temple promises and the life to come. Alive in Kerrianne and the children. Was that how her sister had put an end to her tears? Amanda felt a subtle gratefulness enter her heart—a gratefulness that took away the most bitter edges of her pain.

When she could not shed another tear, Amanda somehow found the energy to pick up the phone and call Blake. She prayed for him to be home, for his news to be good. Right now she could use his arms around her—his and the arms of two innocent children who had not yet faced death.

❄ ❄ ❄

Blake scrambled for the phone where it lay on the kitchen floor by his knees. "Kevin?" he said eagerly.

"It's Amanda." Her voice came across very small, weary.

"Where have you been? Why weren't you at the courthouse?" Even to him, he sounded accusing.

"I tried to reach you," she said. "I left a dozen messages on your cell. They didn't know where you were at work."

"I really needed you there." Blake let his anger show, though in his mind he wondered if her presence could have possibly made any difference in the outcome.

"I couldn't make it. I—"

"You promised! Doesn't that mean anything?"

"Don't be angry, Blake. Listen to—"

"I don't want to listen. I lost the children! Now Paula says she won't let me see them. The judge asked where you were!"

"I was at the hospital."

Fear shot though him—and guilt, too. Guilt that he hadn't been as concerned for her disappearance as he had been for his own suffering. "What happened?"

"Adam's dead."

"No!" he gasped.

"Yes. But suddenly I find I don't really want to talk about it with you." Amanda's voice was cold. "I'm really sorry about the kids."

The phone went dead in his ears.

Blake shook his head. *What a jerk I am!* Paula was right—he should have known only something big would have kept Amanda away. Their once-bright future now lay in ruins, and he had only himself to blame.

He punched in her number, his shaking fingers making several mistakes and forcing him to redial. When the call finally did go through, the phone rang and rang and rang.

Amanda stared at the phone she had just set onto the receiver. Set there gently as though placing a baby in a cradle.

"Oh, Mara!" she whispered. "Kevin!" Fresh tears streamed from her eyes. Not only for the children but for the relationship she'd thought she shared with Blake. She was angry at him for doubting her, for not believing in her. If he thought she was . . . well, like Paula—undependable and self-serving—then he had no place in her life.

I can't think about this now!

Amanda flew to her bathroom and grabbed a toothbrush. From her room, she collected pajamas and a change of clothes. Stuffing everything into her book bag, she raced to the door. Kerrianne needed her now, and Amanda would be there for her sister.

She heard the phone ring and paused in her flight. Blake,

probably. But she was angry at him and wanted to stay that way. The anger buoyed her, gave her strength when she had none left. The anger helped her forget Adam. Forget Kevin and Mara.

What about Blake? Would it help her forget him?

At the dance he'd said "We won't," and she knew now that he had meant they wouldn't lose what they had between them. They wouldn't allow anything to get in the way. That included stubborn pride . . . or anger.

The phone rang again, then a third time. *Let him wonder where I am.* She opened the door, knowing her answering machine would pick up after the fourth ring.

Riiiing.

Dropping her bag, she ran for the phone. "Hello?"

No answer. Had she picked up too late? Was this a defining moment, one she would regret for the rest of her life? Was this the moment they would never be able to get past? The moment she had chosen anger and pride over love and forgiveness?

Then she heard the faint breathing sounds. "Hello?" she said again.

"'The itsy bitsy spider crawled up the water spout,'" Blake's voice sang over the phone, softly and wobbly at first, but gaining strength. "'Down came the rain . . .'"

Tears fell again on Amanda's cheeks, but this time they were tears of relief, of intense gratitude—yes, gratitude to the Lord for giving her Blake, to Blake for trying to make up, and even to herself for reaching the phone in time.

"I love you, Amanda," he said hoarsely.

"I love you, too."

"I'm coming over to talk."

"I'll wait right here."

He hung up, but Amanda held the phone to her heart.

Chapter Twenty-Six

The first three days were easy. Paula felt the same pride in her children as she had felt when they were first born. Friends came to visit and offer support, and Kim watched the children while she was at work. Kevin was helpful with Mara, keeping her smiling when she became fussy.

Things soon changed. At the end of the third day, Kim told her to find another sitter. Paula didn't see why Kim couldn't do her this favor. After all, she was on vacation for the Christmas holiday. And it wasn't like she and her son were going anywhere. She noticed that Kim went out of her way to avoid her children, as though afraid of them, and that *really* bothered her. It wasn't like they were sick or stupid, or even ugly. They were better than Kim's son, who did nothing but boss Kevin around and who laughed when his puppy knocked Mara over. Mara didn't seem to mind, but it irritated Paula.

Paula missed a day of work to find a sitter. When her boss threatened to fire her if she missed another day, she quit. She didn't need that job anyway. Waitressing paid better, and she could do it at night. With her looks, it was easy to get a job—as long as she made sure she didn't put down any references to her old jobs. The managers were jerks at those places, too, and she'd had to quit all of them.

With her new job, she was able to find a neighbor girl to come in to watch Kevin and Mara in the evenings until it was time to put them to bed. Paula figured once they were in bed, Kim surely wouldn't mind watching them while they slept.

A week later, the day before Christmas, Kim cornered her in the kitchen before she left to take her son to the mall to see Santa. "You should have been paid by now," she said. "Where's the rent? You said you'd pay it last week."

Paula hadn't meant to be late, but everything cost so much more than she'd planned, though the state at least helped her with some of it. Others had also been generous, especially the people at Sub for Santa, who had made sure she and the children would have a nice Christmas. "I'll get it for you next week," she told Kim. "It's been tough with Christmas and all. You know I had to quit, and the new job doesn't pay till next week."

"I know you're not paying for Christmas." Kim's eyes held no sympathy. "Didn't you get paid at the old job?"

"Only a little. I—I had to buy formula."

Kim shook her head. "I don't think so. I saw the free coupons you had for that. And what about your tips? I'm sorry, Paula, but I can't let you stay here for free. I need money to pay the mortgage, or you'll have to leave so I can get someone who will pay."

"It's okay for you to say that," Paula retorted. "You get child support. I don't."

Kim shrugged. "Look, you had a good place for those kids. You could have let them stay there until you had some money—and a plan."

"I have a plan. Besides, that stupid cousin of mine wouldn't let me see them!"

"Whose fault is that? From what I saw, he was willing to work out anything. You're the one who went over there and made a scene. In fact, if you let him see the kids, I bet he'd even come up with your rent money."

Tears began in Paula's eyes. "Why are you being so mean? I thought you of all people would understand the importance of being with your children."

"Your tears won't work on me," Kim said, her face rigid. "I let you stay here, I've done what I feel I could to help you, but you aren't holding up your end of the bargain."

"It seems like you hate my kids. You never talk with them, play with them—nothing. I don't treat your son that way. What did my kids ever do to you?"

There was a slight softening in the hard line of Kim's mouth, but she still spoke firmly. "They haven't done anything to me, but I can't get involved. I can't let myself care about them. It took me four years to get my son out of foster care, to get this house, a steady job. I can't risk that now. I *won't*. It would be different if I thought you were willing to do what it takes, but I don't think you are. I saw what you brought home the other night, and I have to say that and alcohol and one of Loony's 'grab bags' don't qualify as nutrition for your kids. Face it, Paula, you went after them, not because you were ready, but because you wanted your own way. You, you, you. I think it's time you thought about them instead of yourself!"

Paula glared at her. "You just don't understand!"

"Yes, I do. I know *exactly* where you've been because I was there four years ago."

"I don't want to wait four years to be with my kids!"

Kim shrugged. "If you don't turn things around, you may have to wait even longer than that. They won't let you keep them if you don't have a place to live."

"One more week, please?" Paula hated begging, but she needed a place to stay.

"One more week." Kim took her car keys from the drawer by the sink. "But don't leave them alone—even if they're sleeping. I can't plan my evenings around them. If I'm going to be here, I'll tell the girl to leave, but if I'm not going to be here, she has to stay. If they're left alone, I'll have to do something about it."

Paula watched as Kim left, fuming at the threat. What would she do, call the social worker? A chill swept through Paula. She might at that. Kim had become more and more outspoken in the past weeks. She didn't seem as in awe of Paula's outbursts or threats as she once had. *Well, I don't need to put up with that. I'll stay a few more days and then leave. I bet Loony will let me stay with him for a bit in his apartment. Probably won't even charge me. Then I can get my feet on the ground.*

"Mommy?"

She turned around to see Kevin standing where the kitchen met the hallway. "Hi," she said brightly. "Did you have a good nap?"

He nodded, rubbing the sleep from his eyes. "Mara's still sleeping. I put a pillow by her on the bed so her wouldn't fall." They didn't have a crib, so Mara slept between Kevin and the wall on one of the two single beds in her room.

"That was good thinking."

"Mara falled off once at Uncle Blake's when I put her on the bed," Kevin said.

"You put her on the bed or Blake did?"

Kevin frowned. "Me. I didn't know her would fall off."

"Where was Uncle Blake?"

"Working on the truck. Mara was sleeping and her woke up. Uncle Blake says I should have told him, but I just wanted to help." Kevin brightened. "Amanda bought a thingy so Uncle Blake can hear Mara all the time, even if he's outside."

"A baby monitor?"

"Yeah, that's it. I like to play with it, but I don't break it."

Paula had never owned a baby monitor, and somehow it bothered her that the monitor hadn't been in the boxes Blake had mailed to her. Did he think he was getting the children back? Well, she'd show him. She certainly didn't need a baby monitor with Kevin around. For being only four, he was a good baby-sitter.

"Are you hungry?" she asked. When he nodded, she got out the large jar of peanut butter she'd bought when he first arrived. She had to scrape the bottom with a knife to get enough for his sandwich. "Looks like we'll have to buy more," she said with a sigh.

"I don't have to eat peanut butter," he offered.

"I'll buy some."

Kevin didn't reply, but that didn't surprise her. He was much quieter than she remembered.

A few days ago, she'd mentioned that he would be going to school the next year. "Will I go to Grovecrest?" he had asked.

"No. I don't think so. Why?"

He shrugged. "I know a teacher there." After that he'd stared down at a tiny sticker book that had come in the boxes Blake had sent and wouldn't look up at her no matter what she said.

Now he ate in silence, and for a long time Paula watched him. She loved the way his hair was growing long enough to curl over his ears, the way his face was beginning to lose its baby fat. She almost couldn't believe he was her son. When had he grown up so much? There was nothing of his father in him, which was probably a good thing because his father was long gone. The last she'd heard, he was working for a railroad in the East. At least he was alive. Mara's father had died of a bad liver a few months before her birth. Paula didn't have much luck with men.

Too bad I never found a man like Blake, she mused. Her mother had once said the fault was hers, and Paula felt anger rise at the thought. *I've done what was right by these kids,* she told herself.

286

Yet seeing Kevin lick his fingers and look hopefully at his empty milk glass, and her with no milk in the refrigerator to fill it, she had to wonder if she was telling herself the truth.

"We'll borrow a little more of Kim's milk," she told him. With a little luck, Kim might never know the difference.

Chapter Twenty-Seven

Day after day passed, and Paula still didn't allow Blake to see the children. Every time he saw the brightly colored packages under the tree, he felt a knot in his stomach. Surely Paula would let him visit soon.

He had finally stopped listening for Kevin and Mara, but the silence in the house when he was alone seemed deafening. The baby shampoo on the edge of the tub twice reduced him to tears. So had the receiver for the baby monitor he'd accidentally left on his dresser.

Kevin hadn't called him again, but Blake didn't cancel the cell phone service in the hope that Paula would relent. He had called the cell number several times—only to get his voice mail. He *had* managed to talk to Paula once more on her home phone.

"At least let me come and take them to church," he'd begged. "You know how important that is, whether you live it or not. They need an anchor." Paula's answer was to swear at both him and the Church.

Only prayer got Blake through each day—prayer and Amanda.

Amanda suffered with the situation as he did. Because Blake was out of school for the holidays and Amanda didn't have to teach, they spent more time together, growing closer.

They also spent some time every day with Kerrianne and her children. While Amanda comforted Kerrianne, who was still in shock and deeply mourning her husband, Blake entertained her children. Being with Misty and Benjamin helped fill the emptiness Kevin and Mara's absence had left in his heart.

Blake celebrated a subdued Christmas with the Huntington family. Kerrianne had insisted upon a dinner and presents. She wanted everything to be as normal as possible for her children, who really weren't old enough to understand their father's death.

Later that evening at his apartment, Blake took his tree down but left the presents he'd bought for Kevin and Mara in a corner of the living room.

A few days after Christmas, two weeks after the custody hearing, he decided to try again to talk to Paula, but her housemate, Kim, answered. "I'm sorry, but Paula moved out."

Blake found it hard to breathe. "Moved out? When? Where'd she go?"

"I don't know where she went," Kim said. "She skipped out yesterday without paying the rent."

"You don't have any idea where she went?" Blake didn't bother to hide the pleading note in his voice.

"Well, the day before she left, she did mention something about a friend of hers opening a restaurant in California. She might go there to work for him."

After he hung up, Blake called Erika with the news, and she promised to look into the matter. "What if she does move to another state?" he asked.

"There's nothing we can do but try to follow up," Erika said. "Still, she came to her counseling session last week—and passed the drug test. That's something, at least."

Blake held onto that slim hope with a prayer in his heart.

"Now we'll see if she shows up for her test tomorrow," Erika added. "If she doesn't, that'll be grounds to take the children back."

Next, Blake called Hal and Tracey, hoping she had gone to visit one of them, but Hal hadn't heard from Paula since the hearing, and Tracey had only talked to her a few times, the last time a few days before Christmas.

"Truthfully," Tracey said, "she wanted more money. So I started asking her some questions, and she swore at me and hung up. I'm really sorry, Blake. Looks like I was wrong about her. I hope you understand. I just so much wanted to have my little sister back. But I'm sure everything will work out."

The apology didn't change the facts, and the assurances made him feel worse. His worry intensified when Paula didn't show up for her weekly drug test.

He and Amanda went to the LDS singles dance for New Year's Eve, but they ended up leaving early and going to Kerrianne's, where the rest of her family had gathered. They played board games until almost twelve, and then Amanda pulled some noisemakers and fireworks from her purse for Misty and Benjamin, who weren't in the least tired, having slept several hours after dinner. Blake laughed at their excitement, but it brought an ache to his heart as he remembered how her "magic purse" had delighted Kevin.

Where were he and Mara now? The not knowing hurt Blake more than he could express. A part of him was simply . . . gone. Amanda reached for his hand, squeezing it with understanding. Blake put his arm around her, grateful for her presence. He didn't even try to consider where he'd be without her support.

New Year's Day dawned cold and crisp, and that evening Blake once again found himself with Amanda at Kerrianne's house. They sat together on the couch in the family room while Misty and Benjamin played in the middle of the room with their new Christmas toys. Despite the noise coming from his siblings, baby Caleb slept soundly in his car seat nearby.

Amanda was thumbing through the fourth volume in the set of children's books Blake had bought her for Christmas. "What are you thinking about so deeply?" she asked him, tilting her head to the side in the way that he had grown to love. "I've asked you a question three times, and you haven't heard me once."

"I'm thinking of hiring a private investigator," he admitted, pulling his attention back to the room. "I have to know they're okay. Paula has to at least let me see them."

Amanda placed her hand on his. "Let's see what Erika comes up with. She has a lot of contacts, and it's only been a few days."

"Paula didn't show up for her test this week," he reminded Amanda. "Or her counseling session. I'm afraid she's moved out of the state." He rubbed his thumb over his right eye, blotting the moisture.

"Maybe you're right—maybe we should hire someone." She bit her bottom lip. "You know, I could go see the woman Paula was living with, get a list of her friends. Someone will know where she is. Then I'll go see her myself. I don't think she'd mind. I'm used to dealing with the parents of the children in my class, and I might be able to get somewhere with her. Even if it's only to let us visit the children there."

"I'd appreciate it."

Deep down, though, Blake had a horrible fear that Paula had gone away somewhere—maybe California, as her roommate had suggested—and he'd never see the children again. He wouldn't watch them growing up, wouldn't be able to tell them that the life their mother lived wasn't normal. He wouldn't be able to teach them the gospel or about Jesus. To teach them to work and pull their own weight.

His chest felt tight with emotion. *It's not fair!* his heart shouted. It wasn't fair that Paula should thrust the children on him long enough for him to really love them—and then rip them away. He knew he'd have his own one day, hopefully his and Amanda's, but what about Kevin and Mara? The uncertainty evoked a terrible, helpless desperation that threatened to consume him.

"My aunt's right, you know," he said softly.

"Right about what?"

"What she said to me on the phone this morning. Paula should have given them up for adoption. Better not to have known them than to have them in danger like this. They deserve a good family."

Amanda hugged him, and Blake clung to her until his desperation faded to a size he could better handle. "Come on," she said at last. "Let's put these kids to bed for Kerrianne. Then we'll call Mitch over to baby-sit while we take her out for an ice cream cone. It's not too late, yet. Things should be open. That will cheer you both up."

Blake pulled her closer for a kiss. "Did I ever tell you how much I love you?" he asked.

"You have," she said, her tone light, "but I am beginning to wonder if you really mean it."

He blinked in confusion. *Just when I thought I was getting this love thing right!*

Shaking her head, she jumped up from the couch. "Oh, don't mind me. Come on, kids. Blake's going to help you brush your teeth while I talk to your mother."

Blake stared after her.

Amanda went into the bedroom where Kerrianne sat on her bed staring blankly at the white wall. She turned toward Amanda as she entered, trying to mask the forlorn expression on her face.

"Are you all right?" Amanda asked, her heart aching for her sister.

Kerrianne nodded. "I just . . . well, I can't remember what I came in here for."

"You were going to show us that brochure of community education classes."

"Oh, yeah." Kerrianne scooted over on the bed and reached for the top drawer in the night stand. Her hand stopped short of the knob.

"It's okay, Kerrianne. You can show us tomorrow."

Kerrianne didn't seem to hear. "This is his night stand," she said. "We bought matching ones right before Benjamin was born. Mine's over there on the other side because that's where I always put the baby bassinet when I start to need one. At about six months or so. Of course, I won't need a bassinet now because the bed's plenty big without Adam. Caleb can keep sleeping with me. Anyway, this is Adam's night stand. I've been using the top drawer. He never had much to put in it anyway. Just his scriptures and lesson manual. I'm not sure what to do with the manual." She looked at Amanda, her eyes glazed. "Do you think they'll ask me for it?"

Amanda shook her head. "I'll take it—if you want." She had helped Kerrianne clean out and put away most of Adam's things during the past weeks.

Kerrianne considered her offer a moment before shaking her head. "No. He was looking at it the night before . . . I want to keep it for a while."

"Of course. Keep it."

Kerrianne pulled her feet onto the bed and pushed herself back until she rested against the headboard. "I'm always so tired, Manda."

Amanda sat on the bed next to her sister, and Kerrianne slid over to allow her more room. "It'll pass, Kerrianne," Amanda said. "It's okay to be tired. You've been through a lot."

"I never thought I would be without Adam. Never. It's so soon. We hardly had any time at all." Kerrianne didn't look at her as she spoke but at the quilt on the bed.

"You loved each other," Amanda said.

"Yes, and I'll see him again." Kerrianne swallowed hard. "Sometimes forever just seems so far away."

"I know," Amanda whispered, placing her arms around her sister. Kerrianne clung to her arms with both hands. For a long moment neither woman spoke.

"Blake and I were thinking about taking you out for ice cream," Amanda said at last. "We'll put the kids to bed first. Mitch can watch them. We won't be long. We know you have church early tomorrow."

Kerrianne shook her head. "Not tonight, Manda. I appreciate the offer, though, and I think you and Blake should still go."

"I don't want to leave you alone."

Kerrianne's eyes as they met Amanda's were full of tears, but she smiled. "I'm not alone. Even when I'm physically alone, I've never really been alone since Adam died. It's been so hard and so awful, but there is peace, too. I know where Adam is. I know his heart is here with me. And so is my Savior."

Amanda began to cry, and this time it was Kerrianne who embraced her.

"I want so badly to help you," Amanda whispered. "What can I do?"

"Well, you can bring me another large slab of that cooking chocolate I always keep in the freezer for emergency cravings. I've eaten practically all of it." Kerrianne uttered a sound that might have been a very small, strangled chuckle. Then she sobered again. "Besides that, you can do just exactly what you've been doing. Be here a little each day, play with the children, talk to me about Adam—it helps to talk about him when I miss him so much."

Amanda nodded and wiped the tears from her cheeks, but

Kerrianne wasn't finished. "And you can be happy, Manda. I want you to be happy with Blake. That's what you can do for me. You can love him and do all the things for him that I would have done for Adam if I had known he was . . ." She trailed off and took a deep breath. "Seeing you happy makes me feel better."

Amanda knew her sister's heart was much larger than her own. So many times over the past few years she'd felt envy for the life her sister had led, but now the situation was reversed, Kerrianne did not seem to hold any envy or begrudge Amanda her happiness.

"I love you, Kerrianne," Amanda whispered.

"I love you, too." Kerrianne drew away. "Now, go. Send in my babies. I want to snuggle with them while they go to sleep. I have a tape here of Adam's songs I thought I'd play for them. And you go out with that man of yours."

"Okay, I will," Amanda agreed. "Maybe being alone with him will remind him that we do have a future to think about."

"He knows that."

"Does he? I don't know. I'm about ready to start giving him jewelry ads. I would, too, if he had any taste for that sort of thing." Amanda rolled her eyes as she got off the bed. "You should have seen a few of the wedding sets he pointed out to Mom when she showed him those ads at Christmas. They looked like clearance leftovers from eight years ago."

To Amanda's delight, Kerrianne actually laughed—a real laugh this time. "I did see, Manda, and it was hilarious. But are you sure he wasn't just joking around?"

Amanda shook her head. "Nope. He was serious." She backed toward the door. "I'll bring Caleb in. He'll be hungry if he's awake."

"Thanks," Kerrianne called after her.

A short time later, Amanda and Blake left the children snuggled with their mother in her queen-sized bed, the strains of Adam's music following them out the door.

Chapter Twenty-Eight

Mara was asleep on the worn couch. She wore the shirt she'd had on the day before, but someone had at least pulled a blanket over her during the night. Even from where Paula lay on the floor, she could see the angelic face was streaked with dried tears. Her brown flyaway hair shot in every direction.

The clock on the wall read after one. *Happy New Year,* Paula told herself. She stretched on her blanket, feeling the ache in her neck that came from not using a pillow. Like it or not, she was getting old.

"Mara needs a diaper when her gets up."

Paula moved her head carefully, wincing at the pain from her hangover. Kevin stood by the couch, his small insect sticker book in one hand, the other pointing at a used diaper on the floor, one that Paula could smell from across the room.

"Yuck," she said. "Did you take off her diaper yourself?"

He shrugged. "Mara was crying. Her bum gets red if it stays on too long. But I couldn't get another diaper on. Her wiggles too much."

Paula felt a pressure building in her chest—a bruising pressure as painful as the ache in her head. "Oh, Kevin," she said, hauling her reluctant body past various plastic sacks, several beer and pop cans, and other party discards until she reached his side. She didn't try to stand—for the moment just sitting there took all the effort she could muster.

"I washed my hands." He pointed to the part of the kitchen they could see from the front room. Sure enough, there was a stool by the sink. "I got some on me. It was gross."

"I'm sorry. You should have woken me up."

"I tried once, but I didn't want you to yell like last night."

"Yell?"

He nodded slowly, staring at her with a carefully blank expression that hurt Paula to see. What had she done last night? She couldn't remember any of it. There had been a lot of people over, she knew. Her friends and friends of Loony. She remembered something about going outside and catching snowflakes on their tongues. It was then she made the decision to move to California. The idea had freed her—though this morning moving seemed more like a burden.

Kevin sat down on the edge of the couch, next to Mara, who moved in her sleep but didn't wake. The book in his hands opened.

Paula thought about putting a diaper on Mara but decided to wait until she awoke. Loony's couch had seen worse. "Are you hungry?" she asked Kevin. Her own stomach was growling.

He turned a page and didn't reply.

Then she remembered there wasn't any food in the house, since what little they'd bought had been devoured by their guests last night. Kevin had probably eaten whatever remains he could find while she was sleeping.

"Hey, honey, I know what we can do," she said, reaching out to touch his arm. "We'll go to the store. I'll buy you some peanut butter crackers."

She thought the mention of those would have sent him jumping for joy—it would have once—but now he just looked at her steadily. "Okay, but Mara needs more milk. And other stuff. Her doesn't like crackers much."

"I thought we still had some formula left. At least enough for a bottle or two." Paula spied an empty bottle then on the couch by Mara, and she could see the formula can on the counter in the kitchen. She forced herself to her feet and took a few wobbling steps in that direction, seeing spilled powder on the counter. Apparently, Kevin had taken care of his sister while their mother slept off the result of her choices last night.

I slept while he paid the price. The thought cut deep into her heart.

Stumbling back to the couch, she put her hand out to steady herself on the armrest, her head pounding painfully and making it hard to concentrate.

Kevin looked up at her, his face frozen. She'd seen this look before during the supervised visits. In fact, if she told the truth, this very expression on her son's face was the reason she had missed the last two visits before the custody hearing. Yes, she'd had car trouble, but that was earlier in the morning, and besides, a friend had offered her a ride. Still, she hadn't gone, unable to bear seeing this solemn expression. Her hand itched to slap it from his face.

Before she could act, the look in his eyes changed, becoming one of pleading—a desperate pleading that wounded her heart. Soon the pleading faded, followed quickly by a sharp, biting hurt that emanated clearly from those innocent blue eyes. Then his face turned dark, sullen, and angry. As his expression filtered through these changes, the size and shape of his face had also altered. He was older now as Paula stared at him. Years older.

This is what he'll become! she thought. Her breath caught in her throat.

This was how her precious son would stare at her in future years.

This was the boy she would disappoint by her failures. The boy who would lose his innocence, who would grow up in a world that had no security and guidance. He wouldn't have the Church as a guide as she'd had growing up—though in the end she'd chosen to ignore it. He wouldn't have Blake to steady him. He wouldn't learn about morals, respect, or Jesus.

Haven't I even taught him about Jesus? The clarity of this thought was an agony in her soul. If he knew anything of Jesus, it was because Blake had taught him. *It should have been me,* she thought.

Yes, here Kevin was, all grown and staring defiantly at her, looking exactly like the teenage children of her friends. Children who were unable to hold down jobs, who spent time in jail, or were beginning broken families of their own that would perpetuate the cycle.

She had never wanted that life for her children. Never. She didn't want them to experience her pain. Paula shook her head, staring at this boy she knew was hers—and yet who couldn't possibly be. No child of hers would have that bleak pain in his eyes, would he?

Oh, what have I done?

More than four years ago, she had ignored all counsel and kept Kevin instead of giving him up for adoption. She loved him more than she had ever loved any other person in her entire life. How could she have given him away? Yet if she had, her precious boy wouldn't be looking up at her right now with that terrible weight in his old-man eyes, clutching the sticker book that was his constant companion, as though it was his only link to safety and sanity.

With a little gasp, Paula turned on her heel and ran from him.

Blindly, she fled into the bedroom where Loony had let her and the children stay for the past week. She fell to her knees by the mattress on the floor that the three of them shared as a bed. She'd promised the judge she'd do what was right for her children. She hadn't been lying at the time. She really wanted the best for Kevin and Mara. But what was right? She wasn't sure she even knew.

Oh, dear God, she prayed silently. *What have I done? What have I done? Please help me!*

Much, much later, after her swollen eyes could cry no more tears, she came out of her room to find Kevin and a diaperless Mara on the couch looking at the insects in his sticker book. Kevin was his four-year-old self again as he calmly glanced up at her. Next to him Mara looked tiny, and Paula wondered if she'd lost weight in the past weeks.

"Come on," she said. "Let's get Mara dressed and then help me put your things in the boxes in our room. We're leaving."

"To the store?" His expression was wary.

"Yes, but then we're going far away from here. A new life. You'll see."

"We're not coming back?" Kevin glanced around the room.

"No."

He smiled. "Good. Mara doesn't like it here."

He didn't question her further about where they were going, as Paula thought a normal child would. Maybe he was too afraid of the answer.

Chapter Twenty-Nine

Monday after work Amanda readied herself for Blake's arrival. Since Kevin and Mara left, they'd spent most of their time together at her place or at Kerrianne's, but tonight he wanted to make a special dinner for her. Anticipation filled Amanda's heart. She would be lying if she said she didn't hope he would finally propose. They had to go on, even if the children weren't in their lives.

She had a surprise for him, too. Right now it was looking at her with large brown eyes from the large cardboard box Mitch had brought from a grocery store. She felt bad about leaving it home alone—even with a hot water bottle and a cloth-covered ticking alarm clock for company—but she wasn't willing to share Blake for the next hour at least.

Blake arrived on her doorstep, looking happier than usual, his face freshly shaved. Even his unruly hair had been slicked down with water. Amanda gave him a hug and kiss, her hand stealing up to fluff the top of his hair the way she liked it best.

He laughed. "You look nice," he said, glancing over her flowing crinkle skirt and matching blouse.

"Thanks." She smiled, and he smiled back. A delicious tension built between them.

"Come on," he said. "Let's go." He took her hand and led her out to the snow-flocked drive.

In the car she said, "I talked to Kim on the phone this morning. You know, Paula's old roommate." She knew the information might destroy their evening, but she didn't want to keep it from him, either. "She was nicer to me than she was to you when you called, or at least more talkative. I like her. I think she's going to make it. She found a new roommate—an older widow—and it seems to be working out for her. Anyway, she gave me a list of friends and their phone numbers. I found one guy named Loony who says Paula and the children were staying with him but left on Saturday."

"On New Year's?" Blake glanced up briefly from the snowy road. "That was only two days ago!"

Amanda took a deep breath. "Yeah, but he thinks Paula might have gone to California. He gave me some names to check out about that."

Blake's jaw clenched as he absorbed the information. Finally, he gave a sigh. "Well, I guess there's nothing we can do about that right now. Thanks for calling. At least we have a direction to look. You sure do have a way of getting information from people."

"I'm just tactful. Sometimes you can be . . . well, a little blunt."

To her relief, he grinned. "Yeah, it's a guy trait, I think. So what did Erika say about it? I'm assuming you called her."

"I left a message, but she hasn't called back. I told her we'd be at your place for dinner. I doubt she'll call until tomorrow, though."

Blake nodded. "Okay, then. We'll wait to hear from her." Then he added more softly, "This evening will be for us." One hand left the steering wheel and took hers, sending a happy warmth to her heart.

At the house he served her chicken and rice with salad. For dessert he made huge banana splits. Amanda eyed them doubtfully. "Didn't you have enough ice cream on New Year's?" she asked. "You don't know what this'll do to my waistline."

He grinned. "It's just this once. Trust me."

"Mmm," she said, digging in. After only three bites, she felt something in her mouth that definitely wasn't a nut.

A ring. She could feel the hardness against her teeth, feel the shape with her tongue. Her heart pounded. Blake was watching her, silent now, his dark eyes alive and intense.

She drew it out of her mouth, stared down at the simple band with the small, shining diamond. A long moment passed. She'd been engaged once right after high school and nearly engaged last year, but nothing had prepared her for the love she felt at this moment.

"Well?" he asked. "It is one of the ones you liked in the ad, isn't it?"

At that point Amanda wouldn't have cared if it had been one of the clearance rejects. She slipped the ring onto her finger, still slightly sticky with the sweet ice cream. "Yes," she said. "It's perfect."

"And?"

"And I will."

Blake sprang from his chair and hugged her, drawing her to her feet. Tears stood out in his eyes. "I know I've been occupied with losing Kevin and Mara," he whispered. "And I'm sorry. But I love you, and I will love you forever."

"I love you, too."

Their ice cream sat forgotten on the table as they began to plan their future. Where they would live, how many children they would have, and what they would do about work. Blake had Amanda laughing at the jobs he said he would soon start applying for: chief bottle washer at the Gerber Baby Food Company, assistant paint chooser for General Electric appliances (so he could do away with all shades of green), or maybe even executive doughnut taster for the police department.

The doorbell rang, interrupting their mirth. Both of them froze, staring at each other. *Funny,* Amanda thought, *doorbells never seemed to hold such power before Kevin and Mara entered my life.*

"It's probably Garth from upstairs," Blake said. "I bet he smelled the chicken and wants some. He's a terrible cook."

Amanda relaxed. "Well, open the door. He'll be the first to hear the good news." She held up her hand with the new ring. "Then we'll go over and tell Kerrianne. We should call my parents, too. And Mitch—and your brother and his wife."

Blake kissed her hand. "Okay, okay. But maybe you ought to run some water over it. I think there's some chocolate from the ice cream trapped in the prongs."

Amanda gasped. "Oh, rats! Can't have that." Glancing at the multitude of pans and dishes piled in the kitchen sink, she added, "I'll just run to the bathroom and clean it." She wanted to check her makeup anyway and make sure nothing was in her teeth. If they were going to start announcing their engagement, she wanted to be presentable.

Yes, and maybe she wanted to do a private happy dance to release some of the excitement welling in her heart. She hadn't been this happy since before Adam had died and the children were taken away.

If only . . .

No, she couldn't think about the search for Kevin and Mara—at least not right now. She'd promised Kerrianne she'd be happy, and she would do her very best to fulfill that promise.

Blake went to the door as the bell rang again, suddenly realizing that Garth always used the door coming into the living room. This bell was from the outside door that opened into the kitchen. *Who would be coming here on a Monday night?* he wondered. Dread shivered up his spine.

As he opened the door, shock filled his entire body. He couldn't move. He couldn't speak. Only his tight grasp on the doorknob stopped him from falling flat on his face.

Paula stood there holding little Mara, who was wearing the pink coat Rhonda had bought for her. His cousin appeared small and weary, her eyes red from tears. At her side Kevin looked like a puffy blue marshmallow in his winter coat. Behind them stood Erika Solos, her hands in the pockets of her long black jacket.

Only a second passed while they studied each other, but for Blake it was an eternity. Then Kevin finally shot at his legs, clinging to him. "Uncle Blake!" he shouted.

Blake fell to his knees and hugged the child until his arms threatened to rebel at the pressure. Kevin didn't protest but clung tighter to his neck.

Blake felt more than saw Amanda come into the kitchen behind them, stopping short as she saw who the visitors were. Kevin wrenched himself from Blake and flew into her arms. Both were crying.

"Here," Paula said, offering Mara to Blake.

"Bk, Bk," Mara said, her face awash with smiles. Her arms went out to him, her body leaning forward.

"She missed you," Paula said. "Look how happy she is to see you."

Mara put her short arms around his neck, her tiny fingernails digging into his skin. Blake held her close, felt his tears wet her cheek.

"Bk, Bk," Mara said again, squealing with delight.

Paula stared at her. "She never learned to say Mommy," she

whispered. Her expression was forlorn, and Blake felt a surge of pity for his cousin.

"She will." He held out a hand to her. "Thank you for bringing them, Paula. Thank you so much. I've missed them more than I can say. Come in, come in. It's cold out there."

Paula shook her head and didn't move.

Erika stepped forward, taking a folder of papers from beneath her jacket. Blake accepted the folder. "What's this?" he asked.

"I'm giving you custody," Paula said, her voice low. "You'll still need to sign the papers and go in front of the judge, but you'll have custody."

"You're giving me custody?" The thought was unbelievable. Blake glanced at Amanda, who stood close to him, Kevin folded tightly in her arms. "But Paula, I know how much you lo—" He broke off. "What happened?"

She shook her head, her lips trembling and nostrils flaring slightly. Some of her newly brown hair fell forward over her pale face—a haggard, suffering face that showed a myriad of new wrinkles around her eyes and mouth. "You were right, Blake. I finally saw myself as you and Mom see me. I should have made this choice a long time ago—when Kevin was born. I still could, I suppose, for Mara, but Kevin loves her so much, and no matter how I want her to be happy, I can't separate them." Her voice cracked. "Besides, I'm not that strong, that giving. I have to know where they are. It's gone too far for anything else. With you, I know they'll be okay."

Tears streamed down Paula's cheeks, and Blake felt helpless to do anything for her. In his arms, Mara was reaching for Amanda. She took the baby and at the same time handed Kevin to Blake. Kevin buried his face in Blake's neck. Mara's innocent giggle filled the glaring silence.

"We'll take care of them," Amanda said at last. "We're getting married." She lifted the hand with the new ring.

Paula gave her a watery smile. "I'm glad. I knew you would take care of them after meeting you that once. I knew I could trust you."

"You can get help," Blake said. "Please, Paula."

His cousin nodded. "I'm going to try, but I don't know if I can do it. And Kevin shouldn't have to pay for my sins."

"You *can* do it," Blake urged. "If you turn to the Lord. I know He'll help you. I *know* it!"

A sob escaped her throat. "I want to believe that, Blake, but right now I don't trust myself. I don't trust that tomorrow I'm not going to wake up and think crazy again. That's why I gave you custody. I know you won't give it back easily unless I'm really ready. I am going to try, believe me, but it's so hard!"

Blake didn't know what to say.

Paula took a deep breath and wailed, "Oh, Blake, how did I get to be so unfit? No, don't answer that." She held up her small hand, willing him not to speak. "I'm going now. I know I'll hate myself forever for not being strong for them, but I'd hate myself even more if I don't let them go. Still, it's tearing my heart out!" With a shaking hand, she touched Mara's soft cheek and then leaned forward on tiptoe to kiss the back of Kevin's head. The boy didn't turn around.

Paula met Blake's eyes, her voice lowering to less than a whisper. "Tell them I love them, okay? Tell them every time you think about it or when they ask about me." At his nod, she turned and ran into the darkness, her sobs lingering behind on the frigid night breeze.

Blake watched her go. He felt guilty experiencing such joy in having Kevin and Mara back while Paula endured such unspeakable agony. There was a time he would have run after her and begged her to stay, but he had a stronger obligation to the children now. Paula would have to find the strength within herself.

"I'll see that she's all right," Erika promised. "I drove them over, so she'll be waiting in my car."

307

"How . . . when . . ." Blake felt too overwhelmed to finish his sentence.

"She tracked me down on Saturday, and it took me two days to get all the paperwork done. I would have called you before but"—Erika shook her head—"you never know if they'll change their mind at the last minute."

"They're really mine?" Blake looked first at Kevin and then at Mara in wonder.

Erika nodded. "Almost. Of course, if she does get things in hand, something might change in the future, but even then you'll always have some legal rights. As for Paula cleaning up, I wouldn't hold my breath. These things take time. She's going to California to work, and I've set her up with some groups there. If she continues to want help, she'll get it."

"I want to know where she is," Blake said. "I'll want to write her letters, send pictures. And I need to contact the Church there. If she can find her faith, she'll be okay."

"I'll do that," Erika promised.

"Thank you so much," Amanda said.

Erika smiled. "All in a good weekend's work." She bent down and picked up a large duffle bag. "Here's some of their things, but you'll have to come and get the rest at the agency tomorrow. I didn't have room to get them in my tin can of a car."

"I'll be there," Blake said.

He took a deep breath as Erika walked away. Only when he shut the door did Kevin lift his head from Blake's shoulder. "You're getting married?" he asked.

"Yep, bud, we are. Is that okay with you?"

Kevin nodded. "Yes. It's *really* okay." Then his attention riveted itself on the presents he spied in the corner of the living room. "Are those for me?"

"Yes. For you and Mara."

Kevin grinned and struggled to get down. "Can I open them? 'Cause Christmas is over already."

"Wait a minute," Amanda said, a gleam in her eyes that Blake recognized all too well. In his mind he called it the magic-purse syndrome.

"Why?" he asked, looking around for her purse.

"Let's take them to my house. I have another present for them there."

"You do?" Blake didn't see how she could have bought them more presents when she hadn't known they were coming home tonight.

She gave him a crooked grin. "Well, actually, I didn't know it was for them at the time I got it. I almost got birds instead but . . . Oh, let's just go!"

Minutes later they were at Amanda's house, the brightly colored packages forgotten on the floor as Kevin and Mara played with the golden puppy she had bought after work at the pet shop.

Blake shook his head at her. "Too big to fit in your purse, huh?"

Amanda laughed and sat back on the couch. "Hey, I was tired of living alone. I didn't know if a certain guy I'm dating was ever going to ask me to marry him."

"You could have asked him."

"Naw. I'm an old-fashioned girl at heart."

"Can he come and live with me at Uncle Blake's?" Kevin gathered the wriggling puppy in his arms.

Blake met Amanda's eyes and she nodded once, silently asking him to go ahead. "Well," Blake began, "we were sort of hoping that in a month or so you and Mara and I could come and live here at Amanda's."

Kevin's eyes widened. "Here?"

"It's bigger than the apartment, you see," Amanda explained. "I know you like being in a room with Mara now, but when you're

309

older you might want your own room. Here we have three bedrooms, plus a whole empty basement to build more rooms if we need to. We'll bring your bed over, of course, and all your toys."

The puppy succeeded in freeing himself from Kevin's grasp. He trotted over to where Mara sat on the floor and flopped his head on her legs. Mara tugged on the long ears, and the puppy turned his head to lick her hands.

Kevin didn't seem to notice the dog's desertion. He leaned forward and curled one arm around Blake's neck, the other going around Amanda's. "Okay," he said, "I'll come live here. But that means I get to go to Amanda's school, right?"

Amanda hugged Kevin, and there were tears in her eyes as she met Blake's gaze. "Yes, Kevin," she said. "It does."

Kevin pulled away, grinning broadly. "Good. Then let's go see my new room."

Amanda picked up Mara and slid her hand into Blake's. Together they followed Kevin down the hall, the puppy tripping clumsily after them.

About the Author

Rachel Ann Nunes (pronounced *noon-esh*) learned to read when she was four, beginning a lifetime fascination with the written word. She avidly devoured books then and still reads everything she can lay hands on, from children's stories to science articles. She began writing in the seventh grade and is now the author of twenty published books, including the popular *Ariana* series and the picture book *Daughter of a King,* voted best children's book of the year in 2003 by the Association of Independent LDS Booksellers.

Rachel served a mission to Portugal for The Church of Jesus Christ of Latter-day Saints and teaches Sunday School in her Utah ward. She and her husband, TJ, have six children. Rachel loves camping with her family, traveling, meeting new people, and, of course, writing. She writes Monday through Friday in her home office, often with a child on her lap, taking frequent breaks to build Lego towers, practice phonics, or jump on the trampoline with the kids. She believes that raising her family is the most important thing she will ever do.

Rachel welcomes letters from her readers. Please write to her at rachel@rachelannnunes.com or P. O. Box 353, American Fork, UT 84003–0353.